Cruel Summer

Cruel Summer

Book One

Lisa Cardwell

Rebel Heart Ink

Lisa Cardwell
Rebel Heart Ink
www.lisa-cardwell.com

Publisher's Note: This is a work of fiction. Names, characters, places, and incidents are a product of the author's imagination. Locales and public names are sometimes used for atmospheric purposes. Any resemblance to actual people, living or dead, or to businesses, companies, events, institutions, or locales is completely coincidental.

Cover art designed by Mariah Sinclair / The Cover Vault

Book Layout ©2019 BookDesignTemplates.com

Ordering Information:
Quantity sales. Special discounts are available on quantity purchases by corporations, associations, and others. For details, contact the "Special Sales Department" at the address above.

Cruel Summer/ Lisa Cardwell. -- 1st ed.
ISBN 978-0-9878805-5-0

To Mom

1

"We're live from outside the hospital where the latest Holly-wood 'it girl,' Chey Morrow, has been brought in. According to an unnamed source, she lost control of her BMW earlier tonight on a slippery stretch of PCH and spun out into oncoming traffic. No reports yet on whether alcohol was a contributing factor..."

The same perky blonde reporter from the premiere flashed a bright smile at the camera like my sudden downward spiral represented the highlight of her day. Disgust flowed through me, and I was tempted to hit mute to stop her spiel, not wanting to hear any more. I was sure, no doubt, there'd be something from an 'unnamed source' who had nothing but a vendetta against me.

The screen split in two, and before the serious-looking anchor-woman could ask a single nauseating question, my finger found the power button on the remote and clicked the dratted thing off, leaving me to glare at the darkened screen. *Alcohol a contributing factor,* my rear. I hadn't been near any all night. I'd been stone cold sober throughout the entire painful ordeal.

I eased down carefully in the cramped hospital bed, wanting to pull the blankets over my head, wanting to drown out the thoughts that were going through my mind, all seemingly being narrated in that stupid reporter's perkier-than-thou voice.

But the standard-issue blanket was too thin to do the type of blocking I needed, let alone keep out any of those faint hospital sounds in the hallway. Pages, beeps of various machines, and voices and footsteps of who knows who loitering near my door drifted in.

I reached behind me, wincing slightly as I moved in a way my body no longer liked thanks to my various new scratches, bruises, and possible fractures to grab one of the extra pillows someone had procured for me. I pulled the flat pillow over my head, screaming silently into the worn fabric that still smelled faintly of laundry detergent, letting out all the pent-up emotion, the anger, sadness, everything that had led up to this brilliant point in my life.

The first hitch of a sob shook me, sending a jolt of pain through my sore ribs. I let it out into the fabric of the pillow, slowly easing it down so I could breathe, glad no one was here to witness my mini meltdown.

If I only had the chance to redo at least part of my summer.

I'd been so naïve when I arrived, thinking the whole time would be about me and my father bonding, hanging out, having fun. All those things I'd missed out on since my parents' divorce nearly a decade ago.

I sniffled away the last of my tears, wiping them away with the back of my hand, glaring at the sight of the I.V. the paramedics had hooked me up to.

Yeah, if I could go back in time, I'd seriously think about smacking that version of me up alongside the head as I issued a dire warning.

Beware of Adriana.

Enough said.

Six weeks before

The metallic red, hard-cased carryon bumped along behind me as I trekked across LAX airport. He'd promised to be the one to pick me up, but I had serious doubts, fully prepared to see some chauffeur or long-suffering personal assistant holding a sign with my name and the keyword on it.

No keyword meant I wasn't going anywhere—except on the next plane back home.

That had been one of Mom's little rules which, of course, I'd instantly agreed to. Truth be told, Mom could have gotten me to agree to almost anything just so I could spend the summer here.

I'd been counting down the days.

It meant more to me than my graduation had a few weeks ago. I hadn't been thrilled at Dad's inability to make it, but I understood his schedule was set seriously in advance, and he didn't have any wiggle room.

As a consolation, he was supposed to have most of the summer off.

I slipped by the couples happily reuniting around me and headed into a no man's land, wondering if he'd forgotten me completely. I was about to pull my cell phone out of my pocket and text a quick message to see where he was when a familiar voice called my name, and I turned around, moments before I found myself swooped up into my father's arms.

I wrapped my arms around him tightly as he lifted me up on tiptoe, taking a deep inhale of his familiar scent, a cologne I remembered buying him years ago for Father's Day as a little girl. A scent that purely reminded me of the sun and the beach and him.

To say I was stunned by the ferocity of the hug may have been an understatement. Some small voice—which reminded me vaguely of my mother's—wondered if a stray paparazzi lurked nearby to capture this happy father-daughter reunion to sell to the highest bidder.

"How are you, Chey? How was the flight?" Dad asked, taking the handle of my carryon as he finally let me go.

I took a moment to look at him, the faded Dodgers baseball cap hiding his dark hair, a hint of stubble on his face. I almost wondered if he'd overslept.

All combined, it might make him a little less recognizable to those around us who barely spared us a quick glance, but to me...I'd know my Dad anywhere.

I fell into step easily beside him as we headed towards baggage claim. "Okay on both counts."

"Good." He smiled like he did in so many family photos. A little lopsided, a little goofy. The smile I'd unfortunately inherited. "Glad you're here."

I beamed. "Me, too."

Very glad.

Fifteen minutes later, the matching red suitcase finally appeared amongst the sea of revolving luggage on the carousel in front of us. I hoisted it off easily and set it at our feet, keeping my hands wrapped around the handle, ready to go.

"This it?" Dad's blue eyes looked a little stunned as he glanced at the luggage carousel then back at me, as if he'd expected a few more matching suitcases to magically appear.

I peered at my meager belongings.

"That's all." What can I say? I traveled light.

"Let me take that."

"Thanks."

He took the suitcase while I dragged the carryon behind me, glad it had wheels and not just its flimsy shoulder strap. Walking alongside him towards the exit, I noticed a few whispered comments being directed our way—maybe someone had seen beyond the stubble and baseball cap, but Dad didn't do anything but slip on a pair of aviator shades and keep moving.

Oh, yeah—I might have forgotten to mention it, but my dad, he's well...sort of an actor.

A well-known sorta actor.

The type who graced People's *Fifty Most Beautiful* issues and *Sexiest Bachelors in Hollywood*. The man had *People's Choice* awards, MTV movie awards, and countless other accolades, but most importantly to me, he was *my* dad.

Or 'estranged' Dad as Mom liked to call him when she was upset with him. Not that he'd forgotten about me, because he hadn't. Didn't.

This trip alone, this summer alone, was proof of that.

A combination Graduation-Birthday-whatever-else-he-wanted-to-throw-in trip. A chance for the two of us to spend some real time together.

A chance to make up for the lack of real father-daughter bonding going on the last couple of years.

Which I understood. His workload was heavy. He was busy shooting films all over the world, which didn't exactly allow a lot of time for on-set visits by his teenage daughter. My school break schedules never really aligned with his time off.

Don't get me wrong, it's not like he'd forgotten about me, because he hadn't. We exchanged emails and phone calls and texts. The occasional visit when he was nearby. Our usual trip to NYC to see the Christmas trees in December and catch a Rangers game or two.

I kept up to date as much as I could, finding tidbits online about his life. I'd learned to DVR anything that mentioned his name. It had become my way of keeping up with him between visits. Made me feel like a part of his life, even when I wasn't around.

In spite of the near-unbearable heat the moment we stepped outside, I couldn't help smiling.

It was official.

I was finally in California, and I was *finally* spending the summer with my dad.

Nothing had come up that meant cancelling the trip at the last minute.

If something even *tiny* had changed in his at-times unpredictable schedules, with reshoots or whatever else, this would have been totally off, and I would have likely been spending the summer either hanging out with my grandparents or being a part-time pizza delivery driver.

Not exactly how I envisioned spending my summer for a second year in a row.

"Which way?"

My gaze got lost at the sight of row upon row of vehicles. The sun glared back from all those windshields. I squinted a little, wishing I'd pulled my sunglasses out sooner, but they were stuck likely in the bottom of my purse which was still in my carryon. I'd just have to suffer.

He adjusted his grip on the suitcase. "Head right, a couple lanes over. I lucked out on the parking spot. Figured you wouldn't want to make a huge trek."

Especially in this heat.

I swore it almost hurt to breathe.

Heat waves rose from the asphalt, creating a mirage as we kept walking, and I realized again how big LAX was and actually how close he had parked.

We came to a stop in front of a silver Escalade, and Dad opened the back hatch while I rooted through my carryon, removing my small black leather purse and iPhone, unable to keep from glancing around me in awe.

It was true. I was really here.

Someone pinch me.

"I thought we'd go home first, get you settled in."

"Fine by me."

"Are you hungry?" he asked as he unlocked the doors. "We can pick something up on the way?"

"I'm good." Food was so the last thing on my mind right now. I wanted nothing else but to go home.

Wow, *home*.

That sounded so...different, especially out here. Go home, un-pack, change, and see what Dad had in mind. I doubted he planned to take me to Disneyland—although honestly, I wouldn't have ve-toed that one completely. But food...hmmm, now that I thought about it, my stomach gave a testing rumble. "I could maybe go for something in a while."

"We'll get you comfortable first then see what you're in the mood for after."

"Perfect."

Even though the air-conditioning of the Escalade struck me as icy, I hoped for a pool when we got to Dad's. I just felt like diving in and cooling off for the rest of the day, even after the brief walk to the vehicle. I mean, I should have known L.A. would be hot during the summer months, but this felt a little extreme.

'Course, not like I had dressed for the weather. Shorts and flip flops would have been such a better choice than jeans and my ancient sneakers. No wonder I felt like I'd stepped foot inside a sauna.

"You okay over there?"

I smiled. Dad must have caught me toying with the air vents, trying to find the perfect angle to cool down. "Fine. Need to get used to the heat, that's all."

"It's not always this hot," he assured me before he turned the a/c from icy to Antarctic.

So much better.

"But it's not going to get any cooler over the next few days, either. Sorry, kiddo."

I had to smile at the nickname I'd grown up with; even at seventeen, I liked hearing him say it. "That's okay. You've got air, right?"

"Absolutely. Trust me, you won't fade away from the heat any time soon." He hooked his phone up to the stereo and punched in some playlist before we pulled out of the parking lot.

The ride to the house turned out filled with traffic jams, my plane having landed at just the right time to put us in gridlock. I surfed through his iPhone music lists and skipped ahead to a couple of better songs. When they were done, he had me switch over to the radio app so he could hear the traffic reports and I could pretend I knew where half the accidents had happened.

I hadn't been to Los Angeles in years, vaguely remembering spending my tenth birthday at Disneyland with both my parents and having a private dinner with Cinderella in matching dresses before Dad went home and Mom and I spent the night at the hotel before flying back east.

So basically, I was one Star Home tours away from qualifying as a tourist.

"Are we there yet?" The GPS screen on the console looked like alien mish-mash. Where exactly were we? Okay, not like I knew one part of L.A. from the other, but still.

"Close," he said with a smile. "It shouldn't be much longer."

My body slumped into the leather seat, and I watched the palm trees and bright-colored flowers pass me by. We'd hit a residential area a few blocks back, and I kept waiting for him to turn into one of the gated driveways we kept zooming by.

Finally, we took a turn off and headed into the Holmby Hills, or so the last sign we'd passed said. I tilted the air conditioning vents once more, smiling as the rush of Arctic air hit my face. Dad, in his dark blue T-shirt and faded jeans, looked like any father, really, out for the afternoon with his daughter. It just happened my dad had a star on the Hollywood Walk of Fame.

No biggie.

I glanced over at him, trying to get a hint of how close we were.

"Whatcha looking at?" he asked, glancing at me.

I laughed self-consciously. "The scenery. It's gorgeous out here."

My attention veered back out the window. The vehicle slowed as we rounded a curve and headed into a nearly hidden driveway, the dark metal gates sliding back effortlessly seconds before we drove up.

Can I just say it's a little odd to be gaping at your father's house?

Yet, I freely admit I did.

I leaned forward slightly as we approached, staring out the windshield at the glistening glass house in front of us.

It was a lot more modern than I expected, with all that glass and a boxy look to it, jutting out at different angles here and there.

The whole thing looked glass from where we were. So much for privacy, I guess.

As we followed the driveway, I could see a balcony or two visible along the back. Hope sorta jumped in me that maybe, just *maybe*, one of those balconies belonged to my room?

How cool would it be to sit out there and look down the hills at night with all the lights of the city spread out below? It'd definitely beat the view out my bedroom window back home of the overgrown apple trees and our backyard.

Dad chuckled as he unlocked the doors, obviously wanting to give me time to absorb things. Or at least, not look like a fool in front of him as I practically drooled. You know, the more I stared, the more I grew pretty sure I'd seen this place somewhere before. Like on TV. Certain of it, actually.

"What do you think?" he asked from the back after he popped the hatch.

'Wow' came to mind. I couldn't quite take my eyes off the house. I never expected him to live in a place like this.

I couldn't believe I would be living here for the next few months.

I turned in the passenger seat to look at him. "It's great. I love it. It's awfully familiar, though."

Which I couldn't figure out, unless I was having the world's strongest case of déjà vu.

"I thought you might recognize it. The last owners filmed part of their reality show here."

Well, that totally explained it.

"It's great," I said again, unable to think of another way to describe the place. Or this whole thing, just being here with him.

"Hoped you'd think so." Dad smiled as he moved by my passenger door, my suitcases looking even more glaringly shiny and metallic in the bright California sunlight. "Well, come on, let me give you the grand tour and get you settled. I know your mom's probably anxiously awaiting your texts."

"How long have you been in this place?" I asked as we headed up the stone walkway to the double front doors.

"A year and a half. Bought it when I finished filming in Australia."

Within moments, he'd fumbled with his keys, gotten the front door open, and we were stepping inside.

Cool air rushed towards us, and I smiled in relief to be out of the heat, even from the brief walk up the driveway. I watched him key the security code into the panel by the door and took a moment to look around. The place appeared bright and airy—the whole front of the house to the right was open concept; the left had a wall and the staircase. I could see part-way into the stainless steel and pale blue kitchen from where we stood.

Two colors that seemed to be the decorators' favorite choice, from what I could see.

It was a lot more homey than I expected from all that glass. There were pale gray curtains and shades in almost every room I could see, and I had the distinct impression that half of them were remote-controlled.

Dad shut the door behind us and set my bags down by the stairs off to the left. He surveyed things, looking more anxious than I'd ever seen him.

"You want a drink?"

"Sure."

He smiled and took off down the hall to the kitchen. I slipped off my sneakers and walked into the living room, surprised to see pictures of the two of us when I was little, not to mention my school photo from last year in a shiny red frame sitting on one of the glass end tables where anyone and everyone could see it.

"Here..."

I looked up to see Dad carrying a couple cans of my favorite soda. "Great, thanks."

"Should we start the tour?"

"Why not?"

I opened my drink and took a careful sip, trying not to spill any on me or the floor as we headed down the hall. The kitchen seemed huge and open with a double set of French doors that led onto the patio. Dad held one open as we stepped outside. A huge pool, the answer to my earlier prayers, glistened brightly in the afternoon sun. A little patch of grass covered the far side, between the pool and the back of the triple car garage we'd parked in front of a few minutes ago. A couple flower beds and a stone wall stood beyond on that side of the yard. To the right was more patio, a fire pit, and some lounge chairs, and another grassy area with flowers. Every few feet were small potted palms and other plants I didn't quite recognize. Everything looked out towards the amazing view of the hills from the back of the house.

We walked further down the patio, past a couple of lounge chairs, the oversized umbrella that seemed attached to a couple of loungers, and the fire pit. A sudden breeze brought up the sweet smell of the flowers planted here and there. He turned.

"See that first balcony?" He pointed to the far side of the house.

I spun—the same one I'd seen from the SUV. From here, though, it was evident there were more than one. More than two, even. There were three, at least, one bigger than the next as they jutted out from the house.

Each one looked like it had its own similar décor, potted palms, flowers, and loungers.

I was definitely going to be spending a lot of time outside this summer.

"Yeah?"

"That one's yours."

I squealed, and he laughed.

"Guess that means you're ready to see your room now?"

"Absolutely!"

We headed back in so he could grab my gear, and then, we headed upstairs. The staircase took a moment to get used to, with the glass sides, you could look straight over and down.

I followed him along the wide, sandy colored hallway with a feeling he had a thing for the beach with the color scheme he had going. All shades of sand and blues with that gray from downstairs here and there.

Soft sandy colored walls? Check.

Even lighter sandy colored hardwood floors? Check.

All he was really missing was a huge painting or photograph of the ocean somewhere on one of the walls. But all the walls we passed were pretty bare, like maybe he hadn't fully decorated the hallway yet.

I still had to pinch myself that I was actually here. If this happened to be a dream, I wasn't sure I wanted to wake up.

Evidently, I missed a bit of the tour guide spiel he was giving, and I quickly peeked into a few of the open doors as we passed. A study with bookshelves lining the walls and a giant leather couch with a lamp towering over the side, perfect for curling up in to read.

A bathroom with yet more glass and chrome in it.

A couple of guest rooms, one in soft grays with the bed facing what I could only guess was the patio doors that led to its own balcony, its mirror image next door done in soft beiges and gray.

Then, we headed up another smaller set of stairs and along another hallway.

"And this one's yours."

I stopped behind him, and he motioned for me to open the door.

A little dramatic, but hey, he was an actor. I'd play along. I smiled and put my hand on the doorknob, pushing on the door.

It gave way, and for the first time in my life, I found myself speechless as I stared at a pale blue wonderland.

The far wall was completely glass, floor to ceiling, and it took me a moment to realize the sliding door off to the side led out to my own balcony, no doubt complete with the hint of lounger and potted plants I'd seen from below.

The huge bed lay in front of another massive window, pale blue satin draped around the posts. A bright blue sofa with white and silver stars covering its surface sat in the corner of what looked like an attached sitting room to the left, with a large, flat screen TV mounted on the wall facing it.

There was a glass desk fitted in the other corner of the sitting area.

Was that really a mini stainless steel fridge tucked next to it?

And a single serve coffeemaker on that little counter in the main room?

I took a step forward and noticed small silver stars on the one wall, barely noticeable until the light hit them.

All in all, the room looked amazing.

I let out a low whistle of admiration as he came in behind me.

"The decorator did a great job."

"Didn't use a decorator."

I turned to peer at him, a frown scrunching my face. Please don't let this be where he introduces me to his latest twenty-something girlfriend who wants to bond—at least in front of Daddy Dearest. Been there, done that. Wasn't up to it again. I had bad flashbacks of a forgettable Rangers game one December and shivered, wishing them quickly away as I cast a weary glance to the door, but the house still sounded silent, like it held just the two of us inside.

"Did everything myself."

I took one more look around.

"I'm impressed." Truly.

He looked up at the far wall where those stars were. "I hope you still like stars. I remember taking you to the Griffith Observatory when you were little."

He did? I smiled in memory. I'd loved that place back then. Even though the memories were faint, I remembered happily walking along with him, holding his hand as we looked up at the stars through the telescopes and went to the Planetarium.

"Love them."

Despite what Mom said, he did show signs of wanting this; I mean, really wanting this visit to work out.

Why else would he do all this?

Knowing he had picked out the bright blue curtains and the glass desk near the windows sorta gave me the warm fuzzies. And he'd painted those stars? Or at least had thought of them and someone else had; it didn't matter, he'd remembered the smallest things about me, what I loved, and that's all that mattered.

Okay, I was still a total Daddy's girl. So what?

I gave him a huge hug as he set my luggage on the bed. "Thank you."

He kissed my forehead, wrapping his arms around me for a quick hug before he glanced at his watch.

"It's the least I could do for you." He smiled and stepped back. "Bathroom's through there..." He pointed to a partially open door. "Closet's there." Another door I hadn't noticed. "I'll let you get settled in. I've got the stuff to barbecue burgers, if you want? Or we could try and get something somewhere."

Let's take the selfish route. My first night in town, and I wanted my dad all to myself. "Burgers sound great."

He nodded, hesitating on his way to the door, and gave me another awkward hug. "Take your time. Unpack, change. Don't forget to call your Mom. She's probably wondering if I've left you loitering at LAX."

I laughed lightly; he didn't know how true that statement was. There was probably several texts already from the moment my plane had landed, wondering how I was and if I'd seen him yet. It was probably a good thing I'd kept my phone on mute. "Will do."

He walked out the door, closing it behind him.

Left alone in my new room, I turned in a slow circle.

This was...*wow*.

I headed to the mini fridge and opened it slowly, surprised to see it fully stocked with water and my favorite root beer and juice.

He remembered.

See?

Mom was so wrong about all of this. She was so sure I'd end up disappointed.

I grabbed the rest of my soda from where I'd set it on my desk in my walking-around daze and headed to the bed to unpack. Best to put things away so I'd have room to stretch out before calling my no-doubt over-anxious mother. I figured a phone call would be more reassuring than replying to her—I picked my phone up and turned it on, checking my messages—twenty-two unread texts.

Maybe a phone call would be better?

I bit my lip, checking the time stamps of when she'd sent the last one. Ten minutes.

Just got home to Dad's. I'll phone you in a few.

I hit send on the text and put my phone down on the dresser before I took a long sip of my soda, bracing myself for the phone call.

I needed a few more minutes to figure out what exactly I should say to put her mind at ease.

"Well?"

I heard the worry in my mom's voice fifteen minutes later. I'd hung up the clothes in my walk-in closet, which seemed bigger than my entire bedroom back home. Not the sort of thing to mention, though.

The bad airline food, yes.

Dad picking me up—alone and on time?

Definitely, as that would have to put him in some sort of good light in her eyes. I mean, he didn't send his assistant or a driver or anyone else.

Just him.

And no photographer in sight.

"All good," I sighed, rolling over on the king-sized bed, a far cry from my ancient twin one at home with the brass headboard I'd had since I was little.

A girl could get used to this.

Easily!

"Really, all good," I added at her silence as my gaze lost itself to the amazing view from my corner window. The pool glistened warm and welcoming below. I'd have to take a swim later after supper.

"Okay. You know I'm just a text or phone call away," she repeated for what I swear must be the billionth time. Enough times to drive me crazy, anyway.

"You'll be my first call. But I know this is going to work out."

Even though I wanted to reassure her, I still heard a small harrumph, the sign that, yet again, she doubted my decision to try a little father-daughter bonding. She would have to get used to it, if I did decide to go to UCLA... I mean, who knows? Maybe I could stay here. Save money if I didn't have to pay for a dorm room.

I'd decided to take a year off, think about what I wanted to do, and where I wanted to be.

I'd gotten almost straight A's through school, so it wasn't like there was anything to complain about. I'd earned a little time off; even Mom agreed on that point. I'd taken extra classes, done tutoring on the side... I needed a break.

We talked for a few more minutes, and I promised to call her in a few days and text every day in between, before we hung up. I lay there, the phone still in my hand, wondering what she had to be so worried about. Dad hadn't backed out at the last minute like she'd kept hinting he would, and I couldn't imagine anything that might ruin the perfect summer I'd been picturing since he'd first suggested the idea of me coming to visit.

I still had that email.

Screencapped.

Had a printed copy in my wallet, folded up. Sometimes, I kept it in my pocket.

Emails could get deleted, and that was one I wanted to keep.

The one reminder that...

"Chey?" Dad hollered from downstairs. "You want to help me grill the burgers?"

I jumped up from the bed, ready to kick off my summer in Los Angeles. "Yeah, let me change. I'll be right there."

2

The next morning, I sat at the granite island counter, fixing my morning java—one teaspoon cream, one and a half of sugar, and five quick stirs. A couple sips, and I'd be as wide awake as I could be.

"You drink that?" Dad asked as he came into the kitchen in a faded T-shirt and plaid pajama bottoms.

Apparently, he still visualized my ten-year-old self. Mom often suffered from the same affliction. I was tempted to tell him I was driving, too, but I figured one traumatic moment at a time.

"Why not? It gets me going in the morning. Besides, I've been drinking it since I was fifteen, two, almost three whole years now."

He wiped his sleepy eyes as he poured his own mug of coffee. "Like father, like daughter, I guess."

I watched in surprise as he followed my coffee regime almost exactly, though he stirred a few extra times.

He gave me a smile over the rim before taking a long sip. "I'm working today, so that leaves you the run of the place."

He took a seat at the counter across from me.

"Great! I mean, not that you have to work, but..." I couldn't quite hide my excitement over the prospect of having a place like this to myself and on my second real, full day in Los Angeles. What could be better?

He chuckled. "I pulled out some blu-rays for you in the living room, if you want to watch them. Plus the Apple TV's hooked up. Netflix, everything's there, all yours. All the passwords you need should be on a notepad on the coffee table."

"Sounds good." I still had a bit more unpacking to do. Hadn't touched my carryon, so I still had to my laptop to take out, plus all my charging cords. My phone could probably do with a quick charge. No doubt Mom would want to check me over on Face Time to make sure I was all in one piece. No matter how many times I texted her, no matter how many pictures, she'd still worry.

The sound of nearing footsteps in the hallway caught my attention, and I turned to see a pretty brunette in jeans and a black T-shirt walking towards us.

"'Morning," she called, smiling as she laid eyes on me.

"Hi." A trickle of unease flowed in suddenly as I glanced back at Dad. I hadn't heard anyone pull up. 'Course, I'd slept in somewhat, and she could have been here for hours already.

Dad jumped to his feet, a grin on his face. I studied him for signs of who this woman might be, but nothing. He still looked like the same hair-mussed father who'd walked into the kitchen a few minutes ago.

"Chey, I want you to meet—"

Oh, man, it was way too early in the day to play nice to one of his girlfriends.

I waited for the inevitable introduction, chewing the inside of my bottom lip as all my plans for my summer started to evaporate in my head.

As she came closer, I could tell she seemed older than the last one; she looked mid-thirties, at the most, with her dark brown hair in a stylish layered cut.

"My personal assistant. Trish."

I hadn't even realized I'd been holding my breath. I could have jumped up and hugged the woman in relief. I smiled and held my hand out. So this was Trish, the woman I'd been talking to on the phone for weeks, getting the details hammered out of my flight and making sure Dad's schedule stayed as clear as possible for the trip. (Mom's rule: if he started working all the time, I was on the next flight home.)

"It's so great to finally meet you."

She gave me a warm, welcoming hug. "Same here. Glad you made it here safe and that he pulled himself away yesterday to pick you up."

I laughed, glancing at him as we separated. "Have to admit, I was surprised to see him there."

Dad feigned shock. "Hey..."

"Your rep's a little less than stellar where Chey's concerned," Trish said.

I liked her already. She turned to me.

"I would have stopped by last night, but I figured you two needed a chance to settle in." She looked at Dad and then at her watch. "You aren't anywhere near ready."

He held his hands up in surrender. "I know, I know...I'm going. You two catch up. Fill Chey in on what I neglected to tell her."

"Which, let me guess, would be everything?" she teased as he left the room. She grabbed his almost empty coffee mug and headed for the sink, dumping out the little bit of coffee he hadn't drunk and rinsed it out, before setting it aside. She opened a nearby cupboard, took a glass out, and poured herself some juice from the fridge. "How do you like Cali so far?"

"I like what I've seen of it."

"Is there anything you need today while he's busy?"

"I'm good." What could I need? I pretty well already had my day planned out—poolside 'til lunch, then inside and watching Netflix and check out those blu-rays Dad mentioned. No need to get sunstroke this early into my vacation. "What's he doing, anyway?"

"He's scheduled to do the start of a press junket this morning. His new movie's getting some early buzz."

My turn to nod, pretending I had any clue what she was talking about. I didn't know all the Hollywood lingo, not exactly like I'd ever really had the chance to learn, aside from the few things I'd picked up online. But we had talked a little over burgers last night, and I knew he was scheduled to do a pile of interviews down at one of the hotels with a couple of his co-stars for most of the day.

The timing wasn't the best, he agreed, but at least, it had been the day after I'd arrived since he'd wanted to be the one to pick me up from the airport.

"You sure you don't need or want anything? I can have lunch delivered here, if you want. He doesn't exactly have a full fridge and pantry at the best of times."

"I'm sure I can scrounge something up." If Dad and I shared any of the same DNA, there had to be the makings of a peanut butter sandwich somewhere around here. And if I felt creative enough and the ingredients were there, I could mix up a batch of my favorite chocolate chip peanut butter cookies as a surprise for later.

"Well, there's a list of numbers by the kitchen phone and in the office. If something comes up, text me first since—"

"Dad's in the junket all morning." Oh, I liked how that sounded.

Trish smiled warmly, obviously pleased I'd caught on. "I'll have him call you when he breaks for lunch. Probably somewhere around two." She checked her watch again.

Dad came in then, right on cue, dressed up in a grey silk shirt and black jeans. His hair had been tamed into the slightly spiky style that had become his trademark over the last few years.

"Looking good," I said with a grin. Now he appeared a lot more like the guy on all those magazine covers.

He smiled, and I caught a glimpse of the famous dimples.

"Got something for you," he said, casting a glance at Trish that said she knew exactly what he was up to, and she moved to take a seat at the counter.

I shrugged, not knowing what he had up his sleeve. I doubted he was about to invite me along to the junket. Didn't seem like a take-your-daughter-to-work sort of activity.

Without a word, he handed me a small, silver-wrapped box from his shirt pocket.

I looked at it for a moment. Maybe he did feel a little guilty he'd missed my seventeenth birthday last year. Not to mention my graduation a couple of weeks ago. Not that I held a grudge; I was excited I was getting to spend more than a few days, or a few hours, with him, which seemed to have been the hallmark of our visits the last couple of years.

If he'd tried to make my grad, it would have been just another couple hours squeezed into his schedule, and his appearance probably would have caused some sort of commotion. So, probably better in a way he hadn't been able to come. There wasn't much to see, anyways—I walked across a stage and got a piece of paper, along with a couple hundred other people.

You see one person do it, you've seen them all.

Besides, I had the footage Mom took of it all stored on my phone for him to look at if he wanted.

I ripped open the shiny wrapping paper, shooting him a questioning look. He just shrugged, but the smirk stayed on his face, like he couldn't wait for my reaction to whatever lay inside.

So totally not suspicious, in the least.

I swore I saw Trish lift her cell phone up, no doubt recording this moment for him, making me wonder just what he was up to.

I lifted the lid to find a key ring nestled there. I recognized the obvious house key, but there was also a distinct car key on there, along with the remote control entry fob. And to my knowledge, the car I drove still sat in the garage back home, unless Mom was borrowing it again when hers conked out.

"What's this?"

"Well, I can't very well leave you alone in L.A. without wheels. This way, you won't have to rely on rides from me or Trish or whoever. I didn't exactly love the idea of you taking Uber everywhere. I doubt your mom would, either."

He must have noticed my eyes start to gloss over as the sharp sting of the tears I was fighting back prickled my eyes.

"Now, it's nothing fancy."

As long as it had four wheels and an engine, I was going to be more than happy. Seriously. I sniffled a little as I glanced back down at the key ring in my hand. I never even thought of having a way to get around here on my own; guess I'd never really thought that far ahead. "Dad..."

"You should be able to blend in easily with this," he said, tapping the keys.

I took them and followed him out the patio doors, through the side of the yard, and out to the driveway. There, parked in front of the garage where the Escalade had sat, gleamed a shiny black BMW convertible.

I must've stumbled. "You're kidding me."

My heartbeat started doing an impressive tap dance in my chest, making me think a heart attack was imminent.

A car.

A brand new car.

"In a good way?"

I wrapped my arms around him in a tight hug. "It's more than good. It's amazing. Thank you!"

The relief on his face that I liked my present seemed obvious—as if there could have been any doubt. A brand-new, shiny car; what girl in her right mind wouldn't be ecstatic over a present like that? "Can I take it out?"

"Of course you can. What do you say you drive us to dinner tonight?"

"Sounds perfect."

"Great. I'll let you check it out." He gave me a final squeeze before letting me go.

I barely noticed him walk back to the house as I squealed and headed around to the driver's side, staring at the keychain in my hand and hitting the button for the door. The trunk popped up, instead, and I laughed to myself. I hit the other button and heard the click for the door.

I stretched my arm out and slammed the trunk down before opening the driver's door and getting hit with the most amazing new car smell. New. The closest my beat-up car came to that happened through one of those 'supposed' new car smell air fresheners from the car wash.

"Hold up."

Trish's voice. I turned back to see her jogging towards me, camera in hand.

"We've got to properly document the moment," she said with a smile.

I grinned proudly as I slid into the seat. Oh my God, this was what Heaven felt like. My hands looped casually around the steering wheel, and that's when I noticed the bright pink bow on the stick shift. I laughed to myself; he really was thinking of everything.

"Can you swing this way?" she asked, breaking me out of my new car owner daze.

I moved like I was about to step out of the car and smiled even bigger. "Like this?"

Oh, I totally wanted to send this one to Mom, but she'd so get the wrong idea, especially on my first full day in Cali. I knew exactly what she'd say, too—*buying my affection. Blah blah blah. Material things can't make up for the time we'd never spent together.*

Blah.

Blah.

Blah.

"Perfect. We'll print off a copy and set it on your dad's desk in a frame. He'll love it."

"I can't believe he did something like this." Reluctantly, I climbed out of my car, running my fingers over the smooth leather of the steering wheel. Okay, so had this been at home, I would have been driving around showing it off. Here, I basically had no one to show it off to—at least, anyone who'd care, anyway. To people here, I would just be another Hollywood teenager driving a pretty car, blending in with all the other Hollywood kids.

"He wanted to. Combination graduation, birthday, and welcome to Los Angeles present. All his idea, really. Took him two weeks to find just the right one."

I turned and walked backwards, watching the sun glint off the finish. I had images of him looking up cars online trying to find one he just knew I'd like, then taking it for a test drive before making the final decision. "It's amazing. I love it."

"He thought black was the most stylish."

I nodded, turning and following Trish back inside the kitchen as I scanned through the pictures she'd snapped on the camera, finding the perfect one to print off.

"It's great. I just can't believe he'd do something like that." The goofy grin wouldn't come off my face no matter how hard I tried to stop.

"Like he said, it's the easiest way for you to get around. Explore the city a little on your own. It's got GPS, so you won't get lost. He made sure it's got the latest everything."

We headed down a side hallway off the kitchen I hadn't gotten around to exploring yet.

"Use your dad's office." She opened the door to our left and waved me in. "Computer's set up, if you want to download the pictures and email them to your Mom?" she suggested. "And to print, just use the photo printer on the glass table in the corner. It's all set to go."

"Okay, great." I sank into Dad's oversized black leather chair behind his glass desk.

"We're off," Dad announced as he appeared in the doorway, jingling his own car keys. "If you go out, just leave me a note. I won't have my phone on, Trish's number's listed everywhere around here, so if you need anything, call her. She can get a hold of me in case of emergency."

"Will do. See ya." I waved as he disappeared down the hall and I heard their voices muffle the further they went. Within moments, I heard the front door close, followed shortly by a vehicle's engine.

I moved the computer mouse, and the jumbo-sized computer screen lit up. I saw Dad—or maybe Trish, but I wanted to think it was Dad's doing—had already set me up with an account on his computer. I clicked on my name beside the twinkling shooting star he'd picked as my logo and waited for the computer to load.

It didn't take long to transfer the pictures to the computer and print them off. I debated on whether or not to send a quick one to Mom, conveniently cropped, of course, to hide the pretty pink bow that would totally give away the whole present thing. Instead, I left the printed photos on Dad's desk for when he came home.

Knowing I had the place to myself, I headed back to the kitchen and made myself another cup of coffee. I went through the cupboards and found Trish was right. Not a lot there, but the standard PB&J fixings, a couple boxes of my favorite cereals, and enough protein bars to get Dad through any emergency. I threw together half of a sandwich and munched on it as I sat at the counter, scanning through my phone. All was silent. The sun wasn't too high in the sky yet, so I could spend some quality time bonding with the pool and the sunshine.

But first...I kind of wanted to explore.

I set my empty mug and plate in the sink to put in the dishwasher later and set about exploring the house. Now that I was by myself, I was able to take my time and wander around, acclimating to my new surroundings.

I wandered around the first floor, taking a closer look at the framed photos hanging on the walls. I recognized some old family shots of Dad when he was younger with his parents. Him fishing with some friends that looked semi recent given the haircut.

I played with the remote in the living room, found the handwritten instructions from Trish on using the voice-activated system.

"Close front living room curtains." I tried out, hanging on to the remote as I looked around the room. With the smallest whirring sound, the curtains slid easily shut.

Well, that would be handy.

I went back through the kitchen, back to the hallway that had led to Dad's office. I followed it further down, finding Dad's home gym just off from his office.

I turned the light on and peeked in. One mirrored wall faced me with a treadmill, elliptical, exercise bike, and a couple other machines I didn't quite recognize right away making a nice row to my right while enough weights to fill a fitness store were to my left. A huge TV mounted in the far corner faced the machines.

Definitely seemed like his man cave to me.

I flipped the light back off and headed to the last room down the hall, moving the heavy barn-style door to the side, revealing a large, dark room.

I stepped forward, fumbling for the light switch on the wall. Finally, my hand connected with it, and the overhead pot lights flickered to life. I turned around and smiled.

Done in shades of gray and black, black and white movie posters hung on one side of the room, with a few of Dad's movie posters framed hung on the right. In front of me were two rows of giant leather couches that I was pretty sure reclined.

And in front of that, the biggest projection screen I had ever seen outside of a movie theater.

I had definitely found my second favorite room of the house.

I took a couple steps forward, finding a mini candy counter on the far corner of the room and another mini fridge with a glass front, filled to the brim with assorted drinks. More controls and a couple throws were on the first couch. I picked up one of the remotes on the couch and studied it for a few minutes, hitting a couple buttons and waiting for something to happen, but nothing did.

No lights.

No sounds.

Nothing.

I figured I'd better stop playing around before I broke something. I could work the TV in the living room or my bedroom if I wanted to watch something. Plus there was always my laptop.

I set the remote back where I'd found it and turned to check out the candy counter. I skipped over the chocolate-covered peanuts, plain chocolate bars, and grabbed a mint chocolate bar from the back before I turned the lights out and walked out of the room.

Talk about surreal, I still had a feeling someone was going to pop up and tell me to stay behind the velvet ropes of this little Hollywood tour.

It still didn't feel real, like I was staying with my dad.

I guess our father-daughter relationship had evolved or something. That was probably typical since I wasn't a little girl anymore.

But still, I mean it's not like I expected him to have tea parties with my stuffed animals—I'd passed that stage a long time ago—and it was cool he was giving me so much independence and all.

I mean, honestly, my mom would never have let me go explore a strange new city all on my own. Like ever.

But Dad had left me all alone, with total permission to take off and go wherever I wanted. I didn't need a twenty-four hour babysitter.

I just didn't really have anywhere I wanted to go.

I was right into the musical episode of Buffy, belting out the lyrics along with Willow, when the doorbell rang. Everything in me froze, hoping whoever stood on the other side of the door couldn't hear my horrible off-key singing. I paused the episode and headed barefoot across the living room to the front door, peering through the peep hole to see a delivery guy in a black T-shirt and matching baseball cap.

I opened the door cautiously, about to tell him he had the wrong house.

"Pizza delivery."

"I didn't order any—"

He looked bored as he held out the cardboard box. "Trish sent me."

"Oh, okay." Guess she'd been serious before. I started to turn to go for my wallet, but he stopped me, putting the pizza box in my hands instead.

"Already taken care of."

By the time I murmured thanks, he was halfway to the red sedan parked at the end of the driveway. I shut the door behind him with my hip and headed back to the living room to turn the television off before going outside to eat. Figured I might as well soak up some sun and have lunch at the same time. I had my cell phone in my pocket and I sorta itched to call Mom to tell her what I was doing. But I kinda didn't think she'd take too well to the fact that on my first full day in L.A., Dad was working. A huge no-no that I planned on keeping my mouth shut about.

Besides, Trish assured me it was only a one-day type of thing and that the next few months were wide open.

I stopped at the counter, set the pizza down and opened the box, inhaling deeply. It smelled amazing. Pepperoni, mushrooms, and peppers. Someone knew my absolute favorite. I put a still steaming slice on a plate, grabbed a bottled water from the fridge, and headed outside to enjoy my private lunch for one.

Dad was late.

The clock on the microwave had read almost eight last time I'd wandered in to check, and that had to be at least fifteen minutes ago. I sat out back, figuring I would seem a little too eager if I waited in the living room. Upstairs looked like I didn't care, but outside, I could hear him pull in and act surprised at the time when he appeared.

I grabbed the next issue from the stack of magazines I'd brought down from my carryon and waited to hear the crunching sound of tires on the gravel stone of the driveway.

By the time I heard a door slam, I'd fallen half-asleep in the lounge chair, the stack of magazines at my side sliding in all directions as I jostled myself awake.

"Sorry I'm late," Dad announced a few moments later.

I blinked my eyes open.

"It's okay. What time is it?" I stifled a yawn.

"Quarter after nine." He walked towards me, pulling off his sunglasses and tucking them in his shirt collar. "Sorry, Chey. Look, I'll drive. I know a great place to take you to for your first meal out in L.A."

"I'm ready to go."

"I'll be five minutes." He tossed me the keys to the Escalade and headed inside.

I sat in the SUV, waiting while he changed and wondered what he thought would be suitable for my first real meal out in Los Angeles. I ran through some of the restaurants I knew about in my head, all of which sounded way too dressy for my jeans and pink tank top ensemble. I was just about to run inside and change when he opened the driver's door.

"Am I dressy enough?" I asked, closing up the mirror on the sunshade. I'd added a fresh layer of my favorite lip gloss since it had faded away since I'd first gotten ready hours ago.

Dad laughed. "Totally. Trust me, this place is super casual."

I breathed a sigh of relief. "Good."

"Sorry about taking longer than I thought," he said as we left the house behind. "We ended up giving some interviews that were lengthier than expected."

"That's fine. I soaked up some sun."

"Trish said she sent lunch?"

"Pizza."

"Good."

I tried to follow where he was going, but I became seriously confused by the time we were a few blocks from home. I had a feeling my GPS was going to quickly become my new BFF.

Soon, he made another turn, and according to a passing street sign, we were headed down Melrose, finally another name I recognized.

"Got any idea where we're headed?"

"Can't say I do," I said, watching buildings and trees blur by as we passed.

"You in the mood for a hot dog and fries, and maybe a celeb or two?"

"Absolutely."

We parked in a small side lot beside the little white building that housed Pink's. From where we were, I could see the bright white patio tables and red and white striped umbrellas. A few people sat out there eating, but it didn't seem too busy for that time of night.

All right, so it wasn't exactly what I expected, but I figured he was doing his best to take me to all the L.A. hot spots. And from his spiel as we parked, Pink's existed as a Hollywood legend itself, dating all the way back to the late 1930s.

We quickly got out of the SUV and headed down the sidewalk towards Pink's which Dad said surprisingly wasn't too busy yet, since the line wasn't halfway down the street.

Dad pulled his wallet out as we reached the back of the line outside. I kept glancing around. It was busy even at that time of day. People walking by. More people joined up behind us, talking loudly to each other. Cars sped past. I kept trying to catch a glimpse of my first live celebrity—my father not included—but so far, I hadn't seen a single one.

Which left me only slightly disappointed. Did the entire celebrity population of Los Angeles all make a mass exodus the second I stepped off the plane?

Soon, we made it through to almost the front of the line—only a couple were in front of us ordering at the counter.

"Why don't you go up ahead, find us a table, and I'll take care of the ordering?"

"You sure?" I asked, casting a look around us. So far, no one was paying us any attention, but still...

"Yeah, go ahead. I'll surprise you with the order. Go on. There's a whole pile of photos around the back I'm sure you'd love to see. Maybe a familiar face or two in there."

I nodded, excusing myself by a couple of tourists ahead of us and turned down the hallway that lead towards the back. There were a few small white tables for two along the wall as I went. Through an open doorway was the room Dad had mentioned with the rows of framed photos on the wall.

Famous faces stared back from every one, and I wondered if Dad had a picture on there somewhere; he must have since he'd said familiar faces. I headed to where it looked like some newer pictures had been hung and tried to spot him staring back at me. I must have lost track of time because the next thing I knew, Dad was beside me, a tray of amazing-smelling food in his hands.

"Grab a table yet?" he asked, looking amused.

"Uh..."

He chuckled. "Don't worry about it. I thought you might have gotten distracted so I snagged one on my way over," he said as he turned and headed to the table he'd reserved for us.

I followed him out of the small room and towards the back open area. One of the back tables with the umbrellas had a homemade-looking reserved sign leaning against the umbrella stand, a simple folded piece of paper with *Reserved* scribbled in black ink.

"You weren't in line long." I sat down as he put the tray on the table and took down the reserved sign, folding it up and sticking it in his back pocket.

He shrugged. "There wasn't that many orders ahead of us."

He took a seat across from me.

"Smells great."

"Some of the best food in the city. I've been coming here since I first came to L.A."

"Really?" I asked as I grabbed a napkin and spread it out in front of me on the table.

Dad put my food in front of me, a hot dog, chili cheese fries, and a drink.

"Oh, yeah. Back then, it was a chance for me to meet someone famous. Now, I come strictly for the food. And tonight, a chance to show off my beautiful daughter."

I couldn't help myself from smiling as I ducked my head. "Do you come here often?"

"Used to. Once a week, at least. Now, it's a little less often." He smiled, grabbing a napkin from the tray. "Place has quite a history," he said as he took a look around.

"I can see that." I bit into my chili cheese dog. Heaven. I totally forgave him for being late. I took a few more bites in silence, just soaking in the atmosphere. It seemed quieter back here for some reason, even though we weren't all that far from the street.

"Are you seeing anyone?" I asked, grabbing a couple fries.

"Are you?" Dad countered, or at least it seemed that way as he reached for his drink.

"Not anymore." I took another bite of my chili dog and looked at the scenery. A couple other people had joined us nearby, but they were too busy with their conversation to pay us any attention.

"Why not?"

Dad seemed very interested, all of a sudden. I so hoped he didn't have plans to fix me up with someone. Talk about embarrassing, having your own father play matchmaker.

I shrugged. "He was too busy."

"With?"

"Other girls."

"Sorry, kiddo."

"S'okay. I'd rather be single, anyways," I said, trying to sound like I meant it.

Besides, what good would a boyfriend be right now when I was spending the summer out here? I totally didn't buy into that long-distance stuff, either. I mean, if that worked, my parents should have still been together, and they obviously weren't. So see, I had a case study of how disastrous a long-distance relationship could be.

"What about you? Anyone new since the Botox beauty?"

Dad started coughing like he was choking on his French fries, and I became tempted to get up and slap him on the back.

"I, uh..." he coughed again, reaching for another napkin from the tray. "Botox beauty?" he finally managed.

"Didn't you ever notice her face never really moved? At least, her lips. She was totally expressionless half the time."

"Now that you mention it..." he trailed off, taking a healthy gulp of his soda, but I could see the grin he was trying hard to hide.

"I didn't really like her."

"What about your mom?"

"I like her, sometimes."

He gave me one of those 'that's not what I meant' looks. "She dating anyone?"

"Doubt it. She lives and breathes business." I paused to stare at a passing car leaving the parking lot. If I squinted, it could have been one of the Hemsworth brothers. On closer inspection as the car got closer, totally not, unless they were currently sporting a blue-tipped windblown Mohawk.

So much for my celeb spotting.

I reached for another French fry.

"Was she okay with you coming here?"

Hmm. Go with the truth, or smooth things over? "I think she was surprised by your offer."

We both had been. Heck, I still carried the email he sent around in my pocket, just to be sure I hadn't dreamt the whole thing.

He wasn't the worst father in the world, but the invite to spend the summer with him had come completely out of nowhere, that's all.

We ate in silence, him devouring two hot dogs and half a basket of fries while I added more ketchup to the side of my basket and dunked a few fries cautiously.

"Thanks," I said finally, my fingers toying with the edge of the napkin nervously, like they were trying to create origami.

Dad looked surprised as he finished off his second hot dog. "For what?"

"Dinner. And well, everything."

Inviting me out here, and most importantly not backing out of it...

"I want this summer to be great for you, Chey."

"It will be," I said with a hopeful smile. It had to be.

3

"An invite?" I repeated, glancing at the piece of paper on the counter that Dad had come down with that morning. I barely knew a handful of people on the west coast, let alone Los Angeles, so how could I get invited anywhere? Unless Dad had gotten involved somehow.

He shut the fridge door with his hip. So that's where I got that habit from.

"Thought you could use a chance to hang out with people your own age. It's tonight, by the way."

"Tonight?"

Nothing like a little last-minute notice.

I leaned on the kitchen counter, swirling my spoon around the last of my strawberry yogurt in the bottom of the container as I looked at the supposed invitation again. I'd barely had a chance to hang out with anyone, spending more time watching Netflix by the pool on my tablet than with anyone three-dimensional since I'd gotten here.

"Hot date tonight?"

He almost choked on his orange juice. "What?"

"You obviously want me out of the house for some reason, so logical thought is you've got a hot date tonight."

"It's not a hot date, it's a..."

Ah ha! I knew I wasn't wrong. There was a woman involved. Mom had the same pattern when she had a date. I either ended up staying the night at a friend's house or hanging out with my aunt.

"If you're going to say one night stand, that's way too much info for me."

He grinned. "Hardly."

I so didn't need the image of walking in on Dad and some woman kissing on the couch—or even worse.

I took the so-called invite. Obviously, it had been emailed over given the unfamiliar email address at the top of the page, making me wonder if Trish actually had a hand this. Maybe she wanted to make sure I had a good vacation, which had to include making a friend or two. I studied the page, which seemed pretty sparse. Time, address, and a gate code.

No names.

Nothing.

"Whose party is it?" Maybe I was too naïve and that's how they handled parties out here lately. Not like anyone could text me an invite, since, well, other than Dad and Trish, who had my number?

"A friend of mine's daughter. Adriana. She's around your age, maybe a little older. Haven't seen her in a while."

Ah. My dad was trying to socialize me. Was this his version of a Daddy and Me play date without the daddy portion? He'd probably already decided he didn't want to spend an entire summer with me on his hands. Okay, so I have a wee bit of an overactive imagination. Creativity runs in the family. Dad *had* written a couple screenplays over the years.

"You might enjoy a night out."

With people I don't know.

I reached for my cell phone I'd left on the other side of the counter and tapped the address in. Bellagio Drive? The only Bellagio I'd heard of before was the hotel in Vegas.

"I don't know..."

"Think about it. But I think you'd have a good time. Might be nice to for you to meet some people. Have someone to hang out with if I'm busy." He must have noticed the skeptical look still on my face. "It's up to you if you want to go or not. I just thought I'd give you the option."

Right.

Because staying at home did not mean I was embracing my glam new life—well, the one I was borrowing this summer. Because even though Dad was Dad, *my dad,* this still didn't quite feel like it all belonged to me.

"I'll think about it," I said when I noticed he was watching me pretty intently.

He gave me a quick hug, tapped the piece of paper on the counter one last time before he headed off to play basketball, and I stared at the invite, already crinkled from how tightly I gripped the corner.

Somehow, I found myself sitting outside at the oversized patio table with the printed directions from Google and a tall glass of orange juice.

I was in charge of my own happiness—Mom's favorite saying. I looked at the map and invite again before I reached for my cell phone.

"Who are you calling?"

I jumped at the sound of Trish's voice.

"You, actually." I turned to see her coming out the patio doors, sliding her sunglasses to the top of her head.

She smiled. "Looks like I saved you a call. What can I do for you?"

I read the address on the paper. "Bellagio Road?"

I looked at the invitation again, then back at Trish.

"Yeah, it's not too far."

That, I knew from the printed directions. In good traffic, it was literally less than ten minutes away.

"Should I really go to this?" I waved the copy of the email, feeling torn. My first Hollywood party, but I'd know absolutely no one. Then again, I wasn't going to meet anyone hanging outside by Dad's pool, either.

See? I was totally making myself crazy with these arguments.

"Why not? Why wouldn't you go?"

"Have you seen my closet?" I didn't exactly sport the season's hottest looks. Or last season's, for that matter. I wasn't exactly the type of girl who lived for fashion. If it was comfortable and I liked it, I wore it.

"Is that all? That's easily solved. Come on."

I followed her inside the house, wondering for a moment if she was going to become my fairy godmother, complete with magic wand and the ability to transform me from Chey to Cinderella—although without the poufy dress.

That so wasn't my style.

Trish's magic wand turned out to be Dad's platinum AMEX card. She promised my matching one was on its way—Dad had ordered me one just before I'd arrived. Along with a supposed new bank card I hadn't seen yet, either.

"He talked you into this, didn't he?" I asked as I got in the passenger side of her car ten minutes later after I'd grabbed my shoes and purse and put my hair into a ponytail.

I probably convinced him that morning I needed drastic help. I couldn't even decide if I wanted to go to a party or not. A tsunami size wave of guilt washed over me. Trish didn't need to baby-sit me. I'm sure she had more important things to do than try to help me fit in.

"I offered." She glanced at me with a warm smile as she pulled out onto the street. "Besides, I didn't think you'd want to go shopping with him. He's in and out of a store in like fifteen minutes, he knows exactly what he wants when he goes in, and once he has it, he leaves. Not much fun in that"

I had to agree with her on that point. "How did I get invited, anyways? I don't know anyone here I'm not related to."

"He's good friends with her parents. He mentioned you were coming out here last week over dinner and that you didn't know anyone. Their daughter was glad to put you on the list."

The list.

That definitely sounded L.A.

"So, what do I need to know?" I asked, picking at my thumbnail.

"Be yourself. Remember, all these kids are just like you."

Sure. I leaned back and watched the palm trees blur by. Just like me, huh? Wasn't so sure about that. They'd probably all grown up together, been to countless different events together, school, everything. They had history.

I, on the other hand, didn't.

My events? The occasional Rangers game with Dad. The once or twice we'd ended up on the screen. Dad's movies had always been a little too 'adult' for me to go to a red carpet for. And he'd always been working when there'd been an invite to something a little more family-friendly.

So I was the new girl...who likely needed to find a way to fit in.

By the time we returned home several hours and several stores later, I was the proud new owner of a nice new L.A.-inspired wardrobe. Shoes that had made me smile the first time I saw them were now in their boxes, waiting to be put on a shelf in my closet. Jeans I'd looked at online were now being pulled out of multiple shopping bags and laid on the bed. Shorts. Shirts. Tank tops. I had enough to nicely fill in my sparse walk-in closet. Plus thrown in were a couple new swimsuits Trish had talked me into since I was spending so much time out by the pool already.

I would have dwindled my measly savings account on the shoes alone if Trish hadn't told me it was Dad's treat and to put everything on his credit card.

Personally, I figured he was experiencing parental guilt over missing my graduation and my first full week in L.A. But hey, I wasn't complaining, not with my freshly stocked closet.

Trish handed me the new sunglasses she'd bought me for the party that night. "I think your Dad's back. Do you want to show him what we got?"

I peered at the stack of clothes covering my bed and grew a little nervous. I could barely see any of my duvet beneath. Maybe he'd say it was too much. "Maybe not right now."

I stuck my hands in my back jean pockets and swayed back and forth on my feet a little, biting my bottom lip.

"I'll go tell him we're back and leave you to get ready. Holler if you need anything."

She shut the door behind her, then I turned back to stare at the bed, the total number of clothes almost overwhelming me. I mean, I thought a new shirt and jeans would be fine—it was only one party, right? But Trish had been adamant Dad would want me to get what I needed for the summer, so...that's what we did, leaving behind many happy salesclerks in our wake.

I headed to my balcony door to see if Dad was out back, but instead, I saw a tall, dark-haired, decently muscular guy in the yard near the garage, staring up at the house. I yanked the curtain back quickly, hesitating about peeking back outside.

All right, there had to be a reason for there to be a strange guy in the backyard.

The conversation with Dad about my somewhat non-existent love life came flashing back, and suddenly, a wash of dread came over me. I really hoped he hadn't decided to play matchmaker. First, the party, and now what, a date?

I pulled the curtain back a little, but he was gone.

I knew he hadn't been a mirage.

I could go to Trish and tell her I saw some strange teenager on the property, or even call Dad on his cell. Maybe this guy was a stalker. All celebs had stalkers, right? This one could be Dad's. One who kinda, now that I thought about it, looked a lot like the pizza delivery guy from yesterday. Oh lord, I'd answered the door, not even bothering to ask how he'd gotten by the gate.

"Chey!" Dad hollered from down the hall, ruining my overeager imagination.

"Coming!" I grabbed my sunglasses from where I'd absently set them down on the edge of the bed and headed downstairs in time to see him disappear from view. Maybe he'd seen the guy, too.

"Dad?" I called, not sure where to go.

"Outside."

Not on the patio. I walked barefoot across the cement stones, enjoying the warmth beneath my feet as I tried to figure out where he was. I rounded the edge of the house, thinking maybe I should have grabbed my cell phone, when I saw the same pizza delivery guy towering over Dad by a good inch and a half, talking away like they were best buddies.

"Chey, come meet someone," Dad said with a big warm smile as he finally saw me and waved me over to join them.

Who was this guy? I really hoped Dad hadn't befriended his stalker...

Or worse.

With that grin on Dad's face, he looked awfully happy for me to meet this guy. Oh, please, do not let this be some bizarre fix-up. I know I'd told him I was single again, but that didn't mean he needed to go out and find me someone. I managed a weak smile as I stopped in front of him, putting my attention squarely on Dad.

"This is Milo."

I turned my head and looked up at him. Wow, was he tall—and extremely familiar. Definitely the delivery guy. The breeze teased his shaggy black hair.

"Hi. I'm Chey."

Dad must have sensed the whole 'who the hell is he' vibe emanating from me. "He's Trish's son."

I think I stumbled back a good step or two. Trish had a son?

"Nice to meet you." *You look nothing like your mother*, I wanted to say.

"You, too." He gave me a half smile then turned back to my dad. "I'll get that taken care of."

"Thanks, Milo."

We watched him walk away, and I glanced at Dad. "He works here, too?"

"Summers. He does some errands Trish can't or wouldn't want to do. He's the one I played basketball with earlier."

Great. Male bonding at its finest? But before I could think of something coherent to ask, Dad beat me to it.

"So, Trish tells me you're going out tonight."

"Yeah, thought I'd give it a shot."

He grinned and ruffled my hair like I was five. "Glad you're going. I think you'll have a great time."

Fingers crossed. But I kept silent.

Great time. Fingers crossed. But I was kind of doubtful of the whole great time aspect so I kept silent.

"I have a surprise for you."

"Will it top the car?" I half-joked.

"It could. I called my stylist, and she's sending someone over to do your hair and make up for tonight."

My jaw dropped. "Seriously?"

I'd figured I'd check through a couple YouTube tutorials to update my usual look. A little more eye shadow, darker eyeliner, and I hoped I'd blend in or at least not stand out so much.

"I thought you deserved the star treatment on your first big night in town. She'll probably be here soon if you wanted to head in and start getting changed." He checked his watch, and I couldn't help doing the same, leaning over his arm to see the time. I had what was hopefully plenty of time to get ready and get there.

"Thanks, Dad." I stood on my tiptoes and kissed his cheek, smiling at his smile.

"I just want you to be happy, Kiddo."

"I am."

By the time Trish had knocked on my door with Veronica, Dad's stylist, right behind her, I was trying not to bite off all my fingernails, a habit I'd never had before.

It hadn't taken Veronica that long to work her magic after she'd paired one of my new shirts with a pair of sandals and a pair of jeans. After a quick introduction, Trish had taken off, Veronica had set her make up bag out, checked what I had, and we'd started talking while she worked.

My usually stick straight, flat hair that I bemoaned most days was in soft waves that looked more natural than anything. Veronica liked what I'd picked up that afternoon and added a few things of her own. My make-up was a little darker than what I normally wore, with a little more glow than I'd ever been capable of creating on my own, but I had to agree with her as she packed up her gear that it looked perfect.

With a good luck hug, she left me to finish getting ready. I fastened my little gold earrings in my ears, took a deep breath, slid my feet into my new sandals, and headed downstairs.

"You look great," Trish said as I came down the last stair.

"Really?" I wasn't normally so self-conscious, but I had no idea who was going to be at this party. Pretty well everyone I knew in L.A. was in the house at that very moment.

I must have looked really anxious. It was the only reason I could think of to explain the next words out of her mouth.

"Do you want Milo to go with you?"

I knew Trish meant that as a good thing, but taking Milo? I barely knew him more than a millisecond.

I looked over at him sitting at the kitchen table, tapping away on a laptop.

"Do you want to go?" I asked politely, fingers crossed he had other plans. I didn't need a babysitter. Even one my age.

He shook his head, not even looking at me. "No, thanks."

There was something in his voice that I didn't quite understand, but I figured he was as thrilled with the invite to tag along as I'd been.

I tugged down the back of my navy blue halter top from where it kept wanting to ride up in the back. "Well, then I guess I'll go."

"You've got your directions and the invite?" Trish asked.

"Yeah." I had made sure I had both upstairs on paper so I didn't need to worry about my phone suddenly finding the only dead zone in Los Angeles or having the GPS in the car suddenly die on me. I needed the pass code to get inside without looking like an idiot or trying to prove who I was to some bored-looking security guy.

The map would be a little less important. If I got lost, I could always call Trish for help or try and use the GPS system in my car. It didn't seem like it would be too complicated, but I figured Trish was my best option, the reason why she was now contact number one on my cell phone.

"You look great, Chey," Dad said as he walked into the kitchen and saw me. "Have fun. You'll do fine tonight."

Right.

After a couple quick hugs from him and Trish, I headed for the front door. If this was Mom's, she'd be telling me to be back before midnight, text when I got there, and text her if I knew I was going to be late.

But there were no instructions from Trish, and Dad had already headed back upstairs to his stylist, the one who'd done my hair and make-up for me so I blended in, or at least attempted to, anyway. Didn't want to look like a complete outsider, even if I was one.

Welcome to my first L.A. gridlock.

For what was supposed to be probably a ten-minute trip tops, I was stuck in bumper-to-bumper traffic on Sunset, wishing I'd taken the alternate route, the one that had looked like a curvy snake on my print out. Instead, I'd opted for what I'd thought would be the easier drive. *Ha.*

The announcer on the radio talked about an accident a mere two blocks away. No wonder I still sat in the same spot as I did twenty minutes ago. Someone a little more superstitious might think this was the definitive sign that this was the wrong thing to do, that I should turn the car back around at my first chance and head home.

But the new me, the one wearing the brand new Fenty and MAC make-up, in brand new jeans that were worth more than one of my pizza delivery paychecks last summer, tapping her sandaled foot inside her shiny new black car, was ready to fully embrace her new existence.

And step one was to go to this party.

Maybe I'd find someone I could hang out with. I think Dad hoped Milo and I would become fast friends, but he wasn't exactly the warm and welcoming type like his mother.

Just as I was about to attempt to use the GPS to find an alternate route that would get me around the accident, the car in front of me started to move.

I took a deep breath and eased further into traffic.

Now or never, there really would be no turning back.

4

I turned into the driveway with the number partially hidden by the ivy and hoped—prayed, even—that this was the right address. I could just imagine trying to key the code in for the party and having some nasty security guy come charging towards me, demanding to know what I was doing.

Luckily for me, the code worked on the first try, and the huge black gates slid smoothly back, welcoming me in. I gingerly put my foot on the gas and crept forward in awe as I followed the curving road up past the gates and up a slight incline.

After one last bend, suddenly, the road opened up.

The driveway, if it could still be called that, spread out like a huge parking lot in front of me, both left and right.

Parked cars were everywhere, and suddenly, apprehension washed over me as I could see the house up ahead, a short trek from where I sat.

Well, it was either a house or some sort of movie set with the size of it. It seemed like there should have been cameras or a film crew milling around, setting up shots or whatever else they do.

But all I saw were a few people around my age getting out of cars and lazily walking up towards the house.

It dwarfed Dad's easily.

Heck, Dad's could have been considered a garage next to this one. If there was a place that seemed old Hollywood, this was it.

What was I doing? I *so* didn't belong in a place like this.

No one had seen me yet; I could simply sneak back out. Not like anyone was expecting me, anyway. I still wasn't sure this Adriana even knew I'd been invited, let alone who I was.

I could just go.

On the other hand, this could be my only real chance to meet people my age for a while.

Well, besides Milo.

I quickly made a deal with myself, hoping it would stop my nerves from making me sick.

If I didn't find a single person to talk to, or simply didn't like it there, I was gone. I didn't need to stay long, fifteen minutes, half-hour tops, and then, I could leave. I could still make the nine o'clock movie somewhere. Or if not, hit a drive thru, get a burger, go home, and spend some quality time on my balcony, watch the city lights for a while. Not like anyone would be checking what time I'd actually gotten home. Dad didn't seem like the type to check the security camera.. If he asked, I could tell him I had a good time, and no one would be the wiser.

I parked my new car alongside a few others off to the side, ending up between a shiny red Jag and another BMW convertible like mine and got ready to make my hike towards the front door all the while thinking calm thoughts. Anything to keep down the sandwich I'd hastily eaten a few hours before at Trish's insistence. As she'd said, I didn't want to get sick or pass out from nerves.

Imagine that little spectacle.

What a way to make a grand Hollywood entrance.

I grabbed my cell phone from the glove compartment and my wallet and stuffed them inside my tiny purse, a gift from Trish.

I slid out the driver's side, adjusting my top one last time before starting to close the door and hitting the fob, locking the doors before tucking my keys into my jeans pocket.

My car door slammed louder than expected. I winced—what a way to announce my arrival. But at least, no one was really around to witness it, right?

"Hey!"

Damn, I was so not lucky.

I spun at the voice to see a tall and pretty brunette in jeans and a bright blue tank top coming towards me from a few vehicles over. I held tighter to my purse, ready to prove I wasn't the outsider I appeared to be.

"Uh, hi," I said quickly, "I've got my invite...right here."

Well, it was there, somewhere. I fumbled through my purse. How could I lose something in a purse this small? I went for my wallet, trying to remember if I'd folded up the invite when I was sitting in the car giving myself a pep talk. Maybe I'd tucked it in my cell phone case? I could just see this girl demanding to know who I was and how I got invited to what was an obvious private party. And me without a recent photo of me and Dad. Shit. I knew we should have taken a selfie before I left.

But what would that prove, anyway? It would look like just another teenage girl taking a selfie with a celeb.

Argh.

The pretty brunette smiled and waved a dismissive hand just as I was thinking of going back inside the car and seeing if it had fallen on the floor.

"No need. If you knew the pass code to get by the gates, you're supposed to be here. I'm Sorche, and you're—" she gave me a quick once over, scanning my face intently for a couple of seconds, an embarrassed hue darkening her perfectly made-up cheeks. "God, no clue. I'm sorry," she admitted somewhat sheepishly.

I blushed, even though I figured I'd better get used to that reaction. I held my hand out awkwardly. "I'm Chey Daniels. My dad's Sean Morrow."

Technically, I was Chey Daniels-Morrow, but since we moved, Mom had decided to drop the hyphen to make it easier for me to blend in. I was more used to being plain old Daniels than having the Morrow tacked on.

"Oh, he's hot! I had a crush on him when I was younger. I just loved his last movie," she said with a big grin as she shook my hand easily and laughed. "Our dads have known each other for years, I think they even share the same trainer," she rattled on. "You're new to town, right?"

Wow. Did I look that out of place, or had Dad simply taken out an ad in the Times? "Just got here a few days ago."

"Cool. Well, welcome to La-La Land."

"Thanks."

"What have you done so far?"

"Not much."

"Well, we'll have to change that. What's the story, how long are you in L.A for?"

I caught her looking back over her shoulder, and turned my head a little to see what she was looking at, but I didn't see anyone.

"For the summer. I just graduated, but I'm taking a gap year..."

"Oh, that's exciting. Me, too. Or at least, that's what everyone else calls it. I'm planning on hitting the audition circuit hard. My new agent is hopeful. I had a guest spot on a pilot we shot a few months ago, so, we'll see..."

"Good luck."

"Thanks."

"I was just escaping the chaos out back for a few minutes." She waved towards the massive double front doors that wouldn't be out of place on a castle somewhere. "Let me be your unofficial tour guide tonight."

"Great," I said as we headed across the driveway towards the house. I took a deep breath before we went inside.

It was surreal as she pulled me through the open giant front door of the house. Immediately, I could hear the mix of loud music drifting towards us, the hum of people talking, and the definite sound of a video game or two being played somewhere nearby, but that noise wasn't what caught my attention.

If I'd been impressed by Dad's house, this one was legit straight out of a movie set. Marble floors, a dual curving staircase leading up to the next level, and in front of the staircases, a statue of a man that was beyond life-size. I was almost prepared to look up and see a painted ceiling, but Sorche pulled me deeper into the house before I had a chance to sneak a look.

"Where is everyone?"

"Most people are out back by the pool or in the pool." She laughed. "There's some people out by the tennis courts, others are hanging in here escaping the heat, playing video games, eating, hanging out somewhere. Most of the little cliques are holding court in their rooms."

"Sounds great."

So far, it wasn't what I expected from my first Hollywood party, but then again, I was barely thirty seconds into it.

Sorche caught me looking around. "First things first, we need to get you a drink, then I'll be happy to introduce you to who you need to know."

Sorche must have sensed my uneasiness; 'course, how could she miss it? I was toying with my purse so much, I'd probably break the strap before we made it outside again.

She pulled me down the hallway, no doubt to keep me from getting lost—or bolting, another strong possibility. This place seriously dwarfed Dad's.

I peeked into a game room where a couple guys were playing some racing game on the biggest flat screen TV I'd ever seen. It took up almost the entire wall. They didn't even glance our way.

She took a turn near the end of the hallway into the huge black-and-white kitchen and opened the double-wide stainless steel fridge. "They've got soda, they've got beer, and somewhere, there's..." she turned to me as if the thought suddenly struck her. "You're not one of those wheatgrass and soy milk types, are you?"

She looked horrified as she asked.

"Not fond of soy, and the only wheat I like is in my cereal," I replied as I leaned against the counter.

"My type of girl." She grabbed two cans of soda.

Drink in hand, I popped the tab and took a small sip, hoping not to spill something on my new clothes or make an idiot out of myself. My goal for the night was to not draw too much attention. Blending in was a good thing.

"You ready to meet a few people, or do you want to hang out here for a while?"

I glanced around the large kitchen that remained surprisingly empty, given the spread of food on the counters. It looked like a mix of pretty much every food a person could want. Pizzas down one end, sliders, sandwiches, little tacos, several salads were in big bowls spaced in between everything. I could have happily spent the night in the kitchen, munching on a slider and watching the scene outside. It looked like there were a few dozen people out there, having a good time.

Maybe if I actually went outside, I'd be one of them.

"I guess I'm here to meet people." I gave a small shrug. "Might as well start."

Just as we were about to walk out of the kitchen, two guys in jeans and T-shirts walked in from the hallway. Their conversation about video games stopped as they saw us. I managed a weak smile, glancing at Sorche.

"Sor! Who's this?" The taller one of the two said as they headed towards the food, looking at me.

Sor smiled, nudging me forward. "Adam, Brody, this is Chey Daniels. She's in L.A. for the summer. Chey, meet Adam and Brody."

"Hi," the one I assumed was Brody said. He'd nodded when she said the name and smiled at me, a smile that wouldn't have been out of place in a toothpaste commercial.

"You two want to join us? We're taking a food break before starting the new Fallout?"

"Thanks, guys, but I'm making sure Chey makes the rounds tonight and gets a chance to meet everyone. Maybe later."

"Yeah, definitely," Adam said, looking at me with a grin.

Sorche nodded noncommittally before she pulled me out of the kitchen, onto the first level of the covered patio. It seemed to stretch the length of the house, with a set of steps halfway that led down to the pool area.

I let out a deep breath. I guess that hadn't gone too bad. I peeked back in and was sure they were watching us as they loaded their plates with pizza.

"You did great, and you don't look so nervous. So come on..."

I followed her down the long length of the patio, seeing different groups of people sitting at tables talking away. I took a sip of my soda as we walked, and my gaze landed on a group farther down the patio, sort of set off from everyone else. One blonde at the table turned to look in our direction, her expression changing instantly the second she saw us.

Or maybe Sorche?

Whatever it was, she didn't look happy.

We stopped at a different table to say hello to a couple more people Sorche knew. Two girls around my age and their older brother who was in town visiting. We made a little small talk, standing there, and I couldn't help but glance back to that table farther down. It looked like the blonde had disappeared, leaving a handful of people behind, including a redhead who seemed busy on her phone, but kept peeking our way, a similar look on her face.

As we walked away from Sor's friends and towards the steps down to the pool, I glanced back.

"What about that one?" I asked.

Sorche turned her head to see where I meant. "Wow. You really want me to throw you to the sharks so soon?"

"What do you mean?"

"Trust me, you can wait to meet them. Especially..." she trailed off as the redhead looked up from her phone and saw us looking over, instantly shooting us a dirty look I didn't understand. Maybe it was more aimed at Sorche? There likely was a history there. "Just trust me, you've got all summer."

"Okay," I agreed, trying to find something to clue me in to what Sorche meant. Other than the dirty look, I didn't see what made them sharks. 'Course, I was the stereotypical fish out of water, a goldfish suddenly thrown into shark-infested waters. If my tour guide was telling me to forget about them, then I definitely would.

Sorche stepped forward, grabbing my arm gently as she passed and pulling me along, almost as if she wanted to make sure I avoided the temptation of going anywhere near them.

I'd barely stepped out of the shadow of the house when something—make that someone, a rather *naked* someone—collided with me. I stood there frozen as he righted me, his wet hands cool on my bare skin before he winked and took off running straight towards the pool, giving a loud whoop before dive-bombing to a round of applause and yells of approval from the groups of people poolside.

I winced as the water splashed up in the air at impact. Instinctively, I took a small step back just as the water landed with a solid whoosh at our feet, splattering my sandals and the bottom of my jeans. At least, it hadn't drenched us. I could have been soaked.

"JT! You ass!" Sorche yelled at him.

JT laughed from the deep end where he treaded water, a huge grin on his face as he looked back and forth between me and Sorche.

She looked at me. "I'm so sorry..."

I stayed back while she marched to the side of the pool, people around her moving out of her way without a word. I had a feeling an angry Sorche might not be a good thing. If a person could have literal steam coming off of them, she would have...easily.

"Get some clothes on. No one wants to see *you* of all people naked, Justin Thomas."

She crouched down at the side of the pool, clearly trying to glare at him face to face. I wondered if he was going to try and pull her in, but he didn't move from where he treaded water several feet away.

"Hey, Sor. Does that mean you'd streak if I grabbed some clothes?" he called, and I could see the mischievous glint in his eyes even from where I stood.

I almost laughed, but looked away just before I caught his gaze.

"Not if you're here," she said pointedly, getting to her feet. She let out a sound of frustration before she turned, rolled her eyes, then headed back towards me. "I'm so sorry. He can be such an ass at times."

She cast a look back over her shoulder where some of the others in the pool were starting to play chicken.

I shrugged, trying to play it off like it was all fine by me. I could feel a few curious gazes directed our way, but I did my best to ignore them. They were probably all wondering what Sorche was going to do. I could see over her shoulder that JT had disappeared from the pool.

"What's the story with him?" I asked as we walked. A set of stone steps at the other end of the pool looked like it led to a long balcony above, and it appeared that's where Sorche was headed.

A lopsided smile crossed her face. "JT?" she asked as we started the trek up the stairs.

It seemed like there were twenty or thirty steps, a number that almost seemed to grow as we climbed.

"The streaker?" I asked as we reached the top and found a long stone balcony overlooking the pool below. Half a dozen empty loungers were scattered around. A few people stood at the far end, leaning over the railing and shouting down to the partiers below.

"That's him. He's harmless, really. My guess is he's broken his twelve days of sobriety." She sighed as she stopped to sit down onto an empty lounger, and I did the same, glancing towards the pool, but I didn't see the dark-haired guy anywhere. Maybe she'd scared him off.

Suddenly, I found myself wondering if my self-imposed thirty minutes were up yet. Sorche was nice and all, but looking around me, I was so in over my head. I mean, the girl in the pink bikini who'd just dived into the pool before we climbed those stairs? I'm sure she was in the movie I saw on the flight out here.

"So how long have you been in town again?" Sorche angled herself to face me.

"About three days."

She laughed in amazement. "Wow, you are a complete newbie. What have you done so far?"

"Unpacked." A shy laugh escaped me, and I tucked a couple of strands of hair behind my ear.

I could see a few people by the pool glance over at us, no doubt trying to figure out who the heck I was and why I was hanging around Sorche. Easy to see she belonged in a place like this. She was completely confident in herself; no doubt if she'd been the one to bump into a naked JT, she probably would have simply shoved him into the pool and spun around to get herself another drink. I'd opted for the deer in the headlights look. Or at least, it sure felt like I had.

"And you've shopped. I saw those sandals the other day." She leaned over and took a closer look at them.

I nodded absently. "Just picked them up today. My dad's assistant Trish took me out this afternoon. I kinda didn't think I'd blend in too well with what I brought with me."

I didn't see a paint-splattered tank top from when we'd repainted the kitchen and matching denim cutoffs blending in easily around here.

"You'd be fine. Really."

Why did her words make me feel like I'd just passed some sort of initiation? Or maybe that's what JT had been before? See how the new girl deals with nudity—if she doesn't freak out or run away screaming, she's certifiably cool and can stick around. Otherwise, *there's the door. See ya.* Maybe I'd learn a secret handshake now that I was apparently part of the 'in-crowd.'

One step at a time, Chey, I reminded myself.

"So you're here for the whole summer, right?"

"Yeah."

"Great." She actually sounded enthused about that little fact, and I wondered if I had made my first L.A. friend.

"C'mon…" She jumped up and headed to the railing. "Let's see, who do you need to know…" She moved her soda down on the stone rail, walking a couple feet ahead so we were more towards the middle of the pool. "Okay, girl in the green bikini is Fiona. She can be nice on her own, but when she's with the entourage…"

"Entourage?" Somehow, I didn't think she meant the old TV show.

A look I didn't quite understand crossed Sorche's face.

"Think Mean Girls. She's practically second in command of that little clique." Sor glanced at me. "Trust me, those are the *last* ones you want to meet."

And suddenly, that table full of sharks made a lot more sense.

"Okay."

"Good." She smiled. "'Course, you kinda met JT already," she said as he surfaced at the far end of the pool and seemed to glance up at us soon as his name was mentioned.

"Right." Like I could forget him. I took a small sip of my drink and studied the people in the pool. A handful seemed familiar, faces that were in the magazines I'd bought at the airport.

"Let's see who else…"

She began pointing to a group of people clustered around tables near the pool. "Pop princess wannabe; little sister of a major rock star…and now…" she turned, "you."

"Which makes me what?" If everyone could be broken down in three word descriptions or less… what was my title? New kid? Misfit? Soon to be outcast?

Sorche laughed. "Probably the most likeable person here." She nudged my shoulder as she pointed JT out again below. "And he, try as he might, is still JT."

I scanned the pool area and caught a blonde staring up at us, or rather, glaring and more at me than anyone.

"Who is she?"

Sorche actually grimaced, which I knew couldn't be a good sign. So far, she seemed to have a pretty good relationship with everyone we'd come across.

"We'll talk about her later."

"Considering the way she's glaring at me, I think I'd rather know now." It's not like I hadn't been glared at before; trust me, I have. But this glare held something behind it, and it totally unnerved me.

"That is Adriana."

Adriana?

"The one whose party this is, Adriana?"

"Unfortunately so. But luckily, there's only one of her. They haven't been able to clone her, thank God. But her little minions try so hard to be like her."

"Minions?"

"We met them downstairs, the shark table? Somehow, she wasn't there. But that look she's sporting, she probably wasn't thrilled about how you met JT. They used to be a thing," she said, turning away from the pool. "Don't worry, used to be is a long time ago, over a year. He's over it...I thought she was the way she was working her way through guys for a while, too. But she *might* still think he's her property."

Sorche pointed out a few more people, before she pushed herself back from the railing. "You must be hungry. I'm famished. I've barely had anything to eat all day."

"I could eat," I admitted, thinking of the food in the kitchen, glad when my stomach didn't grumble in response. My nerves had abated a little bit so I felt more comfortable to try some food. That was the bad part of my lovely anxiety I had to deal with sometimes—anxiousness caused nausea or worse, feeling like I was about to pass out.

"Why don't you stay up here? I'll fix us some plates. You aren't allergic to anything?"

"Nothing I know of."

"Great. Be back in a few."

Sorche left to raid the kitchen and get us something to eat, and I was stretched out on the lounger, listening to the music blaring from unseen speakers somewhere overhead. About to take the last sip of my drink, I suddenly realized who the figure heading straight towards me was.

The streaker.

Except now, thankfully, he was clothed—well, was semi-clothed—in a pair of dark red surfer shorts, with a faded shirt draped over his shoulder.

A teensy rush of panic washed over me. Sorche had left for who knew how long, and I was here all on my own about to be—

"Hi there."

His voice interrupted my thoughts, and I found myself staring up at him.

I took a not so very discreet slurp of my soda. "Hi."

He sat on Sorche's unoccupied lounger and used the edge of his shirt to dry his face, his damp, ink-black hair falling forward and covering his electric blue eyes.

"Sor told me I need to apologize about before," he said once he was done and his bright blue eyes met mine.

"What?" Okay, so maybe I should have thought that instead of saying it. But I'm not sure what I was more shocked by—Sorche making him apologize to me, or him actually finding me and doing it.

"She's worried I may have unnerved you a little and made you uncomfortable." He let out a deep breath as he studied me. "So, I'm sorry. I'm not used to having new faces around. Our little group is pretty tight."

Great.

I mentally thanked Dad for picking out such an exclusive group to get me into. That might just explain the dirty look I had received from that little entourage.

"It's okay."

He tilted his head slightly.

"Sorche said it's not." He leaned over and grabbed my soda can before giving it an experimental shake, like he was trying to see if any remained. "By the way, I'm JT. I don't think we've officially met."

"Chey."

But he already knew that, obviously. I mean, he'd found me and all. No doubt Sorche had filled him in. I found myself wondering what she'd said.

"So we're cool?"

"Yeah, we're cool."

"Great." He smiled that mischievous grin he'd had in the pool. "You wanna take a swim?"

I laughed. "Not really."

I didn't have a suit, which I figured wasn't a point to bring up, given what he'd been swimming in—or without—less than an hour ago.

He laughed, a deep sort of sound that suddenly made me feel happy just hearing it.

"Damn." He played with the soda can for a minute. "Well, I'll let Sor fill you in on things. See you around, Chey."

And with that, he took off, leaving me staring after him in awe. Like, what was all that about?

By the time Sor came back with a plate of food and a fresh round of drinks, JT had reached halfway down the steps and headed back to the pool. She didn't look surprised by the fact I'd had company. She simply handed me the plate with the mini rolled sandwiches and dropped beside me.

"That's who I meant to warn you about earlier," she said as she pulled her cell phone out of her pocket.

"JT?"

"The one and only. Thank God for that." She laughed. "He can be a little hyped up at times. Now, I need your number." She held her phone out to me.

I set down the sandwich I'd just grabbed and keyed my cell number in for her before I opened my purse and handed her my cell for her to do the same.

"You got any big plans this summer?" she asked as she took a sandwich and ripped off a piece of pita roll.

"Not really." Dad hadn't exactly mentioned anything yet.

"Well, I'm just the one to fix that." She gave me a wicked smile before popping a bite-size piece of roast beef into her mouth. "I guarantee this will be your most memorable summer yet."

Having Trish pass me on my way up the driveway had been a surprise. I hadn't left the party 'til well after one with Sorche, and by the time I'd gotten home, it struck closer to two. I wished she'd stopped to chat as she drove by, instead of giving me a simple wave. It definitely made me wonder if something more were going on between her and Dad as I parked in the garage. Otherwise, who stayed that late?

I headed upstairs to my room and changed before going to find Dad. I threw my sleep tank over my head, the grey one with *Princess* scrawled in glittery gold writing and the matching satin tiara-covered lounge pants before I slid my feet into the Tweety Bird slippers I'd gotten last Christmas and headed outside where Dad chain-smoked by the pool. I thought he'd given up that gross habit a couple years ago.

Guess I was wrong.

I waved the smoke away and curled up on one of the nearby chairs, as close as I could be without the stink billowing in my face.

"Tweety," Dad said with a smile.

I nodded, playing with the bottled water I'd grabbed on the way outside.

"Are you dating Trish?" I blurted out. That was the only logical conclusion I could come up with for her leaving this late—or early, whichever way you wanted to look at it.

Okay, so totally less than tactful, but still...

I looked at him expectantly.

He tapped out his cigarette on the cement beside his chair. "What gives you that idea?"

"An inkling?" I shrugged, leaning forward to pull a piece of fuzz off my slipper.

Besides, Milo seemed to be hanging around, and Dad wasn't exactly that into kids. Me excluded, of course. He'd told me that several times, and I knew it was true, because he never, ever dated anyone who had a child. I figured I was all he could handle; that, or he just didn't want me to get jealous if he was playing Daddy to someone else.

"She's my assistant, Chey." He put his lighter and pack of cigarettes on the ground. "A friend. Nothing more."

"Then what's the deal with Milo?" I knew I sounded a touch jealous, but when you spent as little time with your father as I do, you tend to get a little territorial. And in the past, I may have—accidentally, of course—spilled red wine on his Hollywood girlfriend's brand-new, white Armani gown. But in my defense, she'd called me a brat. And I'd been twelve at the time, still fresh off my parents' divorce and well, pre-hormonal, so you can see, I was totally justified.

Now, she's happily married to some stunt guy, so all's well that ends well, right?

Besides, Mom has told me time and time again that my dad is a player. And hey, every player needs a ref, don't they?

Good thing I'd brought my black-and-white striped T-shirt with me this summer.

Dad sighed and looked straight at me. "Milo can use the extra cash, and Trish could use some time off. Works out perfectly."

I had a feeling we'd see about that.

"Tell me about the party," he said, changing the subject easily.

"Not much to say." Or that I wanted to share right now, anyways. Telling him the most memorable moment by far amounted to my collision with a naked teenage guy didn't quite seem the way to go.

"But you had a good time?"

I twisted off the cap on my water, thinking back. "Actually, yeah, I did."

If it hadn't been for Sor, I probably wouldn't have. But I'd have to see if Sorche was just being nice to the newbie or if she actually wanted to hang out this summer. I hoped she wanted to be friends, because thinking back to some of the looks sent my way, it proved enough to make me consider staying home and poolside for the duration of my stay.

5

"You've had three calls already this morning."

Trish greeted me as I padded across the tiled kitchen floor in my slippers, the Tweety heads bobbing with every step. I glanced tiredly at the clock on the microwave. Twenty minutes to noon. Well, it was summer, after all. I was allowed some sort of beauty sleep, right?

"Who?" I tried unsuccessfully not to yawn. Who knew having a bit of a life could be so draining?

"Sorche, I think. You left your cell phone down here last night. I just saw her name flash by on the screen."

I tried to pour some coffee, but Trish stole the pot away from me, pointing instead towards the pitcher of orange juice on the table. I sighed. So much for me being wide awake any time soon.

Trish poured a small mug of coffee that I hoped was for me.

I picked up my cell phone from where she'd pointed on the counter. Someone had thoughtfully set it on the charging pad. I scanned the log. She was right—three missed calls from Sorche.

"Her dad's some music producer, I think." I yawned, waiting for my eyes to adjust to the bright light streaming into the kitchen. Hard to think back to our convo last night when it seemed like my brain still snoozed upstairs. "She was sort of my unofficial tour guide last night."

Trish held the mug out to me. I set my phone back on the charger and grabbed the coffee gratefully.

I took a long sip, wanting to stretch it out. I could feel the haze around me starting to fade as the caffeine kicked in. I took a second sip before putting it down. "Where's Dad?"

"Out on a run with his trainer."

I smiled knowingly at Trish. "So he left you behind on Chey duty?"

I can't believe he thought I needed someone to be here when I woke up.

She laughed. "I'm hardly babysitting, Chey. I sent out a few faxes. Grabbed your phone by accident. You left it outside on the table, and I thought your father had gotten a new one. And I made breakfast, because I figured you'd be hungry when you finally got up."

"I'm starving," I admitted.

"Good. The pancakes should be done soon."

Dad came in half an hour later, freshly showered and smelling like a mix of soap and aftershave. He kissed my forehead as he slipped into one of the chairs at the table.

"So, tell me all about the party. You were pretty tight-lipped last night."

"I was not."

He arched an eyebrow.

"I was tired."

"You're wide awake now." He grabbed a slice of toast from the plate on the table. "How'd it go?"

"Not bad. I think I made a new friend." Wow, that sounded like I was back in kindergarten.

"Does she have a name? Or is it a he?"

Ha! "Her name is Sorche. She said you know her dad."

He nodded. "David. She'll be good for you."

Glad she had the fatherly seal of approval. "Why do you say that?"

"Sor's been around the scene long enough to help you navigate things."

Great, she was the friend version of GPS.

The cell phone on the counter beeped, interrupting our conversation, and Trish held it out to me. I grabbed it from her and headed outside. "Hello?"

"Finally, I got you. I kept getting your voicemail all morning."

"I just got up."

"Typical teen, sleeping in after a late night of partying." Sorche's laugher filled my ear. "Anyway, I was wondering if you were up for doing something today."

"Today..." I repeated slowly.

"You said your summer was free...I've got the day off so I thought we could do something. Do I hear a yes?" she asked before I had a chance to really think.

I glanced back through the patio doors. I doubt I had any plans here.

"Sure," I said, making a decision to take charge of my own life for once. "Where do you want to meet?"

"Why don't I swing by and grab you? Say in about an hour? I've got a short yoga session in ten minutes so maybe we'll hit a movie or something?"

"Great, see you then. Do you need my address?"

"Nah, I'll grab it off my dad's computer. See you soon."

I clicked the phone off and headed back into the house. "Guess I'm going out this afternoon."

"Sorche?" Trish asked from her spot at the kitchen table.

It looked like I might have interrupted their convo with my quick return.

"Yeah, we're going to a movie."

"Sounds good." Dad took a sip of coffee. "You need to get out of the house more."

I grabbed the rest of my coffee, deciding to ignore his comment. I'd gone out last night, and I was going out this afternoon; what more did he expect? "I think I'll go upstairs and start getting ready."

I sat on the front steps an hour and a half later, looking at my silent cell phone and beginning to think I'd been punk'd. Like *ha ha, the popular kids want to hang with you*, then don't show. I was thirty seconds away from deciding to give up on Sorche and go spend my afternoon by the pool when I saw a vehicle stop at the gates.

I rose to my feet wearily, thinking it might be Milo. But then, he'd just let himself in if it was him. I hit the remote on my keys, and the gates swung open in response, letting the candy apple red SUV zoom in. I immediately recognized it from the parking lot last night.

Sor honked the horn, and I hurried down the steps, my purse straps dangling from my fingers.

"Love the wheels," I said as I opened the passenger door.

"Thanks. One of my graduation presents. You missed having a big blowout out here, huh?" she asked as I got in.

"Guess so."

She sped out of the gated driveway. "We'll make it up, I'm sure. Now, I know we'd planned on the latest movie, but..."

I waited for my newfound friend to tell me my all-access pass to the land of young Hollywood had suddenly been revoked and kick me out just outside of Dad's gates.

"We got a better offer."

We? But I came up with a better question. "Which is?"

"I'm so glad you asked. Charity modeling gig. Primo clothes. Top designers and modeling scouts are rumored to be in attendance."

I shifted uneasily in my leather seat. "Uh, good?"

"You're not excited? Why aren't you excited?" She cast a bewildered glance in my direction.

"I'm not exactly into modeling."

Okay, truth be told, I'd never modeled before. Well, unless you count trying on the clothes my grandma sent me for Christmas every year in front of Mom and her favorite digital camera.

"Why? I mean, what do you want to do?"

"I really haven't decided yet." Just because everyone else I knew seemed to have their entire futures mapped out ahead of them didn't mean I needed to follow the pack—or so I kept telling my mother.

And now...

"Well, then, it's settled. You have to go, if for no other reason to strike it permanently off your list of options."

I sighed. I wasn't exactly the modeling type. I glanced at Sorche who looked so excited about this little idea as she expertly maneuvered the Los Angeles streets. 'Course, modeling like this was probably something she did all the time. Me? I could go my entire life without ever walking the runway.

I just knew that a) my nerves would get the better of me, and I'd become the klutz of the millennia, and b) I just wanted to stay low-key right now. Why embarrass myself in front of who knew how many people?

"Do I have to?"

"I guess not." She frowned. "I just figured it'd be fun. You know, part of your L.A. experience."

A rush of guilt hit me like a blow to the stomach. Sor was just trying to inject some fun into my summer by doing something I totally wouldn't be able to do back home. "How did I get asked to do this, anyway?"

She smiled, glancing at me for a moment. "Well, I forgot the rehearsal was today, and when they called to check to see where I was, they asked if I knew anyone who could come in as a last-minute replacement since a couple people had backed out for some reason and I said I had the perfect candidate. Told them all about you, and they said you were in."

Butterflies started to appear in my stomach. I was *in*. "Couple hours, right?"

"Absolutely." She looked back over at me as she rounded a corner. "Worse-case scenario, we have to catch the late, late showing."

"All right, count me in."

As soon as we arrived at the hotel, I started getting a bad case of nerves, especially when I heard a testing blast of loud music from down the hallway. But since I figured this was a good start to my 'living the L.A. experience' this summer, I kept silent and followed my new friend through an open door and into a maze of hallways.

At least, Sorche knew where she was going because frankly, I became completely confused after the second turn up a short flight of stairs. There was no signage on the walls saying which direction to go for what.

We went through a set of double doors and clearly found ourselves in the right place as we began to weave our way past the racks of waiting clothing and the half-dressed women talking excitedly about the clothes with their names on them. Needless to say, I felt totally out of place and stuck as close to Sor as possible, not wanting to find myself faced with the inevitable 'who are you and what are you doing here?' question. I saw enough curious looks thrown my way to keep my head down and stick close to my unofficial tour guide.

Sor circled around one rack, and I realized she was following the tall blond guy dressed in all black with a clipboard in hand. Finally, she tapped him on the shoulder.

"We're here," she informed him as she slipped her denim jacket off and draped it over her arm.

He spun and looked at us, his eyes lighting up when he saw Sor.

"Darling!" He kissed her cheek then turned to look at me. "And this must the one and only Cheyenne..."

"Chey, please," I said quickly. Mom only called me that when she was royally ticked off.

"Chey it is, then." He smiled as we shook hands. "Sor was right."

I almost started to ask about what but managed to keep my mouth shut and just glanced at my friend instead.

Sor just grinned at my misery as she slung an arm over my shoulders. "I said you'd look great. Besides, what better way to spend an afternoon or two?"

"When is the show, anyway?" I asked, caution strong in my voice. Sor had neglected to leave that little detail out.

He looked at Sor then at me. "Why, tomorrow afternoon, of course. We start at one...today's the last run-through, and I cannot tell you how thrilled we are to have you, Chey. We were scrambling for a couple last-minute replacements after the twins backed out."

"Total serendipity that you came into town at just the right time," Sorche added, giving me a big smile as she looked around. The excitement literally radiated off of her.

Oh, it was serendipity, all right.

Sorche was clearly in her element.

"You two are at the far end of the room, second last rack." He checked his clipboard. "And Chey, you can see the stylist first if you want."

Oh, great. Me first.

What did that say?

Sor gave me a little half smile. "Come on, let's see what we got."

Our rack sat right at the end of the room by the last few remaining empty chairs. At least, we weren't wedged in between a large group of people. I let out a deep breath in relief and perused the clothes hanging there. Most of the rack seemed dedicated to Sorche, but I found my three outfits easily. One was a pastel multicolored silk sundress, another a set of jeans and a simple T-shirt that looked like it could have come straight out of my revamped closet, and the third looked a little more club-style, with black capris and a metallic silk halter. Since I was filling in, I had less than half the stuff Sorche did and breathed a silent sigh of relief. There was a curtained-off change area, and I pulled a folding chair out to sit down and wait to see what I was supposed to be doing.

Sor looked at me as she rooted through the clothes. "You have to be more excited."

"It's just not my idea of a great time," I tried to explain. A few girls our age were down at the other end of the room, doing the same as Sorche, and I just felt, I dunno, like I totally didn't fit. Sorta like that old Sesame Street game, one of these things is not like the other? Put a big blinking neon sign above my head because that was me.

"Well, what is?"

"I don't know..." I reached for an abandoned magazine nearby, which she quickly snatched out of my hand.

"No time," she chastised. "You've got hair and make-up, and you need to get into your first outfit for the run-through," she said, taking hangers off the rack and holding them out to me.

The same hanger that I just noticed had a number attached to it. The dress had the earliest number. Nineteen. At least Sor had a matching dress in lavender marked twenty. "Fine."

"Hold on...don't forget the shoes."

For the first time, I glanced down and noticed the shoe boxes lined up in a perfect row beneath the rack.

Taking the hanger from her fingers, I stepped into the curtained-off area, yanking it shut behind me. I couldn't believe I'd been roped into spending my afternoon like this—and in a dress, at that. Better not think that I had to repeat the experience tomorrow.

In front of an audience.

The sooner we started, the sooner we'd get it over with.

I came out in the knee-length dress, amazed it fit; after all, not like I had given them my sizes beforehand. I stowed my clothes beside Sor's under the makeshift table and looked around to find her, but she was already across the hall in hair and make-up, gabbing away.

Once again, I felt like the total outsider.

I stumbled out of my thoughts as a tall, skinny redhead shoved me aside.

"Hey, watch it," I muttered, watching her go by.

Sor appeared at my side, shaking her head at the girl. "Come on, Chey. Time for make-up."

"Who was that?" I asked as she pulled me away. I could still feel the instant dislike radiating off the redhead. Almost like she'd targeted me for some reason. There was something kind of familiar about her, and I wondered if I hadn't seen her at the party last night, hanging around the pool area.

Was she the one with the cell phone?

"Never mind. We've got to get you to hair and make-up. I'm so excited we're doing this." She almost squealed and jumped up and down in excitement.

I splashed a smile on my face for her benefit. Besides, I didn't want to lose the first friend I'd made in L.A. over something as simple as spending a couple afternoons wearing expensive clothes. I mean, hey, there were worse things I could be doing, right?

Just because I didn't envision my future full of runways didn't mean I had to ruin it for Sorche.

"So cool," I said as we headed into the make-up room.

The space was brightly lit and filled with a bunch of make-up stations in a long line, dividing the room right down the middle. A few girls around our age and some twenty-somethings were at the other end of the area, getting made up.

As I glanced around, my gaze landed on the guy at the far end of the room, talking with who I assumed was one of the stylists, clad in the all-black look I'd seen earlier.

JT.

"What's he doing here?"

"Modeling. You didn't think it was all women, did you?"

Sor sounded surprised that I hadn't expected to see him.

Well, now that she mentioned it, I hadn't really given it much thought. 'Course, the only guy I'd seen since we walked into the dressing room had been the one with the clipboard... Guess I should have realized we were only in the women's dressing room.

As if sensing us, JT looked up at that very moment. He flashed me a boyish grin, highlighting his pearly whites, and I forced a weak smile back as Sor shoved me into the empty make-up chair, and I suddenly found myself with a plastic cape draped over my shoulders.

"Chey, this is Enrique. Enrique, my new friend, Chey." Sor made the introductions as she lowered herself into the chair beside me.

"Nice to meet you," I said, meeting his cocoa eyes in the mirror.

Enrique gave a barely perceptible nod. "You've got the look."

"Isn't that a Roxette song?" I asked, hearing JT's instant snort a few feet away. Not my fault my mom loved old music from the eighties. Besides, when had JT gotten so close?

What was he eavesdropping through the open doorway?

The stylist rolled his eyes.

"You're hilarious. Now I'm seeing a blank canvas." He leaned in close enough that I caught a strong whiff of cinnamon breath. "That's rare," he confided in a hushed tone.

I looked quizzically at my reflection. Same dark blonde hair and nude lip gloss I'd had on when I left the house. So I hadn't gone make-up crazy, but I usually didn't. Besides, who would have seen me in a dark theatre, anyways? Sor's lucky I didn't come out of the house in my pajama bottoms with the flamingos on them and a hoodie.

"What do you see?" Sor asked, spinning her chair to face mine and tapping her finger on her glossy lips thoughtfully. Well, until Enrique shot her a dirty look, and she quickly lowered her hand.

"Don't ruin that make-up."

Clearly, Sor had gone to make up while I'd been in the dressing room, trying to get organized...and more than that, get my courage up.

"Sorry." She shrugged and grabbed a bottled water from the table and a straw. "So?" she prompted.

"I see..." He began wrapping my hair around his fingers, holding it against my head.

I prayed he wasn't about to say curls.

"Loose and flowing...some slight waves...natural, but without me, you'd never create it."

That made me laugh, and he smiled. I knew I liked Enrique. "Sounds good."

"Sorche, hand her a water. She's going to be here a while."

He wasn't't kidding. It took him almost forty-five minutes before he had my hair the way he imagined it. By then, the room had filled up with the other models ahead and behind us.

I tried not to move as Lola, the make-up woman, did my face once Enrique had finished with me. So weird having someone else do my make-up. No one but me had ever lined my eyes, and it took a while to get used to. I'd even asked Veronica to let me do that when she'd done my make-up.

"Sor tells me your dad's an actor."

I leaned my head back against the neck rest, trying not to tell her it tickled when she lined my eyes, like a thousand little feathers dusting my skin. "Yeah, Sean Morrow."

The pencil stopped halfway across my right eyelid, and I was so tempted to open them to see the look on her face. Surprise? Disbelief? Who knew what kind of rep Dad really had? But I sorta figured I'd rather not be impaled with the charcoal-black eyeliner, so I waited for her to speak.

"Really? He doesn't look old enough to have a daughter your age."

Great, I passed for an old-looking seventeen and he, a young thirty-eight. Quite the pair.

I shrugged, the most I dared to move for fear of getting myself poked in the eye.

"He and my mom married young, I guess."

That must have satisfied her as the pencil started to move again.

I breathed a silent sigh of relief and hoped I wouldn't get a lot of questions about Dad. I mean, I knew some stuff about my parents' relationship. They'd met in L.A. and got married before he hit it really big...but the rest, well, I figured that was a convo Mom was saving 'til I jumped over twenty-one.

"So you don't live in Cali?" she asked as she stopped lining my eyes, and I risked opening them again.

I was tempted to come up with some witty reply about Swiss boarding schools when Sor caught my eye; she must have sensed my slight annoyance. "Nope. We moved back to where my mom's from. Buffalo."

That seemed to satisfy Lola as she went back to finishing up her last-minute touches. Finally, she deemed me ready and pulled the cape off. "Perfection."

Following a couple of blinding photographs by a bored-looking twenty-something with a dark ponytail and a huge camera, I trailed behind Sorche out of the room.

"Where's nineteen and twenty?" someone yelled from the front of the line.

I grabbed Sor's hand and pulled her along, through the dressing room and out into the hallway already packed with models looking less than enthused we weren't in the desired spot, all ready.

"Right here," I called.

The line of teenagers and women parted, and we slipped through. The guy with the clipboard smiled as he saw us.

"You're up after this group." He smiled warmly at me, and I had a feeling the next words out of his mouth were going to be something about me cleaning up nice.

I leaned by Sorche, trying to see where it was we were headed. Four steps up to a glossy black stage and runway. All the better for me to stumble on.

"Watch," Sor whispered, nudging me in the ribs.

The two blondes ahead of us marched up on the stage while the song changed. They walked—or rather, strutted—to the beat of the song down the middle of the runway into the crowd of tables, before separating at the end and heading back up the stage.

"Think we can do that?"

Sor looked at me hopefully. She must have thought I'd bolt.

Which really wasn't that bad of an idea. But I think I'd passed the bolting stage when we moved a few steps ahead. If I tried now, I'd definitely create a scene.

"And go..." Clipboard Guy whispered, giving us both a gentle shove forward.

6

Several deep breaths and twenty-four hours later, we found ourselves suddenly on stage. All the practicing in the world the day before couldn't have prepared you to face a room full of expectant faces. From the side, you couldn't tell how full the room really was, and now, I had an up close and personal view. Every table, every seat, appeared filled.

Over two hundred people.

I'd taken the time—or made the mistake, whichever way you chose to look at it—at counting the tables yesterday. At least ten chairs per table. And more than twenty tables.

I tried to keep my eyes straight ahead and stay in sync with Sorche as we replicated what we'd spent hours doing yesterday, perfectly mimicking the two blondes in front of us, right down to the exact turn at the end of the catwalk and the slow stroll back.

I was sure I recognized a couple of famous faces at the tables up front, but I couldn't make myself slow down to take a quick peek. The end of the stage couldn't come soon enough.

"Did you breathe at all out there?" Sorche asked with a giggle as we headed back to the dressing room to change.

"I think so," I said optimistically.

I wasn't sure.

I'd just kept reminding myself to put one foot in front of the other and stare straight ahead, try to keep a somewhat natural smile on my face, ignoring the fact there were so many eyes on me.

I didn't take drama in school for a reason—I didn't exactly relish being in front of a crowd.

Sorche shook her head, obviously trying not to laugh at newbie me. She grabbed her next set of clothes then looked at mine hanging there with the glossy sign that said 'Chey Morrow' that had been there to greet us early that morning. "I'm thirty-two, and you're forty-four. So you've got a little wait."

"Good."

I sat on the folding chair and took in the flurry of activity around us. Before I knew it, Sorche had changed and headed back to the line-up. I took that as my cue to get into the jeans and T-shirt, careful not to mess up my hair and make-up before going back to the line myself in a routine that went on for the next two hours.

As I stood in line in the hallway once again, taking calming breaths and straining to see Sor ahead of me, I heard a few murmurs from the girls behind us. Every once in a while, I could feel their gazes on me, and I fought the urge to turn and ask 'what?'

I didn't quite get it. There'd been a few more additions to my clothing rack when we'd arrived that morning after a quick breakfast of Starbucks coffee, the most I could stomach without fear of getting sick. I'd figured the additional clothes had been because someone else had backed out. No big deal, right?

I hung the last hanger on the rack. The dressing room felt a lot less crowded now than it had been for the last couple hours. I even had to admit I'd had a good time, better than I would have thought when I woke up that morning fighting back a case of nervous nausea.

Kinda fun playing dress up. I even wished Mom could have seen me. I think she would have loved to have seen me in a dress for once. But I hadn't told Dad or Trish, for that matter, about my newest activity, not sure I wanted them there to witness any possible disaster. Besides, this was a one-time deal, and the only souvenir I would take with me was the glossy program Sor had presented me with upon arrival, with my name and photo inside among the list of participants.

The photo being one of those last-minute shots they'd taken yesterday before we'd left.

They must have had a printer on standby for those last-minute changes.

I headed back towards the comfy chair in the make-up room where I could see down the hallway for Sor's inevitable appearance. About to pick up a discarded issue of IN STYLE, I saw a man pass by and peek into the room, smiling when he saw me. I figured he had to be another one of the male models. Dressed in faded black jeans and one of those T-shirts I'd seen half the models wearing, his shoulder-length, jet-black hair had been pulled back in a small ponytail. He didn't look a day over thirty.

I smiled back, and he walked in. I just hoped he didn't ask me where so and so was, because I hadn't exactly met that many people yet that I could put faces to names. Other than Sor, Enrique, and Lola...I'd be out of luck. But I guess I could direct him to one of them for more help.

"You're Chey, right? Sorche's new friend?" he asked.

I nodded, taking a seat on one of the empty make-up chairs to wait for Sor to finish changing. She had one outfit left before we were out of there.

"I'm Rico Vanetti."

The name set off bells in my mind.

Rico Vanetti - the designer. The one behind all those T-shirts and half the outfits we'd worn this afternoon. The one who a lot of the other models were talking a lot about. I vaguely remembered Sorche telling me he was there somewhere, but she'd never bothered to point him out to me. I'd pictured someone older, a lot older.

"Hi, nice to meet you," I said, putting the magazine down on my lap. I couldn't quite figure out what he was doing talking to me, but I figured he must have had to wait around for everyone to finish so he could take the clothes back to wherever he kept them. He was probably just being friendly and killing time.

"Great to meet you. I gather you're new to town?"

"Is it that obvious?" I asked, slightly embarrassed. Had Dad sent out some kind of announcement or something? Or even worse, did I just look that out of place?

He laughed, taking a seat beside me in one of the empty chairs. "No, not at all. But I'm pretty familiar with the 'it' crowd around here, and I'm sure I'd remember your face."

So I hadn't exactly made the rounds, or as Sor called it, had my unveiling. I think she had big plans for that one. "I've only been here a couple days, really. Staying with my dad for the summer."

"Sounds fun."

"I hope so," I admitted, glancing at my freshly painted nails. They'd been done a copper color that morning while I'd waited to get into make-up.

"Do you have any big plans while you're here?"

"Not really."

A slight, uneasy silence settled as I felt him studying me closely.

"You're a very attractive girl, Chey."

"Thank you."

He nodded.

"The clothes worked beautifully on you." He leaned forward. "More so than on some of the others." He studied me again. "In fact, you just might be perfect..."

Right as I was about to ask "perfect for what," I saw Sorche heading our way, and he must have, too, because suddenly, I found a business card pressed into my palm. Before I could look at it, Sor had reached my side, shaking her hair out before pulling her glossy dark locks back into a ponytail. I slid the card into my jeans pocket, deciding to forget about it for a moment. Especially with Sor so close. My gut instinct said it wasn't a big deal, so why make it one?

"Nice talking to you, Chey. Great job in the show, girls."

"Thanks, Mr. Vanetti," Sor said as he left us. "You ready?"

I still had my eyes locked on him walking away. My fingers tapped my pocket absently, wondering what exactly was going on.

What was I perfect for?

I snapped out of my fog as I realized I hadn't answered her.

"Absolutely."

"Did you pick up your bag of goodies for modeling today?"

For the first time, I noticed the navy canvas bag in her hand. A rather large, heavy-looking bag.

"No..." I said slowly. There really should have been a neon blue sign above my head blinking 'innocent newbie.'

'Course, with the way JT kept staring at me every time he saw me, there may have been.

"Second room off the hallway, just past the dressing room. I'll wait." She smiled, dropping into the seat Rico had been in.

I followed her directions and found myself in a small room filled with tables covered with bags. The guy with the clipboard was lounging against the far table.

"Chey, there you are. I was wondering when you'd come pick yours up."

I gave a weak smile. "Sor just reminded me."

"Glad she did." He checked his clipboard then leaned over to get a bag. "You can grab a set of sunglasses, too," he said as I took the bag and looked where he was pointing. A rack half hidden by a pile of black totes.

"Okay."

"You impressed a lot of people today," he said as I looked over the styles of sunglasses, trying to spot a pair of aviator ones like Dad's.

"Did I?" Had he seen me talking to Rico?

"You did." He confirmed. "We've got another fashion show in a few weeks for another charity out in Malibu. Sor will have all the details, if you're interested. We'd love to have you back."

I finally spotted a pair of aviator shades with metallic lenses and lifted them off the rack before he handed me a case for them.

"Thanks, I'll think about it," I said, but really, deep inside, I wasn't sure this was anything more than a one-time thing. Without Sorche's pushing, I wouldn't have even done it in the first place.

I sat in Sor's SUV, my bag taking up my entire lap as I rummaged through it, getting more and more amazed by the minute. Make-up. Three bottles of perfume, and not those little sample ones I tended to get at the perfume counter, either. One of them was Mom's favorite, and I smiled, thinking I could bring it home at the end of my vacation and make it a nice surprise.

We also got gift certificates to restaurants and a free facial and a mani/pedi that I thought I'd give to Trish for helping me out. I opened a box and found a watch glistening up at me.

"What is all this?" I asked in amazement. It felt a little like Christmas.

Sor glanced over casually as she pulled out of the parking lot. "It's called swag. Isn't it great?"

"Uh, yeah." But I still didn't get why we'd—or make that me— had gotten any of it. "But it's a lot of stuff."

"It's a thank you for doing the show." She stopped at a red light behind a silver version of her SUV. "Enjoy it."

Seemed a little much for a couple hours of playing dress-up, but I kept silent, stuffing the watch back inside the bag and then setting the whole thing down by my feet.

"What are we up to next?" I asked, glancing out the window.

Sor headed down Rodeo. I hoped she was going to suggest we'd stop to eat soon. I was starving. I'd barely managed to drink a couple glasses of juice that morning, afraid of making myself sick if I tried to eat anything that actually resembled food.

"Mom texted me and offered to take us to a celebratory lunch for looking so great at the show. You mind?"

"Not at all."

Turned out, lunch was being held on Sorche's back patio.

"Wow," I muttered as I followed her inside the house. Smaller than the one the party had been held at, but still way bigger than Dad's. I tried to remember what it was Sor's parents did again. Acting, directing? Agenting? I didn't want to say something that made it seem like I hadn't been paying attention.

Music, I suddenly remember. I think her dad was in music.

Sorche smiled at me as she dropped her canvas bag on top of a beige suede couch in the living room.

"It's not the fabled Spelling residence, but it's home," she said as we walked across the spotless foyer and headed past the winding pale marble staircase.

I followed closely, trying not to stop every few steps to gawk. The place looked straight out of an old movie set on those black and white TCM movies Mom watched sometimes.

I shook my head in awe. "It's…"

I didn't know where to start. As much as I loved Dad's place, I'd pack my suitcase and move right in here if asked.

"Been featured in a handful of magazines. Mom's publicist makes sure to send someone over with every redesign."

"I can see why."

"Hope you girls don't mind," Sorche's mom said as we walked out a set of French patio doors in one of the living rooms, done all in white. "Every place I went by was packed, and I thought we'd do just as good with take-out."

Sor glanced at me.

"It's fine," I replied as I looked at her mom.

She looked like an older version of Sorche, but not by much. She had Sorche's same brunette color and the newest layered hairstyle that fell just past her shoulders. Her nose was a little thinner, and I could see the smallest hint of smile lines around her eyes when she smiled at us.

She wore a pair of black jeans and a blue v-neck T-shirt.

She waved for us to have a seat at the large stone table under the beige canvas awning. "I'm so glad to meet you, Chey. I've heard lots about you from your father and now from Sorche."

The rush of warmth crept on my face. I hadn't known Dad talked about me to his friends out here or at least often. "Thanks, Mrs. Maxwell."

"Call me Sydney, please. Have a seat. You two looked great up there on stage today. Sorche told me you were really nervous, but I couldn't tell at all. You were both so poised up there, so professional. Did you have fun?"

Fun.

Nerve-racking, panic inducing fun.

"Yeah, it was a good experience."

Sor sat beside me and lifted one of the covers, revealing Chinese food. I breathed deeply, feeling my stomach rumble lightly in response as my mouth began to water. I couldn't wait to dig in.

"Yeah, I think Chey here made a good impression, don't you?" Sor asked as she settled into her chair and started taking more covers off of the food. Rice. Dumplings. Sweet and sour chicken. More dishes I wasn't too familiar with but which smelled amazing. I couldn't wait to start adding something to my plate and dig in.

Sor's mom, er, Sydney handed me a plate. "Hope you don't mind? I had a craving for sweet and sour chicken all during the fashion show. I wasn't too big on the finger food they were serving us."

"Don't mind at all." In fact, it reminded me of Mom's irregular Friday night Chinese dinners. I scooped some of the egg noodles onto my plate and eyed the chicken that Sorche was adding to her own.

"So Sean's been hiding you away all this time," Sydney said with a smile. "What did you have to do to get out here for the summer?"

I laughed as I helped myself to some spicy chicken. "Graduate, apparently. I think he thought it would make up for missing my birthday the last couple of years."

Not to mention the graduation.

That was still a little bit of a sore point. Even though I tried to pretend it wasn't.

It was one of those one in a million moments in my life, the type I'd always imagined having both of my parents at. Except I hadn't. I'd had one, and one empty chair.

"What's he have planned for you two so far?" Sydney asked, handing me another plate of food to try.

I took the plate of some sort of chicken and veggie dish and added a few pieces to my plate before setting it down.

"He really hasn't said much," I said as Sor poured us each a tall glass of ice water. "I'm sure he'll come up with something, though."

Sydney smiled. "Well if he doesn't, I know Sorche here will have plenty enough to keep you occupied this summer. And I'm sure we can come up with something for you two girls to keep busy." She glanced at me. "You and Sor should spend a weekend in Malibu while you're here. I have a place out there, have a girl's getaway weekend for a few nights," she suggested, digging in to her food. "Knowing Sean, you'll need a break from him at some point."

I held my smile as I nodded, glancing at my new friend. I kinda hoped I wouldn't have to take her up on that offer.

Dad had to clear his schedule for some father-daughter time sometime, right?

Sor dropped me off from a long celebratory lunch, and I headed through the back patio doors, hearing Dad's voice carrying down the hallway the minute I stepped inside. I set my gift bag down on the hall table and contemplated going to see him.

I wanted to tell him all about my day, fudging the truth a little from 'I'd been the one modeling' to 'Sor had dragged me to see a charity fashion show.' Which was the truth, really—I'd just had an insider's view of things. I knew if I did tell him how I'd really spent the afternoon, he'd burst out laughing at the thought of me on the runway. I wasn't always the most graceful one in the family. When Sydney had called me poised and professional walking the runway, for a moment, I'd wanted to ask if she was sure who she was talking about.

Even watching the footage she'd taken on her tablet, I couldn't quite believe that was me. She'd promised to send me a copy of it later to show Dad. But I had a feeling I'd keep it stored in my cloud account for a while.

I grabbed a bottled water from the fridge and tiptoed down the hall, sure he'd be off the phone soon. Well, I'm assumed it was the phone; I didn't hear a second side to the conversation.

"My schedule's clear..."

Something stopped me on the other side of the partially open door, just outside of Dad's view. My stomach started churning, and I took a gulp of the cool water to try and settle it down. Why did I have the feeling I wasn't going to like what I overheard next? I eased back closer to the wall, trying to stay as silent as possible.

"Two days or three, it doesn't matter. As long as it takes to make sure everything's worked out when I leave."

I must have moved more than I thought because the door squeaked as I slightly brushed against it, and I froze, swearing under my breath.

Dad suddenly turned in his chair and saw me, his eyes widening in surprise as our gazes met, obviously not expecting it to be me standing there. I guess he figured I'd be gone for the whole day and not just part of it. Either that, or he'd have closed the door.

"I'll call you back in a few, alright? Chey just came home. Okay, talk to you then."

He clicked the phone off and waved me into his office. He looked a little paler than he had just a few short seconds ago, but I played it off as just being my eyes adjusting to coming in from outside.

Somehow, I took a couple of sheepish steps forward, toying with the water bottle in my hand. "Sorry to interrupt."

"It's okay." He motioned for me to take a seat across the desk. "Did you have a good afternoon with Sorche?"

"Yeah," I answered automatically as I sat down across from him, wishing I'd brought in the tote bag as it would have given me something more substantial to fidget with or show off, or give us another topic of conversation to go with, other than what had that conversation I'd inadvertently overheard been about?

I saw him watching me, trying obviously to read my expression.

"You're going somewhere?" I asked in a fog. That was the only thing my brain could latch onto.

Dad sighed as he met my gaze, and I could tell he wished I hadn't overheard what I had. I had a feeling he'd wanted to come up with a better way to break the news to me.

I watched him lean back in his chair, a sheepish expression on his face. He broke our gaze for half a second, scanned his desk, then looked back at me.

"Something's come up...totally out of the blue."

"Right," I said, trying not to sound as hurt as I suddenly felt. The promise of not working while I was here seemed to fly out the window the moment anything came up.

Anything important, I should say.

That's what it felt like, at least.

Things that didn't quite matter—

Birthdays - *check.*

Graduation - *check.*

Summer just us together hanging out - *check.*

Chey - check

Everything was more important than me.

"It's just business, Chey."

Just business. Which obviously meant I couldn't tag along. And I was *just* on my summer vacation, fresh from graduating high school.

No biggie.

Hell, who cared it was the first time I'd been to California in seven years, or that this was supposed to be father-daughter time?

Father and daughter time I'd been jipped of for how long?

Too long. My mom's voice rang out in my mind, and I couldn't help agreeing with her.

"I can tell you're upset..."

Wow, he must be a gifted mentalist, right? I almost wanted to laugh thinking of my fortune from the fortune cookie I'd stuck in my wallet. *'Good things come to those who wait'* evidently no longer described me.

"Forget it. It's fine." I ignored the burning of tears starting to rear up and blinked rapidly, not wanting him to see them.

"I can't get out of it, but I promise it'll only be a few days."

'Course he couldn't.

And *promise.* He sure liked to throw that word around.

"You'll never even know I'm not here," he continued. "I'm sure Sorche has all sorts of plans for you two. You've been pretty well inseparable since you met."

"Sor's working." Well, technically, according to our over lunch convo, she was auditioning, but what was the difference? Busy spelled busy. So what was I supposed to do?

"And you haven't met anyone else to hang out with?"

Besides Trish and Milo? I wanted to counter.

Who else was I supposed to meet?

Where was I supposed to meet anyone?

"Not really."

Okay, so now, I was feeling really lame. My cell phone should have been filled with the numbers of the rich, famous, and wanna-bes, as Sorche had called them at the party. I couldn't help but think she threw wannabes in the same class as the sharks she'd wanted me to avoid.

My schedule should have been booked solid. I should have been the one telling my father I didn't have time for him—not the other way around. Maybe this was exactly what Mom wanted to protect me from.

She'd love to know how right she was.

"Like I said, it's no biggie," I said softly as I stood up. I needed to get out of there before the tears really began to fall and I ended up messing this whole thing up beyond repair.

"I'll make it up to you."

Yeah, how exactly was that going to work? Another BMW? Maybe another closet full of designer clothes? Or a platinum AMEX all of my own?

No, thanks.

Not interested.

I started for the doorway, wishing my cell phone I'd left on the hall table would go off and give me an excuse to get out of there. If he clearly didn't want me there, then I didn't want to stay any longer than necessary.

"Don't bother. I get what's most important to you around here." And clearly, at that moment, it wasn't me.

"Chey, it's not like that."

I paused and turned around, crossing my arms over my chest as I lifted my chin, staring at him defiantly.

Just how was it?

"Not like what, *Dad*? It sounds like you're about to jet off somewhere for a couple of days."

I motioned to his phone sitting on the corner of his desk as I tried to keep from throwing a tantrum a two-year-old would have been proud of.

"Look, it's a couple days, three, tops in NYC."

I could hear my mother's voice saying *see?* right now.

"Uh huh. You promised me—not to mention *Mom*—that you weren't going to be working this summer, but here you are, *again*. First, it was the press junket, and now this. What else is going to pop up? I'm amazed you managed to tear yourself away from whatever—or whoever—to pick me up at the airport in the first place. So you know what, *Dad*? Don't bother doing me any favors. Go to New York, go for a day, go for a week, you know what? Go for the whole damn summer, for all I care."

With that said, I turned and hurried out of the room before he could stop me and see the tears starting to fill my eyes. I almost wished I'd slammed the door behind me for good measure as I hurried through the house, grabbing my keys and my purse, trying to find a spot to seek refuge.

Somehow, I ended up in the dark garage, my vision still blurred with tears. I let myself into my car and sat there in the dark for a while, letting the tears fall. All I knew right then was that I wanted to get away from him, far away. Maybe I could go to the mall or something. Any place I could lose myself for a couple of hours.

My summer vacation was going downhill at a rapid rate. Faster than I'm sure even Mom would have predicted.

I knew the smart thing would be to call Mom and cut my trip short, head home. I could go work delivering pizzas again. That would keep me busy.

But part of me, ninety-nine percent of me, really, wanted to stay.

If Dad didn't want to be a part of my plans, then fine, I'd come up with Plan B.

And I knew for a fact Sorche would love to help dream up a Plan B.

I went to reach for my cell phone to text her when my hand brushed a folded up piece of paper in my purse. I would have laughed if I wasn't already feeling so miserable. I picked up the paper and unfolded it, noticing how worn it had become from being in my purse for so long.

I spread it gingerly across the steering wheel, carefully smoothing out the wrinkles while doing my damnedest not to hit the horn. The last thing I wanted to alert anyone where I was. Not that there was likely anyone looking for me. My phone had been remarkably silent since I'd gotten in the garage. If he'd been concerned, he could have phoned or texted, but there was nothing.

Emails got accidently deleted. Same with screen caps. That paper was proof he'd wanted to spend time together.

The same paper I'd shown Mom before I'd pleaded for her to let me go on this little trip.

Even in the darkness of the garage, I knew what the email said. I had it practically memorized after all.

He was so proud of me and all my hard work. So happy I was graduating top of my class. So happy I had a bright future ahead of me. He was so sorry he wouldn't be able to make it, things just conflicted too much, but he'd be there in spirit. Maybe if Mom would let me, I could come out to California for the summer so we could spend some time together?

I still remembered my conversation with Mom on the way to the airport.

"I don't want you to be disillusioned." We were barely out of the driveway before she started in on things.

"How am I going to be disillusioned?"

"You don't know him like I know him, Chey."

"That's my point! I'm almost eighteen, and I barely know my own father. Why not give me a chance to see what he's like? What's the worst that can happen?" *I really shouldn't have asked that.* "It's a great opportunity. I can see a different city, I can check out UCLA. Really sink my teeth into the California thing."

"That's what I don't want you doing, either, Chey. It's different out there. Just don't get so caught up in everything. It's easy to do."

"Chey?" I heard Trish's concerned voice from the side door to the garage as I came out of my thoughts.

"I'm fine," I called in the darkness.

I was.

Really.

I just wanted to be alone with my pity party.

I quickly folded the paper back up and stuffed it inside my purse before she could see it.

Her soft footsteps grew louder as she neared, before the passenger door opened and the overhead light flicked on, startling me with its brightness.

"You don't sound fine," she announced as she dropped into the passenger seat beside me and, thankfully, closed the door, which extinguished the overhead light.

My vision slowly returned to normal as the darkness of the garage once again enveloped us.

"Let me guess, he sent you to either make peace or tell me I'm on the next flight home?" I asked, not bothering to look over.

"Neither, actually. He doesn't know I'm here."

"I seem to be falling under that umbrella myself." I fell back against the seat, my hands grasped around the leather steering wheel.

"Look, I know he hasn't been your perfect version of a father so far, Chey, but give him a chance, okay? He's got a lot of stuff going on." Trish's voice came out soft.

"Then why invite me in the first place?" I countered angrily, my voice rising. Just once, I wanted him to try. For me. No other reason. Just me. Was that really so damn hard to ask?

"Why don't I get you dinner reservations somewhere? You and Sorche can have a night out." She offered. "I'll see if there's any good shows tonight, maybe someone you'd like to see in concert? I have connections. I can get you two a hotel room for after even, you can crash some place fun."

My fingers traced the grooves on the steering wheel. "I don't know. I think I'd be lousy company."

I mean, if I was going to ruin my friendship with Sorche, it might as well be over something a little more worthy than my crappy attitude at the moment.

"Well, I'm not Sorche, but I do have a couple cartons of ice cream in the freezer inside and access to a pretty cool theatre room. We could wallow there for a while," she offered, and I could see the concern in her eyes as she looked at me. It seemed like something Mom would have done if she was here.

"No Dad?"

"Not a single sighting, I promise."

"Deal." I could do with a healthy dose of mocha fudge ice cream and a hundredth viewing of one of my favorite movies.

7

The two days before Dad left for NYC felt different from my first few days in Los Angeles. I'm pretty sure he thought I must be hormonal or something after my semi-outburst (which I wasn't, thank you very much), so I made sure we kept our distance. I didn't feel like arguing or being told I needed to go home. Because I was pretty sure that would be his go-to response if we had another fight.

So I spent my afternoons by the pool or swimming laps. Sorche was busy with some auditions, so it was just Trish and me most days as I did my best not to spend more than a moment or two with my father. Heck, I even got used to seeing Milo around the house and did everything to ignore the sting of jealousy that he was spending more time with my own father than I was.

The morning Dad left, I climbed out of bed before the sun was up, tied my hair back in a ponytail, and headed downstairs to see him and Trish off in my pajamas.

Dad looked at his suitcase waiting by the door. "You sure you'll be okay?"

Was that a note of apprehension in his voice?

"I have all the numbers and Milo's a phone call away," I assured him.

Not that I was counting down the minutes to the second he got on the plane or anything, but suddenly, I was looking forward to a few days on my own. I could really get settled in, adjust to my new surroundings, and get to work on my tan, even though I had the pretty good start of one already thanks to all the time I'd spent in the water the last few days. Not to mention try and forget that little argument—it's not like either of us had actually apologized, but it hovered like a little black cloud hanging over the house, giving the place an air of unease.

Trish smiled as she came in from the kitchen, a small bottle of orange juice in hand, and I was glad she was going with him. I had the feeling they'd talked about her staying behind, but I wasn't a baby in need of a babysitter.

"He's on twenty-four/seven Chey duty. Nothing will happen," she assured Dad, wrapping an arm around my shoulders for a quick side hug.

He nodded. "I know. I trust Milo with my girl's life."

Oh, goody. Didn't know he and Milo were that close.

We heard the beep of a car horn, and Trish checked out the front windows. "Car's here."

"I'll give you a call once we land," Dad said as he gave me a hug goodbye.

My first hug in days, definitely not as strong a hug as when he'd picked me up at the airport. I pressed a quick kiss to his cheek as he pulled back.

I nodded, taking a step back so they had room to get their bags together. "Sounds good. I'll stick close to the house today."

Trish put the juice in her oversized purse for the ride to the airport. "Don't think of it. If you and Sorche want to go out, go ahead. We can get a hold of you on your phone."

"She's right," Dad agreed as he opened the door and motioned for the driver to come and help with the bags. "Don't hole yourself up at home because of me. This is your chance to be free."

He cast a smile my way, and for a moment, all the tension between us seemed to fade away.

I laughed wearily. Words I wouldn't repeat to my mother. "I'll be fine. Maybe I'll go crazy and go out for dinner on my own."

"Good." Trish gave me a quick hug. "You need anything, call Milo. He'll come right over."

"You sure he's okay with this?" I asked quietly as Dad headed out the door with the driver, each carrying a suitcase. I noticed Dad had taken Trish's carryon.

"Milo's fine with it. Besides, it'll give him an excuse to earn some of the money your dad's paying him." She smiled as she headed to the door. "Shouldn't be more than three days, I promise. Talk to you soon."

"See ya. Have a good flight." I waved as they loaded the last of the luggage in the car and got in.

Before I knew it, they were past the gates, and I hit the button on my remote, making sure they locked up behind them.

I stepped back inside and shut the door behind me.

All alone.

The house was really quiet after Dad left with Trish. With at least seventy-two hours of alone time ahead, I had my take-out menus to occupy me. Trish had taken me grocery shopping so the pantry was fully stocked in case I got the urge to cook. We'd joked that was probably the most food the house had ever had in it since Dad had moved in.

Milo was indeed on speed dial on every phone in the house and newly added to my cell phone as of the night before, and I just knew he'd be putting in the occasional surprise appearance to check up on me so I wouldn't be totally on my own. Besides, I had no doubt it wouldn't take all that long for Sorche to stop by.

I grabbed my breakfast bagel along with a bottle of orange juice and headed outside for some air and to watch the sunrise, way too keyed up to fall back asleep any time soon.

I dragged one of the oversized chairs off to the side, more under the umbrella, and sat down, propping my bare feet on the other chair, and leaned my head back, setting my drink and bagel on the table and let my eyes drift closed.

The sound of the phone ringing woke me up, and I blinked my eyes open to find the sun high in the sky. Guess I'd missed sunrise by a couple hours. Oh, well, there was always the one tomorrow.

I stumbled inside and grabbed the cordless off the wall. "Hello."

"What are you doing?" Sor asked.

I propped the phone against my ear. "Not a lot."

I had the feeling Sor wanted to take advantage of my free time and do something— which was totally cool with me. Checking the time on the stove and seeing it was almost lunch, I opened the fridge and pulled out the makings of a salad. I'd managed a few bites of the bagel hours earlier before falling sound asleep, but that wouldn't last me long.

"Good. I've got to do something with my mom this afternoon, but you free later?"

"Most likely," I replied, looking for the leftover chicken I knew I'd seen last night. We'd bought one of those rotisserie chickens just before we'd left the store, and I knew Milo and Dad had made themselves sandwiches after their basketball game...but I was hopeful there was still something left

"Cool. I'll come by when we're done. Say four-ish?"

"Four-ish."

She laughed. "See you then."

I clicked the phone off and started shredding my lettuce when the phone rang again. I grabbed it immediately, figuring it must be Sorche wanting to change times or something.

"What did you forget?" I asked as I picked up.

"Chey?" a confused voice asked.

I blinked at the unfamiliar male tone. Definitely not Milo calling to check up on me. "Uh yeah, who's calling?"

"It's Rico Vanetti."

I almost dropped the phone. "Mr. Vanetti, hi. How did you get my number?"

I set my knife down before I hurt myself by dropping it on my foot.

"Where there's a will, there's a way." He chuckled. "Besides, I know some people in your circle."

I barely knew I had a circle.

"Oh, okay." I slid onto the kitchen stool and tried to find a logical reason why Rico was calling me. I glanced at the time on the microwave. Just before eleven.

"What can I do for you?" I asked, trying to remember if I'd accidentally gotten a piece of Vanetti clothing in my swag bag. I didn't remember seeing anything like that in there. But maybe it had been rolled up or something?

"Can we get together? I wanted to finish our conversation from the other day."

"Mr. Vanetti...I don't understand why you'd want to meet with me," I said honestly as I glanced around the empty house. Maybe I was still half asleep and this was a dream. Any minute, some llama or something was going to walk into the kitchen. Wasn't that the way all crazy dreams went?

"I told you before, Chey, you were perfect—"

"For what?" I interrupted him, immediately feeling like an idiot.

"To be the 'Face' of *House of Vanetti*."

My grip slipped on the phone, and I managed to catch it before it hit the floor. My hand shook a little as I put the phone back to my ear.

"The 'Face'?" Even to me, that sounded important. Mega important, and something that shouldn't be offered to a newcomer like me. I barely took photos as it was. The occasional family photo at Christmas or whatever. Hell, I wasn't even that big on selfies...there was less than a handful on my phone at any given time. "I don't know..."

I raked my teeth over my bottom lip in thought.

I could hear the smile in his voice when he spoke. "An hour. That's it. If I haven't convinced you of your amazing future by then, feel free to walk out, and I'll go search for someone else who isn't as fresh or perfect for this."

Should I? I mean, going to a meeting didn't mean I'd officially signed on as the new 'Face' of Vanetti. I scrunched my nose up. Well, one hour proved doable. "When?"

"Are you free today? My afternoon's clear."

The clock on the microwave informed me I had more than enough hours to kill before meeting up with Sorche. "Yeah, okay."

"Great."

He gave me the address, and I scribbled it down on the inside of a pack of gum I found in one of the kitchen drawers, knowing I'd have to check my phone's directions to make sure I knew how to get there.

"Guess I'll see you in a couple hours," I said, and we said our goodbyes before I hung up, pressing the phone against my chin as I reread the address again.What had I just gotten myself into?

I didn't know what to wear to meet up with L.A.'s hottest new designer. My little online search I'd done after I'd hung up the phone had been eye opening. The stars who wore his clothes was like a list of who's-who in Hollywood.

And he was interested in me?

I couldn't believe it.

My closet suddenly seemed a little lacking, so I threw on the jeans I'd worn to the party and a clean black T-shirt, pulled my hair back, and added a pair of heeled sandals which amounted to about as good as I could get without calling Sor. I didn't exactly want to confide this to her yet. I mean, we were friends; I just didn't think we knew each other well enough for me to rock the boat with this piece of news.

Like, newbie takes title of 'Face' of *House of Vanetti?*

Not exactly something to bond over, especially when said friend was an aspiring model.

Halfway there, I stopped at a drive-thru, for a second time that day, deciding maybe something caffeinated would help with my nerves. Then I thought maybe some air would help, so I put the top down on the car and headed back in traffic, making it there in good time.

I parked the car in the first available parking space I found and looked at the large, bright white building that matched the address on the gum wrapper. Not exactly what I'd pictured. It was about five stories high and sort of a shoebox shape. For a moment, I asked myself just what the heck I was doing there when a glass door opened and Rico stepped out and waved at me.

I waved back in surprise. He must have been keeping an eye out for me to appear so fast.

Either that, or he'd wanted to make sure I wouldn't bolt.

Which I definitely couldn't do now that he'd seen me.

I took a deep breath, looked at my empty iced coffee container, and pulled my keys out of the ignition. Now or never.

I stepped out of the car and took a deep breath, relaxing a little as I headed towards him, hitting my key fob and hearing the familiar sound of the doors locking behind me. "Hi, Rico."

"Hi, Chey. You're early."

"Wanted to make sure I got here on time," I said as he held the door open for me. "Still learning my way around Los Angeles."

I slipped off my sunglasses and tucked them in the collar of my T-shirt.

The strong smell of freshly brewed coffee hit me the moment I stepped inside, and I took a look around us. The floor was bare cement; up ahead was a huge circular reception desk in a matte silver. On the bright white wall behind the desk hung a huge version of what could only be Rico's logo.

To either side of the door were tall potted palms. To the left was a small waiting area with leather chairs and a glass coffee table. To the right, it was set up like an office with a huge conference room you could see into behind a set of glass walls.

Further back down a hall, I could see racks of clothes that looked like the ones from the fashion show.

"We'll go in the conference room, it'll be more comfortable," Rico said. "Can I get you a coffee? Latte? Something else?"

"Coffee's fine."

He told me to go and wait for him so I went inside the conference room and took a seat in one of the plush, bright red leather chairs that surrounded the large table. Through the glass, I could see him talking to the blonde woman behind the reception desk. He took a couple files from her before nodding and heading my way.

Somehow, I had a feeling this could take longer than expected.

I glanced at my cell phone really quick, debating on canceling my four-ish plans with Sorche. If she went by the house and I wasn't there, that wouldn't be good. I tapped the screen to bring up the keyboard and texted a quick message. *We might have to get together later than planned* before turning my phone off and stuffing it back into my purse.

"Coffee will be here shortly," Rico said as he came in the room. "Have you eaten? We were going to order out a late lunch."

"I'm fine," I said, feeling a touch of nerves as he sat down in front of me at the glossy black table. After he'd called, I'd put away the makings of my salad and gone for a quick drive-thru breakfast which had consisted of an extra-large iced coffee and two hash browns. All that I'd felt I could stomach at that point.

"I really don't get why I'm here, though."

Or why he called me 'the Face.' Los Angeles was full of beautiful people. And they were a lot more qualified for something like this than me.

"The *House of Vanetti*'s about to do a massive launch in Los Angeles. I've been looking for months to find the perfect girl to be the official face...and then, I saw you. As they say, the rest is history."

"Me?" I repeated blankly.

"Yes, you. You're perfect for it."

Sure. Plain old me would be perfect for it.

The conference room door opened, and the woman from behind the front desk walked in, carrying a tray of two coffees and a plate of biscotti. She gave me a smile as she set everything down on the table.

Evidently, Rico realized I wasn't convinced.

"You're a fresh face, Chey," he continued as I helped myself to the cup in front of me.

Fresh or naïve, take your pick. Sorche was going to kill me. She was the one with all the modeling aspirations. Not me.

"I should be. I've barely been here a week." I cracked a smile as I added cream and sugar and the woman left the room, closing the barn-style glass door behind her with a welcoming smile in my direction.

Rico smiled.

"I like your sense of humor," he commented as he set the file folders on the table out of the way of our coffee cups. "I think you've got the perfect look to be the new face for *House of Vanetti.*"

I shifted in my seat. "I honestly don't see it."

I took a sip of my coffee. I stared at my reflection every morning in the mirror, and not once had I seen model material staring back at me.

"Let me show you." He sorted through the file folders and peeked in the middle one before sliding it across the table to me. "Take a look at those."

The heavy manila folder had his logo etched in copper front and center. I pushed my coffee away before I pulled the folder towards me, wondering what lay inside. I lifted the cover to find a stack of photographs, and a quick look told me they were from the fashion show the other day. I racked my mind trying to remember if I'd seen a single photographer, but the spotlights had been so bright, it would have been hard to remember another flash. Besides, I honestly hadn't really been looking. My main focus had been on staying upright.

"I didn't know anyone had photographed the show," I said, looking at the folder full of glossies. There were photos of everyone. I paused on one of Sorche walking the runway alone. She was amazingly photogenic. Poised. Cool. Perfect.

Me, on the other hand...not so much, I realized on the next shot of the two of us together. I could see the deer in the headlights look in my eyes even if the rest of my face looked carefully masked.

Rico nodded. "There was some local press covering the event, and a few of the photographers I know were kind enough to share their shots."

He picked up a couple of the photos I'd discarded and looked them over.

"It's a lovely offer, Rico." I met his gaze straight on. "But really, I don't see anything that shows I'm destined to be the next 'it' girl." Zit girl, maybe. "Sorche would be a much better choice."

He shook his head, an emphatic 'no.' "I know the two of you are friends, and I'm fond of her, too. But she is not new, fresh, or vibrant."

"And I am?" I asked in amazement.

"You don't see it. But I can. The camera can." He opened up a glossy red folder and took out a handful of photos. "See if *this* set doesn't change your mind," he said as he spread them out in front of me. "This girl is destined to be an 'it' girl, Chey."

I pulled a few of the photos closer, ready to argue that another set wouldn't change anything, especially my mind. But the girl in this set was beautiful...she was everything Sorche had been in that first set...this girl was...

Me.

Well, I think it was me. The girl wore the clothes I'd modeled at the benefit.

I remembered the slight struggle I'd had with the side zipper on that dress.

One of the outfits that had suddenly been added to my side of the rack that morning.

Was Rico the reason I'd suddenly had more to wear in the fashion show?

"Now you see what I see. What everyone at that fashion show saw."

Right then, I was seeing a whole other me. One that I think my father could be—would be—proud of.

'It' girl, huh?

I could tell Rico thought he was swaying my decision given my silence.

"I'm still not sure," I said, even as my gaze never left the photos. Even if I wanted to, I still would have a little convincing to do on the parental front. "Besides, I'm camera shy," I argued weakly, finally looking at him again.

He smiled, looking at me then back at the photos. "We can work on that. But I can wait. You, Cheyenne, will be worth waiting for. Trust me, this city is going to love you."

That's what I should have been afraid of.

"Do you have a few minutes? I wanted to give you something."

I checked my watch, surprised to see I'd been there almost an hour already. "Yeah, I've got time."

"Great. Wait here."

I watched him say a few words to the receptionist then head towards the back to where I couldn't see him anymore. I finished off my coffee and waited, my nervousness coming back. I grabbed a biscotti from the plate and broke a piece off, popping it into my mouth and chewing slowly just to give myself something to do.

I didn't have to wait too long before he came back with a large glossy white gift box in hand.

"For you," he said, presenting it with a flourish.

"Mr. Vanetti…"

"Rico, please," he said with a big smile.

"Rico, I can't accept this," I said quickly. I mean, a gift? I hadn't even said yes yet. Or even that I'd seriously think about it, although I think he kinda knew I was thinking about it. A lot.

"Think of it as a welcoming gift. Your first summer in L.A is something to celebrate." He laid the box across my lap before he perched himself on the corner of the table. "Tell me if you like it."

Well, I supposed it would be totally rude of me not to take the package now. I lifted the bright white lid on the box and found three T-shirts nestled in shiny silver and copper tissue paper, colors I was beginning to realize were everywhere around the building. I pulled the tissue further back, revealing a black, a red, and a white T-shirt, all with the metallic graphic designs already becoming familiar as Rico's.

"These are a few of my test pieces."

I looked up at him in surprise, my mouth hanging open. Test pieces?

"Don't look so shocked. I have others, but I thought you'd like these. Wear them in good health."

I was more than shocked as I looked at the shirts again. Rico really wanted me to be 'the Face,' didn't he?

"So what all does the being 'the Face' entail?" I asked as I carefully put the lid back on top of the box.

He smiled, evidently pleased I'd asked a question and stopped saying no. "A small photo shoot, and you'd be seen in my designs when you and your friends go out." He shrugged. "Nothing too much, really."

I tapped my nails against the side of box. It didn't sound that complicated, did it? Still...

This was definitely something I'd need parental input on.

"Thank you, Rico, for everything. I'll talk to my dad as soon as he's back in town," I promised.

He took the box so I could get up. "Give me a call either way, but I hope he'll agree. You're the perfect choice for the line and the new store, Chey."

I headed back to where I'd parked the car, stopping in my tracks at what I saw. JT leaned against the driver's door, blocking my way of any quick escape. I kinda wished for a can of pepper spray to chase him away.

"You're everywhere, aren't you?"

I peered at JT as I neared. The guy was hot. The downside—he knew it, and he tried to use it to his advantage.

"Sounds like you did pretty good in there," he said, nodding towards the building.

I shifted the box against my hip. "How would you know?"

"I was in there visiting my cousins." He stared at me, and I must have looked as confused as I felt. "Rico's wife is my cousin?"

"Oh..." There were more family connections in this town than I could keep straight.

"So, like I said, I heard good things about you in there. Face of Vanetti...that's huge. Lotta girls are going to be pissed to lose it out to you..."

"I haven't agreed yet," I said quickly.

He looked perplexed, something I hadn't expected from him. "Why not?"

"Let's see, first off, there's Sorche," I started, about to tell him all about her modeling ambitions.

"Piece of advice, Daniels," he cut me off. "Don't live your life for your friends." He played with the key ring in his hand. "Do what's best for you."

I stared in awed silence, the box beginning to slip out of my grasp. He reached out and effortlessly took it, setting it inside the convertible. He'd rendered me totally speechless. I don't think that had ever happened before, at least in California.

I had to admit he was right, though. The chances were pretty good that I'd leave after this summer, maybe come back to go to UCLA, but realistically, I'd never see Sorche again. Or at least, she'd never want to be seen with me. What was the expiration date on our friendship, anyway?

"It's a great op, and you'll kick yourself later if you turn it down. Plus—" he finally pulled away from my car, brushing close enough that I caught a strong whiff of his citrus cologne. "Chey?"

I barely had my finger on the unlock button. "Yeah?"

"You're perfect for it."

He didn't elaborate.

I'd had enough advice for one day. Seriously.

Life in L.A. was starting to get complicated.

Way too complicated.

I watched him walk back towards the building as I started the car. Checking my texts, I saw I was supposed to pick up Sorche in half an hour, but right now, I kinda wanted some time to myself, to process and all that. I texted a quick reply that I was running late before I headed out.

I grew tempted to go by Pink's and pick up an order of fries and a milkshake to go. Nothing like drowning my nerves in thick chocolate goodness, but I kinda wondered if that was the diet of an 'it' girl—or future 'it' girl.

I wanted to tell Mom all about this sudden unexpected twist, but the thing was, I wasn't all that sure she'd be happy for me. It's not like she wanted me to have a miserable summer. I knew she was hoping that, for once, Dad wouldn't disappoint her, or more importantly, me, but she never understood that he didn't disappoint me that often up 'til now.

See, I knew what he was like, and I'd learned to live with it. I think Mom's issue was that I'd had to learn to deal with it in the first place.

So finding out I was a candidate—the only candidate, it seemed—for something like this, she'd say it had all the markings of Dad's handiwork all over it. Even if Rico had never once mentioned my father...or my last name.

But I have to admit, I kinda had that little inkling myself. Dad knew a lot of people and could make things happen. I just wanted to believe that this was one thing I'd done on my own, without anyone else's outside influence.

At the next traffic light, I pulled down my visor and looked in the mirror.

Was that the 'Face' of the *House of Vanetti* staring back at me?

8

Sorche jumped into my car almost as soon as I pulled into her driveway. She settled in, turning to drop her purse in the backseat behind us, her phone in her hand. She looked excited. "Well?"

"What?"

She practically bounced in her seat as we moved through traffic.

"What was this mysterious meeting of yours?" She wiggled her eyebrows. "I want all the details, especially if it involves a guy."

I laughed as she turned down the volume on the stereo.

I knew she figured JT would be caught up in it somehow. All right, so he was, but not like he'd been part of my plan all along; he'd just sorta appeared out of nowhere.

First the party, then the lounge chairs, the fashion show, and now this.

Kind of seemed like a habit of his.

"Hate to break it to you, but no guy involved."

She laughed. "Okay, so I was wrong. No JT. So what was it? Did your dad want to have one of those 'talks'? You know the type, no drinking and driving, no distracted driving, no drugs, no unprotected sex?"

Now that she mentioned it, I was a little glad we hadn't had a chance to have any of those talks. Hard enough to go through that with my mom, but to listen to my estranged father give me his version of the ol'sex talk...well, talk about uncomfortable. Especially considering the clips of his make out scenes on YouTube. 'Course, knowing him, he'd probably pass that off to Trish now. I mentally crossed my fingers he'd figure Mom had already given me all the talks I'd require and stay clear of any uncomfy topics while I was here. I mean, we could talk about anything; just not that stuff...

I gripped the steering wheel a teensy bit tighter. "Nope. He's out of town, remember?"

"Okay, fine. Secretive or what?" She skipped a couple songs on the playlist.

"Not that secretive. I just don't wanna talk and drive, that's all."

"Fine. Pick a drive-thru. I'll have an ice cream cone, and we can talk."

The closest McD's we passed appeared packed, so Sor gave me directions to a place a few blocks away. Soon, we settled in at a small outdoor café where Sor was greeted by the owner with a kiss on the cheek. She quickly introduced me, and we were soon led by one of the waiters to one of the best tables outside, out of the direct sunlight and in the cool shade of a large potted palm. I ordered an iced coffee, Sorche a regular coffee, and we decided to split the ice cream brownie combo.

In moments, the waiter was back with our coffees and told us it wouldn't be long for the rest of our order.

Sorche waited 'til he'd left, taking a long sip of her coffee before she spoke. "Well? You want to tell me what's going on before I start imagining some truly horrible and hideous things." She leaned back in her chair for a moment. "Adriana and her entourage sighting?"

I laughed as I opened my purse beside me on the oversized chair and took out Rico's card. I hadn't mentioned it at all to her since I'd gotten it, but now, that whole saying about burning a hole in your pocket was making a ton of sense.

I held it out to her.

She set down her coffee and wiped her hands off on a napkin before she took the card, her mouth falling open slightly as she saw the name emblazoned on the front. "Whoa."

She raised her eyes to mine, clearly a hundred questions ready to be asked.

The waiter chose that moment to arrive with our dessert and two spoons. I thanked him and grabbed a spoon, working a trail down the river of whipped cream. At least, I was getting some of my chocolate fix.

Sor just stared at me, expectantly, leaning back in her chair, the card still dangling from her fingers.

"He handed it to me at the charity show when I was waiting for you to finish. First, I thought he was lost or looking for someone, then when he gave me his card, I thought he was just one of those slimy agent types you see in all the movies and TV shows. But then you walked over, and I realized who he was..." I took another bite of ice cream. Sorche barely blinked watching me. "Actually, all I knew was he was the designer. Then I got home and looked him up, and it turned out he's—"

"The hottest new designer in Los Angeles?" she finished, looking back down at the card again. "Exactly."

"So?"

"Then or today?"

"He was who you were meeting with?" Her eyes widened, and she finally almost put the card down. "So tell me what he said, word for word."

"I had 'the look'."

She smiled, lifting her gaze from the card. She still hadn't touched the ice cream yet. "I knew it!"

"Knew what?"

"You had 'the look'! Didn't I say you were perfect for modeling?" She tapped the card against her palm. "I wonder if I can convince him to give me a finder's fee. After all, you wouldn't have been at the show if I hadn't brought you..." She looked thoughtful for a moment.

"Sor!"

She laughed. "Sorry. But wow. Tell me what else he said. I'm dying to hear."

"He called this morning and asked to meet me. So I went..." I stopped for another bite of ice cream, my mouth suddenly going dry. "He's opening a new store somewhere here. He said it's going to be the signature for his brand-new line, and he still didn't have a face for it until he saw me..." I blushed. Even repeating it didn't make it seem any more real. I mean, me?

Why?

"What did Rico give you when you said yes?"

"Actually..." I drew the word out so it sounded a lot longer than it was. Who knew whipped cream and drizzled chocolate sauce could be so yummy? I slid another spoonful in my mouth.

All right, so I was derailing answering Sorche's question. Maybe it was an outsider thing. She'd probably been asked to be 'the Face' or at least model a hundred times before.

This felt all so freaking new to me, I wasn't sure about anything.

I mean, truthfully, just between us, I still kinda figured the rug would be pulled out from under me at any moment and I would be on a plane back home. It's why every night I laid in bed figuring out how to fit my new wardrobe into my suitcase.

Sor stole the sundae away from me. "Not another bite until you tell me what's up."

"Other than the sun, the sky, the moon, and that weird cloud over there that looks strangely like a paw print...nothing." I motioned to the cloud with my spoon and reached forward again, but she inched the ice cream back towards her.

"Chey..."

"Seriously. I haven't agreed to anything yet, and honestly, I'm not sure I want to do it, either."

If I hadn't thought her jaw could drop any further, I'd just been proven wrong.

It was like I just told her the tooth fairy really looked a lot less like Tinkerbell and a lot more like her mother...

Stunned.

And in a rare occurrence for Sorche since I'd met her, speechless.

"Okay, say something because now, you're freaking me out."

"Why wouldn't you want to do it? Are you insane? Think of everything. The clothes...the photo shoots...the attention. Oh my gosh..." She shook her head in utter disbelief. "I'd kill for this."

I scooted back just a touch at those words.

"Not literally," she said quickly as I discreetly slid my hand over the nearest knife on the table.

I cracked a smile and laughed before I stole back a spoonful of melting ice cream. "I just don't think this is my type of thing."

She grabbed her first spoonful of ice cream as she studied me. "Give me one solid reason you won't do it."

"For one, I think you're better qualified."

"Where do I figure into this?" She looked confused as she swirled her spoon around in the whipped cream.

"Rico had pictures from the fashion show. Some were of you."

"Are you kidding? You'd turn down 'the Face' of Vanetti for me?"

The wide-eyed disbelief clearly said she thought I was insane.

"Not for you," I clarified, feeling very stupid all of a sudden, sorta like I had when JT decided to give me his unsolicited advice earlier. "It's just that I never really thought of doing anything like this in the first place."

"Uh huh."

"And I keep thinking JT could have talked him into it."

I mean, it looked like he was close to his cousins. Who knew what kind of influence he had on the guy? Not to mention Sorche had told him to apologize to me. Maybe he thought this would be a way to make things up to me.

"Right, because he has that much pull."

"You don't think it's some weird scheme of his?"

"I'm not saying he isn't a complete manipulator when he wants to be, but this? No way. He'd be saying he discovered you himself. Trust me. I've known him forever." She looked at me. "We go way back, kindergarten at the very least."

"Okay." I cut off a hunk of brownie with my spoon and chewed thoughtfully. Maybe I had the wrong image of JT in my head.

"Does that mean you'll do it?"

"Only one hurdle left."

"Your dad?"

"I wish. My mom."

Sor gave me a sympathetic look. "She'd really be upset?"

"I think it goes totally against her 'don't fall into the L.A. life-style trap' speech she gave me on the way to the airport."

"Ouch."

I nodded, stuffing more brownie goodness in my mouth. "So you can see why she's the last person I can tell right now."

"You're going to have to tell her some time, though, aren't you?"

Honestly, if I could help it? I'd wait 'til I stepped off the plane at home, with my ads tucked snuggly under my arm, before I said a word.

Sor and I spent the next couple days together, hanging out usually at my place. I didn't want to risk missing a call from Dad, even though he said he'd get a hold of me on my cell if it was something important. Aside from a few texts from him and Trish that first night, things had been pretty quiet. Though he did call around midnight every night, which I always thought was to make sure I was at home.

Sor looked up at me as I hung up the phone after a rare lunch time call while we took a break from the pool, enjoying a couple cold root beers and the air conditioning up in my room.

"What's daddy dearest have to say?"

"He's still stuck in meetings. Might be an extra day." I shrugged. "He asked how I was doing living on take out..."

"Did you tell him you're doing really, really good?"

I knew exactly what she was referring to.

"I haven't mentioned it to him. I want to talk about Rico's offer in person."

"Definitely the best way to do it." She stretched her arms over her head as she yawned. She set the remote down on my little coffee table and headed into my bedroom.

I turned Netflix and the TV off and followed her.

Sorche moved to my balcony door, pulling back the curtain to look outside. "Who's he?"

I had a feeling who she meant without even having to look outside. "Milo. Remember I told you my dad said he was stopping by?"

She made a thoughtful sound, and I earned a quick glance over her shoulder. "You're not related?"

"To Milo? Hell, no."

"Interesting," she mused, glancing back out the curtains.

"Why?"

That made her turn to look at me, her mouth falling open slightly. "You cannot be *that* blind?"

"To Milo?" I repeated, scrunching my face up at the thought. Milo. Trish's son, *Milo*. I guess he was okay-looking. Tall, dark hair, not bad arms. Certainly wasn't creepy or anything, just well...not really my type.

And yes, that may have to do with the fact he spends far more time with my father than I do.

"Yes, to Milo. He's what, around here twenty-four/seven sometimes according to you? He's pretty cute, and he doesn't just have six pack abs...they're eights. Can you believe it? I didn't think that was possible."

"Calm down. I doubt he..." I paused, her comments swirling through my head. Just how good vision did she have if she could tell that from up here? "You looked that close at his abs?"

I hadn't seen Sorche give a guy more than a passing glance in the time we'd known each other.

"Hello? There are more males around here than just JT. I don't get why you're so obtuse to that fact."

"Obtuse?"

She blushed. "'Word of the day' calendar from my grandmother at Christmas. Can I help it if I take a look at it sometimes?"

I stuck my hands in my pockets and peeked out the window again. Maybe I really was blind as I tried to see him as a guy and not just a guy standing between me and my father. "I guess he isn't half-bad."

"Guess that's as good as we can hope for now that you've been tainted by JT."

"Tainted?"

"Absolutely." She nodded. "Though he's a much better choice than Adam."

I laughed. "Do you want me to set something up?"

I glanced back out the window. He seemed totally oblivious to the fact he was being ogled from above.

"Hell, no! I don't need a set up. I'll just bump into him in the kitchen or something. Why? Is he seeing someone?"

"We haven't gotten that deep into our personal histories."

"Chey!" she almost whined.

"Hold on, I'll text him and ask." I had to laugh. "Seriously, not that I know of. I haven't seen him with anyone."

"Hmmm..." She peeked back outside again, but he'd disappeared towards the patio doors, which meant he'd be in the house within moments. Suddenly, she turned to face me. "Maybe I should get us a couple more drinks. What do you think?"

I *think* I had a fully stocked mini fridge just feet away, complete with root beer and all. But I stifled a laugh and ran a hand over my still damp hair.

"Do what you want, Sor..."

I smiled as she grabbed her cover-up from the chair and headed downstairs.

Apparently, Sorche just missed Milo. He'd set a note on the kitchen table and was sauntering—her words, not mine—out the front door by the time she'd reached the landing. We drowned our sorrows in root beer floats before she grabbed her gear to head home for a dinner out with her parents.

"Listen, if you do agree to Rico's offer, and I still think you'd be crazy to pass it up," Sorche said as she slid her sundress back over her head, covering up her bikini. "We have to go out and celebrate. I mean it."

I laughed as we walked around the side of the house towards her SUV parked in front of the garage. "Deal."

"Good. Because seriously, I see exactly what Rico does. And you're in Los Angeles now. You're Chey Morrow, for crying out loud...use that to your advantage." She laughed at what had to be the look of disbelief on my face. "Seriously, Chey. Things are different out here. Especially for us Hollywood kids. Get used to it."

Hollywood kids.

The words sent tiny shivers through me.

I guess I really was one if Sor thought of me that way. Hmm.

I rubbed my arms absently. "Guess you're right."

"Good. Call me once you say yes, and I'll plan the perfect celebration."

"You'll be the first one I tell."

Hell, she could be the only one I tell. I waved as she drove through the gates and left me, yet again, alone.

Kicking at the gravel with my toe, I headed back around the house to do a few more laps in the pool before heating up the leftover Chinese food I'd ordered last night.

9

To say I was surprised to come into the darkened kitchen a couple nights later and find the shadow of someone sitting in the chair would be an understatement. I almost screamed and reached for the lights when my Dad's hoarse voice filled the silence. There went the need for trying to figure out how to use a rolling pin to defend myself. I'd taken karate when I was little, but aside from the cute little white outfits, I barely remembered anything but being allowed to yell and hit stuff.

"Chey, could you leave the lights off?"

"Sure, Dad."

My racing heart slowly returned to normal as I headed for the fridge and a late night glass of orange juice, wishing I'd kept my mini-fridge better stocked. But the last few nights, I'd done a pretty good job cleaning it out as Sor and I talked over Face Time and watched crazy videos on YouTube.

"I didn't expect you back tonight. Can't sleep?" I asked, trying to be conversational and act like he hadn't just stripped a decade or so off my life with that scare.

"Got in a couple hours ago. Was going to ask you the same question."

I shut the fridge door with my hip, debating on whether or not I should join him. He didn't exactly give off that 'wanting company' vibe. "Little restless."

I heard the kitchen chair being pushed back across the tile floor. Maybe I'd read him wrong.

I circled the table and set the carton of juice down and grabbed one of the empty cups on the surface, already laid out for my breakfast in a few hours.

"Insomnia?" I asked, pouring my juice.

"You could call it that." Dad took the carton and poured his own glass, and I caught sight of the luggage under his eyes. Didn't he sleep at all in New York? But before I could ask, he suddenly looked up at me.

"There's, uh, something going on..."

He took a long sip of juice, and I thought he was debating on what to tell me.

"I thought everything was good."

My hands wrapped snug around my glass, an effort to hide their sudden tremble. I still saw him as the guy on the big screen. The guy I secretly measured every crush against. But I'd never seen him more down, not even during the divorce. So I grew majorly worried.

"It's been better. I'm not about to lose the house, but I need a hit, Chey. I'm not getting any younger." He stared into his juice. "I need to pull a Travolta. Re-invent myself."

"But what about your trip to NYC? I thought that was for your next project?"

"It's a bit part." He took another swig of his juice, and I caught sight of his couple-day-old stubble in the moonlight creeping in from the patio doors.

"Shit, Chey. I didn't want you to see me like this."

Almost as if he'd read my mind, he rubbed a tired hand over his chin.

"It's okay," I said quietly, trying not to be too obvious as I took a good look at him. In the weak glow, he seemed older than he did in the light of day. There were lines beside his eyes I didn't remember, and he just looked tired.

Exhausted.

And not so much like the Daddy I remembered.

I glanced away, toying with the stem of my glass.

He reached over, patting my hand absently. "Not exactly the way I wanted your vacation to go, kid."

I shrugged. Hate to admit it, but I was used to it where he was concerned.

"It's okay, really."

I wanted to tell him I was old enough to handle it. That I was almost an adult. I could handle a dose of the truth, that everything in Hollywood wasn't perfect. That he wasn't exactly the face that stared back at me from the covers of those glossy magazines I kept in a box in my room. I figured everyone had secrets. Look at the doozie that had just been dropped into my lap.

"You going to go up?" he asked.

"I'm not that tired."

He nodded. "You wouldn't mind if I headed up to bed? I think everything's catching up to me, and I might finally be able to sleep."

"Go ahead."

I barely noticed him get up until I felt him kiss the top of my head, and I quickly wrapped my arms around him.

He went up to bed, but I wasn't exactly in the mood to sleep. I didn't have a clue about any of this. Not even an inkling. And here I'd thought I sorta knew my own father. Turned out, not even close. Definitely not the right time to share my good news with him. When I'd hugged him, I'd caught the strong scent of beer on his breath, barely masked by the juice, but hadn't said anything. What was there to say? If he wanted to drown his thoughts in beer...

I headed up to my room a while later and went and sat on the oversized lounger on the balcony. I draped my fuzzy robe over my bare legs and looked out at the lights over the city.

Thankfully, where my lounger was remained isolated and Dad wouldn't see me as I sat there if he decided to venture outside. I didn't want him to turn around and start worrying about me the way I was starting to worry about him.

He was a workaholic. Without that, who was he? Maybe that's the reason why he wanted me to consider UCLA, so he'd have his daughter close by. Now that his career might be winding down, he suddenly wanted to become my father. I could hear Mom's sarcastic reply—'well, that's great, honey; it's only an itty bitty too little, too late.' And deep in my gut, and in the dark recesses of my mind, I couldn't stop myself from agreeing with her.

He still didn't see I needed a dad. Not a friend, or someone to set me up with the 'cool kids.' I didn't need to drive a shiny new BMW. I didn't need the latest clothes. What I really needed was to hang out with my father and get to know the little things I didn't know about him.

I pulled the robe off my legs and wrapped it around me just as the sun started to rise. Maybe the one thing that would perk Dad up, other than the light of day, would be my news?

Yet, maybe not.

Honestly, I debated on just calling Rico myself and telling him it was a no-go, but then, I didn't want to run into him somewhere with Dad and have it come up. If Dad figured out the real reason I'd never brought it up...that might be something neither one of us could get over.

After our late-night confessional session, I really wasn't sure how to bring up Rico's offer to Dad. I mean, he really had enough on his mind without me adding to it with something so insignificant. But when I called Trish a few days later, she told me it might be just the thing to distract him.

I hoped so. It's why we concocted the perfect plan to sway his opinion.

I opened the oven door and peeked inside. Lunch was warming in there 'til he made an appearance. I grabbed what we needed to eat outside on the patio and loaded up the large wooden tray I'd found stashed inside one of the cupboards.

"What's all this?" Dad asked as he walked around the side of the house.

I'd been outside for the last half-hour, adjusting the patio umbrella to give the right amount of shade and trying to make everything perfect, which explained why I'd folded the bright red and white checked cloth napkins I'd found in a kitchen drawer into neat triangles on each plate.

"A girl can't make her father lunch?" I asked as I finished setting the table.

I figured outside felt a little more relaxed than inside. I mentally thanked Milo. He'd been helpful keeping Dad out of the house while I took the time to get everything ready. They'd gone for a run on the beach, and I'd worked on the food. Oh, all right, so I hadn't exactly barbecued the chicken—that had been from the store—but hey, presentation counted for something, right?

He gave me a one-armed hug and pulled me tight to his side. "Well, it looks great."

I smiled. "Thank you."

I motioned for him to sit down. When I'd told Trish my plan, she'd doubted he'd have any objections over my newfound modeling career. Okay, not career. Stint. That sounded better. Not as if I had any great lifelong goal to have my face stare back at me from the magazine rack.

"Are you joining me?"

"Ha ha. Funny. Of course I am."

I went back inside and pulled everything out of the oven, careful not to burn myself with the steaming-hot serving plates. Setting everything on the tray, I double-checked I had everything. Barbecued chicken. Green salad I'd made myself, and baked potatoes. An all-around solid lunch to try and talk Dad into letting me do something that was *so* not typical Chey behavior.

He took his plate off the tray, and I sat down.

"So, what's the real reason behind all this?"

"I got a job offer." Might as well come right out with it, like the adult I wanted to be.

"I didn't know you were looking."

"I wasn't, really." I took a nervous breath. "It sorta came up unexpectedly."

"What is it?"

"Kinda like modeling, but it's not."

"Acting?" He gave me that half-smile of his.

I burst out laughing. "No. I don't like being in front of crowds, you know that."

"You inherited that from your mother."

Probably.

"What's the deal, then?" he asked.

"You know the designer, Rico Vanetti?"

I tried to look like the food in front of me was interesting. But my stomach was doing its own gymnastics routine, and the last thing I felt like was eating, or even attempting to.

"I've heard of him." Dad shoveled a few bites of baked potato in his mouth, looking at me expectantly.

"Well, he wants me to be the face of his new ad campaign."

"Sounds like a big deal."

"It's not that big of a deal. It would only be in L.A." Thank goodness for that. "I think part of it is because I'm hanging around Sorche. I mean, without her, I never would have been at that fashion show in the first place. And since I'm the new kid on the block, apparently, I'm fresh." I shrugged. "It's not a big deal if I do or don't do it."

Dad put his fork down and leaned forward on the table. "Why not?"

"Because—"

He cut me off before I could sprout off the reasons I had given Sor. "Chey, is this something you really want to do?"

I toyed with my napkin. "It might be fun."

The more I'd thought about it the last few days, the more excited I'd become. It really was a great opportunity for me. Something I'd never even imagined would ever happen, and here it was, on the proverbial silver platter.

"And it would be a good first step for you into the L.A. scene," he said. "A good way to get your name out there and network. I don't see a lot of cons to it, so why haven't you agreed yet?"

He studied me rather intently.

I smiled sheepishly, bowing my head. "I thought maybe you'd object?"

It came out as more of a question than I'd meant it to.

"I'm not your mother; I thought we agreed on that. You've got a lot more freedom here. And this sounds like too great of an opportunity to let slip away. So go for it; you have my blessing."

"Really?"

"Really."

I couldn't help myself as I rushed around the table and gave him a huge hug. "Thank you, thank you, thank you!"

"Don't thank me. It was all you on this one." He smiled up at me. "Now, let's eat. After this, we'll call Rico together, see what we have to do to get you named the official 'Face of Vanetti'."

I don't remember much of the actual meal after that point. I'm sure I ate. Food disappeared off my plate. Dad talked about something, probably one of the stories he liked to tell about being my age and working on his first movie set. I pretty well had it memorized so I could nod at all the appropriate parts.

After lunch, I handed him the card Rico had given me, and he dialed the number on the speakerphone. I curled up in the leather chair opposite his desk and twisted my hair nervously around my finger. I knew Dad said it was a go, but I couldn't help thinking what Mom would say about all this; after all, her big speech on the ride to the airport had been to keep myself out of the whole L.A. scene.

And here I was, about to throw myself straight in the center of it.

Part of Rico's pitch had been about me being seen out and about wearing the clothes so I could get his name out there. I knew I should have run it by Mom first, then Dad. But I was in L.A., and there was barely any chance that any of this would get out of the area, right? Mom seriously wasn't about to step foot in California, so I was pretty safe on that front.

"Rico Vanetti."

"Rico, it's Sean Morrow, Chey's dad. We've got you on speaker-phone."

"Sean, Chey, hello. I hope you're calling with good news."

Dad chuckled and looked at me. "I think you should ask her that."

"Okay. Then, do I have a new face for the line?"

I tucked my foot tighter under me, glancing nervously at Dad. He just nodded. I leaned forward so Rico could hear me. "If you still want me—"

"Welcome to the *House of Vanetti*, Chey. We're glad to have you."

"What all do we have to do to make it official, Rico?" Dad asked.

"I'll start making plans. Chey, you'll have to come down and pick the closet clean. I'll see if I can get you and Sorche some invites to the hottest places in town."

"Sounds good," I said, my excitement betraying me in my voice. I think it went up a couple octaves in just two words.

"What about contracts?" Dad smiled at me.

"I'll fax it over this afternoon."

"Great. We'll be in touch."

"Look forward to it. See you soon."

"Done deal."

I'm not ashamed to admit I squealed. For something I hadn't exactly wanted when it had first been offered, I was beyond thrilled to be part of it now.

"I'm happy for you, Chey. What if we went out tonight to celebrate?" He must have noticed my slightest hesitation. "You've already got something planned?"

I didn't, exactly; in fact, I wasn't too sure what Sor had up her sleeve. "Sor mentioned something about a bonfire..." I shrugged. "But I can cancel, and we can—"

"No, no, you go. Meet some new people. Celebrate your deal with Sorche. I'm sure she'll be thrilled for you. We'll go out another time. What do you say; you leave Thursday open for a date with your old Dad?"

"Absolutely. Thursday is all yours." I gave him a hug. "I'm going upstairs to call Sor, tell her it's official."

"You girls have fun tonight."

"We will."

I shut the office door behind me, leaning against it for a moment as a rush of exhilaration ran through. I couldn't wipe the grin off my face as I did a mini happy dance before running upstairs to tell Sor the good news.

10

"It's some of the same crowd as the other night," Sorche explained as we pulled into a parking spot at the beach. "We'll put in a brief appearance and move on. We've got lots to celebrate."

It didn't take long to find the party from the parking lot. A short trek down a well-worn path, and we found ourselves suddenly on the beach. A group of people milled around, sitting on blankets or lounge chairs. The crowd seemed in full party mode, laughing and talking, and truthfully, I hadn't felt this much of an outsider since I'd parked my car at the first party. At least this time, I could put names to a handful of faces, and I had Sor beside me.

I recognized Adam twenty feet away, adding some more fuel to the small fire started in the fire pit on the sand. The bonfire suddenly roared to life, the flames rising higher.

"I'm going to grab us a spot over there..." Sor pointed to a nearby bench. "You want to get us a couple drinks? There should be coolers scattered all around here."

"Yeah, no problem." I watched her head to the bench then looked around for one of those coolers she mentioned.

"Hey, Chey."

I turned to see Adam beside me; he was taller than expected. "Adam, right?"

He nodded, the corners of his mouth lifting into a smile, obviously pleased I'd remembered him. "Good to see you out here."

"Thanks."

"Need help with anything?"

"Sor said she'd stake claim on a bench spot if I could find us some drinks."

"The closest cooler is probably just behind where Sor's headed...I'll show you."

He started walking, and I played catch up.

"Nice night for a beach party," I said as we passed a group of guys carrying more wood towards the bonfire.

"Yeah, it is."

Someone called his name, and he gave me an apologetic smile.

"You okay from here?" he asked.

We were halfway to where Sor sat talking, and I could see the cooler just opposite of where they were. "I'm good, thanks."

He took off back towards the guys with the firewood with a last wave in my direction. I headed to the cooler to grab something for Sor and me. With a glance over, I saw her chatting with a couple people who'd joined her. Since I still didn't feel comfortable enough to plop myself down and dive into whatever convo they were having, I dug through the assorted cans and bottles to grab a couple waters from one of the coolers for myself and made my way down the beach with my cell phone.

I kicked off my flip flops once I found a great spot away from everyone, a nice secluded area down past the lifeguard stand where I could still hear the faint remnants of the party going on and I could dig my freshly painted toes into the sand. This felt more like what I pictured my California vacation would be—stretched out on the beach, surrounded by the sounds of the ocean. Just, this particular version exchanged a group of partying teenagers for my father.

I slid one of the earphones into my ear and scrolled through my growing list of songs, trying to find something to suit my mood. Didn't feel like Mom's collection of eighties songs she'd given me for my birthday. Finally, I found a half-decent playlist I'd put together since I'd been in Cali and hit play, stretching my legs out on the sand, digging my toes into the warm coarseness.

My solitude didn't last five full songs before I saw someone approaching from the corner of my eye. Sorche must've realized I'd taken off and wanted to haul me back to the party.

Imagine my surprise when I looked over and saw JT a few feet away.

"Hey," I greeted, trying not to look too startled.

"Hey. Why'd you take off?" he asked, dropping unceremoniously—and more importantly, uninvited—on the sand next to me, a half-full bottle of something in his hand.

I shrugged.

For some reason, I was intensely aware of his presence. Of the sand that had dried to his bare arm at some point in the evening. I kept my gaze straight ahead as long as I could.

"Just wanted a little space," I said as I tried to figure out just what he was doing there—*with me*. I mean, there were tons of people around the bonfire, so why would he come after me?

What was this, Fate? Or something a little more sinister, a little more engineered by a well-meaning friend who wanted to try and play matchmaker? I didn't want to crane my neck to see if Sorche was peeking around the lifeguard stand or something, watching us.

"Are you applying for the role of stalker or something?" I asked with a smile. He seemed to be everywhere I was. Almost enough to give a girl a complex.

He burst out laughing and fell backwards on the sand, his eyes dancing as he peered at me.

He stayed that way for a moment before sitting back up on the sand. He put the bottle down beside him and ran his fingers through his hair, before resting his elbows on his knees and looking out at the water.

Great. I think I just totally humiliated myself. I must look like the biggest self-centered seventeen-year old this side of the L.A. city limits. I brought my attention back to my phone, turning down the volume and scrolling through the songs, trying to keep my attention anywhere but on his penetrating gaze.

"I wouldn't quite say stalker," he replied.

"So you *are* following me." I risked a sidelong glance at him.

"What if I am?" he asked coyly, taking a gulp of his drink and studying me, the hint of a smile tugging at the corner of his mouth.

"I'd have to wonder why," I said honestly. I didn't get this. Didn't get...was this some sort of test? See how far he could push the new girl? Some sort of initiation or something?

"You intrigue me, Chey."

Why, because I was an easy target? Being new and all, I barely had a clue what went on, and more importantly, I hadn't built immunity to his baby blues.

"Really? Why?" I asked, trying not to sound as curious as I felt.

"Seriously. You're different, and I kinda like that."

Different.

That was supposed to be flattering? I turned away, though the tap-dancing butterflies in my stomach waited anxiously for him to elaborate.

He didn't say anything, just stared out at the surf. I wasn't big on awkward silences, so I asked the first thing that came to mind.

"Did Sorche send you?"

She had done it before the night we met, but I couldn't have been gone long enough to warrant a search party, even of the JT variety.

"No. Why?"

"Just wondered."

Because as flattering as it was having the latest Hollywood bad boy under twenty following me around (a headline courtesy of my last Google search), it just wasn't something that ever happened to me. As much of a flirt as he was, I so wasn't his type. I wasn't falling at his feet. I wasn't one of the big players on the Hollywood scene, I was just...me. Plain old Chey Daniels, well Daniels-Morrow.

"I hear you finally signed on with Rico."

I nodded, wrapping the cord for my earphones around my iPhone. So much for listening to any music with him around. "I did. Well, unofficially. I still need to do the paperwork."

"Congratulations."

"Thanks."

More silence between us, not quite awkward, yet not totally comfortable, either.

I wished Sorche would text me or something. There existed some sort of intangible with JT that I needed time to figure out. And I thought the best way to do that would be with some actual distance. More than a few inches, I realized when I glanced down and saw a lot less sand between us than before. When had he moved closer? I could have sworn when he first sat down that there'd been at least a foot of space between us.

"So you wanna head back?" he asked.

Before I could answer, he stood, stretched a hand out, and yanked me to my feet. I was so surprised and unprepared for the jolt, I toppled into him. And judging by the subsequent grin on his face, I'm sure the sneak planned it that way. I stayed close just a millisecond longer than necessary before I stepped back.

"Yeah, let's go," I suggested quickly. Only because I didn't want Sorche to worry about where I'd disappeared to—absolutely nothing to do with the fact that I really wasn't sure I wanted to be alone with JT much longer.

But by the time we headed back to the bonfire, I doubted my new best bud had even noticed I'd ever walked away. She still sat in the same spot, talking away as she texted something on her cell phone.

Just then, mine buzzed, and I caught her glancing our way before she slid her cell away and went back to her convo. Guess I was the lucky recipient of a new text message. Maybe she had noticed my little disappearance, after all. 'Course, it seemed more likely she'd noticed my reappearance with JT at my side.

I looked up at my new—er, bodyguard? Shadow? Stalker? Friend? None of those seemed all that likely, though stalker could have a slight tinge of possibility.

"I think I can handle things from here," I told him, noticing how the light from the fire changed the intensity in his blue eyes, making them almost the same violet-blue that burned at the hottest part of a flame.

"You sure?" He looked amused, the slight breeze playing with his hair, and he lifted a hand to brush it back.

I forced my eyes not to follow the movement.

"Hundred percent." Couldn't be more sure if I tried.

"Okay, then. There's something I wanted to ask you..."

His lips were moving, and I'm pretty sure I was hearing things, because he totally didn't ask me out, did he?

I grew well-aware he was staring, the rich blue flecks in his eyes darkening while he stood there, patiently waiting for my...answer?

"Uh..." Me, eloquent as always.

"It's okay," he said, obviously thinking I was brushing him off.

My hand instantly reached out, grabbing for his sleeve to stop him from moving.

"No, wait. You surprised me, that's all," I rattled on quickly, before I lost my nerve. I kept my hand on his arm to keep him from walking away. "'Course, I'd love to."

Love to what, I'm not sure. I really hoped it didn't involve an extreme sport of some kind since I enjoyed keeping my body all in one piece. It functioned better that way.

"Cool." He nodded as he stuffed his hands into his pockets. "Looking forward to our date. Talk to you soon, Daniels."

Date?

He'd *seriously* asked me out?

I watched him walk away back towards the rest of the guys around the bonfire before I pulled open my cell phone to read Sor's text.

What's up?

At that point, I sure wished I knew.

11

"Are you free this afternoon?" Dad asked as he came outside with his morning cup of coffee.

Dressed in his jeans and a faded black T-shirt, he had cleaned up from the first glimpse I'd had of him heading out for his morning run when I'd opened up my balcony doors.

I stopped pouring the mini box of cereal into my bowl.

"Absolutely." I scooped a couple Lucky Charms marshmallows into my mouth. "What do you have in mind?"

I was hoping for the beach; I couldn't wait to go back to the ocean and feel the warm sand between my toes. After one night, I seemed to have become horribly addicted.

The water. The sand. The sound of the waves hitting the shore.

It was just perfect.

Dad smiled and handed me a white envelope from his pocket.

I looked at it a moment. "What's this?"

"Open it."

I ripped open the flap and peeked inside. It looked like tickets. Tickets could be promising. I pulled them out, gasping in surprise. Baseball.

"Uh, wow..." I mumbled, staring in disbelief. He wanted to take me to a baseball game?

"Not bad, huh?" He sounded excited. Really excited.

I managed a smile as I looked up at him, tapping the tickets against my palm. "Great. I've never been to a pro baseball game before."

So not exactly my perfect idea of father-daughter bonding, but I'd take what I could get. Especially when who knew when there could be another urgent business trip in his future. Although, hopefully now that I had Sorche and this whole 'Face of Vanetti' thing going on, I wouldn't notice the absence so much.

"The game's today."

I peeked back at the tickets. I hadn't even bothered to read the date and time when I'd first seen them.

"It's a late start. So if we want to beat traffic and everything, we could leave here early, say around four. Or earlier."

"I have to drop off the signed contracts at Rico's this morning, but I should be back in time," I assured him. Rico had asked if I could drop them by in person, and I'd said I'd be happy to.

"Good. I'm taking Trish to lunch so I'll meet you back here later."

"A date with Trish?" I asked, acting as innocent as possible, but I'm sure my smile must've been a dead giveaway.

The news thrilled me. Trish was great. And so much better than the last couple of females he'd been linked with, including the one or two I'd had the unfortunate luck of meeting over the years.

He laughed as he took a sip of his coffee. "It's a business lunch."
"Right."
"I like being single, Chey."

"So do I, Dad." I smiled at him. Didn't mean I didn't date, though.

I was still sitting there staring at the baseball tickets when the doorbell rang.

"I'll get it," Dad said. "Trish probably forgot her key again."

I noticed the smile on his face as he headed inside to get the door.

I swiveled back in my chair. Okay, so baseball wasn't really my favorite sport ever. I enjoyed hockey a little more, but it so wasn't in season. But as I looked at the tickets again, I couldn't help smiling to myself. He *was* trying. Probably wanting to make up for that disastrous NYC trip. And besides, after his little late night talk when he told me what was really going on, I couldn't feel angry at him anymore. He should have just come out and told me; I would have understood that he needed to go.

Maybe we could have found a way for me to tagalong with him, or at least we could have Skyped or something.

"Hey!"

I spun around in surprise at Sorche's voice. "Hey...what are you doing here?"

She smiled as she came over and took a seat at the patio table. "Heard you were dropping the contracts off today. Figured that warranted a visit."

"Do you want a coffee, Sorche?" Dad asked as he came back outside.

"I'd love one, thanks, Mr.—"

"Just Sean," he said as he headed back inside, and a moment later, I could hear him digging through the cupboards.

"Just Sean. Thanks," she called as she looked over what I was holding. "What are those?"

"Dad's taking me to a game this afternoon."

"Ooh." She pulled the tickets from my hand. "Great seats. My dad would be so jealous."

Dad laughed as he walked outside, obviously overhearing her comment. He handed her the coffee. "I think you're right. If you two girls are good, I'm going to go pick up Trish for lunch."

I raised an eyebrow.

"Business lunch," he repeated for my benefit.

I grinned. "We're fine. I'll be heading out to Rico's soon, anyways."

He paused in the doorway. "Oh, Milo was supposed to stop by to drop some papers and stuff off, so if you see him, just tell him to leave everything on my desk. I'll get to it soon as I get back."

"Will do. If he's not here before we leave, I'll put a note on the hallway table for him."

"Thanks, Chey."

We watched him head inside, and I pushed my cereal bowl away, glancing at my friend. "Okay, so why are you really here?"

"I brought you a good luck present." She smiled. "You aren't going to drop off your contracts dressed like that, are you?"

I looked down at my slightly faded pajama bottoms and scruffy T-shirt I'd slept in. "No."

I gathered my bowl and my empty juice glass and headed inside, Sorche right behind me.

"Thank God." Sorche smiled in relief.

"I'm not that bad, am I?"

"No, but those pants..." She cringed, and I laughed.

"C'mon up, you can help me get ready. I'm not sure what I should wear."

"Looks like I had perfect timing."

Sor set her bag down on my dresser as we settled in. I dug my favorite pair of jeans out of the closet and tossed them across the top of my empty desk, glad Sorche was there for styling help. I mean, what was I supposed to wear for this? I didn't want to go over the top, but I didn't want to look like I'd just rolled out of bed and grabbed whatever was clean, either.

I didn't want Rico to take one look at me walking through the doors and decide he'd just changed his mind. "What do you think?"

She followed me inside my walk-in closet now a lot more crowded than when I'd first arrived. I hadn't even imagined needing half this space.

Sorche smiled as she looked around. "Now this is nice."

"Thanks."

She thumbed through some of the hangers on an upper rack 'til she found something she liked and pulled down a couple T-shirts.

"You probably couldn't go wrong wearing one of Rico's." She held both the bright red T-shirt and white one out towards me as if testing to see which one looked better. "Maybe go red, it's bolder. It'll make a statement."

"Yeah?" I looked between the two shirts. Now, I never would have thought of that.

Statements?

Bold?

I just would have gone for whichever one I thought I looked better in that day.

She nodded, handing me the hanger with the chosen shirt before putting the other back in its spot. "I like your place. It's cool. Mine's so perfect sometimes...it's like I'm afraid to move something out of place."

"Really? I like the look of yours."

She shrugged. "Mine was a decorator's concept. You said your dad did this for you. Big difference."

"I guess." I laid the shirt on top of my jeans. "So, you're serious about going with me to Rico's?"

I didn't want her to think I required an escort or a babysitter or something as equally childish. I'd driven there once before, and I was reasonably sure I wouldn't get lost on the way.

After all, the directions were saved in my phone.

"You're dropping your contract off today, right? I'm here for moral support." She pulled her digital camera out of her tote. "And to document the occasion."

"Sor, it's just a couple pieces of paper," I said, trying to convince myself as I opened up the desk drawer and pulled the file folder out. I did a quick check to make sure I'd signed the papers in all the right places and Dad had, too. Those little neon paper markers came in so handy.

I flipped the folder closed again and set it beside my clothes.

"Right." She nodded solemnly, leaning past me to tap a brightly painted nail against the folder. "Papers that could change your entire life."

I stuffed the contract into the manila envelope Trish had given me. "The only thing it changes is it gives me a little more spending cash of my own this summer. That's it."

"You're so under dramatic."

That made me laugh.

"Yeah, well..." I gave a shrug in response. Dad had the drama genes in the family, apparently. "I'll get changed, and we can get going. I have no idea what time Dad wants to leave for the game."

"You've got hours," she assured me. "It's a late start." She glanced around the room. "I'll be right back; I left something downstairs."

She left the room, and I grabbed my clothes and headed into the bathroom to change. By the time I'd returned, finishing the last loop of the elastic on my ponytail, Sor was back and sitting on my bed, a large, sparkly gift bag in front of her.

"I got you a little something," she announced before I could say a word, and she pushed the bag towards me.

"Sor, you didn't have to do anything."

"Oh, please, you have to commemorate." She smiled. "The 'Face of Vanetti' deserves to celebrate." She held the bag out to me. "Take a look. I hope you like it."

I sat on the edge of the bed and took the bag. It was filled tight with tissue paper and heavier than I'd expected. I managed to move some of the tissue aside before putting my hand in, coming into contact with a cool, smooth surface. I shot her a questioning look, but she simply shrugged, camera in hand, waiting for me to pull whatever it was out. "What did you get me?"

"Not saying a word, you'll just have to see. But be careful. It's breakable." She held onto the sides of the bag while I put both hands in and managed to find the edges.

I pulled out the black and silver make-up mirror with the mini lights around the edges.

"I have one in blue," she said as she cleared a spot on my dresser. "I thought what better gift for the new 'Face of Vanetti' than a mirror?" She smiled at me. "You like?"

I followed her over and set the mirror down. It was gorgeous.

"I do." I gave her a hug. "I've never had a mirror like this before."

Honestly, the only mirror I had back home that didn't fit in my purse was the one attached to my dresser.

"Good." She stepped back. "I figured the most important thing for a potential 'it girl' is a good mirror." She turned to look at me. "You really don't mind me tagging along to Rico's? I just thought it'd be fun to go with. Moral support and all that."

"It's fine. Besides, I'll be glad to have the company." Probably help keep my nerves at bay. I scooped up my keys, ready to head out while she went back to the bed to grab her camera and purse. I noticed her hesitate as she looked out the window.

A good minute passed while she stood there, practically rooted to the spot.

"Sor?"

"Hmm?" She totally seemed not to hear me.

I moved beside her, peeling back the curtain to peer outside. All I saw was a topless Milo putting a few boxes down on the patio.

"Seriously? Milo?" I hadn't heard her mention him since the first time she'd seen him, and figured she was over whatever little instant crush she'd had.

I caught sight of the time on my alarm clock. "C'mon, we've gotta get going. I promised Rico I'd be there before lunchtime. Can you pull yourself away from the eye candy out my window or—

"I'm coming. Jeez, a girl gets a modeling contract and already, she's a diva before the first photo gets taken."

"Don't make me open up that balcony door and invite Milo up here..." I teased as I grabbed my keys and the envelope with the contracts and headed downstairs.

While Sorche went ahead to my car, I circled back toward the kitchen. I found Milo out on the patio. "Hey. Dad said just to put the paperwork on his desk."

He nodded as he glanced up at me. "Yeah, sure. Where you going?"

I lifted the envelope up. "Just have to drop something off at Rico's."

"Right. Mom mentioned something about that, congrats."

"Thanks."

"There she is," Rico greeted as he came out of the conference room at the same moment I walked up to the reception desk.

"Hey, Rico. I'm just dropping these off."

I blinked at the sudden blinding flash from Sorche's camera as I raised the envelope holding my signed and authorized contracts from Dad in my hand. I waved my hand in front of my eyes, waiting for the little dancing spots to disappear.

"Sorry, don't mind me." Sorche gave a little half-wave and ducked behind a nearby rack of clothes where she quickly disappeared from view.

I could have sworn I heard an excited squeal from her direction, but Rico quickly motioned for me to come with him back inside the conference room.

I followed him as he took the envelope.

"All signed," I assured him, suddenly realizing this was for real. Sor was right—those papers suddenly held the power to put my life on a whole new course, for this summer, at least.

"Good. Great. How's it feel?" he asked with a smile.

"A little unreal, and it hasn't even really started yet," I admitted, tucking my hands in my back pockets awkwardly. I glanced towards the glass windows looking out into the reception area. Still no sign of Sorche. I hoped she wasn't getting into any trouble out there.

"Have you celebrated yet?" he asked, taking a seat.

"Not really. Sorche and I went to dinner last night. Dad's taking me to a baseball game this afternoon."

"Sounds fun."

"I hope so." I managed a weak smile and noticed the designs for the first time spread out across the table. "Oh, wow..." I stepped closer for a better look.

"You like?"

"I do," I answered honestly, looking at the one closest to me. I may not have been a girly girl, always in dresses, but even I would have loved to wear the simple blue halter dress with the diamond pattern sketched out in front of me in varying shades of blue.

"I've been working on these all week." He glanced back at me. "You're going to be a hit once you're unveiled, you know."

A nervous laugh escaped before I could stop it. "Unveiled, huh?"

"Oh, we have big plans for this launch, Chey. Especially now that we found our perfect face." He looked back out the glass wall where we could see Sorche scanning the racks, taking pieces out to hold up to herself.

"Take something," he said, motioning back towards the racks outside.

I smiled. "You mean like a coffee cup?"

I hoped he meant like a coffee cup. Or even a mouse pad. I could really use a new one for the wireless mouse on my laptop.

"If you really want one, sure, but I meant from the racks. You said your dad's taking you out. Find something to wear if he takes you someplace special. Consider it part welcome gift, part first official assignment."

"Rico..."

"Go before Sorche calls dibs on all the best pieces. Now, don't argue with your new boss." He lifted the envelope with the signed papers inside.

"'K, boss." I saluted him. "If you say so."

Sorche looked up as I came to stand beside her.

"See anything you like?" I asked.

"Tons." She hung a midnight blue sundress back on the rack. "What did Rico say?"

"Not much. Just he'd probably call later this week to schedule some stuff. Things are going to move quickly, apparently. Guess it's good my schedule's pretty wide open."

"Cool." She flipped through the skirts. "I wish his store was open already."

She sighed as she studied one skirt thoughtfully.

"Well..."

"Well what?"

"He told me to pick something," I admitted a little sheepishly.

She squealed.

Rico laughed, and we both glanced up, startled to see him leaning on the rack across from us, his arms crossed and resting on top. "Sorche, you've got great taste. Want to help me find something special for Chey? I think left to her own devices, she'd say she'd do well with a simple tank top."

Sorche grinned.

"I'd love to." She glanced at me. "He's right, you know. You'd say you can wear the tank top and those jeans and be fine practically anywhere."

Before I could argue that it was true, he headed to a rack on the far side of the room. "Now these over here are brand-new, just arrived yesterday, so you're the first ones to see them."

Sor oohed and aahed as I trailed behind her.

Rico looked at me as I finally caught up to them, already flipping through the hangers and studying pieces. "Now, be honest and tell us if you don't like something we choose."

"Okay."

I thumbed through the rack in front of me while they pulled bits and pieces out and held them against me as I tried to get over my sudden anxiousness. I vetoed the ankle-length skirt, fearing my ability to walk in my new three-inch sandals I had bought shopping with Sorche, but I loved the jet-black skirt Rico picked, cut on an angle which would fall above my knees in the front and slide past them just a touch in the back. I found a great electric blue shirt to match.

"Done," I said happily.

Rico just smiled as he took the shirt from me.

"For now." He glanced at Sor who was staring longingly at the same shirt in a metallic red. "Take it."

"What?" she asked, snapping out of her thoughts, a stunned expression on her face like she didn't quite believe what she'd just heard.

"For helping Chey. It's yours." He swiped the hanger before she could say anything. "You girls hang out for a few minutes. I'll get these boxed up for you."

I put the boxes with our new clothes in the back of my car and slammed the trunk down, unable to stop myself from taking a quick glance around for a JT sighting as I headed to the driver's side. Sorche opened the passenger door as I slid inside the car.

"You have time for one more stop?" she asked.

I glanced at the clock on the dashboard. "More than enough."

I doubted Dad and Trish had even sat down for lunch yet. And I'd texted Dad when I'd parked the car before going to see Rico to check for the time. Apparently, we weren't even going to leave 'til after three, so I definitely had a couple hours to kill.

We'd barely walked in the doors of Sorche's favorite smoothie place when she grabbed my arm and pulled me back behind an arrangement of plastic plants. "Stay here."

I looked at her like she was crazy and watched her peek around the leaves. It was like something out of a bad movie, except I had a feeling the wrong thing to do would be to laugh.

"What are we doing?" I followed her gaze and saw a tall, statuesque platinum blonde near the counter, checking her iPhone.

"Who is she?" I tried to remember her from the quick rundown Sorche had given me the night we met, but the more I looked at her, the more I was sure we hadn't met.

"Trouble," Sor replied in a low voice.

From the way she gripped my arm, I figured she wasn't kidding. I peeked through the foliage again. She did look sort of familiar.

"Sor?" I tried again, prying her fingers off my arm. Ouch, she had sharp nails. And even worse, they left a noticeable mark. I rubbed my arm, hoping to draw back the circulation and get the indents to fade. "Who is she?"

"One of JT's many admirers and once considered the top choice to be the 'Face of...'"

Uh oh.

I didn't even need to hear the rest of the sentence to know I had two major strikes against me. "So I doubt she's going to be a member of my fan club?"

"Wouldn't count on it. Best thing to do is ignore her. All she wants is attention, and JT won't give her any. *You* won't give her any, and I'll try not to leak any nasty rumors about her," Sor said with an evil grin. "Of course, if TMZ should happen to showcase one or two bright and early tomorrow, I swear I won't have any clue where they got them."

I could almost picture the halo glistening brightly over Sorche's head, propped up on one side by a sparkly little red horn. I laughed, though I kinda worried just how joking Sor was. I didn't usually have to worry about my new best friend, but at this moment? Color me concerned.

"All will be fine. Come on..." I hooked my arm through hers and marched to the empty counter.

I could feel the girl shooting daggers at my back as we ordered our extra thick smoothies. I did my best to ignore her while I pulled a twenty out of my wallet and handed it over to the girl behind the counter, feeling Sorche just waiting to pounce. I hoped figuratively and not literally.

"Well, well, well, if it isn't the new 'Face of Vanetti'," the girl said as we walked to the other end of the counter to wait for our drinks.

"News travels fast around here," I said to Sorche as I took my change.

The blonde huffed, and I realized she was practically beside me as the air shifted. "Rico's obviously lowered his standards."

I tried not to let her comment faze me. I gave a one-shouldered shrug, reaching for my drink on the counter. "He didn't seem to think so..."

Sorche nodded her agreement as she grabbed a couple paper-wrapped straws from the dispenser. "I think he used the terms 'fresh' and 'vibrant' to describe Chey. Not 'stale', 'overexposed', and 'over-bleached', Adriana."

I bit down on my lip so hard to keep myself from laughing out loud that I could taste the slight metallic tinge of blood.

Adriana's blue eyes turned to ice.

"He's a flash in the pan, anyway..." She looked straight at me. "Enjoy your fifteen minutes, Wyoming."

"Ouch." I turned back to Sorche who rolled her eyes at the snarky comment. "Was that supposed to be painful?"

"First encounters with her usually are." She leaned past me. "Looks like Fiona's taking her out of here."

I looked behind us to see a brunette with her heading towards the doors, dropping their smoothies in the trash on the way out. "Glad to see she travels nowhere without an entourage."

"You'd have to with an ego that big. It'd be hard to walk upright, otherwise." Sor smiled. "You handled her well," she said as we took our drinks to a nearby empty table and sat down.

"Let's just say I'm no stranger to dealing with jerks."

I knew all about them, unfortunately. I'd gone to school with several from fifth grade 'til now, and they hadn't changed. Or if they did, they only got worse over time.

"I'm impressed." She smiled.

I shifted in my chair a little, looking at the door then back at Sorche. "So you and Adriana..."

"I was friends with Adriana for a long time," Sorche confided over her smoothie. "Then I got tired of her games and her personality and her entourage."

I nodded. "I'm not too fond of them, either."

"They're her little 'yes' girls. I swear one of them only breathes if she thinks it's okay with Adriana." Sor laughed a little. "I'm so glad you're more real than she is, and I'm sorry if I somehow put you in her crosshairs."

"I don't think you did. I somehow managed that all on my own."

"I don't think JT's attention helped with that. They were a 'thing' for a while there about a year ago, and I don't think she handled being dumped well."

"Control issues?"

"Clearly."

Sorche picked up her cell phone and scanned her texts. I set my phone down and glanced around the small shop. Only a couple people sat at tables, mostly twenty-somethings, the occasional mom with a baby stroller in the corner. But other than that, the place was pretty empty.

She texted something to someone then picked her smoothie back up. "Drink up! We are celebrating, after all."

"That, we are."

She lifted her frothy strawberry drink. "To this being Chey's most memorable summer yet."

"Hear, hear." We clinked plastic cups.

And to that being my only encounter with the wicked witch that was Adriana, I added silently.

If only my luck would have held out.

12

Dad's car was already back in the driveway when I got home. Sorche took off in her SUV with a wave, and I hurried inside, trying to get upstairs without bashing my boxes into the walls. I had the uneasy feeling I'd find more than the skirt and shirt inside with the way Sorche and Rico had been whispering. Making it into my room, I slid the boxes onto an empty shelf in my closet and shut the door behind me.

"You home?" Dad's voice traveled down the hallway a second later.

I peeked out the doorway. "Hey, just got here a second ago. Sor wanted to grab a drink on the way back so we stopped for smoothies."

"That's okay. Can you be ready in half an hour? That way, we can leave earlier and avoid some of the heavy traffic. Just heard there's a couple traffic delays on our route."

I looked at his scruffy sneakers; obviously, he wasn't dressing up for this, so I didn't really need to, either. "I can be ready in fifteen."

"Meet you at the car. I have to see what all Milo brought over."

"Okay."

I ducked back into my room and peeled my shirt off, grabbing a fresh pair of jeans from where I'd left my clean laundry piled on my armchair last night. I grabbed one of the first T-shirts Rico had given me from the closet and quickly changed before I touched up my make-up in my new mirror and added a baseball cap—we were going to a baseball game, after all—and headed downstairs, sandals in hand.

The house appeared empty when I got to the landing, so I grabbed my cell phone from the hall table and locked up before I hurried to the garage.

"Are we ready?" I glanced in the backseat, half-expecting Milo to be sitting there; he was around often enough lately, I'm sure Dad would think nothing of inviting him along.

And I hadn't thought enough to check how many tickets Dad had bought.

Dad held out an envelope. "The tickets are inside. Let's go."

We left early enough that we got to the stadium with more than enough time before the game started. Like a lot of places in Los Angeles, I hadn't been there before. And I really wasn't that big of a baseball fan, but Dad didn't know that. Actually, the more I thought about it, the more I realized he didn't seem to know a lot about me. Trish probably knew me better than he did in some ways. I ignored the small stab in my chest at the realization.

My feet were killing me by the time we found our seats near the dugout.

"We having fun, yet?" Dad asked, adjusting his new baseball cap he'd bought on our way in.

Must be his lame attempt at hiding himself. But hey, who was I to judge? I had the same cap on my head, the old one I'd worn there fastened to one of the belt loops on my jeans.

"Will be if you buy me a drink," I suggested as the drink vendor went past us. Nothing like spending the afternoon with Dad and a couple thousand other people. Father-daughter bonding at its finest. But at least, he was trying; I had to give him props for that.

"No problem."

Within moments, he had my drink in hand.

"I thought you'd enjoy this," he said, handing the icy plastic bottle my way as he watched the players stretching on the field.

"I am."

Well, I'd try. I took a small sip of the cold liquid to relieve my dry mouth from the hike we'd taken to even get there, then set my drink down by my feet and tried to get comfortable. Soon, he started talking about the various players, and I tried to follow along as best I could as he pointed them out on the field.

By the time the game was underway, I'd already noticed a few curious stares directed at us. It didn't help that much when I caught a brief glimpse of a cell phone aimed our way. I slid down deeper in my seat, adjusting my hat and wishing Dad would do the same, and tried to lose myself in the game being played in front of us.

We'd been sharing a box of popcorn when the first person approached us. As he crouched down beside Dad, I thought at first Dad was buying us a couple more drinks or maybe even a hot dog. But when I looked over, I saw him scribbling something on the guy's program.

Dad caught my eye and winked.

"Sorry kiddo," he said as the guy walked away. "I was hoping that wouldn't happen much today."

"It's okay," I lied.

Sitting there beside him, I watched as he signed autographs and posed for pictures with all the adoring fans during lulls in the game. I plastered a smile on my face that became faker and more plastic as the afternoon wore on.

I had to wonder if this wasn't part of what drove my parents apart. Mom got tired of sharing him. I could kind of see where she came from—there really was no time for just the two of us to hang out.

I munched on a handful of popcorn, watching some guy from the home team hit a homerun. At least, I think it was a homerun. People around us were standing up and cheering and hi-fiving one another. So I joined in, acting as excited as anyone else, though I seriously had no clue what we were all so excited about.

Dad shot me an apologetic smile as he signed one more autograph and handed the paper back to the woman who was still staring at him as she walked back to her seat a few rows behind us. I was almost worried she was going to take a tumble since she was watching him more than the stairs.

I had the feeling she was a tourist. She had that same awe about her that I did the first few days in town. The same awe that was slowly fading away, being replaced by something I didn't yet understand.

"You didn't have a good time, did you?" Dad asked a few hours later as we walked out of the stadium amongst a swarm of happy people.

I didn't want to lie, but I didn't exactly feel like telling the truth, either. "I guess I'm not really a baseball fan. Sorry, Dad."

I tried to stick as close as possible to him, knowing if I lost him in this crowd, I probably wouldn't be able to find him again. There were way too many guys in baseball hats and sunglasses to ever be able to spot him without having to yell for him. And imagine how many people would stop and turn at that. At least, I had some idea where he'd parked, and I had my cell phone. I could always text him an 'I'm lost' and wait for him to find me.

He handed me the car keys as we made our way across the parking lot. "How about I make it up to you?"

"No outdoor sporting events involved?" I asked as I hit the button on the remote as we neared the Escalade, unlocking the doors.

"None." He looked at me suddenly. "You're having a good time, right?"

Why did I have a feeling he didn't quite mean just the baseball game? "Now that we're no longer watching baseball, absolutely."

You couldn't fake the wattage of my smile.

Dad laughed. "Okay, so you're not the sports enthusiast I am. I know that now."

"Just baseball. It's so..." I shrugged, trying not to tell him it was one of the most boring things I'd ever watched in person; it was just so drawn out. Why did they need nine innings? "Not my thing."

"That's okay. We've got time to find something we can do together." He opened my door for me. "Besides, I think what I have in mind for tonight is definitely more your style."

I watched him walk around the vehicle, trying to figure out what that cryptic comment meant. I took off my new baseball cap he'd bought me and tossed it into the backseat before running my fingers through my hair. It felt nice to be out of the heat and not surrounded by people.

Dad slid in the driver's side and slammed the door behind him. "You up to going out tonight?"

"Yeah, of course." I aimed the blast of icy air conditioning at my face as he started the engine.

"Good. We should have just enough time to get home and clean up before we need to be there."

"Be where?" I tried to get some piece of information out of him.

"You'll see." He just smiled at me as he pulled out of the parking lot, and I can safely say I was very glad to leave the stadium behind us.

I didn't have that long to change, because Dad had given me a strict hour time limit to get into something 'nice' and be back in the vehicle. I'd hopped in the shower, washed the sunscreen and popcorn smell off, gave my hair a quick wash, and slipped into my favorite fluffy robe to dig through my closet. But the second I stepped out of the bathroom, I heard the familiar ping from the computer.

I slunk onto the desk chair, my heart thudding as I saw the invite to web-cam with Mom. I couldn't very well say 'no.' Her 'Mom radar' would have gone off the charts, so I hit 'yes' and waited.

Suddenly, Mom's face stared back at me, our familiar pale yellow kitchen wall behind her. *Deep breaths*, I told myself. Remembered that yoga breathing Sorche had taught me, which totally came in handy at a moment like this. I had the biggest fear she'd take one good look at me and know everything wasn't as it seemed and that she'd have me on the next flight home.

"Hi, Mom." I tried to sound as cheerful as ever.

She smiled at me for a moment.

"Something's off," she declared.

I hated how well my mother knew me.

"No, it's not. Everything's fine."

Lie. Total, complete lie. If I was like Pinocchio, my nose would be straight across my room, past my balcony, heading for the pool and the hills beyond the fence.

Silence.

She totally knew I was lying.

The silence was her trick to guilt the truth out of me. A trick that had worked surprisingly too well in the past. I tried my best to stare innocently at the camera.

"Dad took me to a baseball game, and we're about to go head out for a late dinner somewhere. I guess I left the laptop signed in while we were out..." I said truthfully.

"All right..."

Long, lengthy pause, of which Mom was probably waiting for me to crack. Well, not this time. I was seventeen and wise to her tricks.

"I'll text you later when we get to the restaurant," I promised, my fingers tapping the side of my mouse anxiously.

"Okay, talk to you soon." I could tell she was scrutinizing my image on her screen. "Have fun tonight," she said after a few moments' pause.

"I will. 'Night, Mom. Love you." I blew her a quick kiss before I closed the connection and let out a relived sigh.

I'd felt a little guilty at the sound of the incoming call and sat right down. My daily emails and texts home had definitely dwindled down to pretty well nothing the last week or so. Just a couple good morning and good night texts here and there. Ever since that mini-blow up with Dad, I was afraid she'd somehow be able to read between the lines and know things weren't as picture perfect as I tried to paint them.

I wondered how bad my acting had been during our brief convo. Although I'm pretty sure some of it she'd write off as my nerves on going somewhere with Dad, I knew she'd now be double-checking there really had been a baseball game this afternoon.

Remembering Dad was downstairs getting ready to go out, I turned the laptop off and ran to get ready myself.

"Are you ready?" Dad called up the stairs.

"Almost!" I yelled back, trying to get my other sandal out from under my bed. I stretched a little more and finally wrapped my fingers around the heel, trying to figure out how it had gotten so far under there in the first place.

Dad had stayed pretty quiet about where he was taking me to celebrate my little burst of good news. I'd also decided to stay mum about the whole date with JT thing. I doubted anything was going to come of it, anyway, so why mention it?

I zipped up my black skirt and added the pair of casual black and blue sandals I'd spent five minutes trying to reach. I'd gone with an almost all-black look, frankly because well, I had no clue where we were headed but I doubted it was back to Pink's. I remembered him saying something about reservations, so obviously, it was someplace special.

I grabbed my little purse and hurried down the stairs. I whistled as I saw Dad standing at the front door, obviously waiting for me to show up. The grey button-down shirt brought out the vivid blueness of his eyes, and the black jeans were a lot more casual than I expected.

Relief flooded me that I wasn't overdressed—or underdressed, for that matter.

"All set," he said as he opened the front door, and we stepped outside into the cooler air.

It smelled like rain in the distance, and I rubbed my arm absently, wondering for a minute if I should run back in and grab a jacket.

"Could you be any more secretive?" I teased him. Not that I minded, because I was having fun even with the baseball debacle earlier.

He only smiled. "You'll see."

"Okay." I was starving, anyways. That popcorn seemed hours ago now, and no doubt I'd used up any and all energy from it on our hike back to the vehicle after the game.

I just hoped they had good food and we wouldn't have to wait in line forever to get there.

Then, I remembered who I was with, and as Sor had been drilling into me lately, everything was different in L.A. Especially for the Hollywood set, which as weird as it still was to me, I was now officially a part of.

We found a nice little parking spot close to wherever it was we were headed to. Dad didn't point out any of the passing restaurants as we drove by, just said it was within short walking distance. I had my arm looped through his as we walked, and I was really glad Rico had pushed me to take some clothes home when I'd dropped the contract off. I could see some of the people who passed by take another look at us and even better, overheard a few comments about my skirt. Rico would be so proud.

"Here we are," Dad announced, hand on the door handle.

I was surprised we'd stopped walking. I looked up to see where we were.

"You're kidding me," I said as I saw the name above the door and glanced at the smoky glass entrance, trying to see inside.

"Nope." He opened the door. "After you."

I may not have moved in the Hollywood circles long, but even *I* knew about this place. Anyone who was anyone ate here. There'd even been a write up on it in one of the magazines I'd brought with me on the flight. Half the owners were celebs, and I'd never in a million years have imagined myself within a hundred yards of this place, let alone eating here with my father.

Dad laughed and pulled me inside after him. "Come on, we're right on time for our reservation."

"Right," I said, like I'd known that all along.

I knew there had to be some perks to having a movie star father. Good tables was one. No waiting in line, another. We were led straight through the restaurant, and I finally had a few celeb sightings of my own. I suppressed my inner fan girl urge to squeal and ask for an autograph or a quick photo on my phone and instead kept walking, following the woman who led us straight to our table—smack dab in the middle of the room.

Talk about being on display.

I could *so* feel people looking at us. In fact, they probably were, but I didn't want to glance around and risk making eye contact with one of my favorite actors of all time. (Three tables over. His poster hung on the back of my bedroom door at home.)

"I hope this is all right?" the hostess asked.

"It's fine," Dad answered, pulling out the chair for me.

I smiled and took my seat, putting the white linen napkin on my lap as I tried to discreetly look around, taking it all in from the dark brown tables with the high back leather chairs, to the dark smoky gray walls and matching booths against the far wall, and the square lights hanging down overhead.

Wow.

This place definitely felt like Los Angeles.

Not that I hadn't been in L.A at Dad's, or at Sorche's, or the party or anywhere else...

But this suddenly was different. *So* different. Like welcome to the world of the real grown-ups.

"You okay?" Dad asked, handing me a matte black leather-covered menu.

I straightened up in my chair a little. "Fine."

"Okay, then." He smiled. "I just thought this might be a lot for you to take in all at once."

"It is a little overwhelming," I admitted, glancing at the condensation appearing on my glass of ice water.

"You look great, Chey."

"Thanks. Rico gave me the outfit."

Along with the orders not to thank him profusely and just enjoy life on the sunny coast. I adjusted the spaghetti strap on my shoulder and looked at the menu, trying to decide what I wanted. I was starving. and everything looked amazing.

"Do you know what you want?"

I lowered the menu. "Haven't got a clue."

Dad laughed. "Trust me to order for you?"

"Of course."

Halfway through our father-daughter date, we were interrupted.

I knew the moment the man in the expensive-looking grey suit appeared at our table and shook my father's hand that something was up, especially when the guy turned and gave me one of those beyond perfect smiles. Teeth that white only existed in toothpaste ads. For a moment, I wondered if he was related to Brody from the party.

Dad smiled at me, and I could see a touch of pride in his eyes. "Quinn, I want to introduce you to my daughter, Cheyenne. Chey, this is Quinn Donovan, one of the executive producers of what hopefully will be my next project."

I smiled as I caught the hint in Dad's words.

"Nice to meet you, Mr. Donovan," I said as Quinn shook my hand.

"Pleasure to meet you," Quinn said as he skirted the empty chair at our table and took a seat. "And please, call me Quinn. I'm not intruding, am I?"

'Course not. Just the first grown-up time I've had with my father in seventeen years. But I knew how important my dad's career was right now, so I took a sip of my diet soda and opted to stay quiet. I was sure Quinn would have his drink with us, make small talk, then take off for the night, leaving Dad and me to stop somewhere for ice cream after dinner. For some reason, I was craving Rocky Road.

"Special occasion?" Quinn asked as the waiter brought over his drink.

I glanced at Dad who nodded. Apparently, I could share my good news. "I just signed a deal with Rico Vanetti for the summer."

"That's great news." Quinn smiled, lifting his glass in the air for a toast. "Congratulations."

I felt a little embarrassed as the three of us clinked glasses. I'd been cursed with shyness, from my mother's side, apparently, and now, couldn't stop putting myself in situations where I was destined to be noticed. It suddenly felt like everyone in the restaurant had to be watching the three of us toasting something front and center.

"Thank you. I'm looking forward to it. Should be fun."

"The experience should add some fun to her summer. I think spending all three months stuck with just me for company would have turned her off Los Angeles permanently."

I smiled at Dad. "I'm hardly housebound."

He turned to Quinn. "She's been hanging out with Sorche Maxwell and JT."

Quinn looked mildly surprised. "Good crowd to be moving in."

I gave a little shrug. I didn't see my friends as a 'crowd.'

"I heard the trip to NYC didn't go as well as you'd hoped," Quinn said, obviously turning the conversation away from me.

I took a few more bites of the food on my plate, paying close attention to stabbing my lettuce just so. Not like I was mentally replacing my food with Quinn's hand. I wasn't that childish, was I? With any luck, he wouldn't nurse his drink longer than necessary. I have to say I felt completely and utterly dismissed by the guy.

"I'm hoping I can salvage something from it."

"I might have something better if you're interested."

I glanced up just in time to see Dad's eyes light up, then flicker back down as he glanced at me. "We'll have to set up a meeting."

"What's wrong with tonight?"

I bit my lip to keep from having a mini-outburst at that little comment. How about the fact he'd just commandeered our dinner conversation?

Quinn looked at me. "Would it be okay if I borrowed your dad?"

I opened my mouth to speak, but before I could utter a word, Dad spoke up. "Chey, you don't mind, do you?"

Oh, like I *could* possibly mind. I couldn't exactly balk. Instead, I shrugged as he slipped the car keys into my hand.

"I'll be fine." The Escalade had GPS; I had my phone. I was sure I could find my way home. If not, I could always call Trish to give me directions. Or Sorche, even. She knew how to get to my place.

Quinn smiled as he rose from his seat. "We'll make it up to you."

Like I really believed that. What was he going to do?

"It's fine, really. Dinner was practically over, anyways." And then, there would have been a tour around town or something, but hey, don't mind me. I'm only the daughter. No one important.

"Can I get you anything else?" the waiter asked, taking my plate, probably expecting Dad to say the check.

I sighed and looked at Dad.

"You stay for a while, Chey. Soak in the atmosphere." He smiled before turning to the waiter. "She'll have a nice slice of Death by Chocolate. Extra drizzle." He looked at me. "You sure you're okay with this?"

For the first time, he looked a little unsure.

"'Course I am, especially now that you ordered me dessert." So I was lying through my teeth. I didn't need to make him feel any worse than I'm sure he felt taking off on me—at least, I hoped he felt.

The waiter brought him the check to sign. Then, after a quick hug for me, he and Quinn left.

I didn't think watching him walk out the door would be the wisest move. What would that look like? A little too pathetic for words, I imagine. And really, right now, I could feel the curious gazes of people around us as Dad and Quinn left the table amongst the familiar murmurings of *isn't that...?*

So instead, I took a sip of my water and pulled out my cell phone, making a show of checking for messages and praying the waiter would hurry up with that slice of cake.

What was he doing? Preparing it from scratch? Just throw the blasted thing in a cardboard box, for all that I cared, and bring it back to the table.

I took another sip of my almost flat soda, having had enough of the tasteless ice water just as the chair Dad had occupied slid back. I doubted Dad would have returned already. Quinn seemed to have something important to talk to him about.

I glanced up, almost not believing my eyes who stood there.

13

"Rico!" I looked up to see none other than the man who had discovered me standing there. I smiled warmly at my boss, feeling a lot better that I wasn't sitting there all alone, the poor daughter abandoned in a strange restaurant no longer. "What are you doing here?"

Actually, I didn't care *why*. I was just glad he was there.

He took Dad's seat and motioned to a nearly concealed back corner. "We were having a quiet dinner out, and I saw your father leave. I wanted to invite you to join us."

"Us?" I looked back at the corner, trying to distinguish the shadows at the table, but from where I was, they were well-hidden from view.

"A fellow designer, my wife, and..." he paused, giving me a lopsided smile. "My cousin-in-law, I think you know him. JT."

I wanted to laugh as I sighed and tucked my cell phone back inside my purse. I couldn't get rid of JT if I tried, apparently. I momentarily wondered if I had a tracking device on me.

"Are you sure? I was just going to head home after my dessert arrived." I jingled the car keys for effect.

"We insist. Besides, we wanted to take you out anyways to celebrate. We'll start tonight."

Well, if that was the case, it would be rude not to go over, at least for a few minutes. Have my cake then take off for the night.

Rico stood and helped me from my chair before waving down the waiter and telling him to send the dessert, along with a fresh diet soda, to my new table.

"Looks like we've got company," Rico announced as we reached his table.

I slid into the booth and found myself instantly beside JT, not expecting Rico to slide in beside me, trapping me where I was. There really was no place to move, except closer to JT. It could be worse, I reminded myself—I could have been stuck sitting there alone waiting an eternity for a simple slice of cake.

Rico smiled at me. "Everyone, *this* is Chey Daniels. My choice for the next big Hollywood '*it* girl'."

"Hi," I said a tad meekly, not used to having so much attention focused on me at one time. And there were a few other faces crowded around the booth now that I was sitting there that I didn't know.

After a few quick introductions, everyone soon went back to their conversations, and I found myself sitting there talking with JT, who for once, acted surprisingly normal. Or at least, more normal than I ever gave him credit for. I chose to ignore the fact my heart beat a little faster any time I needed to scoot closer to him when Rico poured the glasses of champagne and began passing them around.

Honestly, I was glad Rico had come over. I'd felt pretty abandoned when Dad had taken off. Sure, I knew all about how important his career was, especially right now, but this was going to be hard to get over. We were celebrating my big news, and he just let Quinn swoop him away. I was sorta seeing what Mom meant; a few more episodes like this and I could, maybe even *would*, become disillusioned about the guy.

Not that I thought he was perfect, because over the years, I'd realized he wasn't. The missed holidays, the time he didn't get to see my first school play. When he didn't come to my sweet sixteen party. Missing my grad. And the piece de resistance, forgetting my seventeenth birthday, which I totally know he did because I recognized Trish's handwriting on the memo in his date book tucked in his desk drawer. It explained my free reign shopping spree.

And the way he'd promised we'd celebrate both our birthdays together this summer, my eighteenth and his thirty-ninth—yeah, I wasn't holding my breath on that one.

I loved my dad, don't get me wrong. He was a great guy. It's just that he wasn't in the running for the world's greatest dad. Sure, he tried. Like the car and having me visit for the summer, but I really don't think he knew what to do with me half the time. Hence his over-eagerness about my modeling, something to occupy my time and keep my focus off my absentee daddy.

Rico slid me a half glass of champagne. "We need to toast our beautiful new 'Face of Vanetti'."

I wasn't entirely convinced of the beautiful part, but who was I to argue with L.A.'s hottest new designer as every Internet search I'd done called him? Blushing, I lifted the glass and clinked it along with the others, feeling a lot better than when I'd joined them.

"Take a sip, Chey. It's a night to celebrate," Lorna, Rico's wife, said with a smile. "Shall we share one more slice of cake?"

I looked at the remains of mine on the table in front of me. JT had somehow procured an extra fork and had been sneaking bites here and there while we talked. "I suppose I could have a couple of bites."

"Excellent." She smiled. "We need one more Death by Chocolate," she told Rico.

We sat there talking for the longest time, Lorna asking what I'd done the short time I'd been in town and telling me all I had to do and see before I even thought of stepping foot on another plane back home. It felt nice to be included, and I found myself laughing along with JT as he told his cousins about something that had happened at the bonfire that I'd missed

By the time we left the table to head outside, the restaurant was dimming its lights behind us, and I wondered how late it was. I hadn't even glanced at my watch the entire time we'd sat there. But for almost the first time since I'd arrived, I felt amazingly relaxed.

We stepped en masse outside into the breezy night, the smell of fresh rain hanging heavy in the air. The streetlights reflected off the small puddles on the street. It must have rained a little while we were all inside. I shivered a little, yet again wishing I'd brought a jacket with me, but I hadn't. Luckily, it wasn't that big of a trek back to the vehicle.

Lorna turned to me.

"You have a ride home, Chey?" She looked concerned about leaving me on my own.

I'd explained all about Dad needing to take off for a sudden, impromptu meeting when we were inside. I didn't want them to think I'd been rudely abandoned for nothing.

"I'll make sure she gets home safe and sound," JT piped up from beside me before I could open my mouth.

"Thanks, JT," Lorna said before she gave me a tight good night hug. "We'll see you soon."

I nodded before JT and I walked away, leaving them at the valet stand.

"Thanks, JT, but..." I started as soon as we were out of earshot. He didn't have to play hero. I was fine.

"You had a glass and a half of bubbly. I didn't. Keys." He stopped, holding his hand out. "You heard me tell Rico and Lorna I'd make sure you got home okay. Don't make me lie to my family."

I sighed. "JT—"

"I'll drive you home, then get someone to pick me up," he assured me.

I pulled the keys out of my bag and pressed them into his hand, earning one of those butterfly-unleashing smiles of his. Though it could have been the effect of the Dom; who was I to know? That was the most alcohol I'd ever had in my life.

"Now where'd you park?"

"Down there." I pointed across the street.

We walked alongside each other in silence. On such a beautiful night out, it wasn't even bad being with JT. We reached the Escalade far too soon for my liking.

"This is it," I said as I stopped beside the passenger door, unable to open it since he had my remote.

He hit the button on the fob, and I heard the loud click as the doors unlocked. I slid into the passenger side while he went around. I found myself shivering as I shut the door.

"You tired?" he asked me as he opened the driver's side.

"No, not especially." I looked at him in the suddenly bright interior light. "You?"

"Not really."

I looked back outside. Too nice a night to waste. "You know, I don't have to be home at a certain time. You feel like going for a walk?"

I wasn't ready to go home, anyways. I doubted Dad would be home yet, and I was a little too keyed-up to sleep. A walk might be just what I needed to help lull me so I could drop into bed once I got home.

He leaned in. "You know, this isn't going to count as the first date you promised me, Daniels."

"Damn." I laughed. "But you want to?"

"Let's see, take a walk with a hot girl, or head home? I'll take more time with the girl." He grinned. "I know a great all-night place for coffee, too."

"Let me guess, a twenty-four-hour Starbucks?" I teased as I leaned over, reaching behind the seat and grabbed my baseball cap from the back. I slipped it on my head, hoping it would tame the strands the breeze had kept toying with as we walked to the vehicle. Of all the nights not to have a spare hair elastic in my purse—or on my wrist, for that matter.

He got out of the vehicle first, and I climbed out of the SUV as he locked it up behind us. I noticed he pocketed the keys, but I didn't say anything. He did promise to be my ride home, and I had a feeling, as odd as it was, that I could trust him.

He slid off his leather jacket and draped it around my shoulders without a word. I gave him a questioning look.

"I'm fine." I was about to hand it back to him.

"Sure you are, Daniels."

He started walking, and I followed quickly.

"Which way?" I asked as we reached the street corner.

He looked down both sides of the street.

"Why don't we go this way?" he suggested, motioning to the opposite direction from the restaurant.

"Sure." The streets weren't that crowded. Cars passed by, but there weren't that many people on the sidewalk. The rain earlier had probably driven everyone inside the restaurants and coffee places we kept passing.

"I know I said it before, but congratulations on *finally* accepting Rico's offer."

"Thanks."

"Glad you agreed."

"Me, too." I could tell I startled him with that response.

We walked in silence for almost half a block.

"Rico has a lot of amazing things planned," JT said at last.

"Yeah?" I carefully stepped around a puddle, trying not to splash him or me.

"Oh, yeah." His smile told me he knew what Rico had in mind, but wasn't about to tell me a word of it as we crossed another street. "How do you like life in L.A. so far?"

I shrugged. Our pace felt comfortable, not hurried. The sidewalks were drying from the rain showers earlier; yet, they were still a little slick in spots. He grabbed my hand to help me over an especially large puddle. "Still getting used to it."

"I'd have thought you would have settled in already, hanging out with Sorche and all."

"She's making sure I have some sort of social life," I agreed, glancing in a few of the darkened shop windows as we passed. I saw a jacket I liked and glanced up at the store name, hoping to remember it in the light of day so I could drag Sorche back to try it on with me.

"Trust Sor to be the life of the party."

"Judging by the way we met, I'd say that was you."

I could have sworn his face reddened a little, but it might have just been the neon glow of one of the signs we passed.

"Like I told you then, I'm not used to new people."

"Sorry about that."

"Hey, it's my fault. It's what too much Corona gets me."

Deciding not to go down the road of questioning him too much and getting him upset, since he was my ride home, after all, I thought I'd better change the subject as quickly as possible.

"So," I glanced at him from under the brim of my baseball cap. "You're related to Rico."

"Yeah."

"You never mentioned that at the fashion show."

"You didn't ask," he said with a grin. "We really didn't talk much that day, anyway. Are we playing twenty questions?"

"Should we?"

He laughed. "No."

I smiled. "Good."

"You know, I like you, Chey."

So he kept saying.

"You like a challenge," I countered. I mean, I figured that much was true.

"Is that what you are?"

"I wonder."

I smiled as we rounded the corner and headed back up towards the restaurant on the opposite side of the street. Soon enough, we'd be back at the Escalade, and our little walk would be over.

Why did it feel like we'd only been walking for a few minutes when if I glanced around and realized how far we walked, we must have been out for at least an hour. And I didn't feel the least bit chilled in the cooling night's air, even when I handed him back his leather jacket. JT most definitely had an odd effect on me.

"You're different."

"I'm new, that's all," I countered.

"That's not it. There's something about you. You're not jaded. You're not demanding... you're just..."

"The next 'it girl'," I said with a laugh, recalling Rico's toast that evening. I still couldn't see it. I had nothing in common with the so-called 'it girls' of the past.

There was that boyish smirk of JT's, the one that said he knew something I didn't.

"No doubt, you've got potential."

We'd stopped walking, and I looked up to see a small café all lit up. "Where are we?"

"I believe I promised you a coffee before I took you home. Welcome to some of the best coffee you'll ever have in L.A." He opened the door and waved me in. "My treat."

"Thanks for driving me home," I said as we sat in the warmth and dryness of Dad's Escalade. The only lights on inside the house were the ones I learned were on the timer. Dad still wasn't home. Must be one long meeting I'd missed.

"Glad to." He turned the screen off on his phone. "Looks like it'll be twenty minutes for my ride to get here."

I nodded. "That's okay."

"You know, tonight still isn't classified as our first date," he reminded me, leaning back against the headrest and turning his head to look at me. Something serious in his eyes had me thinking...

"Oh, really?"

There was an assuredness about his nod. "Saturday good for you?"

"I think I can pencil you in."

"Good."

I laughed softly and leaned over to turn on the satellite radio, flipping through Dad's presets until I found a half-decent station.

"You don't have to stay out here and wait with me."

"And leave you alone in my driveway or sitting on my steps?" I raised an eyebrow. "You really want that role of stalker, don't you?" I teased. "Besides, if my dad pulls in and finds you out here alone...that's a hundred questions I don't feel like answering tonight."

It had to be nearing three in the morning or so, I guessed. I really didn't want to take a look at the time.

"Suit yourself."

We listened to music for a while before he leaned forward and looked out the window, towards the gates. "I think I saw headlights on the other side of the gate."

I turned to look, and sure enough, it looked like a car sat there waiting. I sighed to myself, suddenly wishing the ride had taken a lot longer to get there. I turned the stereo off, and he handed me the keys.

"I'll let him in," I said, about to hit the gate button on the keychain.

"Nah, I'll just walk to the gate. It's fine," he said as he stepped out and the door shut loudly behind him, breaking the sudden silence.

"I'll walk you down," I said quickly, throwing my passenger side door open and stepping out, suddenly not ready to say good night.

The rain was starting to fall again, and I pulled the baseball cap off, leaving it on the seat before I moved around to where JT stood. In the glow of the headlights, he looked like he should be on a glossy poster, in his untucked button-down shirt and jeans, his jacket wide open, his hands stuffed deep in his pockets, and the corner of his mouth lifting into a smile.

"Chey..."

"I have to let you out, remember?" I held up the remote, glad to have that as an excuse.

"You just don't want to see me go."

I laughed, avoiding his eyes. "Yeah, right."

"Mmm..."

I watched as he closed the distance between us. The rain began to fall harder, and the front of his hair started to stick to his forehead. I was just about to reach out and brush it back when he stopped in front of me.

A hint of a smile cornered his lips, and our eyes met. He leaned down just a touch, and I could feel the warmth of his breath against my skin, smell the faintest hint of coffee.

Before I knew what was happening and could even think about a protest, his thumb was on my chin, his fingers coiling beneath, tipping my head up. Then came the briefest meeting of our eyes, before his mouth came down on mine.

And it was...

Well...

Too many words come to mind. Amazing. Awesome. Mind-numbing. Tempting, because as soon as our lips separated, I wanted to kiss him all over again.

I took a teeny step back, all the better to think clearly. "What was that?"

JT looked amused. "I like to think it was what they call a kiss. A pretty great kiss."

"Right." I was back to my one-word answers, so that clear-thinking thing? Totally not working.

I blinked as the Uber driver flickered his lights.

"Looks like he's impatient." I slid back another half-step.

"Looks like he just cost himself a nice tip," he mumbled as we headed towards the gate.

I hit the remote, and the gates moved back, letting JT through.

"'Night, Chey."

"'Night."

I watched the gates close behind him as he walked towards the car waiting at the end of the drive, and I didn't move 'til its red taillights disappeared in the distance. My lips still felt the sting of JT's kiss as I headed back up to the house and noticed the door still open on the Escalade.

I jogged over, grabbed my hat, and slammed the door, locking it behind me as I headed for the front door, my mind still replaying the last few moments with JT. A smile played on my lips as I ran a hand over my damp hair that was beginning to plaster itself to my head, but I didn't care.

14

"Chey!"

I whirled around at the sound of JT calling my name and found him running towards me, the gates shut behind him, the car long gone. And the front driveway illuminated only by the suddenly flickering outdoor light above my head.

"What are..." I started to ask as he stopped in front of me, our faces level since I was still on the step.

And just as he was about to answer, 'Girls Just Want To Have Fun' began blaring from somewhere around us. I blinked, trying to figure out where the music came from, when his mouth opened and the words tumbled out.

"JT?" I repeated as the muffled sound of my phone's ringtone broke me out of my dream and I pulled the pillow over my head, wanting to drown it out—forever if possible—but it kept going. I reached down alongside the bed, trying to find the evil device that was still blaring that song. Next time, I was making sure it was on vibrate before I fell into bed.

"Hello," I rasped, keeping the pillow over my head. It felt like I'd just closed my eyes. Who in their right mind would be up already?

"Hey there."

Sorche.

Sounding way too perky for... I fought the urge to lift the pillow and see what time blinked on the clock on my bedside table. Whatever it said would still be too early for my liking, anyway.

"What do you want, Sor?" I rubbed my tired eyes.

"Uh oh, did I wake you up?"

"What do you think?"

"I'm thinking at quarter to one in the afternoon, I was sure you'd be up already."

I lifted the corner of my pillowcase. Sure enough, sunshine was trying to break into the room through the unevenly closed curtains. I groaned and rolled over, fighting to keep my eyes shut and hang on to the last remnants of sleep.

"Late night?" She sounded very amused.

"Kind of."

"I knew it!"

"Knew what? That I wished I slept 'til three?" I sat up when I realized trying to fall back asleep proved beyond futile and leaned against the pillows, wiping the sleep from my eyes.

"What did you want, Sor?" I repeated.

If this could be a quick convo, maybe I would be able to grab another half hour of sleep. Not that I hadn't slept well; it's just I kept dreaming of JT and that kiss, and I kinda wanted to go back to it.

"Oh, right. I was going to ask if you'd seen something, but obviously, no, you haven't."

"Seen what?" She wasn't making any sense.

"There's a JT mention in the online gossip this morning. It talks about spotting him walking around with a mystery girl late last night."

I grew more awake with every word I heard. "Mystery girl?"

I could almost see her nodding. "There's a picture, too."

"Oh, my..." I slid out of bed. "Sor..." I waited for her to elaborate while I took a seat at the glass desk and waited for my laptop to boot. There was no way my eyes were awake enough to try to make sense of anything on my phone.

"It's from the back, apparently. It's posted a couple places online already."

Now I groaned, my world feeling a little lopsided, and not because of any champagne-induced hangover.

"Why aren't you saying anything?" she asked.

"Because I'm hoping I'm dreaming." Seriously. I even pinched myself, to no avail. All I got was a nice, stinging pink spot on my forearm.

"Chey, relax! You're a mystery girl. That's it, that's all."

Why was my gut saying it was a mystery soon to be solved?

"So, was that your first date?"

"Sorche..." Shouldn't she know the use of her full name meant I wasn't in the mood for this?

"Oh, come on, you have to fill me in. Without me, you wouldn't even know about the supposed mystery girl."

"Can you send me the link?"

The computer finally booted, and I hurriedly opened my browser.

"Already e-mailed it over."

"Thank you."

I checked my e-mail and clicked the link, finding instead of the blurred image I'd been hoping for, a crisp, clear, and in color shot loaded onto my screen. The one saving grace was that it was us from the back, so there was no way of telling it was me. I'd forgotten he'd grabbed my hand when we'd hit the more puddle-laden part of the sidewalk. And had I really been leaning that close to him?

Yikes.

"Great," I muttered, completely having forgotten I still had the cell phone pressed against my ear.

"So?"

"Well, the short version is Dad took me to a baseball game yesterday, and it was horrible. I'm just not into it. I give him props for trying, but we would have been better off going to the Pier or something."

"Hate to say it, Chey, but your dad doesn't seem to be the Ferris Wheel-riding type."

I know. That was my problem. The more the summer went on, the more I kept thinking our two worlds just didn't mesh.

"How did you get from a baseball game to being JT's mysterious new girlfriend?"

"I'm getting there. Anyways, to make up for the horrible experience at the game with all these fans coming up to him for autographs and picture taking and just generally ignoring me, Dad took me out to dinner. But then, this producer guy came by the table, and before I knew it, Dad had to go off with him for an impromptu meeting. I stayed behind for dessert, Rico came over and invited me to his table. JT was there, and he walked me back to the car afterwards."

My abbreviated version. I figured driving me home and the kiss was on a need-to-know basis, and at the moment, Sor didn't exactly need to know.

"They must have snapped it then," I continued.

"Must have," she agreed.

"I didn't even know anyone was following us," I said as I automatically right-clicked, saving the photo to my hard drive.

"With the lenses some photographers have, they don't need to be right behind you anymore. Or could have just been someone on their camera phone. Some are pretty good quality even at night like that."

Over a moment of silence, I could hear Sorche doing something on her own computer.

"Did you read the blurb?" she asked.

"No, why?"

"Nothing."

"Just tell me," I said, fighting with my mouse to get it to scroll up the page.

I heard her small sigh. "Nothing big. They just call you 'the mystery girl seen walking with JT'. And then, they try to figure out who you could be, that's all."

"*Great.*" I leaned my forehead against my hand, tearing my gaze off the screen.

"If you don't want to go out tonight, we can just binge something on Netflix and hang out at your place. Sound good?"

I stole a glance at the photo again. I really didn't feel like going out and solving the mystery for them quite yet. "Yeah, sounds good. See you about eight?"

"Works for me," Sor agreed before she hung up.

I clicked the phone off, cradling it in my hand as I stared at the screen a moment longer before moving the pointer upwards and clicking on the little red *x*.

"I'm sorry about taking off last night," Dad said the moment I stepped into the kitchen.

"It's fine, really. And I made it home safe and sound."

I headed for the fridge, craving something to eat. I should have still had some yogurt left. Java could come later; I was already wide awake courtesy of Sorche and her informative phone call.

I desperately wanted to change the subject before he could ask about my drive home last night and I could accidentally spill the news about JT.

"How'd the meeting go?" I asked, even though I still kinda didn't care.

He'd abandoned me on our father-daughter date—not so easy to get over, even if he did apologize. I grabbed the last strawberry yogurt from the fridge, closed the door with my hip, and grabbed a spoon from the drawer.

"Good, I think. Our conversation was really promising. We met up with a couple more producers and a screenwriter they're planning on working with over drinks."

"I'm glad it went so well." I should have gotten a nice little gold statue for keeping the bitterness out of my voice with that remark.

"What are you up to today?"

"Sor's coming over later. Besides that, nothing big planned." I slipped onto my favorite stool at the counter. "Unless *we* have plans?"

Okay, slightly pointed question, but after ditching me last night, maybe he'd want to make it up to me. And I could put Sor off; she'd understand.

He set his coffee cup down.

"No, you and Sor hang out. Enjoy yourselves. The place is yours." He smiled like he was doing me a big favor.

Before I could answer, Trish came in from outside, taking off her baseball cap, one that looked remarkably like the one Dad had bought himself yesterday. "'Morning, Chey."

"'Morning," I replied. "So you two are working again?"

Yeah, so not my fault if a little disdain had crept into my voice. This *was* my ruined summer vacation, after all.

Trish's face immediately turned apologetic. "He's got a conference call in an hour. I'm just here to help him set it up."

"You know me, Chey. I'm terrible with technology," Dad piped up.

Somehow, I managed a weak smile. That wasn't the only thing he was terrible with.

"You guys have fun." I unhooked my feet from where I'd wound them around the legs of the stool.

"You, too," Trish said, a look of understanding in her eyes that I doubt Dad even noticed.

"I'll just be outside." I gathered my yogurt and a section of the paper, ready to leave them alone to talk business.

Trish shot Dad a look. "You didn't give her the message?"

I looked between the two of them, the paper pressed against my chest. "What message?"

"Rico's sending someone to pick you up this late afternoon for an hour or two," Trish informed me.

I stared at Dad, watching as his neck flushed red. I hoped in embarrassment. "Dad didn't say a word."

"Sorry, Chey. It slipped my mind," he said meekly.

"Right." I put down my barely touched yogurt, feeling the urge to get out of there before I said something I knew I'd end up regretting. "I'll go up and change. I'll wait outside, so you know, I don't bother anyone."

Trish hurried down the hallway beside me as I stormed off.

"I'm sure it really did slip his mind, Chey. Rico left a message on voicemail at eight this morning. No one actually talked to him...if I didn't check the messages first thing every morning like I always do, we all could have missed it."

"It's okay. I'll throw something on and wait out back."

"Don't be mad at him, okay?" she said with a pointed look towards the kitchen.

I turned to see Dad thumbing through the paper at the counter, looking as if nothing had happened. I sighed to myself. "He's hard to stay mad at."

She gave me a half-hearted smile. "Let me know what happens today. I'm so excited for you."

At least someone in this house was.

I smiled at Trish and gave her a quick hug.

"I'll text and let you know what's up," I said before I headed for the stairs and my escape.

What was it they called Romeo and Juliet? Star-crossed lovers? I was starting to think Fate was getting its kicks having me run into JT *everywhere*, including my own house.

"Well, if it isn't the 'Face of Vanetti'," he greeted as he walked down the stone pathway towards me in the backyard.

I tilted my head back, rolled my eyes, and wondered why the gods were so against me. What had I ever done so wrong in my life to deserve this? I just wanted to avoid him—and the world—for a little while, not wanting to have this 'mystery girl' thing spiral out of control, which some part of me knew it could. And probably would, at some point.

"Hi, JT."

He smiled, and the traitor deep within myself smiled back. Had he caught the bit about the mystery girl? But I figured he probably didn't read the gossip sites.

I grabbed a couple more magazines from the patio table and set them beside me on the lounger, needing something to fidget with since I didn't have my cell phone handy. Of all the times to swear off my phone, but I didn't want to read any texts or keep checking for more info on the mystery girl speculation.

Gah.

Why was I so nervous all of a sudden?

"What are you doing here?" I asked. "Did you forget something last night?"

That would be logical, really. I'd just have a bit of explaining to do to Dad if he did, especially if it was in his Escalade. I glanced back towards the house, but neither he nor Trish were visible. They were likely already holed up in his office, figuring out the set up for a conference call. Besides, they probably didn't care much after they'd buzzed him through the gates. I remembered Dad being sure to mention his name with Quinn.

"Rico told you he was sending someone over, right?"

"Right." When I replayed the message for myself, I'd assumed Lorna. Okay, I might have *hoped* Lorna, because other than her and Rico, I knew no one at *House of Vanetti*.

He held his arms out.

"Meet your chauffeur," he informed me, his boyish grin spreading across his face, making his eyes light up

"Funny." I thumbed through the magazine on my lap.

"Seriously." He pulled his cell phone from the clip on his jeans and held it out to me. "Call if you don't believe me."

I really didn't feel like calling Rico and looking like a total naïve fool. So honestly, that was enough to convince me. "What does he want?"

"For me to take you over there."

"I could drive myself." I stood and started to pick up my magazines, ready to head in to drop them inside on the kitchen table and hopefully get rid of my new...whatever he was calling himself in the process. He wouldn't follow me up to my room, would he?

I snuck a look at him. Suddenly, I wouldn't put that past him.

"I'm sure you can. I've seen your car." He smirked. "Really, today, I'm just the errand boy."

"What do you get out of it?"

"More time to hang out with the next potential 'it girl'."

I sighed, "Stop calling me that."

"You prefer mystery?"

I stopped in my tracks and spun slowly to face him. He had an innocent look on his face, but those blue eyes of his were lighting up with laughter.

"Funny." I rolled my eyes.

"What? I read, too, you know."

"Skimming for mentions of your name?"

"You think I'm that shallow?"

"I think you can be that arrogant." He probably had Google alerts and all sorts of notifications set up, never mind picking up an actual newspaper.

He laughed. "Point taken. But no, Rico told me about it this morning."

"Rico?" For the first time, I wondered if he'd set it up. After all, Rico had mentioned being all about the publicity. JT was his cousin; it all sorta added up in a bizarre way.

And me being a mystery... Well, *he* could be the one to solve it.

Guess I'd just have to wait and see what Rico had to say.

"Fine, let's go," I said, dropping the magazines back on the patio table and using the edge of the tray of empty glasses to weigh them down.

"Right now?"

"Yeah. I was just waiting."

"Take your pick," Rico said with a grand sweeping gesture as he led me and JT into what he'd deemed the storeroom. The room was edged in racks of clothes. More than I'd ever seen at Rico's before. Mix and match. Stuff already put together. It was like something out of a warped fairytale, and I'd been picked to play Cinderella.

And I had a feeling JT thought he'd be just perfect to play my Prince Charming.

"There's so much."

The awe in my voice could be deemed more than apparent as I started to flip through the T-shirts in the first rack, and I had to admit I was totally overwhelmed. I thought when Rico met us at the door, he wanted to go over the contracts or talk scheduling or something, not plan to clothe me for the rest of my life.

"It's called a storeroom for a reason," JT cracked.

"Ha, ha." I picked up a bright red T-shirt with black and silver flecks across it. "I like this one."

"Keep going," Rico said, looking amused from the other side of the rack. "Think summertime, Chey. Think parties. Clubs. You need more than one little T-shirt. You're getting first dibs on what's going into the new boutique. Don't be so choosy."

The man had a point.

I rummaged through the clothes again, this time taking a few more shirts, a pair of shorts, a tank top, a couple camis. Rico looked thrilled when he took them from me and hung them on a separate rack opposite me, and I noticed the card taped to the front said CHEY in big, bold copper letters.

I could feel Rico and JT staring at me and knew I couldn't go to a really late lunch with them without at least attempting to fill that barren rack with my name on it. I kept going, moving from rack to rack, trying to take at least one or two pieces from each one.

JT moved closer, taking the hangers out of my hands and putting them with the rest I'd picked out. I didn't want to think about how much they were going to cost, but maybe I should.

"Rico, I think that's enough," I said when I looked over and saw the rack was close to half-filled.

"You can't be photographed in the same outfit everywhere. That's not what I hired you for. The more you have, the more work you're doing."

Okay, now that was demented logic, but who was I to argue?

JT pulled himself up to sit on one of the long tables grouped together in the center of the room. "I told you, Rico. You're going to have to shove clothes in her arms."

"I just—" I tried to explain before Rico cut me off.

"Chey, this part of what the 'Face' does. You need to be seen out in my clothes."

"Out where?" The words slipped out before I could stop them. I mean, I doubted anyone was going to photograph plain old me walking down the streets of L.A. All right, correction, if I was with JT, then I was guaranteed to have a few shots taken. Hmm. Was JT just a publicity vehicle? I looked at him again, but he wasn't wearing anything Vanetti.

Rico smiled. "I thought you'd never ask."

Ah ha! Now we were getting somewhere.

"There's a brand new club opening up next week, and both of you are on the VIP list."

JT and I exchanged looks. "What?"

Evidently, this was the first he'd heard of it, too.

"I thought you two were getting along so well last night that you wouldn't mind." Rico looked at the two of us. "Unless the mystery girl thing this morning scared you off?"

I wasn't sure who he meant with that comment.

"It's okay." I moved around the racks and pulled myself up on the table beside JT. "I guess I should get used to it."

After all, it was something my dad dealt with for years. If he could handle it, so could I.

"Good. It must have been a slow night in L.A. for that to make news. I apologize for not warning you earlier about the overzealousness of the press."

Rico smiled as his assistant, Todd, came in.

"I confirmed the booking with the photographer for Saturday. Does that work for you, Chey?" Todd asked.

"Absolutely." I nodded, a tingle of excitement washing over me. My first shoot.

"So don't stay out too late Friday night. We need you here bright and early," Rico added.

"Don't worry. I'll be sound asleep by midnight."

When the clothing rack was deemed full enough, we headed across the street to a little Italian place on the corner to grab a late lunch. As soon as we walked in, the most amazing smell of pasta and pizza hit us, and I swore my stomach almost rumbled in response.

A waitress came over and seated us near the back. We'd apparently missed the rush, and most of the circular tables with bright red table cloths were open. She handed us our menus, took a quick drink order, and disappeared from our view.

JT sat across from me at the small circular table and Rico to my right. After we'd gone through the menu a couple of times, Rico sharing what was good, what was even better. We decided to go with the pasta. Almost as soon as Rico had closed the menu, the waitress appeared with our drinks and took the menus, promising the food wouldn't take long.

I sank back into the cushioned seat and took a sip of my lemonade before pulling out my cell phone to check for messages. Nothing. Blissfully quiet. I'd been slightly worried Mom would have somehow caught sight of that picture of JT and immediately with her spidey sense recognized me from the back.

I turned my phone over and set it on the table beside me.

Soon, we got to talking, and Rico told me how he'd gotten interested in fashion as a kid and how he'd gotten started going to one of the best fashion schools in California.

The food arrived, and we kept talking, and I learned that JT's parents had helped by investing here and there while Rico and Lorna put things together to create a small design house.

JT kept watching me as I twirled the pasta around my fork, and I tried my best to ignore him, until Rico got a text he was needed back at the offices. He picked up the check and headed off.

We finished our meals a few minutes later and followed suit outside.

"What?" I asked finally as we left the table and headed back into the sunshine. I thought about calling Sorche to see if she could pick me up, but she was probably busy with auditions. She'd had a few booked this week.

"I'm just wondering if you remember we have a date on Saturday, or do you want to cancel now that you've got your photo shoot."

"Can't I do both?"

He smiled as we headed to where he'd left his car. "I'm holding you to that, Daniels. Mind if I crash the shoot?"

I shrugged as I slipped into the passenger seat. "He's your cousin. Do what you want."

"You were on three entertainment shows."

Sor sounded proud, like the poor, misguided teen she'd taken under her wing was finally showing off the lessons she'd learned.

I shut the door to the theater room and kicked off my flip flops.

"No. The *mystery* girl was," I countered as I flopped on one of the leather chairs beside her.

I'd caught the end of one of the shows when I came home, where whoever had filmed the footage had been behind us. All you could see was the back of my hair under my new black and silver baseball cap. I'd thought that little pic online was going to be the end of it. Apparently, I was oh so wrong. This afternoon's rumors ranged from 'some A-lister in a wig'—uh, was my hair really *that* bad?—to some unknown girl he'd picked up at a club, the unknown being the only right thing in the entire story.

"Well, the mystery girl was—is—you. Just have to wait for the mystery to be solved."

"Maybe there's nothing to solve."

Sor's mouth fell open in disbelief. "What?"

"You know there's nothing really going on between me and JT." Nothing but one kiss, anyway. "Any female photographed near him is the next potential girlfriend."

See, I knew I'd been right all along. Stay clear of one JT. You know, the more I thought about it, the more JT could stand for *Just Trouble* instead of Justin Thomas.

"And how are you going to go about that?"

"L.A.'s a big place." I shrugged. "Besides, I'm only here for a couple more months. We couldn't be that serious."

I couldn't be that serious. We hadn't even had a first official date yet.

Yet? Oh, man, I was in *so* much trouble.

I could tell by the look on Sor's face she didn't believe a word I said, either.

"Fine. But you *are* Sean Morrow's daughter. You *are* going to be photographed, you know. And don't forget about that little deal you just signed with Rico."

"That's different."

"*That's* what is going to get you splashed across pages around here. Rico is hot, hot, and hot."

I slid down in my seat, reaching for the bowl of popcorn on the table wedged between our chairs. "Still, different."

The knock on the theatre door interrupted our convo.

"What?" I called, certain it was Dad or probably Trish wanting to see what we were watching.

The door slid open, and there stood Milo. "Hey, your dad's sending me out for pizza."

I caught the smile on Sor's face the second she laid eyes on him.

"That's nice," I drawled.

He let out a dramatic sigh. "I'm assuming you want some."

"Whatever Dad ordered is fine with me. Sor?"

"Pepperoni. Anything but anchovies."

"Got it." He smiled, and I noticed it was totally directed at Sor. "You find all the controls?"

I held up the remote. "Think I can handle it."

"Cool. Nice seeing you, Sorche," he said before he slid the door shut.

I twisted to look at my best friend. "Spill."

It wasn't quite a question; more so a demand.

She took a sip of her iced tea, trying to look so innocent, I was sure she could sprout wings at any second.

"Spill what? I don't think your dad would want iced tea all over his carpet."

"You know exactly what I'm talking about. I saw that look between you and Milo, not to mention that goofy expression on your face right now."

"Does it mirror yours when you talk about JT?"

I did my best to look indignant. "We're done talking about me and JT. Answer the question. What's going on with you and Milo?"

She sighed as she set her drink down on the table. "He was outside one day when I was heading to my car. We started talking, and I..." She glanced at me somewhat sheepishly. "I asked him to grab something to eat sometime."

I blinked. How could I have missed something so major? "Okay, so..."

"So we had dinner. Then he took me to the movies the other night."

"You're dating Milo?"

Her gaze darted away from mine up to the dark screen. "We're not exactly dating. More like hanging out. And besides, he's not that bad. You just don't know him."

"I didn't say he was that bad. I just think it's..."

"It's?"

"Interesting. You and Milo."

"Yeah. Me and Milo," she repeated, sliding down in her seat. "No biggie. So start the movie already," she demanded as she stole the bowl of popcorn out of my hand.

15

Music filled the stairwell.

"Where are we?" I asked, Sor close beside me as we took the steep stairs down hesitantly.

She'd barely said anything when she'd shown up at my door two hours ago in an Uber other than she was taking me out for the night. I wasn't sure I really wanted to—it was the night before my shoot, after all—but Dad was out at some charity thing, and she'd had a point. What was I going to do? Panic and make myself sick? Or go out and think about something else for a while?

"Forgotten."

Hmmm. It felt like *we*'d been forgotten as we headed down the narrow stairs. The hallway had a Goth feel to it. Shimmering, blackish-red fabric covered the walls, and the small, flickering lights barely lit the hallway.

"Are you sure this is a *music* club?" Because at this very moment, I totally doubted it.

Black velvet curtains covered the entrance into the actual club.

"Name?" the beefy bouncer in head-to-toe black and who had blended into the background 'til that moment asked.

For a moment, I'd wondered if he'd stepped out from behind the curtains when I wasn't looking.

"Sorche Maxwell and Chey Morrow," Sor replied casually.

The curtains tugged back, obviously meaning we proved worthy of admittance. I stepped down the last two black carpeted steps into another world where we were met by another beefy bouncer who quickly wrapped hot pink wristbands around our wrists before we could take another step deeper into the crowd.

"Where are we going?" I looked at the large group of people. There didn't look to be a lot of tables, just people milling about on the edges while others danced.

"We're going to have a good time." She spun and tapped my nose. "Come on, relax. This is the night before your big day, and we should have fun."

She was right; I needed some time away from home. I was learning to give up on the vision I had for my summer and just go with what was happening. And what was happening right now spelled out that Sorche wanted me to go out and have fun.

"Besides, wait 'til you see why I brought you here." Sor headed to the bar along the back and jostled our way to the front, ordering two plain sodas and setting her cash on the counter.

A pushy guy in a too-tight black shirt forced his way into the line-up, knocking me into my best friend. "Why?"

I turned to give him a dirty look but he didn't even look my way.

"You'll see. But JT should be here soon. I told him I was taking you out for the night, and he said he'd swing by."

She grabbed our drinks, and we headed towards the front where a new band was taking the stage. I took a sip of my cold drink as we weaved through the growing crowd around us, and I did my best to stick close to her.

"Aren't you going to tell me anything?"

"Have fun!" she shouted over her shoulder and laughed.

The band started to play as we made our way to towards the stage. I didn't understand why she was so determined to be front and center until we got there. I stood against the worn black metal barricade, its paint scraped off in places no doubt by overzealous fans, amazed when I saw who played lead guitar. Our eyes locked, and that knowing smirk of his crossed his face, the one I always thought had been a little smug. Then, he turned to his fellow guitarist, sharing a microphone stand.

Sorche squealed and elbowed me. "Doesn't Milo look hot?"

"Doesn't he?" I repeated, still surprised by what I was seeing, when the guy beside me raised his beer in the air, sloshing it all over.

I stood there stunned as the cold liquid hit my bare arm, frozen in place, but the guy didn't pay me any attention at all.

I took a step to the side and Sor grabbed my hand, helping to pull me away and tighter up against the barricade.

"What a jerk," she shouted as if he could hear her above the music.

She shot him a deadly look as she started digging through her bag. She handed me a plastic pack of tissues to try and dry off although I wondered what good it would do me since I could feel the fabric of my shirt on my arm starting to stick to my skin in spots.

"Thanks." I handed her my drink and did my best to rid myself of the beer that still trickled down my arm, leaving an icky, sticky coldness in its wake. Finally dry or as much as I could reasonably get, I unfortunately still reeked of the guy's cheap draft.

Sor shot me an apologetic look as she handed back my plastic cup and turned her attention to her boyfriend on stage. I finished off my drink, hoping to cool my nerves, before I pulled my cell out of my wristlet, amazed I was getting full bars inside.

'*Where are you?*' I texted JT and hit send. He should have shown up by now, shouldn't he?

Sor said he knew where the place was. I tucked the phone into my hip pocket, hoping to feel it vibrate as I watched my possibly someday step-brother rock out on stage.

It seemed like an hour later when the guys finally stopped playing, and I turned to see Sor beside me, a huge smile on her flushed face.

"Well?" she asked, her eyes almost twinkling in the stage lights as she glanced over my shoulder where Milo was no doubt lingering still.

"They're great. Shouldn't they have played longer?" I asked as they all disappeared out of view behind another curtain. I watched as a few other guys popped up on stage, taking away instruments and moving things around.

"Set break," she informed me. "C'mon, let's grab another drink then get back up here before they start up again."

"Right. Because you're the typical rock-star girlfriend."

She grinned. "Hardly. But he does look damn hot up there."

We got back in the line-up for the bar, this time with me digging through my wallet for the twenty I knew I'd thrown in before we left when I heard Sorche's gasp beside me, which was surprising given how loud it was in the club. "What?"

"You aren't going to believe this..."

And suddenly, I knew exactly what she meant when I saw who was coming towards us, entourage firmly in place.

Adriana.

My stomach dropped at the mere sight of her. Based on my unfortunate past experiences, all I knew was the best thing to do would be to avoid her at all costs.

I totally recognized what she was, and that was trouble.

With a capital *T*.

"Funny seeing you here," I said as she stopped in front of us.

Her lips curled into a smile that seemed as fake as her hair color. "Isn't it? I don't usually go 'slumming', but I guess this must be the big new place to be if you and Sorche are here."

Sor moved closer. "Amazed they let you out of your cage before midnight. Thought most reptiles were night creatures."

Adriana huffed and took another sip of her drink before taking a sniff of the air in my direction. "What is that Chey, eau de wannabe? Or maybe poseur?"

A couple of the entourage giggled.

I licked my dry lips. "You know something, Adriana? Why don't we call a truce—I won't have a single thing to do with you, and you don't have a single thing to do with me. Deal?"

She looked at me for a minute, as if considering. "Fine, you're not worth it, anyway. You'll be more *forgotten* than this place will be."

"Wow, good one." I rolled my eyes, ready to turn away and head back towards the stage, when I was suddenly jostled and a lot closer to Adriana than I ever wanted to be.

It seemed to happen in slow motion, the drink in her hand upright one moment then tipping towards me the next. The cold liquid soaked quickly through my thin top, turning the white parts transparent and causing it to stick to my skin, making me chilled with its iciness. How many ice cubes had she put in that thing?

"Ooh, oopsies." Adriana laughed. "You shouldn't bump into people like that, *Wyoming*."

"She didn't bump into you. You bumped into *her*."

"Sorche!" Adriana sounded shocked and pouted her over-glossed bottom lip. "Please, just because we're no longer BFFs doesn't mean we need to turn on each other, does it?" She looked at me. "Besides, *she* knows it was an accident."

Her glare practically dared me to say otherwise.

But I knew the truth; she'd calculated it right down to the perfect moment to do the most damage. Her goal was apparently my ultimate humiliation, making me look like one of those wet T-shirt contestants on spring break. My only saving grace was the shirt hadn't been completely white.

"Yeah, fine, total accident."

"Come on."

Sorche pulled me through the crowd, me too stunned to do anything but follow. I noticed a few people staring our way, and I hurried to keep up, wondering where it was we were headed. I apparently was going to give the band quite a show of my own at this rate. I didn't even dare glance down, just kept as close to Sor as possible, using her as a shield to keep me as covered up and out of people's view as possible.

Milo looked surprised to see us by the barricade from his spot on stage where they were setting up a couple more instruments. He hurried to the edge and crouched down, looking concerned. "What's up?"

Sorche sighed, glancing at me before turning back to Milo. "Some bitch we know and loathe threw her drink on Chey."

Milo's eyes widened as Sor took half a step sideways and he caught sight of my shirt. "Wow, okay...look, come back here..." He jumped down off the stage and headed to where the barricade had a gate in it, pushing it open enough for us to fit through. "You can use our dressing room and try to get that dry. If not, I've got a spare shirt in my bag you can wear, Chey."

I smiled for the first time in what felt like forever. "Thanks."

He nodded.

Sor navigated the mazelike hallways like a pro, leaving me to wonder how many times she'd been here. The club was small, cozy, intimate, and not the kind of place I'd expect Milo to play—if I'd expected Milo to play loud, brash rock music.

"I'm sorry, I'm sorry, I am *so* sorry," Sorche said as we took over the small dressing room, its walls covered with faded photocopied ads of bands playing there, the dates stretching back over a decade. The newer ones, the colors still somewhat recognizable, hung nearer the door.

"It's okay." Total lie. I smelled like a mix of everything behind the bar. Draft on my right arm and my entire front a mix of Adriana's drink, which the longer I wore it, the stronger it became.

Sor glanced at me as we tried to wring out as much as we could onto the paper towels.

"I'm sorry. We should have stayed at your place," she grumbled the last part as she patted the silk dry with another set of dry paper towels. The ledge in front of us sat littered with crumpled, wet paper.

"It's okay," I repeated, hoping she'd get the message.

"Seriously. I wanted to take you out to have fun, not be harassed by Adriana." She sighed. "I think that's as good as it's going to get."

She didn't look happy as she surveyed the damage to my shirt.

"I just hope the alcohol will fade away, or I'll have to trash it."

I tossed another wadded-up pile of paper towels on the mess and glanced at our reflections in the mirror.

I couldn't look more pitiful if I tried. My mascara and eyeliner was smeared under my eyes, probably no doubt from the impromptu beer shower, my shirt was no longer white, half of it wrinkled beyond measure from us trying to get the drinks out of the fabric.

It was about as lost of a cause as I was at that moment.

A knock interrupted our convo, and Sorche went to the door, pulling it open slightly. "Hey."

I heard Milo's low voice but couldn't hear exactly what was being said. Next thing I knew, Sor had shut the door and had gone over to the assorted bags in the corner and started digging through a large green one. "Here we go."

"What?" I asked as she pulled a plastic shopping bag out.

"Milo asked how you were, and I said the shirt was kinda hopeless. So he said you can use his spare..." She handed me a folded-up black T-shirt. "And put that one in this. There's a bathroom down the hall if you want to try and clean up better."

Five minutes later, I'd scrubbed my arm and chest as best as I could in the cramped small bathroom. I slid Milo's band T-shirt over my head, my still-damp one tucked inside a crumpled shopping bag by my foot. Sorche stood guard at the door, almost like she thought Adriana was going to burst inside any moment.

"We'll go back to my place first. Get you cleaned up, then we'll all go grab something to eat." Sorche looked at me like she was afraid I was ready to break out in tears at any moment.

"Maybe I should just go home." It was getting late. It seemed our little Adriana adventure had ruined Sor's plans of watching Milo play the full set tonight.

The only plus was it kept my mind off the absent JT, until well, *now*.

Sorche shook her head. "Please, I feel craptastic enough right now."

I sighed. I couldn't have my best friend feeling like that. "Are you sure we won't run into your mom?"

The last thing I wanted was Dad to get a report of my newfound 'scent.'

"Please. She's at some charity gig. Won't be home before two a.m. We're safe for a while."

I gathered my stuff. "Where did you want to go?"

"I don't know. We can just grab something to eat from some-where..." She shrugged. "My treat."

"Sor—"

"Seriously. Gotta salvage the night somehow."

She gave me a weary look, and we headed out to the wings to watch the end of Milo's second set. I had to admit the guys were pretty good, and I was happy to be out of the range of anyone's plastic cup.

Once they were done with their encore, they practically raced off the stage, getting their gear together in what I figured had to be record time. I could only hope that was their ritual and not some-thing because of me.

By the time the band had most of their equipment loaded up in-to a van, I was sitting in the backseat of Milo's car, his guitar case leaning on the seat beside me. I dropped my plastic bag and purse by my feet as Sorche piled in next to him up front.

"So are you sure you guys want to get something to eat?" I asked, thinking again home was probably my best bet. "I kinda have to have a somewhat early night."

"Don't worry, your head will be on your pillow before dawn." Milo put the key in the ignition.

"I need it there before 'before dawn', thank you very much."

Sorche turned to me and laughed. "Relax."

"She's right, Chey. We're just gonna go grab something to eat. You'll be home before one. I guarantee a good eight hours of sleep."

I didn't feel like telling him I'd already set my alarm clock for seven in the morning. I'd probably have to adjust it when I got home.

I was nursing a crushed heart thanks to JT, the remnants of my soaked shirt—unfortunately, it was one of my favorites I'd picked from my last trek to Rico's—and the fact that Adriana was causing me trouble. Plus there was that hint of nerves over the fact it was quickly approaching well past midnight. Maybe the best thing was to talk them into dropping me off at home.

"I thought your little boyfriend was going to show tonight," Milo commented as we headed down Sunset.

I kicked the bag with my foot. "He didn't make it. Didn't give a reason, either."

Sorche shook her head at his question. "Maybe he got lost, or his cell phone died. He could have missed all your messages."

"Right." All logical explanations. But I didn't want to believe them. He knew my cell; he could have called me from anywhere.

"Oh, well...it's no big deal, right?"

I nodded. "Right."

After a pizza at some restaurant I'd never heard of, Milo was pulling through the familiar gates of home.

"See, home early," Sorche announced as she got out of Milo's car, leaving the door open behind her.

I grabbed my bag with the probably ruined shirt in it as I stepped out. I doubted anything was going to get rid of the stench of alcohol. I couldn't even ask Trish what to do about it, not wanting to risk this getting back to Dad or Mom. Maybe I'd let it soak in the sink overnight and pray for some sort of miracle.

"Thanks Milo." I leaned in and waved at him.

"No problem." He gave me a rare smile, and I slammed the back door.

Sorche smiled at me as we walked to the front door. "All right, so have fun tomorrow, and if you get nervous, text me. I'll make sure I've got my phone handy all day."

"Thanks."

"Sorry tonight sorta went downhill for a while."

For a while.

Yeah.

I pulled my keys out of my bag. "Not your fault. Thanks for taking me out. I'd probably be a nervous wreck right now, otherwise."

"Good." She gave me a quick hug. "Sleep well, 'it girl'."

I laughed as I unlocked the door, and she skipped back to Milo's car.

"Don't stay out too late," I called after her.

"Yes, Mom." She waved one last time before she slid into the open passenger side.

I leaned against the door after I heard Milo's car pull away. The night hadn't gone as well as I'd hoped, and I pulled my cell phone out one more time, looking at the 'no new messages' staring up at me.

Great, just great. I thought I already had one guy in my life I couldn't count on. Now, it was starting to look like I had two.

16

"First shoot this morning, huh?" Trish asked as I stepped out onto the patio to find her and Dad already having breakfast at the outside table.

I took a seat while Dad fixed me a cup of coffee just the way I liked it and set it in front of me.

"Yeah."

I had two hours in which to fully wake up and lose the slight fog I was still moving around in. I should have been a good little model-wannabe and headed to bed before the sunset, thus guaranteeing Rico wouldn't take one look at me and hit speed dial for Adriana to come take my place. But my nerves hadn't let me fall asleep 'til well after two—all right, to be fully honest, a lot closer to three-thirty, which gave way to nightmares of the Adriana variety.

"You're here early," I said, watching Trish slather a piece of toast with raspberry jam.

"Wanted to be here for moral support," she said with an easy smile.

"You want anything?" Dad asked.

I shook my head. "I don't think my nerves can handle anything more than coffee."

He patted my hand reassuringly. "You'll be fine. You're a natural."

I just hoped I wasn't a natural disaster. Did this man ever see my school pictures? I hadn't taken a good one since second grade. Oh, well, at least with Rico's photographer, I was sure there would be more than two shots to choose from, unlike the school ones where you were forced to pick between 'horrible' and 'what planet did I beam down from?'

"Just relax and have fun," Dad continued, oblivious to my mini meltdown. "That'll come through the camera and from talking to Rico. That's what he's looking for from this new line *and* from you."

Great pep talk, coach, I felt like saying, but swallowed the urge with a large gulp of coffee.

"I guess I should finish getting ready. I still need to grab a shower before I head out of here."

Dad surprised me by standing and giving me a bear hug that reminded me of the one I'd gotten the day he'd picked me up at airport. "Good luck, Chey."

"Thanks, Dad."

"You know I'm proud of you, right?" he asked as he pulled back.

I did now. But I put a small smile on my face. "Of course."

I heard Trish clearing her throat and turned to see her holding out a small narrow black jewelry box, a silver bow on top of it. "Can't let you leave without opening this."

"What is it?"

"A little good luck present," she replied. "Open it. I don't want to hold you up on your big day."

I sat back down and took the box from her, carefully opening the top. Inside lay a gold charm bracelet.

"Oh, wow..." I lifted it up, and the charms dangled. A palm tree. A camera. A small diamond star. "Thank you!"

"Told you she'd like it," Dad said, nudging Trish.

I looked at the two of them. "Is it from both of you?"

"Sorta. It was Trish's idea to get you something, and we both picked out the charms," Dad explained as he took the bracelet from me and slipped it on my wrist, closing the clasp easily.

"I love it." I played with the star absently. "But I gotta go."

I gave them each a hurried hug before I tore off upstairs to get ready. I wanted to get there as early as possible and hopefully miss any traffic problems. I'd had enough bad luck last night; I didn't want any carrying over into today.

By the time I got to Rico's, the place was as busy as I'd ever seen it. Stepping inside to no one sitting behind the desk, I could see Lorna talking away to a couple people in the conference room. Further back, Rico and his assistant were going through the racks. People I'd never seen before rushed around, and the back door to the building lay propped open, letting in a warm breeze that ruffled my hair, even clear across the vast room.

"'Morning," I called, not sure what I should do or who I should go to.

"Chey! Don't just stand there. Come here," Rico called excitedly as he motioned me over.

"Just give me a sec to finish my coffee." I took a long last sip, hoping for the java to awaken my senses more than they already were.

Not to mention, I didn't want to risk knocking the coffee all over Rico's expensive clothes with a sudden bout of nerves-induced clumsiness. Pretty sure stained wasn't the look he was going for.

I trashed the cup in the wastebasket as I passed and weaved through the long tables to where Rico stood pulling out various pieces of clothing and laying them out on the tabletops. I stuck my hands in the back pockets of my denim cutoffs and tried to look casual like I wasn't suddenly completely out-of-my-mind nervous.

I was suddenly thankful I wasn't a nail biter. I wouldn't have had any left by that point.

Rico glanced at me from the corner of his eye, a teasing smile lifting the edges of his mouth. "Coffee may not have been the wisest choice."

"Why not?"

"I think it just revved your nerves." He laughed easily, his dark eyes twinkling. "Relax, Chey. This shoot is going to go smoothly, and we'll have fun, I promise. Take a look..." He waved towards the clothes covering the different tables. "See if you like what I've chosen."

I moved from table to table, stunned at how talented Rico was. There were T-shirts like the ones I had sitting in my closet paired with jeans, dressier shirts, button downs paired with tank tops, and the dresses were amazing.

Two sundresses, one a metallic copper that I was already in love with. The other looked a lot like the one I'd worn in the fashion show.

Rico's assistant, Todd, brushed by, and I turned in time to see Rico nod at whatever Todd was saying. "All right, Chey, it's time to get started. You ready?"

"Ready as I'll ever be," I lied. Now that he'd said that, my nervous butterflies were making their appearance full force.

"Good." He grabbed a couple outfits that were draped on the nearest table. "You need to try these on," he said as he held the wooden hangers towards me.

I barely got a chance to look at what was in my hand before he spun me around and pushed me towards a curtained-off cubicle in the middle of the room that I knew hadn't been there before. Was that where I was supposed to change?

"Uh..." was about all I could get out before the curtain swished back closed behind me.

There was a little black leather bench in the corner, and I sat down, hanging the clothes on the mini-rack set off to the side. No mirror anywhere. Obviously, Rico wanted to be front and center for the grand unveiling.

Here we go, I thought as I slid my sandals off and pulled my shirt over my head.

"Which one first?" I asked as I looked at the brightly colored collection of fabrics in front of me.

"The red dress," I heard Lorna call.

Easy enough to find.

I stepped out of my denim shorts, laid my own stuff on the bench, and carefully pulled the dress off the hanger.

It was gorgeous. A dark, matte red silk with a spaghetti-strap top that widened out at the waist. I slid it on carefully and found it was longer than I expected, falling halfway to my ankles. I did up the side zipper and peeked from the corner of the curtain to find Rico and Todd waiting nearby.

"Any problems?" Todd asked, probably fearing I'd caught the silk in the zipper or, much worse, broken it.

"No." I took a deep breath before I pulled the curtain back and stepped barefoot back into the midst of the workroom, trying not to look as nervous as I felt. My fingers were trembling, and I bunched my hands into fists to try and calm my nerves.

I stopped a few steps away from Rico. He stood with his fingertip tapping his chin. He motioned for me to turn around, so I did, slowly turning away and whispering a silent prayer as I glanced up at the ceiling, putting a weak smile on my face as I turned back to face him, bracing for whatever his reaction might be.

Somehow, I wasn't sure the total silence was a good thing.

Then, Rico smiled at me. "Perfect."

He looked very pleased.

I let myself inhale a deep breath, the smile on my face relaxing as I moved to look in the full-length mirror they'd set up while I was changing, trying to figure out where he'd gotten perfect from. After all, I was still me, messy ponytail still in place. But when I saw the reflection staring back at me, I had to admit that *maybe*, I was a little too hard on myself. Rico's clothes could make anyone gorgeous.

Suddenly, Todd produced a stool for me to stand on while he crouched down to examine the hem.

"Is it too long?" I asked as I watched him toy with the ends of the dress, pulling a box of pins from his pocket. Leave it to me to be shorter than your average 'it girl.'

Rico shook his head in answer. "Don't worry, Chey. We're fitting it to you, not the other way around. That's why we wanted the dress first. While we get everything put together for the shoot later, the dress can be altered."

"Later?" I thought this was supposed to be more of a test shoot than the real deal; at least, that's what Sor and I had figured over the webcam, but suddenly, this felt a lot more real than a practice run, especially when Lorna appeared with a smile and carefully pulled out my ponytail, fluffing my hair out.

Todd pulled a pin from between his lips and concentrated on folding the fabric by my left knee. "The photographer's coming by in two hours. They're already working on the set up on the roof."

The roof? My heart rate suddenly ratcheted up a few notches.

Should I have mentioned my teensy, tiny aversion to heights?

"Great. Love rooftops," I said, hoping I sounded more confident than I suddenly felt.

I looked back down at Todd and found him marking something on a post-it before slapping it on a dress bag.

"That's it. Let's try the black dress next, Chey." Rico held out his hand to help me down.

I slipped on a pair of yoga pants Lorna had given me on my way to the dressing room after the final fitting for the last dress and pulled my T-shirt over my head before I headed back into the main room. Rico was laying out a handful of designs on a nearby empty table, and attached to every page was one of the pictures of me from the first fashion show.

"Enrique's just getting set up."

"What's all this?"

He pulled out a chair for me, and I took a seat. "These, Chey, are my latest designs. All inspired by you."

The beginnings of a heated blush crossed my face, and I set my tote bag down at my feet, pulling a couple of papers closer. More amazing dresses. Each matched a color I had on in the clipped photo.

"Wow, Rico, I can't believe this." This still seemed so unreal to me, I had to keep from pinching myself every time I stepped out of my little cozy dressing room.

"Which one do you like best?"

He moved more sketches in front of me. I noticed little swatches of fabric attached to each at the bottom. I stopped myself from reaching out to touch them.

My eyes moved from sketch to sketch, still in awe that I'd inspire anyone to create anything.

"It's hard to pick," I replied honestly, though I was partial to the black and white, one-shouldered design right in front of me. It seemed similar to the red dress I'd first tried on, with the same flared skirt.

"Just what a designer wants to hear." He smiled as he took a seat beside me. "Enrique should be done soon, and then, we'll get to work. That okay with you?"

"Fine." I reached for another design to examine. I was a little more at ease and couldn't wait to get in front of the camera. 'Course, that was now. Who knew what I'd feel like the moment I had the lens aimed my way? I'd probably want to run for the safety of my dressing room.

A knock came at the door, and I looked up to see Todd standing there.

"Enrique's all set up and awaiting our *face*."

I stood up anxiously, brushing a hand over my yoga pants absently. "Okay, then…"

That was clearly my sign to go.

I followed Todd out of the room and through the back, up a small flight of stairs I didn't know existed, into a make-up room where Enrique was busy opening up a huge plastic case with enough make-up tucked inside to make Sorche jealous.

"There you are. Have a seat." He motioned me in with a warm smile.

Todd took off, leaving us alone, and I took a seat in the large black plastic chair, noticing there were a few photos taped around the mirror, one of me from the fashion show and a couple shots of another model.

"What are those for?"

Enrique set out a handful of brushes before grabbing a couple small eye shadows and setting them in front of me on the counter.

"Those, my dear, are the look we're going for. That's the hair…" He tapped the model's photo, then mine. "And that is the make-up look. Just a little more dramatic."

He smiled, testing a small amount of eye shadow on the top of his hand. He picked up another and repeated the process over top then nodded to himself, pushing the other shadows further back. He leaned against the counter. "Nervous?"

Who, me?

"A little."

"Relax. You're in good hands."

"You're doing make-up, too?" I asked, trying to get comfortable and forget what I was about to do.

He nodded. "I'm a bit of a jack of all trades. Lorna figured you'd probably be more comfortable with just one of us working our magic."

I laughed anxiously as he pulled a few more tools out of the make-up case. How well she knew me already. "She's right about that."

I sat in the make-up chair, a plastic cape draped around me, while Enrique played with my hair. I had my cell phone in front of me, and I scrolled through the incoming messages. A couple good luck ones from Sorche and Dad and three from JT, reminding me he'd see me after the shoot that night. I had a feeling he had a standing invitation to come by the shoot, but wasn't going to. Maybe he thought he'd make my nerves worse.

But I didn't feel like listening to him right now. If he'd left me a message an hour ago, that meant he was still alive and I didn't need to think he'd disappeared off the face of the Earth, even if he'd bailed on me last night.

The phone vibrated again, and a brand new message from Sor popped up, asking what I was doing.

I smiled and texted her back a reply, taking a couple quick selfies and one of the photos on the mirror to show her the look they were going for, and set the phone back down just as Lorna came in, carrying a couple of steaming coffees.

"How's our girl?" she asked as she held one out to me.

Enrique looked up.

"She's good. Very quiet, though." He nudged my shoulder, making me laugh.

I smiled at him in the mirror in front of us. "Don't want to disturb a genius at work."

He laughed and went back to trimming the ends of my hair.

I looked into the blackness of my coffee. I couldn't lean forward to set it down or move much, not without risking jostling Enrique and losing a handful of my hair via an accident with his scissors.

"Just wanted to make sure nerves aren't getting the best of you." Lorna leaned against the table in front of me.

"I'm okay right now."

"Good." She smiled, glancing at my cell as it beeped again, signifying another incoming message.

I glanced down and saw JT's name again, sighing softly to myself as I covered the screen as quickly as I could.

Lorna sat on a nearby chair. "So JT isn't around today."

"So I noticed." I flipped my phone over as carefully as possible while trying my best not to move, wondering if she'd recognized his number on the incoming calls list.

"Something happen between you two?"

"Not really."

"I'm butting in," she said, before taking a sip of her coffee.

"No, you're not. You're his family, and I work for Rico, so..."

"So?"

I let out a deep breath. "Sor and I went out last night and..."

I glanced in the mirror, wondering what I should and shouldn't confide in Lorna. Adriana didn't seem like an option. She'd been a shoe-in to be the face of the line before I arrived...or before she got in trouble, or both. I never really asked. And I really didn't want to know.

She was just something I'd have to get used to and hope she moved on to another target soon. "He was supposed to join us and never did, couldn't even be bothered to call or text."

"I'm sorry."

"Don't be. I think, though, he thinks we're still on for tonight." I tapped the back of my cell phone absently.

"Well, you could be busy, you know. After a first photo shoot, we should celebrate. Take you out for a nice meal somewhere... Rico and I would love to do that, you know."

Enrique leaned forward. "And what about me? Aren't I helping to make the photo shoot a success?"

Lorna laughed. "And you'd be invited, of course." She smiled. "What do you say, Chey?"

"Let me think about it?"

She nodded, getting to her feet. "I'll go grab the wardrobe and start to bring it in. Rico's decided we're going to start with the black dress and work from there." She set her mug of coffee down. "How long do you think you'll need?" she asked Enrique, who was still snipping away at random ends.

He leaned forward, and I caught his smile. "Hair is almost done. I just need about twenty minutes to curl it. I'd say another twenty for make-up. Tell him she'll be dressed in forty-five. Work for you, Chey?"

I met my own anxious stare in the mirror. "You're the boss."

I peeked over the edge of the rooftop. Wow, we really were high up, weren't we?

Not like we were up super, super high—it wasn't like people looked like ants and cars looked like toys—but it was far enough for my liking.

I was suddenly *very* glad for the high ledge bordering the four sides of the building.

Something cool and soft wrapped around my shoulders, and I glanced over to see Todd smoothing the edges of a shawl around me.

"You gotta keep warm," he said with a smile.

He'd clearly mistaken my trembling over the height as being chilled.

"Thanks. I'm just not used to heights." I nodded towards the edge.

Todd leaned forward beside me, looking down with a shudder. "Honestly, me, either. Best thing to do is look straight ahead."

"I'll keep that in mind."

"You can wait over there. It shouldn't be much longer." He pointed to a few directors chairs lined up off to the side of the chaos going on.

I followed his directions, picking up a small bottled water and a straw since I was under Enrique's strict orders *not* to muss up his hard work, and took a seat in one of the empty chairs. Lorna joined me and handed me a magazine to flip through while we waited for Rico to make the last few adjustments to get his vision just right.

"We're ready for you, Chey." Rico motioned for me to join him.

I set down my mini bottled water with the pink bendy straw and headed to the doorway they were using for the set of shots.

I waited for them to put the small towel that I'd sit on down so not to get the dress all dirty.

Rico led me to the perch, a towel the exact same color as my dress marking the spot I was supposed to occupy. "Have a seat."

The moment I sat, Rico went to work and began to fan the dress out around me, creating a slight wrinkled effect with his hands in the skirt, and Enrique joined us, toying with my hair, adding a touch of spray as he tousled it.

Tousle, by the way, my word of the day. It was the look Rico and Enrique had agreed on before I'd even arrived that morning. I had to admit with the breeze up there on the roof, it proved definitely a wise choice.

"Are we ready yet?" I heard the photographer call out.

Enrique handed me my shoes, a pair of strappy metallic heels, and stepped away.

In the blink of an eye, I was suddenly all alone in front of the camera, a dozen or so pairs of eyes staring straight at me.

My heart leapt into my throat, and I pushed aside my urge to get up and bolt.

I bent forward to slide one of my shoes on while the other dangled from my finger, suddenly aware of the loud click-click-click of the camera.

I glanced up, startled, as the music that had been on low since we'd moved up to the roof grew louder as someone cranked the volume.

"Lean forward, Chey...let the shoe dangle more...arms folded across your lap. Great!"

The photographer, whose name I suddenly remembered as Jeff from a quick introduction on the stairs, came towards me with the camera.

For one moment, I was absolutely terrified, and then I remembered Dad's words that morning. *Have fun.* And realizing how unreal it was that I found myself in the midst of my first photo shoot, completely on my own for what seemed like the first time in my life, I burst out laughing to rid myself of the last butterflies in my stomach.

"Perfect!" Rico called, giving me the thumbs up from over Jeff's shoulder.

My smile grew bigger as the click-click-click of the camera picked up speed.

I carefully put the red dress back inside its dress bag, glad to see it hadn't gotten dirty from me sitting on those steps for so long. It had seemed like an eternity. After one last check, I carefully zipped up the garment bag. The rest of the clothes from the shoot were back on the rack outside of my curtained-off dressing room, but this one, my absolute favorite piece, I'd kept inside with me for the entire set of changes, almost as if for luck.

It was the one piece of clothing that had made me feel different, like I wasn't just playing make believe anymore.

Slipping it over my arm, I slung my tote bag over my shoulder and emerged back into the middle of the room to find Lorna, Todd, Rico, and Enrique all applauding, almost a re-enactment of the scene when we finished the shoot, when the entire crew had started to clap.

I blushed and bowed my head, embarrassed by the unexpected attention. "You guys are crazy."

"No, we aren't," Lorna said, stepping forward. "We're proud of you."

She gave me a tight squeeze around my shoulders.

Rico nodded his agreement. "I've seen some of the shots on the camera already, Chey, and they are *amazing*."

I hung the dress bag back on the rack with the other clothes from the shoot. "Thanks."

Lorna nudged Rico, and he stepped forward, pulling the bag back off the rack.

"Take it." He put the dress bag back over my arm.

I stared at him, dumbfounded. "Are you serious?"

I glanced between them all, not believing it. I had to admit taking the dress off the first time had been a little like Cinderella losing everything at midnight. I'd been afraid that once I put the other clothes on, I'd lose whatever magic I had in the dress.

He nodded, and so did Lorna. "You never know when you might need something dressy to go out in, and you need something Vanetti to wear for that occasion. Besides, it's already tailored to you." He beamed at me. "It's yours. Consider it a perk for a shoot well done."

I smiled sheepishly, looking at the two of them. "Well, then, I thank you."

"No problem," Lorna said. "We'll give you a call when we get all the photos back in the next day or two. I think they're going to turn out great."

"I hope so."

"You sure we can't take you out for a celebratory dinner?" she asked as we walked towards the front door.

I brushed my fingers through my hair. "Thanks for the offer, but I just want to go home and relax."

Who knew a shoot could be so stressful? Besides, I also had JT to deal with. According to the text message I'd gotten halfway through the shoot, he was coming by tonight whether or not he heard from me.

17

"How was the shoot?" Dad asked the moment I let myself in through the front door.

"Tiring," I said with an exhausted smile as I set my dress bag over the back of the arm chair before heading off towards the kitchen in search of a much-needed bottle of orange juice.

Dad followed. "You can recoup tonight."

He took a seat at the counter. I noticed the pile of take-out menus in front of him. One thing about Dad, unless it was grilling out back, he rarely seemed to cook. Having a gourmet kitchen like this seemed like a total waste.

I took a long sip of my cold juice before turning back to him, shutting the fridge door with my hip. "Actually," I said as I twisted the cap back and forth on the bottle. "I have a date."

Dad looked amused. "Already?"

"Ha. It's just JT."

"Ah, *just* JT."

So I had mentioned him a few times, but not in the 'I'm interested' tense. "He asked, and I figured it's the only way to get rid of him."

Besides, once he got over his little infatuation, he'd move on to better; I was sure of it.

He laughed and went back to his menu. "I guess I don't need to ask whether you're in the mood for Chinese, huh?"

"Sorry." I kissed his cheek as I went past him. "Though, you could leave me some noodles and rice in the fridge for a midnight snack?"

"Consider it done." He noticed me grabbing the dress bag. "More clothes?"

I blushed again, clutching the dress to my chest. "Rico spoils me. This one's a dress, in case, you know, I go anywhere dressy."

"We'll have to find a place for you to wear it. What time's JT coming over?"

"Eight-ish." I'd texted him when leaving the shoot, saying I needed more time, and eight worked better than the seven we'd originally planned on. I wanted as much time as I could get. Besides, I still wasn't over his no-show last night. And just because I'd said eight-ish didn't mean I wouldn't suddenly come down with the flu from being on that windy rooftop all day.

"Can't wait to meet him."

I stopped in the doorway. "Dad, you're not going to do anything weird, are you?"

"I won't do anything weird." He rolled his eyes at the look of worry that was no doubt on my face. "Fine, I'll hang out in the garage and work on my car. How's that?"

"Great."

As promised, Dad was working on his car in the garage when JT pulled up. I could see from my spot on the front steps Dad was going to pull out one of his father cards and want to meet my 'date' from the way he stepped back from the car and watched JT park.

I scrambled off the steps and hoped Dad wasn't about to interrogate him or something else equally embarrassing before I could get to them.

JT was already out of his car by the time I reached it, and even worse, he headed straight for my father, as if he were a magnet.

"Uh, JT, I'm ready."

He totally didn't seem to hear me.

"Is that a classic '69 Mustang?"

Dad wiped his hands off on the rag he'd had draped over the side of the car and tucked it into his back pocket. "One and only. Bought it at auction in Scottsdale a couple years ago."

By now, JT stood inside the garage, leaning over the car on the opposite side and staring under the hood in what could only be awe. "It's a beaut. I always wanted one."

Dad laughed. What was this? Instant male bonding over cars?

And weirder yet, was I supposed to feel this instantaneously jealous? I mean, JT hadn't even looked at me, and I knew from my webcam chat with Sorche that I looked pretty darn cute. I'd modeled half the clothes in my closet, and we'd settled on my new copper-colored, Rico-given T-shirt and the jeans I'd bought when we'd gone shopping together. Casual but with enough style I'd fit in anywhere JT planned on going. My garage included, apparently.

I strolled towards them, swinging my purse back and forth with every step.

"How does she handle?" JT leaned over even farther.

I stood next to my father and looked under the hood myself, like I understood what they were talking about. I knew enough to get by, thanks to a 'girls and cars' class last semester, but if they went beyond the basics, I'd soon be utterly clueless.

"Pretty good," Dad answered. "Hey, Chey," he said as if he just noticed I was standing there.

"Hi, Dad." I smiled brightly.

"You two ready to go?"

I lifted my gaze to see JT smiling at me. "Guess so."

"I have only one rule," Dad said, stopping me before I could even move.

I bit my lip. This was the first he'd mentioned any rule, and I was a little apprehensive, to say the least. Did I suddenly have a nine o'clock curfew? I had to call home every time we left a place? We could only go to public places? JT had to be fingerprinted before we left, and Dad was going to dust my clothes for prints when I came home? All right, so I hoped that last one was just my imagination going into overdrive.

"Have fun," Dad said with an easygoing smile.

JT and I looked at each other. I relaxed and carefully gave Dad a quick side hug, not wanting to get any grease and grime on me.

"Be careful," he said into my hair before he pulled back. "Have a good night, guys."

"We will."

"Oh, hey, wait a sec. JT?"

I hesitated. We'd almost made it completely out of the garage.

"Yeah?" JT turned to face him.

I tilted my head upwards, staring at the rafters in the garage, wondering what he was going to say now.

"We're going to a movie premiere on Thursday. Would you like to join us?"

Movie premiere? That was the first I'd heard of that. But I kept silent and turned, catching Dad's smile. What was he up to?

"Yeah, that'd be great. I have something in the afternoon, but I should be free by about six."

"Great. I'll give Chey the details later to text you. You guys have fun."

JT nodded, a smile on his face. "Thanks."

We headed back to JT's car, and I gave a quick wave over my shoulder, still trying to figure things out.

"I heard you had a soft spot for Pink's." JT opened my door.

"Yeah, I'm a big fan of—"

"The chili cheese fries. I did a little investigating." He held up a bag he'd had in the back seat. "I thought we'd go stake some beach and have our dinner there. What do you say?"

"No cameras?"

"Tired of them already?"

"I think I've had enough for one day."

He laughed. "Well, all I've got is my camera phone, but I could be talked into leaving it in the car."

That made me laugh, and I brushed my hair back out of my eyes. "Nah, I think I can make an exception."

"Sorry I didn't make the shoot."

"That's fine." And actually, I might have been a little more nervous if he'd been there. A girl could only have so many people watching before it started to give her an even bigger complex.

Plus, I still wasn't all that sure about what had happened last night. "So, why didn't show you up last night?"

He glanced at me. "I figured you'd ask about that."

I nodded. "Well?"

"I wanted to. Seriously." He turned the radio off. "But then, I had some family stuff come up with my parents. I thought they were out for the night, but I came down to go and there they were, wanting to make sure I was still..." he paused. "Hanging in there. I guess they found out I had a couple drinks at Adriana's party, so..."

"That's what they said?"

"That's what Mom called it. I wanted to call you guys or text, but I couldn't get out of the damn room, and by the time they were done, it was after midnight, and I figured you were probably at home sound asleep and didn't want to wake you up before your shoot. I figured you'd probably forgive me even less at that point."

I sighed to myself. It sounded like a really good excuse. And I kinda actually believed him. I watched the breeze blow through his hair we sped down the road. "It's okay. I just wondered where you were, that's all."

"Did you guys have fun? I heard Sor's boyfriend was in the band or something?"

"Yeah, he is. They're good; we'll have to go see them sometime." I hesitated, wondering how he was going to take that *we*. I'd meant it more me and Sorche, not me and JT. But when I stole a look at him, he was smiling, like that sounded good to him.

"You're quiet."

"I'm the quiet type." I took a fry out of the bag to munch on. "Which beach were you planning on?"

I almost sounded like I knew the difference.

"Well, if you can stand the airplane noise..."

"Really?" I couldn't see us having a great night hanging out on the beach if we had to shout over the sound of incoming planes overhead. Sure, it might be a weirdly Californian thing to do, but I think I'd rather pass.

He broke out in a big grin at the look on my face. "All right, change of plans. We can head somewhere else. Sorche take you to the pier yet?"

"To do what? Push me off?" I teased.

He stole a look at me and reached over, taking a couple fries out of the bag. "I meant the rides and stuff."

"Sounds fun," I commented. "Is that what you had planned, though?"

"Well, you shot down my beach idea. I just thought I'd take you somewhere you hadn't been yet."

"Surprise me."

A mischievous grin spread across his face. "Surprise, it is."

After ten minutes of driving, I was getting hungry with the smell of the food wafting up towards me. Considering I'd barely eaten before the shoot—I'd been so nervous, and all I'd had since was that bottle of orange juice and a couple of fries—I was hoping he'd stop somewhere soon, or else I'd likely end up eating all my chili fries as he drove. "So, where are we headed?"

He laughed. "You'll see."

"Cryptic, huh?"

He glanced over. "You did say surprise you, so trust me. Plus it has one of the best views of the city."

The next thing I knew, he'd taken another abrupt turn off and parked. I looked up and saw a beautiful tree-lined path, gravel crunching under the tires as he followed the well-worn drive.

"Home sweet home."

"Wow."

His lips lifted up into a sweet smile as we rounded a slight curve. "That's the reaction I was going for."

"So this is what you had in mind, huh?"

"Well, yeah."

He pulled the car off the gravel road onto a patch of grass, near a small stone wall, and parked the car before we stared out over the hills.

"I didn't know we were practically neighbors."

I set the bag I had been holding down between us. We were perched on the far end of what was JT's parents' property, overlooking the Hollywood Hills and everything below. If I'd thought the view from Dad's was great, this one proved nothing short of breathtaking. I swear I could even see our place way off to the right, but I'd never seen it from this altitude, so who knew, for sure?

"Lots of stuff you don't know about me, Chey."

"So I'm noticing."

JT opened the bag and pulled out his hamburger. "How'd the shoot go?"

"Good. Rico seemed pleased." I took the burger he'd gotten for me. "Just hope the pictures turn out as good as he thinks they will."

"You know Rico wouldn't lie to make you feel better. If he said he was pleased, then he was. He's been raving about you since he saw you at the fashion show."

"Yeah?"

He nodded. "Yeah."

I swiveled as much as I could in my seat to look at him. "You know, I always thought it was odd Rico just came up to me out of nowhere. Like he knew me, almost."

I caught a flush of red on JT's neck as he grabbed a few of my fries.

"Really?" His voice sounded muffled by the mix of fries and chili.

"Yep. You wouldn't have talked me up to him or anything, would you?"

"Chey..."

"Did you?"

He glanced at me and set his half-eaten burger back in its wrap. "I might have mentioned you once or twice after the party that night."

I must have looked surprised because he kept talking.

"Sometimes, I crash in Rico and Lorna's guesthouse out back. It's an arrangement we've had for the last two years. Works out great."

"You know, you're not exactly the same guy who was skinny dipping the night I met him." I grabbed a couple of my chili fries. It didn't matter they were barely lukewarm—they were still one of my absolute favorite things about life in L.A.

"True. I'm a lot more sober." He took a large gulp of his drink. "Damn, brain freeze." He slammed the cardboard cup down so he could rub his temples.

I couldn't help but laugh before I took a cautious sip of my own soda. I had to admit this was nice. The view was amazing. And the company not too bad, either. I was seeing a side of JT I never ever thought existed.

"You gotta be careful," I jokingly warned.

"Yeah, because cold drinks are so hazardous to your health." His grin looked teasing.

"So why did you bring me up here, anyway?"

"To show you the view...and more importantly, what's yours."

"What's mine?"

"This."

I looked up in time to see him gesture to L.A. spread out in front of us.

"All of Los Angeles is mine?" I couldn't keep the skepticism out of my voice.

"Look, you're new to all of this." He stared out at the view. "Me, it's been mine since I blinked open my eyes and wailed 'I want my mommy'."

I laughed, ducking my head so my hair fell alongside my face and hid my expression. Maybe he was more right than I wanted to admit. I kept trying to justify to myself that I belonged, when in fact, I did, whether I wanted to or not. All because of my father.

Sometimes, I wondered how different life would have been had I grown up out here...

"Seriously."

The word broke the lengthy silence between us.

"I believe you."

"And when it was all there for the taking, I took. Believe me. So do a lot of us. So would you."

"Probably," I agreed. "But I haven't yet, and kinda don't plan on starting."

Part of my deal with Mom. I had to stay me and not become another typical Hollywood Kid out here.

He leaned in front of me, his thumb tilting my chin up to peer into my eyes. "I'd say we'll see about that, Daniels."

I know the last thing on Earth I wanted was to like JT, even remotely, and even worse, fall for him. Like, could it get any more cliché? Naive teenage girl falling for the walking definition of the quintessential Hollywood bad boy. All he needed was the leather jacket and a motorcycle.

I had a sneaking suspicion he already owned both.

"Can I ask you something?"

"Sure."

"Why'd you go to rehab in the first place?" I'd done a bit of Googling and had turned up a bunch of articles, mostly tabloid stuff, but I figured it was better to hear it straight from him.

He went silent for a few minutes as he stared at the lights slowly coming on in the houses on the hills below.

"Stupid stuff." He started to rip the corner off the paper bag, shredding it into tiny pieces.

"Like?" I pressed gently. Maybe I was pushing too much. This was the most we'd talked one on one. Maybe not exactly the best time to delve into our life stories.

"Like, I was fifteen, sixteen, partying like I was twenty-one. Twenty-two. Twenty-nine, even." He didn't even look at me. "I liked my Corona and lime. When I had my first motorcycle accident, I broke my ankle in two places and had to have a plate put in. That's when I added a cocktail of pain killers to the mix."

"Wow." I hadn't quite expected him to be so blunt about it all.

"That was the first go around. The second time, I was back on the painkillers, and my parents talked me into going, saying it might be what I needed to get my acting career going again."

"So you still want to act?"

I remembered seeing him in movies when I was like nine or ten and he would have been about my same age at the time, but really nothing since then. 'Course, I hadn't made the connection at the party. Back then, he'd gone by Justin, and he didn't really resemble the skinny little kid with the big blue eyes anymore.

"Yeah. Actually had a few auditions again this week." He straightened up and looked at his empty cup. "You done?"

I looked at the remnants of my drink, completely unaware I must have finished it in the last few minutes. "Looks like it."

"Good. We better get going, anyway. It's getting late."

I stuffed the garbage back into the paper bag. "I don't have a set time to be home."

Suddenly, I didn't want this to be the end of our first date.

He shot me a smile. "That's good. There's still one place I want to take you tonight."

It was hours later that I sat on the front steps, JT next to me. Dad's car was gone, and the security lights were yet again illuminating the house, giving it that warm and cozy, not to mention inhabited, feel.

"Thanks for tonight." I held the half-eaten cotton candy he'd bought me before we'd left the Santa Monica Pier.

He scuffed his sneaker against one of the stones. "Glad you had a good time. I didn't want to risk us getting another 'mystery girl' mention, so I went low-key."

"Low-key was great."

Actually, low-key was pretty much perfect. Matching baseball caps pulled low, and he kept his sunglasses on half the night.

Despite my fear of heights, which I guessed maybe I'd conquered that afternoon on the rooftop, I'd loved riding on the Pacific Wheel down at the Pier. But my favorite had been the vintage carousel. JT, however, favored the rollercoaster, which somehow, I survived without getting ill. We must have ridden it half a dozen times or more before he finally decided to move on to something else. Maybe he'd been smart waiting 'til after we'd done the ride thing to get me the cotton candy.

I caught him looking at me. "Seriously. It's probably the best first date I've been on."

Hands down, it beat going to a movie or hanging out at someone's house watching them play video games.

The corner of his mouth tugged up in a small smile as his eyes met mine.

Suddenly, all I wanted in the world right then was to kiss him.

I gave in to impulse and leaned over to kiss him. I could smell the mix of his citrus aftershave and the salt air we'd spent so much of the night in as my lips touched his, an almost static-like zap of electricity hitting me as I tasted the cotton candy on his lips.

He pulled back with that amused grin on his face, his forehead leaning gently against mine for a second before he pulled further away. "I knew you liked me, Daniels."

"It's the cotton candy. Gets me every time."

He looked at the blue tuft still in my hands. "I'll remember that."

18

The phone call from Lorna a few mornings later had woken me up, but I hadn't pushed myself out of bed to catch it before it went through to voicemail. All I knew from her message was she hoped I'd had a nice weekend and if I was available, could I come down to the offices that morning? Short and sweet and totally not telling me anything.

I had a feeling the photos were back, and Rico either wanted to, a) congratulate me on a job well done, or b) tell me he was very sorry I wasn't at all photogenic and Adriana was now taking over, and how soon could I return my unused *House of Vanetti* wardrobe? Also, where could he send the bill for the rest of the clothing?

I *really* needed to work on my optimism.

Parking in my usual spot outside Rico's offices, I grabbed my cell and tote bag and headed inside. The place was calmer than it had been on the weekend, and I felt a lot more relaxed when Lorna waved at me from behind the desk, wearing the identical red T-shirt I'd worn out with JT on our date the other night.

"Hi, Chey. You're early."

"Too early? I can come back." I motioned back to the door. I could drive around, get a coffee, kill some time until they were ready for me.

"No, it's fine. Go on back. Rico's in one of the back rooms looking over the photos."

I paused, about to go over there. I searched her face for a sign of what the pictures had turned out like, but she simply smiled and waved me back. Darn it, I was hoping for some sort of idea what they had turned out like, but her expression was almost neutral. Not helpful at all.

I still didn't budge.

"Go on. He can't wait to see you."

That didn't tell me anything.

I headed back and found Rico in a small office off to the side. I hesitated, gathering my nerve. Even from where I stood outside the doorway, I could see the oversized table he sat in front of covered in shots from my shoot.

"Rico?" I wasn't sure I should disturb him. He looked busy and all, but on the other hand, Lorna had told me to go right in to the back office.

"There she is!" He stood and hurried towards me. "My favorite model. The camera adores you."

I smiled in relief as he gave me a hug, glad he was pleased. I was afraid none of them would be usable, even with the extreme use of Photoshop.

He took my hand and pulled me into the room, closer to the photos that littered the table.

I was almost afraid to look.

"Sit. Take a look at these." He pulled another chair up. "Can you stick around awhile? Todd's waiting for the final mock-up of the billboards to be delivered. He'll be back soon."

I couldn't stop the *huh* that came out of my mouth. Nobody had mentioned billboards. I'd known there were going to be print ads in the papers. Obviously, they'd be online, and he'd wanted to paper the windows of the boutique with huge colored posters while they finished the inside in the next week or so, but this?

A billboard?

A larger-than-life, down-the-side-of-a-building billboard like he'd just said while I was sitting here silently freaking out? Totally made my head swim.

He must have sensed my...slight freak out.

"Only a few scattered strategically around the city. Nothing to worry about." He patted my shoulder gently.

Yeah, if I wasn't the worrying type. Unfortunately, that was another lovely gene I'd inherited from my parents.

"By this time Friday, your face will be everywhere," he continued on, clearly not noticing my sudden bout of panic.

I swore the room swam around me. It felt like I was drowning—the lack of air, the feeling of panic; yet, I found myself nowhere near the water. I felt Rico's hand on my arm and realized I was still standing.

"Come sit. Do you want a soda? Some iced water? Coffee?"

"No, no. I'm fine." Though I admit I wobbled a little as he led me over to the bright red vinyl couch against the wall. I fell back into it just as Todd made his way into the room, a large cardboard poster tube in his hands.

"Am I late?" he asked after giving me a quick hello.

"Right on time. Well, let's take a look." Rico smiled, turning to me. "We had a tough time choosing."

I found my nails digging unconsciously into the armrest and tried to loosen my grip before they could do any damage to the furniture as Todd carefully pulled the poster out and began to unravel it. My lungs started to burn from lack of oxygen, but I wasn't going to be able to breathe until I saw more than the tip of the skyline.

I watched in awe as it unfolded, noticing something funny. My shoe was at the top. Which meant...I tilted my head.

"Upside down," I said, breaking my silence.

Todd looked horrified, and Rico simply laughed as they righted the poster. Before I knew it, the whole shot was on display, and the only thing I could do was gape. The girl staring back from the poster was gorgeous, and I fought back the little voice that said she couldn't possibly be me.

"Is that me?" I couldn't believe the words came out of my mouth as I felt my face turn fire-engine red.

Todd gave me a rare smile. "That *is* you. And this is the look that's going on how many billboards across L.A.?"

He turned to Rico.

"A dozen, at least. That's what we had booked before, but now, looking at this, maybe I should try and wrangle a few more. Print ads of different shots are going in the paper next week. The digital ads are going to be finalized before the end of tomorrow and start running a few days after...just bits and pieces to get some early buzz. Before you know it, Chey, you're going to be a household name around here. But mum's the word, okay? I want these to make the biggest impact possible."

I stared at the image, my vision just a little blurry around the edges as I locked on the girl staring back at me from the glossy surface. I heard Rico's voice as if in the distance, and suddenly, there was a cold bottled water in my hand.

"Take a sip, Chey..."

That light-headed feeling was back again, and I took a long sip of my iced water Rico had procured for me, not tasting a single drop of it as I stared in awe at the glossy image.

Rico and Todd conversed in front of me, but I didn't hear a single word they were saying, my attention solely focused on the image staring back at me, still hanging in Todd's grasp.

The Vanetti logo was transparent in the skyline above my head, but I couldn't take my gaze off my face. It was like staring back at a total stranger.

19

I walked in around in a daze for a day or two after seeing the mockups. As much as I tried to tell myself this was just something fun for the summer, it suddenly felt a lot more real after that.

Like pinch yourself 'til it hurts so you realize it's not a dream real.

Thankfully, I had Sorche to distract me. She'd been busy with her mom for a couple of days, but we were finally getting together to go shopping.

We wandered around The Grove while I tried to find the perfect birthday gift for my father. What to get a guy who could buy himself anything in the world he wanted? After a couple hours of searching, I really should have had more ideas than I did, which so far amounted to a big fat zilch.

"Any ideas yet?" Sor asked as we walked out of yet another store, more shopping bags in hand.

Okay, so I couldn't find anything for Dad other than a couple new workout T-shirts; didn't mean I couldn't splurge and buy a little something extra for me—especially when that morning, a courier had dropped off my first check from *House of Vanetti*.

"Not a one." I followed her down the sidewalk, weaving through the crowds and into another of Sor's favorite places.

"You'll find something. You've got at least another week, right?"

"Right." That's why Trish had taken me to lunch the other day after I'd gone by Rico's to see the mock-up, to talk over the plans for Dad's birthday, which thanks to her and the event planner she'd hired, was pretty well all taken care of. Except for my gift. Thankfully, I had Sor to bounce ideas off of. But I figured I wanted something more substantial than just workout gear he could buy himself.

"How'd the date with JT go?" she asked as we walked into another clothing store.

I shrugged. "Pretty good."

I didn't feel like telling her his spiel of 'this was all mine now' because I knew she'd agree. She'd already told me several times I needed to step into it more. But I was still a little leery about stepping in too far, afraid the door would slam shut behind me. Maybe I'd listened to Mom's warnings about the L.A. lifestyle more than I realized.

Or maybe I was just plain scared.

I didn't want to consider that option.

"Be honest, is it infatuation or what?" Sor asked as we began to look through the racks of shirts and she started draping a few hangers over her arm.

I sighed, noticing a couple people looking our way, more than likely due to recognizing Sorche.

"I don't know. I'm only here for the summer, remember?" Which seemed to be starting to pass by at an alarming rate. I didn't even want to think about how much time had already zoomed by. Days had turned into weeks pretty quickly out here.

"So you keep stubbornly insisting." She pulled a last halter top off the rack and added it to the stack of hangers in her hand. "You wanna wait here? I want to try a few of these on."

"Go ahead." Least I could do was wait. She was helping me try and find the perfect birthday gift for Dad. Something I'd completely forgotten about 'til Trish reminded me. Bad daughter that I was. Just proved how quickly time was moving.

I found a leather chair outside the dressing rooms and held onto Sor's shopping bags while she disappeared behind one of the doors with her armful of clothes. She was having way better shopping luck than me.

Before I knew it, the door swung back open, and she walked out barefoot, adjusting the black slacks and a silvery purple halter top as she stopped in front of the full-length mirror.

"What do you think? Will it work for your dad's party?"

"Looks great." Trish had booked some great club for the night; I'd never heard of it 'til she'd brought up the website on her cell phone at lunch, but it was gorgeous inside. Had a bit of a retro feel to it in the VIP area, with the half-circle booths, but it was the perfect spot for Dad's big birthday bash.

She smiled. "What are you wearing?"

"I thought I'd go with something Rico gave me." I decided not to mention the red dress or the photo shoot out in public, just for the simple fact there were way too many people around and, knowing my luck, someone who shouldn't overhear would.

"I should've known that, huh?" She laughed as she headed back to the dressing room. "Just let me try on a couple more things, then we can get something to eat."

"Sounds good." I was starving, and every time we passed by a restaurant, my stomach threatened to rumble.

"Ooh, come on, the fountain should start soon," Sor said as we stepped back into the bright mid-afternoon sunshine a couple minutes later, more shopping bags in hand.

"What are you talking about?" I felt clueless. Didn't the fountain run all the time?

Sor shook her head as she grabbed my wrist and began pulling me through the early afternoon shoppers. "Every thirty minutes, the fountain dances. Come on, it's one of my favorite things about shopping here."

I sighed and went along with her. And sure enough, we were still making our way towards it when the music started. Dean Martin, if I was guessing right. I vaguely recognized the voice from those old movies Mom and I watched sometimes on TV.

I stood beside Sor and watched the fountain dance, amongst a growing crowd of spectators, most I assumed were tourists, given the amount of phones pulled out and aimed at the fountain. Was it odd I suddenly felt above camera phones? Even so, I pulled mine out and snapped a few shots of the fountain and had Sor take a quick one of me with the fountain background to text Mom.

When the show was over, Sor clapped and grinned. "All right, lunch time. My treat. What do you feel like?"

"Whatever isn't packed," I said as we crossed the street and headed past an outdoor café already filled to capacity. I didn't feel like having to stand in line forever just to be seated.

"Let's see what we can find."

Half an hour later, we were sitting at a nice table at The Cheesecake Factory, menus in front of us while the waitress dropped off our drinks. I tensed as I saw Adriana in the distance and lifted my menu a tad higher, but Sor gave me a puzzled look, no doubt think-ing I was avoiding JT before she followed my gaze.

"Shouldn't she be, oh I don't know, busy tormenting small chil-dren or something?" Sor commented as she turned back to me.

"I wish." Out of the corner of my eye, I saw her get closer. So far, it looked like she hadn't noticed us. Maybe we'd get lucky and she wouldn't. "Maybe she'll just keep going."

No such luck.

I should have crossed my fingers...and my legs...and my toes and anything else I could have crossed.

I caught sight of the black and red Manolos beside our table as I pretended to scour the menu before I looked up at the sound of her indiscreet cough.

Talk about crying out for attention. "Hi, Adriana."

Her eyes narrowed as she ignored me. "Sorche. *Wyoming.*"

Wow. I never expected that much venom out of something that wasn't wearing snakeskin and could be classified as a reptile. May-be I should have taken a closer look at the shoes.

"It's Chey," I corrected her, trying to keep my voice light and sugary sweet. As Mom always tried to tell me, letting anyone see they got to you was giving them the upper hand. Something I was sure Adriana already had enough of.

She huffed slightly. "Whatever. I hear you're getting a bill-board."

Oh, she was allowing herself to acknowledge my presence.

"More than one," Sorche said before I could utter a word, and I was glad she was the only one I'd confided in. But then again, how the heck had Adriana found out? Rico had said mum's the word, and I couldn't see Sorche talking to her, period. "What are you do-ing this summer, Adri?"

"Other than counting down Chey's fifteen minutes?" Her smile looked sweeter than the cheesecake I'd seen go by our table earlier.

"Keeping up on my auditions and the party circuit. I hear your dad's having his what? Fiftieth birthday this week?" She tilted her head to look at me.

"Thirty-ninth, actually." I smiled back just as sweetly. "Shame you won't be there."

"Actually..." She stood straighter, an almost evil grin crossing her face like I'd fallen right into her trap, pulling out her cell phone. "Mom got the invite this morning, so I guess I'll see you two there." She looked giddy. "Have a good lunch. I'd go with the salad, much more slimming," she said as she walked away, giving a little finger wave.

I waited 'til she was out of earshot. "Okay, tell me she's joking."

"About what?"

I didn't mean the salad. "The party. I mean, did you get an invite?"

Sorche nodded. "Trish had one sent to me, and Mom got hers a month ago, at least. She's really looking forward to it. So if her mom got hers this morning...she may have been on a secondary list." No doubt that comment was meant to console me.

"She really wouldn't come, would she?" I asked, my gaze on her retreating back.

"I doubt it. She's probably just trying to tick you off. C'mon, forget Adriana. She's not worth the energy."

"Yeah, you're absolutely right," I said with a determined smile on my face as I turned my attention back to the menu.

She could try all she wanted, but I wasn't going to let Adriana ruin anything for me.

20

The next few days flew by. Sorche took me with her to her yoga classes, and Dad and I actually managed to fit in a couple sessions of rollerblading at the beach. We even snuck in a late night snack down at Pink's. I'd promised Trish I'd keep the two days before Dad's party open to help her out with the last-minute preparations. We had to pick up the goody bags in the afternoon and make sure they got to the club bright and early the next morning.

Sitting in the living room with Trish, my cereal bowl in hand, I ate while she double-checked the to-do lists on her tablet.

"Do you have any idea what you're going to get him?"

I shrugged. "I still have time. Besides, does he really need anything but my smiling face there?"

After all, this was the first time in years I was spending the day with him. Usually, I had to mail the package to whatever city he was filming in. Or like last year, send it to Trish's 'til he got back from the latest shoot.

At least now, I knew who the M. signature on the delivery confirmation was.

Milo.

Trish laughed. "I think that's all the gift your dad needs."

I was about to down the last of my cereal when the cordless started to ring.

"I'll grab it." I jumped to my feet, setting my bowl on the coffee table as I swiped the phone off the edge. "Hello."

"Chey! I've been trying to reach you everywhere."

An excited female voice greeted me, one that I knew right away wasn't Sor. Or Mom, thankfully.

"Lorna?"

"That's me. I tried your cell, texting you, and even called Sorche trying to track you down."

I instantly felt bad over making her do all that trying to get a hold of me. I thought of my cell phone sitting upstairs on its charger. "I guess I must have accidentally turned the cell off when I plugged it in when I got up this morning. What do you need?"

"I hope you're free this morning, because two hours from now, your first billboard's going up."

The phone slid out of my hand and hit the coffee table with an echoing thud, loud enough that Trish turned to look at me from where she sat working at the corner desk.

"You okay, Chey? Something wrong?"

My mouth was suddenly terribly dry, and I couldn't even form the words to tell her. My mouth opened, but nothing but a wisp of air came out.

I could hear Lorna's voice calling my name from the phone, and I reached out to grab it, putting it back to my ear and prayed my voice would be there. "D-did you say billboard?"

Trish came over and guided me back to the nearest chair, since I must have looked like I felt—like I was about to pass out. I managed a weak whispered *thank you.*

I was totally light-headed as Lorna spoke.

"I thought Rico told you. The proofs were so amazing, we went straight into mock-ups with the billboards and rushed them. The first one's going up this morning. I thought you'd want to be there to see it."

"I can't believe this." I blinked, suddenly feeling very unprepared as my heart thudded erratically in my chest.

Trish moved around to stand in front of me, looking seriously concerned. She took the phone, and after a few seconds of conversation, broke out into a big smile. "That's terrific news. We'll see you there."

She clicked the phone off and beamed at me. "This is so exciting for you, Chey. Go up and change. I'll get my keys and borrow your dad's camera. See if you can get a hold of him. He should still be at the gym. He could probably meet us down there. I can text him the address on the way. I'll meet you in the driveway."

I managed a nod as I put my hand on the armrest to push myself up to my feet. I didn't know which I felt more at that moment— numb, panic, or sheer terror at the thought that this was really happening. Sure, the photo shoot was one thing, but to have the product of that photo shoot suddenly taking up the side of a building meant a whole other matter. Some part deep inside kept screaming *I want my mommy.* Or Daddy.

Less than an hour later, Trish and I were in the front of her black Audi convertible, the roof down as we stared up at the side of the appointed building, with Sorche in the backseat. Apparently, Trish had called her in for moral support—which to be honest, I totally needed right now. As I watched the two guys climb up, I began to realize this was very, *very* surreal.

"I can't believe your dad is going to miss this," Trish said as she checked the camera one more time before aiming it at the crew who were about to start putting up the billboard.

"He said he'd be here the moment he could," I assured her, trying to stay cool and calm, but the nerves dancing in my stomach could give the entire cast of *Dancing with the Stars* a run for their money.

I shifted to look at Sorche who moved to sit on top of the backseat, ready to record the moment for posterity—or blackmail, which would probably be the more useful and wiser choice.

Right now, I'd pay a pretty penny of my modeling fee—more words not in my vocab 'til this mistake-filled summer began—to keep this hot little bit of footage from reaching my mother's hands—or inbox before I had the chance to explain. I had a feeling Mom and I better have a little chat over Skype sooner than later, before she somehow found out on her own.

Trish nudged me. "Come on, Chey. Aren't you the least bit excited?"

I tilted my head back and watched the progress on the billboard as they smoothed up one more section on the wall. I could see the edge of my dress, and I thought I knew which shot they'd used, slightly different from the one on the mockup I'd seen. This was one of the first where I was leaning against the doorjamb, my shoes dangling from my fingers. My aviator shades would cover my eyes, and my hair would be slightly windblown, helping to give me that whole 'mystery girl' look.

"Okay, a little," I admitted as I pulled my own phone out of my purse to take a couple shots. It wasn't every day that a photo of me was being put up on the side of a building. But then again, life in Los Angeles was pretty much like nothing I'd known before.

I did my best to shove all my nervousness and self-doubt aside, leaning back to watch the rest of my red dress slowly appear on the wall. And as I watched, I had the perfect idea of what to get for Dad's birthday. While Trish snapped and Sorche filmed, I made a quick call to Lorna, who turned out to be pulling into a parking spot just down the street to watch the progress, too. She thought it was a great idea and told me she'd have it delivered before the party.

I ended the call just in time to see the last three pieces go up on the wall to a round of applause from Trish and Sor.

"I'm sorry I missed it, kid."

Dad set down the large paper-wrapped bouquet on my bed and kissed my forehead as I texted Sorche. She was going to upload the video she'd shot so I could do something with it. What, I wasn't quite sure. I figured I'd tell Mom before I emailed it to her. I don't think she could handle the shock of following a link to see me grinning back at her from the side of a building. She'd end up at the front door before I knew it. And who could blame her?

"It's okay. Trish took a lot of pictures, including ones of me standing nearby and pointing up at it." I tilted my head back to look at him as he took a seat on the edge of my bed. "Plus, there's still a few more going up." Seven, at last count according to Lorna. "You can catch one of those."

But it wouldn't be the same, I bit my lip to keep from saying. Instead, I continued on, finally putting my dormant acting genes to good use. "How was your morning?"

"Long." He stretched his legs out in front of him. "I brought you your favorite Fire and Ice roses." He carefully lifted the taped cover and pulled them free of their wrap.

In spite of the small rush of disappointment that he hadn't missed my big moment for something major, like getting a part at the last minute, or having some sort of power meeting with Quinn or whoever, I smiled as I took the flowers, inhaling their strong, sweet scent. The little girl inside me, the supposed inner child, was smiling, almost jumping up and down to get my attention, almost as if to say *see, he still cares.*

Yeah, but just not enough to be there for *my* big moment.

"I know they don't make up for missing out on the billboard. But I did drive by on my way home. You look great up there. A total natural." He kissed the top of my head. "I'm proud of you, Chey."

Those words *almost* made up for him not being there, I thought as I took the empty vase from the top of my dresser and headed into the bathroom to put my roses in water.

Keyword: *almost.*

I was still upset he'd missed my big moment, and for what? An extra hour with his trainer and a business lunch?

He still didn't say what the big excuse was...what topped *my* moment.

But as I put the flowers back on the corner of my desk and patted the ever present e-mail in my shorts pocket, I knew I was in California because Dad wanted me there. And even if we weren't spending 24/7 together, we were still spending more time together then I ever would have gotten back at home.

21

"I've already had calls about you," Trish said with a warm smile a few mornings later as I walked into the kitchen in my pajama shorts and tank top.

Dad was on a conference call—again—so I was left on my own to make breakfast, which I didn't mind. Better than watching Dad dig around the cupboards, coming up with protein bars and flavorless oatmeal like he had that one morning, before he'd decided we'd be better off going out somewhere for pancakes.

I grabbed the carton of eggs and the butter from the fridge, dropped a dollop of butter in the empty frying pan on the stove before adding a couple of the eggs. I put some slices of bread into the toaster and hit the button, before grabbing the frozen hash browns out of the freezer and putting them in a separate pan on the stove.

"What? Me?"

Total surprise. I mean, why would anyone call about me? Okay, so I guess it wasn't like I was some deep, dark secret. My baby picture had been splashed across the cover of People magazine when I was born, and I guess they'd covered the divorce and all…I had the bookmarked Google searches to prove that fascinating little tidbit. But still, I couldn't believe anyone had *any* interest in an unknown like *moi*.

She nodded. "You look surprised. *Really* surprised."

"Why wouldn't I be?" I put the eggs and butter back in the fridge, grabbing the juice and putting it on the table. "Why are they calling?"

"After the billboard, people asked people who might have had an idea who you were, who contacted me since I'm your dad's assistant. You don't have anyone, so I thought I'd take care of it—unless you want to find your own somebody to handle things?"

I laughed as I finished scrambling the eggs I'd thrown in the pan and put them on two plates. I double checked the hash browns and turned the heat up a little. The toast popped up, and I set them on a platter before putting it on the table.

"I thought Sor was kidding when she said I'd need a publicist and an assistant."

"Rico said you're destined to be the next 'it girl' from the start. Looks like the ball's already begun rolling."

Down the hilly streets of San Francisco at full speed, if the stack of messages that were piled on top of the kitchen counter were any indication.

I grabbed a slice of toast from where I'd just set the platter on the table.

"Seriously?" I took a bite of my toast.

"Every phone call, email, and fax this morning is about you."

"It's all been for Chey?"

Dad's voice startled the both of us, and we turned to see him standing in the doorway, his cell phone in hand. I caught the look that flashed across his face at Trish's news. All the calls, all the everything, had been about me and my billboard, not Dad's possible new deal.

I ducked my head in embarrassment and felt Trish's hand brush my shoulder. Instinctively, I knew she'd seen the same thing I had. The silence seemed like an eternity but probably didn't last more than a few painful seconds.

"That's great, Chey," he finally said, and if anyone didn't know better, they'd think he sounded genuinely happy, but I caught the slightest strain in his voice.

"Thanks, Dad." I turned my gaze away, making a show of looking at my watch. "You know, I forgot I have a couple errands to run. Be back in a while," I said as I quickly scooped my keys off the table and hurried out the open patio doors. "You guys have breakfast, the hash browns will be done in a few. I probably made more than enough, anyways."

Okay, that was a total lie; the only errand I needed to run right then was to get away from my father's disappointment.

I was halfway to the garage and sweet escape when Trish caught up to me.

"He's a big boy, Chey. He'll get over everything."

I nodded, glad I had my sunglasses on to mask my glassy eyes. At least, I was getting good at holding my tears back. But I wasn't sure my voice wouldn't betray me, so I stayed silent.

"You want to go for a drive? Check out the billboard? Maybe they've put up some of the others?"

I took a deep breath.

"I think I've seen it enough." For a lifetime, actually.

"C'mon, I'm not going to let you spend the day moping around. Not the behavior of a girl getting the number of invites you are."

My curiosity won out in spite of everything. "Yeah?"

"I have a folder of messages and emails on your bed waiting for your perusal."

"Maybe I should get it and take it to Sor's."

Trish smiled, a look of relief crossing her face. "That sounds like a great idea. I'll go grab it for you."

Half an hour later, I was holed up in Sorche's bedroom. I'd caught her mid-yoga routine when I arrived at the door. She'd quickly ended it, though, when she heard about my horrible morning. Now, the bright blue folder from Trish sat in her lap, and I was sprawled out on top of her bed, the bowl of chocolate chunk ice cream she'd gotten me in hand. I may have forgotten all about my late breakfast, but it could never be too early for ice cream.

Sor swiveled in her modern office chair, a piece of cherry licorice dangling from the corner of her mouth. "So, let me get this straight. Your dad is having issues because you're suddenly one of the hottest things going?"

She closed the folder on the stack of papers thicker than I'd imagined.

I stretched out a little more, adjusting the pillow behind my head

"Pretty much. You should have seen him." I traced patterns in my ice cream before spooning up a chocolate chunk. "I mean, I know he tried to sound cool about it, but the man isn't *that* good of an actor."

"He sounds awful selfish, Chey."

"Selfish?"

"What would you call it? Totally unsupportive, at best?"

"Blind-sided. He could never have thought this little modeling thing would take off like this."

"When Rico said the pictures were amazing, you should have known."

How could I have known anything? I was still maneuvering blind.

I didn't want to argue about Dad with anyone. Especially when, deep down, I knew Sorche was right. He *should* have been happy things were going well for me. Not my fault his career was where it was. He should have been making use of his time off and spending some of it with me, like he'd promised in all those impassioned phone calls when he and Mom had been working this little trip of mine out. *Or had that been acting, too?* a little voice in the back of my mind rang out.

Instead, I felt relegated to the back seat while he did whatever he deemed necessary to keep things going for himself.

"Chey?"

"Sorry." I finished off my ice cream and set it aside. "Any good invites?"

"There's a few that have definite potential. I put them on the top. But I think I know what you need."

I looked at her skeptically. Right now, hiding from the world— and more importantly, my problems—seemed like *numero uno.* "What do I need?"

She smiled. "An afternoon with me. We'll go drive around, maybe hit up Rodeo. We can play tourist. Come on, I know you're dying to check out Grauman's Chinese Theatre. Then we can find someplace cool and low-key for lunch. My treat."

I sighed, getting to my feet as she grabbed her purse and her car keys. "No more Dad talk?"

"Not a word."

After spending the afternoon walking all around the Hollywood and Highland Centre, Sor drove by Rico's new store on the way back. The huge windows were covered in the graffiti version of the ads to keep anyone from seeing inside before the great unveiling. The *House of Vanetti* logo was imprinted all over the photos, and the sunglasses I'd worn in the shots reflected the logo back in a hologram finish. All in all, pretty impressive, I had to admit.

"See? Do you think Adriana could've gotten half this much attention?" Sor asked as she parked across the street and motioned to the windows.

I knew she was trying to make me feel better, and I appreciated it. But right now, all it was doing was making me wonder if I'd done the right thing agreeing to any of this in the first place. Not just Rico's offer, but coming to L.A. for the summer.

I managed a small smile. "Probably not."

At least if she did, she'd probably handle it oh so much better than how I was currently dealing.

Maybe it was time I adopted a bit of JT's attitude—like he said, L.A. was at my feet right now, and maybe it really was mine for the taking. And what better time to start?

Even if Dad didn't exactly acknowledge his less than stellar performance in the role of supporting father, it didn't mean I needed to ruin my summer over it. I was a big girl; I could deal. Besides, opportunities like this didn't come around that often.. I wasn't about to blow it.

"You're right."

Sor smiled. "Good. I know just the thing to pick you up."

"Here we go..."

"Seriously, this is good." She reached into the backseat and pulled out the folder from my bag. "Top sheet."

I lifted the cover and looked at the faxed-over invite. Some club opening that would be thrilled for the newest 'Face of Vanetti' to make her appearance.

"Yeah?"

She nodded. "Totally. Forget your dad. It's not happening, right? Do something for you." She tapped the paper. "This sounds like the perfect night out. Take JT."

"Don't you want to go?" I looked at the date.

"Already have plans, my dear," she said with a mischievous wink as she pulled the vehicle back into traffic.

"Oh, no, Milo?"

"Not saying a word."

But the grin on her face told me the truth.

"Good, keep it that way," I said with a laugh as I opened the folder back up and looked at the sheet. There was an RSVP thing at the bottom. I supposed Trish could confirm I was going.

"Well?" she asked as I put the folder back where it had been.

"Yeah, yeah. I'll go. It's part of working for Rico."

"Good. Besides, once you're totally unveiled, I've got a few spots we can hit, too. I was an 'it girl' once myself, you know." She laughed as we pulled in traffic.

It was true. Around her sixteenth birthday, Sorche had suddenly caught a lot of attention for a photo spread she'd done with her mom in some big magazine, and she'd been labelled the 'it girl' for a good few months until the next one had arrived, some actress with a partying habit that made JT's bad boy days look positively saintly.

Adriana.

22

Everything was pretty well taken care of for Dad's party.

Thanks to Trish and the event coordinator she'd hired, all we had to do was show up and have a good time. I invited Sor to come along—since obviously, Milo, was going to be there—and JT, too, so I wouldn't be sitting at a table all by my lonesome. Not the look for your next 'it girl.'

Besides, it gave me the perfect opportunity to wear my favorite new red dress.

I stood in the front hallway, the large package the courier had dropped off an hour before resting against my legs. Lorna had not only had the poster from the shoot framed for me, but wrapped, as well. I'd added the sparkly, black and silver metallic bow, and taped the card underneath, waiting anxiously for Dad to come down.

For once, it was me waiting for him.

I'd decided to forgive him for the other day, for missing my big billboard launch. All I knew was it wasn't worth ruining his birthday over.

"Any time now, Dad," I called upstairs, hearing the clock down the hall chime seven-thirty.

The car was going to be here soon to take us to the club for the party, and I wanted to give him the present before we left. I think that was one reason Trish had said she had things to take care of, even though the coordinator had assured us that morning that everything was perfect.

I heard his footsteps near the stairs and looked up to see him jogging down the steps, doing up the buttons on his black silk shirt.

"Happy birthday, Dad."

"Thank you, Chey." He stopped at the bottom of the stairs and smiled, glancing down at the package I was holding. "What's this?"

I carefully lifted it up. It was heavier than I expected it to be. "My present."

"You didn't have to get me anything."

"Come on, I've gotten you birthday presents since I was in diapers. Well, back then, I wasn't exactly the one picking them out."

I smiled as he took the frame from me easily and walked to the couch.

I felt a little too nervous to sit, so I pulled out my phone and snapped a few shots of him before I perched on the edge of the sofa.

"Can I open it now?"

I nodded eagerly. "Really wish you would."

He laughed and pulled the card away. I'd opted not to go sappy. Instead, it was a short and sweet, standard issue 'happy birthday' card. He smiled as he read it before he set it up on the corner table. "Chey, you didn't need to go to all this trouble."

"It wasn't much trouble."

Once the idea had hit, anyway. I was afraid I'd have to go with JT's suggestion of an assortment of car rags and waxes for the classic car, a gift which didn't seem to shout *from your loving daughter*. But JT swore it would be practical. I wasn't sure I wanted practical.

I put the phone in recording mode and watched as he tore the wrapping paper off, his eyes widening as he saw the framed poster. Not quite the one on the billboard, but instead, the first shot of the day. He stared at it in silence for a while, and I finally turned the recorder off, before putting the phone down in my lap.

The silence was starting to get to me.

"Do you like it?"

So maybe it wasn't the perfect gift I'd thought it was. I should have gone with a gift card or something a little more Dad-friendly. Maybe I should have had Trish take me down to some of his favorite stores and I could've picked up something new, something that was the latest version of something he already had. At least then, I'd know he'd be guaranteed to like it.

Or ask Trish to get something she knew he'd love. That likely would have been the safest bet.

I was ready to reach out and take the framed print away, saying something about taking it home with me, when he looked up at me suddenly and I saw the unshed tears in his eyes.

"It's beautiful." He looked down at it again, shifting the frame slightly. "*You're* beautiful."

"I thought you could hang it in your office or wherever. There's a lot of space down that hallway."

"That's the perfect place for it." He rose, the frame clutched against his chest.

"Where are you going?" I asked as he moved by me.

"The office. We might as well hang it now, right? That way, it won't get damaged leaning against the wall somewhere or lying on top of the desk where something could drop on it."

I let out an inaudible sigh and followed him past his movie posters that lined the downstairs hallway and into his office. I took the frame from him while he stood in the middle of the room, studying the walls. At last, he moved behind his desk and pulled down one of his first movie posters.

My jaw dropped as I realized what he was doing. "Are you serious?"

Okay, I *really* needed to work on that 'thinking and not speaking' bit.

"Why wouldn't I be? This way, I can show off my beautiful daughter to anyone who comes in here."

He leaned the framed movie poster against his desk and took my frame from me. Thankfully, Lorna already had it set for hanging. Within seconds, it was on the wall, looking like it had always been there.

"Looks great, doesn't it?" He leveled it a little before stepping back beside me.

I had to agree. "Looks perfect."

"Almost as amazing as you do tonight."

Dad turned and wrapped his arms around me in a tight hug, and for a moment, I felt like I did when I was a little girl, like everything was right in the world.

But the moment was broken by the sudden and loud echo of a car horn from the front of the house, no doubt the driver, tired of waiting with the limo at the gate.

"Ready to party?" Dad asked as we left the room and he turned the light off.

"Ready," I said as I took one last look over my shoulder at the poster hanging there. A definite sign that even if Dad didn't say it often, he was proud of me.

23

The limo door opened, and Dad stepped out first, turning to help me out. There were a few paparazzi outside, snapping happily away as we made our way to the double black doors of the club.

"Happy birthday, Sean," one of them called as we passed.

"Thank you."

"Who's that with you?"

Dad smiled and took my arm, posing us for the photo. "This is my wonderful daughter, Chey. She's in town to celebrate with me."

More flashbulbs went off, and I managed to smile, wishing I'd thought to wear my sunglasses against the sudden unexpected glare.

I blinked, waiting for my eyes to adjust.

"Who are you wearing?" a woman called from the corner.

I wasn't sure whether she was paparazzi or someone who just liked my dress.

"Rico Vanetti," I answered, squeezing Dad's hand tightly, feeling more than slightly overwhelmed at all the attention.

"Thanks, guys." Dad gave a quick wave, and we headed to the door that miraculously opened when we neared.

"You handled that like a pro," he confided once we were inside.

"Yeah?" Honestly, my heart was racing, and I was doing my best not to show the way my hands were shaking now that I'd let go of his.

He nodded. "Absolutely. C'mon. Let me show you off."

We walked deeper into the club, through the foyer that had HAPPY BIRTHDAY spelled out in giant silver balloons. Inside the club itself, the lights were already going above us, casting multi-colored streams on everyone below. There was a fair number of people inside, at least fifty or more that I could see milling around. Waiters in black suits made their way around, carrying trays of drinks and food. Trish had set up light snacks early on, and then the big birthday meal at midnight for those who stuck around.

I followed Dad through the crowd, nodding at a couple of now familiar faces until he stopped at one group in particular. Two actors who starred on some of my favorite shows and their wives stood there by one of the tables.

"Happy Birthday, man," one of the actors said with a big smile, giving Dad one of those one armed guy hugs. He smiled at me as he pulled back.

"Thanks, glad you guys could all make it." Dad smiled and nudged me further into the group. "This is my daughter, Chey. She's out here for the summer and just signed a really nice deal with Rico Vanetti. Some of her billboards for his new line just went up this week."

"That's great news, congratulations," one of the wives said.

"Thank you."

"Whereabouts?"

I rattled off the street where the first one went up, and she said she'd go by to take a look, congratulating me again on such a big deal, saying how much she liked Rico's work. I wasn't sure whether or not Rico wanted me unveiled per se so much yet, but I guess it didn't matter now that the boards were up. The ads would come out any day now, and as Sorche had told me in a text, my whole world was about to change. Especially when the store opened.

We chatted for a little while until I caught sight of Trish near the bar in a great little black dress, looking at her iPad. I excused myself and headed over to say hello. I knew somewhere nearby would have to be Milo, and with him, Sorche. I hadn't seen a sign of them yet, but I figured they had to be around somewhere. Sorche had texted me when she was getting ready that Milo was going to pick her up.

The club was filling with people, and I caught sight of the curved booth up front in the VIP area that served as the gift table, already covered in boxes wrapped in blue and plaid wrapping paper.

"Hey. You look great!" I said as I gave Trish a quick hug.

She really did, in a black, spaghetti-strap dress and her hair down, and even more important, she looked a lot more relaxed than I'd seen her lately. I think she was as stressed about the situation with Dad as he was.

She blushed at my compliment. "You are a liar."

"Hardly."

"Tell me, did your dad like the gift?"

I slid onto the empty stool next to hers. "He loved it. It's already hanging up in the office behind his desk."

"See. Told you it was a winner of an idea."

"You were right." I ordered a Coke from the bartender and swivelled to look around. "So, where's Milo and Sorche?"

"I lost sight of them earlier. I think they might be up on one of the VIP balconies."

"JT?"

I wasn't sure how I felt about that hopeful tinge to my voice. I liked him, but there was still that *something* I wasn't sure about. I couldn't figure out what it was. Maybe it was that whole Hollywood dynamic.

"Haven't seen him, but it's still early. Why don't you go see if you can spot Milo and Sorche up there? I'll send JT up when I see him."

"Sounds great." I gave Trish one last parting hug before heading off.

I climbed the winding staircase drink in hand, careful not to bump into anyone coming down. A few newly familiar faces passed by saying hi, and I nodded back, keeping my eyes out for my friends.

Once upstairs, it didn't take long to spot Milo and Sor, sitting a table on one of the balconies, overlooking the party below. I waved and headed over.

"Finally!" Sorche greeted me with an easy smile. "I saw you and your dad come in, but then, we lost sight of you."

I took a seat at one of high-back leather chairs at the table and set my drink down. "You guys look nice."

True to her word, Sor was wearing the outfit she'd bought at The Grove while Milo wore a black, button-down shirt and a pair of dark jeans.

"Thanks." Sor smiled as she looked back down below. "So far, no sign of the wicked witch."

"Sor clued me in about Adriana," Milo commented, making a face as he picked his cell phone up off the table. "She sounds like trouble."

"Yeah, she's definitely not one of my number one fans."

Milo grinned at me. "Isn't JT auditioning for that role?" he teased as Sorche nudged him.

"And here I thought you were heading up my fan club."

"I'll leave that to JT."

Milo left us to go wish my dad a happy birthday, and Sor and I opted to stay upstairs and people watch. It was like watching one of those red carpet shows, except live and in person without the overbearing commentary.

I propped my elbows on the railing and contemplated the top of Dad's head as he talked to a group of guys. Looked like the same ones he'd been with when I'd ditched him earlier, except a few more had joined in, that Quinn guy included. I knew I shouldn't instantly dislike the man, but I did, simply for the fact he'd stolen my dad away.

"Where's your mom?" I asked Sorche.

She gave a barely audible sigh and leaned forward, peeking below.

"Last I saw, she was heading to one of the booths." She shrugged. "You can't miss her when she reappears. Glittering gold sundress."

I snuck a small sip of my drink, watching more people stream through the doors, when my eyes locked on a tall blonde I truly didn't ever want to see join the party. Sor must have noticed her at the same time because she gave an awful nudge to my ribs.

"Ouch." I rubbed the sore spot.

"Sorry, but look who just walked in."

"I saw."

And I couldn't help but notice she'd brought the entire entourage with her. Fiona. And a couple other girls I didn't know by name, but remembered holding court at that first party. The same ones who'd been giving me the dirty looks even then. What were they all doing there?

The invitation had likely just been for Adriana's parents, which Adriana I guess interpreted as anyone else they felt like including. Including her and anyone who worshipped her enough.

A sudden warmth against my back caught my attention, and I turned my head to see JT there.

"Joining the party, or just sightseeing?" he asked as he squeezed in next to me, wrapping his arm casually around my shoulders.

"I'm being social."

"Looks more like anti-social." He smirked at me. "Quite the turnout, huh?"

"Looks like it." I studied the growing crowd below.

The DJ had jacked up the volume on the music, and I was suddenly glad we were up there instead of in the midst of the growing swarm of people below. I remembered Trish saying the place could hold up to five hundred. At the time, I'd thought that would leave us with a lot of empty space, but now, I was thinking we were going to be cramped.

This was a far cry from the birthday parties I was used to at home where the biggest amounted to a few dozen packing into someone's backyard for a pool party.

"Come on, let's join the party." JT pulled on my hand, tugging me to my feet.

I took a look around VIP. There wasn't that many people up there yet.

I looked at Sorche, who was already adding the reserved sign to the middle of our table with my name on it.

"Why not?" I grabbed Sorche's arm, pulling her with us. If I had to face Adriana, I didn't want to do it alone.

We were actually having a really good time, the four of us danc-ing near the DJ booth. He'd begun to play a list of Dad's thirty-nine favorite songs, including a dozen or so I'd never heard before. I fig-ured Trish had done a lot of research until Milo confided he'd 'bor-rowed' Dad's iPad and scrolled through it 'til he'd found a favorites' list.

I laughed and danced with Sor to a classic Madonna song. We hadn't spotted 'her evilness' once, and I was glad to just enjoy the party with my friends. I saw Dad a couple times, dancing to a few of the songs before heading to a table around the dance floor, alt-hough I didn't see Trish anywhere around. I hoped she wasn't 'working' tonight. She'd put enough work in for this party with the planner, and she should have been with Dad, enjoying everything.

Sor and I left JT and Milo on the dance floor, and I grabbed a glass of something from a passing waiter, downing half of it in a single gulp before I felt the fizzy burn of the champagne down my throat.

Sorche laughed at my suddenly wide eyes. "Let me guess, not the sparkling water you thought it was?"

"Far from it." I laughed and set the empty glass down as we inched through the crowd. I was feeling hot from the sudden crowd of bodies around us, and the thought of a splash of cold water sounded like Heaven.

"I think I'm going to go check my make-up," I said to Sor as she grabbed a glass from a passing waiter.

"Okay. I'm going to wait here for Milo..."

I found the glossy black door for the women's room down a small, narrow hallway and pushed my way in. Oddly enough, it wasn't that crowded, and I went to the backside of the double bathroom where there wasn't anyone.

A couple handfuls of icy water later, I was feeling a lot more like myself and ready to go find JT when I heard the door open on the other side of the room followed by the clicking of heels on the tile floor. I was about to make my move for the door when someone spoke.

"You know why she got picked, don't you?"

I tensed, immediately recognizing the voice.

Adriana—the star of several of my recent nightmares.

Don't panic, I told myself, trying to find a spot to disappear into so they wouldn't see me if they peeked around the edge.

I scanned the area quickly, trying to find either a route of escape, or a place to hide.

No escape.

But there thankfully was a place to hide.

A whole line of empty stalls.

I tiptoed as quietly as possible towards the closest one that wouldn't be visible from the other side of the room, sliding gratefully inside and out of sight, closing the door silently. I held my breath, praying it wouldn't make a sound.

Thankfully, not a single squeak.

I pressed my suddenly sweaty palms against the chilled metal of the door and strained to hear what was going on while praying I wouldn't have to breathe for the next several minutes.

Of all the luck, I would have to be in the washroom when *they* walked in.

Why did I have to have the worst luck in the world when it came to Adriana?

"She's a good-looking girl."

Well, thank you, Fiona.

"This city is *full* of beautiful girls," Adriana said, her annoyance coming through loud and clear. "If her daddy wasn't who he was, she'd be just another wanna-be clinging to Sorche and throwing herself at JT's feet."

Hey! I didn't throw myself at JT. If anything, it was the other way around. He pursued me, thank you very much. I wished these two would hurry things up. My legs were starting to hurt from the weird way I was standing, my legs spaced wide apart so I could hopefully not be seen.

"Her daddy?" Fiona asked.

"You don't know?"

Evidently, there were some advantages to keeping Mom's name.

"He's..."

I heard something drop on the counter, and I clenched my firsts to keep from giving in to my urge to open the door *just a little* and peek out. Couldn't they hurry this little convo up? I mean, as much as I loved hearing people bitch about me, it was tiring, especially in these heels.

I took a quick breath and hoped no one would decide to head my way. I didn't need to be discovered like this by the bitch brigade. I could just imagine Adriana's scathing comments.

"He's hot."

"Please. He's past his prime. He should be doing infomercials or something."

I rolled my eyes, my nails digging into my palms to keep myself silent. I had a great remark in mind about her only starring role being in *Girls Gone Wild*, but that'd give me away.

And I didn't want that.

I heard a click that I figured had to be her compact.

Finally.

Maybe now, they'd leave. The room would be good; the club even better.

"Let's find JT. I know I saw him earlier. Maybe we can talk some sense into him."

I heard their heels clicking once again across the tiles, and I waited 'til the door slammed shut to take a deep breath. No sounds filled the washroom, so I risked leaving the bathroom stall.

I went to the sink and washed my hands before I pulled my comb out of my purse, trying to fix my hair. Or more to the truth, calm my nerves and keep myself from going after little Miss Hollywood.

I just had to hope Fiona and Adriana weren't about to make a return appearance.

I'd just put my comb away when the door opened, and I jumped at the sudden intrusion. My heart thudded wildly in my chest as the footsteps neared the corner, and I squeezed my eyes shut, not wanting to see Adriana finding me.

"There you are!" Sorche called, and within moments, she was standing beside me.

My heart rate slowed in relief as I glanced at her in the mirror, hoping she wouldn't notice how freaked out I really felt at the moment.

"I wondered where you disappeared to. I peeked in here earlier, but it didn't look like anyone was here. JT's talking to your dad, so I knew you two hadn't run off."

I managed a weak smile as I rooted through my clutch.

"I went outside for some air," I lied.

Sor looked at me like I was completely zoning her out, which I kinda might have been. "Chey?"

"Sorry."

"Did something happen?"

Hmmm. No, just high school gossip reaching a whole new level of bitchiness. Adriana should patent it; she'd make a fortune. Or another one.

"I think I want to go home," I said as we left the restroom and headed back towards the party.

"Why?"

Why? Because I wasn't so sure Adriana wasn't plotting my untimely demise, that's why. There were way too many balconies in this place I could end up toppling over while she sipped her drink and made shocked expressions when I plummeted to the ground. I'm sure she'd even deliver a touching eulogy while hitting on JT and managing to convince Rico of her potential to replace me.

I wouldn't put it past her to volunteer to Photoshop her face on my body herself.

Yeah. She should win an Emmy for outstanding younger actress in the role of a...

"Chey!"

Great. Dad. I couldn't escape him. It was his party, after all.

"Hey, there." I pressed a kiss to his cheek. "How's my favorite birthday guy?"

He smiled. "Good. Even better if I could grab a couple pictures with my beautiful daughter." He looked at Sorche. "Mind if I steal her away for a few?"

"All yours. I'll find her later."

Sor waved as we moved away, and the crowd swallowed her up.

I followed Dad through the crowd towards where Trish waited alongside a photographer, cameras in hand. I noticed a few other more 'official'-looking photographers loitering about and tugged down the hem on my dress. More butterflies. I still wasn't used to being in that big of a crowd and possibly having every set of eyes in the room directed my way.

As we walked, he grabbed two champagne flutes from a passing waiter and pressed one into my hand. A quick look told me he had the real stuff while mine wasn't fizzy in the least, unlike my earlier drink.

LISA CARDWELL

"Go over. I'll be right there," Dad promised as someone called his name and he gave me a nudge towards them.

I joined Trish at the bar where she seemed to be spending most of the night. "Has the cake arrived yet?"

"They're prepping it in the kitchen. Takes a while for that many candles, you know."

We both laughed and turned to look at Dad talking away with a fellow actor I'd seen on TV tons of times.

"Your dad said you seemed down earlier." Trish glanced at me.

I sighed and looked down into my flute of white grape juice that Dad had handed me and wished I'd grabbed one of the flutes of real champagne instead. Yeah, I knew that whole 'alcohol doesn't solve problems' speech; yet, at that moment...

I'd love something to take off my Adriana-induced edge.

"I'm trying to keep a smile on my face. It's Dad's party."

"What's going on?"

I debated on telling her the truth, but I figured she'd get it out of me, eventually, so why waste time? "You know Adriana?"

"Name's familiar. Point her out to me."

I wished I didn't have to. I looked upwards at the balconies and alcoves above us. I spotted her immediately, my eyes narrowing as I saw who she was laughing with.

JT.

As in *my* JT.

A total moment of possessiveness flooded over me, but she'd torn me apart, at least verbally. Wasn't I supposed to get the guy, in the end? Or was L.A. that warped that a good girl couldn't get the guy?

I pointed her out as quickly and discreetly as possible so she wouldn't see.

"Ah, yeah, I recognize her." Trish turned to look at me. "What's the problem?"

I leaned in close and gave her the abbreviated version of her showing up pretty well uninvited as far as I was concerned, concluding with Adri tearing me to shreds and now cozying up to my...JT.

Trish glanced back up at the balcony and shook her head, clearly not impressed with what she heard. "She's just jealous, Chey."

That much was obvious.

She set her glass down on the bar top. "Look, don't let her get to you. All she wants is attention. Don't waste yours on her."

Dad came over then, halting the conversation, which I was thankful for. "You finally ready to take some photos?"

"Absolutely." I took his hand and followed him over to where the backdrop for the club was set up.

We posed for a handful of pictures, the perfect distraction for two women in matching black pantsuits to come out with the cake on a rolling table. I joined in as everyone sang 'Happy birthday', but my jaw dropped as I saw the second cake, the one that read '*Happy Eighteenth Chey*' on the cart beside his, eighteen silver and gold candles burning brightly, just waiting for me to extinguish them.

Dad wrapped an arm around my shoulders. "Surprise!"

I managed a weak smile as another set of flashbulbs went off. Surprise, all right.

Soon, Dad and I were busy cutting the first slices while the two women who'd brought the cart out stood nearby, ready to take over. Sor held the two plates out beside me, and I caught a glimpse of Adriana lurking behind her. I slid the pieces of cake onto Sor's plates and contemplated practicing my knife-throwing skills and aiming it at Adriana.

Instead, I plastered a fake smile on my face. "Did you want a slice?"

She peeked over Sor's shoulder.

"I couldn't possibly eat a slice that big, Chey." Picture wide-eyed, innocent blink here. "That would last me a week."

Yeah, right.

I wanted to take the few steps towards her and strangle her pretty little neck, but Sor must have sensed my thoughts because she shoved a plate in my hand and grabbed my arm before I could take my first step towards a midnight mug shot.

"C'mon." Sorche lead me away.

"Damn, she's annoying." I fought the urge to look back over my shoulder. I didn't want to see her gloating face that she'd driven me away from my own cake-cutting.

"Makes her night to see you all riled up." Sor stopped in front of a booth with a silver 'reserved' sign on it. I slid into the black leather banquette and Sor followed, obviously wanting to keep an eye on me.

"What is her problem?" she asked as we caught Adriana's attention focused our way.

I turned away.

"I'd go with I exist, the fact I'm here and breathing, and not to mention the 'Face of Vanetti' as the icing on her cake."

Sor giggled.

"I think you nailed it." She pushed her fork through the cake on her plate. "On to better subjects, what did you wish for?"

"What do you mean?" I cut a forkful of my own cake and took a bite. I was guessing this was the white chocolate Trish had mentioned as a back-up when she'd asked for my opinion on a cake tasting. Sneaky woman.

"When you two blew out the candles back there."

"Honestly?" I'd forgotten to wish for anything when I blew out the candles. I'd been a little too surprised to think of something. "Nothing."

"Only you would forget to make a wish."

"What else could I wish for?"

"I thought for sure Adriana being led out of the party by security would be number one on your list."

Now, it was my turn to laugh. "Hey, do you have a lighter? We can grab a fresh slice of cake and one of those candles and have a do-over?

JT chose that moment to slide in across from us at the table. "So this is where the party's at, huh?"

"For the moment. At least 'til her royal highness of bitchiness takes off." Sor toyed with the straw in her drink. "She unnerved Chey so much, she forgot to make a wish."

I rolled my eyes as JT raised a questioning eyebrow in my direction. He stole my fork and helped himself to my slice of cake. Never mind the fact he could have just headed over to where the two women were still cutting slices for the hungry party guests.

"You guys don't need to baby-sit me," I offered.

I was sure she'd rather be hanging out with Milo than me at the moment. I wasn't exactly radiating 'happy party girl' vibes. Like I said, my acting skills hovered somewhere around nil.

Sor laughed. "Who said we were babysitting?"

JT nodded, forkful of cake halfway to his mouth.

"Besides, I prefer the term bodyguard." He grinned. "Emphasis on *body*."

I laughed and took another sip of my drink. "What could she do?"

Really, other than ruin an evening with her mere presence.

Milo arrived at our table a few moments later, and I slid around the curve in the booth so he could sit beside Sorche, and I ended up beside JT.

"Where have you been?" I asked.

"Arranging a little birthday present for you."

"What?"

He smiled. "Notice anything, or maybe, *anyone* missing?"

I scanned the crowd. Dad still stood near the bar talking away, Trish beside him. So it wasn't them. "No clue."

He smirked. "Oh, come on. Who *don't* you see?"

Sor grinned, catching on before I did. "You didn't?"

"I did."

My mouth fell open slightly as I looked back around the room. "You got rid of Adriana?"

If he had, I'd never liked him more.

Milo nodded, leaning forward to be heard over the music. "Happy Birthday. Mom thought she was bringing the evening down after you left the cakes, so I went over with one of the bouncers and asked her and her group *politely* to leave. This is a private party, and they weren't on the list."

"No way!" I laughed. "Milo, they *were* invited. Well, her parents, anyways."

"They left after a few protests. But Mom said to tell you to enjoy your night, and we don't have to stick around if we don't want to. Happy Birthday."

I couldn't help laughing. "Let's get a fresh round of drinks."

Because suddenly, I was back in a celebrating mood.

Two rounds of sodas and a sip of champagne later, I was ready to go. Dad and I did a few more photos, and it looked like he and Trish had settled in to partying for the night since they were finally dancing by the DJ booth, his favorite songs being replayed.

Sor and Milo were planning on hanging around for a while. I think Milo was too interested in the big midnight meal to leave before it.

"Shall we go?" I asked JT as we left the noisiest area of VIP.

"Why not?" He smiled, taking my hand. "I've got a few ideas where we can go."

"Great, let's get out of here. I could use some air."

We walked outside the club into what looked and seemed like at least fifty flashbulbs going off. I lifted my hand to block the un- natural white flashes that kept springing in my front of my eyes like fireworks. It seemed like the number of paparazzi outside the club had multiplied since Dad and I arrived.

"JT, is this your new girlfriend?" someone shouted.

"Isn't she—"

"How was your father's party, Cheyenne?" someone else called.

Apparently, the only one in this crowd who had done his homework—or bothered arriving on time.

I was aware of JT grabbing my hand, and suddenly, we were off.

"Can you run in those?" He ducked his head near mine as he motioned to my brand-new heels.

"Sure." I laughed. I hoped. Well, it was a unique way to break them in.

He flashed me a devious grin, and just like that, we were mara- thon runners taking off on the final stretch. I could hear a few peo- ple chasing behind us, their shoes echoing on the pavement. A rush of fiery adrenaline shot through my body, helping me pick up speed and keep up with JT. I couldn't help laughing at the absurd- ity of all this. I almost risked a glance backwards, wondering how far they planned on chasing us.

And for what?

I had no clue where JT was headed. I still didn't know where we really were. If we survived this, I was going to sit down with a map of the city and really, *really* study it this time. No more just blindly following the GPS system for me. All I knew was I was holding onto his hand for dear life, praying I didn't stumble over a crack in uneven sidewalk.

We ran for what seemed like forever, or at least two and a half blocks, before he pulled me into a tiny alley. We chased halfway down before going inside an open door. I blinked, startled to find us in the middle of a small restaurant.

JT smiled at a passing waiter who must have been used to crazy, out of breath celebs running from the crazed paparazzi—or at least, JT's sudden appearance.

"Kitchen's open," he informed us as he carried two plates of something that smelled delicious past us.

We headed down a small hallway and through the swinging kitchen door. We weaved through the tall silver racks of pots and pans, skirted around waiters carrying plates, and emerged out of breath into another side alley. "Where are we?"

He grinned and pointed across the street. "Parking lot."

I saw his car in clear view and smiled. "You're insane."

His eyes lit up, and I glanced behind me. In the far off distance, I could see a couple cars heading slowly down the alleyway, no doubt on the prowl for signs of us.

"That'd be our search party. C'mon."

We ran for his car. Thankfully, he had a convertible, too, so he could jump over the driver's door. With me in a dress, there was no chance of that, so he had to lean over and unlock my side. I slid in, and he pulled the roof up as the car lurched forward.

"Stay low..." he said with a boyish grin as we zoomed out of the parking lot and into traffic.

I slid down a little bit in the passenger side, double checking my seatbelt. "Does this happen often?"

I strained to see out the back window, but it was hard to look over my shoulder when JT kept turning every block or two. Finally, I gave up and decided to stare at my side mirror, watching for any signs of our followers.

He laughed, reaching over and patting my leg reassuringly for a second before putting both hands back on the wheel. "Don't worry. I took a stunt driving class last year."

I'm not afraid to say my heart leapt into my throat with those words.

"Did you pass?" I swear he took that last turn onto the interstate on two wheels. *Two.*

I just knew we were going to end up...oh, I didn't even want to think about it, our photos on the ten o'clock news, pictures of a fiery crash in the background.

"What do you think?"

Truthfully? I didn't want to think. Or open my eyes to see the cars we were leaving in the dust. I heard his laugh echo around me.

"So stunt driving is a regular part of your repertoire?" I managed to ask between taking big, hulking breaths of air. I was pretty sure I'd been panic-attack-free for nearly eighteen years, give or take twenty-seven days.

Leave it to JT to break that record.

"Jeez, Chey. Relax. You're a little tense."

A little? Ha!

"It's not every day I'm being chased by paparazzi with a wanna-be stunt driver at the wheel."

"Now who said I wanted to be a stunt man? Sure, I like driving, and I like speed, doesn't mean I want to spend the rest of my life as stunt guy. Racing cars, maybe."

We rounded one more corner, and my shoulder knocked into his.

I had to admit I liked his voice. Kinda soothing. Kinda, well, kinda likeable. Which was trouble. I didn't want to like him. I didn't care if he planned to frame our no-doubt future tabloid cover or make the paparazzi photos his lock screen. I wanted nothing to do with the biggest pain in the ass I'd met in my life—or so I kept telling myself.

Not matter how many butterflies were unleashed inside me every time he was around. Or when I heard his voice. Or how I had the silliest urge to smile every time he said my name.

"We'll be fine soon."

"Great." I peeked around, seeing the unfamiliar scenery flashing by. "Where are we headed, anyways?"

"You ever been to Malibu?"

"The closest I've been to Malibu is Malibu Barbie, and that was almost a decade ago."

He looked at me and broke out laughing, and I found myself smiling at the sound.

"Well, then let me be the first to introduce you to what it has to offer."

24

JT walked us through the dark, three-story beach house, and I gratefully pulled my shoes off as we reached the back sliding doors. He slid them both open, and suddenly, we were just a few feet away from the sand and ocean.

"Wow."

He smiled at me. "You like?"

"It's nice." Total understatement. Amazing wouldn't even quite cover it, but I didn't want to sound too in awe.

"Go grab some sand or a chair. I'll get us some drinks."

I stepped outside into the warm night air and set my shoes down on one of the chairs by the doors. Taking a few steps off the warm stone patio, I smiled as my feet touched the cool sand. Instinctively, my toes curled, and I sighed happily as I took a few more steps towards the water. I was tempted to wade straight out 'til the waves lapped against my legs.

I heard JT come up behind me, and I turned to see him holding out a bottle of iced tea.

"So, where are we?" I asked, hoping we weren't exactly in the midst of a B and E.

He grinned and threw his arms out. "My place."

"Right," I said, taking a seat on the sand far enough away from the water to avoid getting wet and opened my drink. After that chase, my mouth was like the Sahara.

Dry as the sand that surrounded us.

Hs shrugged as he sat down beside me, opening his own drink and taking a gulp. He seemed as thirsty as I was.

"Seriously. After my last time in rehab, Mom and Dad thought I could do with a getaway from the L.A. lifestyle. They thought being away from everything would be good for me. So here I am."

"They do know how close Malibu is to Los Angeles, right?"

I heard him laugh as I watched the waves lap at the sand. The chase seemed hours ago, although my heart still wasn't beating its regular rhythm. I kept waiting for someone to pop out of nowhere with a camera.

"'Course. But this way, I could look like I still had my independence, and they could pop in and check up on me unexpectedly. Or send their friends to do it for them." He pointed to the two neighboring houses that were dark. "Trust me, my first month here, I had more people showing up just to say hi than I did in L.A."

I smiled. "My mom would do the same thing."

He set his drink beside him in the sand and leaned back on his elbows. "Sorry about before, you know...the chase and all. You're not exactly dressed to go running around the city."

I brushed my hair out of my eyes as I turned to look at him. "It's not your fault. I guess we could have left separately."

Although I wouldn't have ever guessed just walking outside of the club together would have caused the scene it had.

"Or out the back way." He smiled as he looked at me. "You know, I don't think Rico ever pictured that dress seeing the sand."

I laughed, looking down at the fabric spread out around me, the tiny grains of sand creating patterns where it lay. "Yeah, me, either. But it's only dry sand. Can't do much damage, right?"

"Right."

We sat there in silence a while, finishing off our drinks.

"You want me to take you home?"

"It's early yet, isn't it?"

I saw his watch light up as he checked the time.

"Almost one-thirty."

I had a feeling Dad's party was still going strong, which meant no one would be home to see what time I came through the door. "You mind if we stay here a bit?"

"Cool with me. You hungry? I know the fridge is stocked."

"Another drink, maybe?" I handed him my empty bottle as he got to his feet.

"You got it."

Two more iced teas later, I was relaxed and could almost forget about that entire party—including Adriana—and the scariest car ride of my life. I left JT in the sand and headed out into the water, lifting the bottom of my dress so it wouldn't get soaked. It was so surreal to be standing there in the moonlight, in the middle of Malibu, of all places.

I saw JT coming towards me in the water. "Your pants are gonna get soaked."

"Don't care." He came towards me. "You know, Rico had the total wrong idea with that photo shoot."

The smile froze on my face.

"What do you mean?"

My heart thudded loudly in my ears, and I wasn't sure I wanted to hear the next words out of his mouth.

"This right here would've made the most amazing shot." He pulled his phone out as if to illustrate the point and snapped a few pics.

I laughed, wedging my dress between my knees before cupping my hands together to throw water at him. "You had me thinking you were on the Adriana side of the fence all of a sudden."

"Please." He tucked his phone away before aiming a handful of water at me, which I tried to sidestep and almost ended up toppling over. Before I could fall butt first into the ocean, JT's hand grabbed mine and hauled me back to my feet.

"Thanks," I said a little breathlessly.

"Wouldn't want to see you hurt," he said softly. "C'mon, I better get you home before sunrise."

I let him hold my hand as we reluctantly waded out of the water and back towards the house. "You know, for a second date, I'd say it *almost* topped the first."

"Second, huh?" He smirked at me.

I nodded, grabbing my shoes and looking back at the water longingly, wishing I could spend the night just stretched out on the sand with JT.

25

I groaned as Trish whirled the blender.

"Sorry," she apologized. "It'll just take a couple seconds."

I glared at the appliance that was waking me up more than the weak cup of coffee beside me.

"I wanna die," I wailed, burying my face in my arms.

I wanted to crawl back upstairs and hide under the covers until this feeling of doom and gloom passed. It felt like I'd barely gotten any sleep last night, or actually, more like this morning.

JT and I had stopped at an all-night place on the way home for an early breakfast where I found out Sor had been texting me like crazy since we'd left. Apparently, there were already rumors out about our little run-in outside the club. I was lucky I fell asleep at all. My total hours of sleep came in at a whopping three since Trish came in and knocked on my door to wake me up. Obviously, she had no idea how much I needed the extra hour or two.

I wondered if Trish had slept at all. She looked comfy and wide awake in her T-shirt and jeans.

"Isn't today the weekly phone call?"

"Oh, no..." I rasped.

Did I sound hung over? Probably. But I wasn't, just majorly sleep-deprived. That run had tired me out. I could sleep for a week if someone would let me. But I already knew I couldn't. And an afternoon snooze by the pool totally didn't sound bad to me. I'd even turn off my cell and ignore any calls from Sorche if I had to.

"Have you told her yet?"

I blinked and took a sip of the coffee, hoping it had somehow gotten stronger in the last few minutes. No luck. I pushed it away. "No."

"Chey!"

"What? I know, I know. It's time she knows what I've been up to out here. But..." I rested my chin on my folded arms and looked at her pouring out the fruit smoothies.

"You're afraid."

"Wouldn't you be?"

I caught her smile before she banished it away as she set the frothy strawberry concoction in front of me. "Much healthier than coffee."

"You've been hanging around Dad too much." But I took a sip of it, anyway. "She could blow a fuse."

"She'd have every right, but I don't think she will. Just tell her the truth."

"She's going to wonder why Dad let me do this."

"Because you're a seventeen-year-old girl, Chey, weeks away from eighteen. You deserved the chance to see what comes of it. If you were my daughter, I'd be proud of you."

"Want to adopt me?" I flashed a smile my orthodontist would have been proud of.

"Chey..."

"Fine, fine. Maybe I'll see if I can catch her online before she has a chance to call."

"Sounds like a good idea."

I grabbed my smoothie and headed back upstairs, wishing I could just throw myself back in bed instead of staying on mom-daughter duty.

I shut my bedroom door behind me and headed for my cell phone lying on my dresser, charging away. I turned it on and texted Mom a quick message that maybe we could Face Time? I set up my tablet and debated going out on the balcony, but the bright sunlight was a little too much for sleep-deprived me.

I put my smoothie beside me and got comfortable in my desk chair, waiting for her inevitable arrival. Part of me hoped that she wasn't going to log on, that she'd text back and say she was out running errands and she'd call when she got home.

But my news wasn't something I really felt like breaking over the phone, either.

The advantage of Face Time was I could see the potential disappointment on her face, not having to try to read her lengthy silences blind like I'd have to over the phone.

Suddenly, there was that familiar noise that she'd logged on.

Too late to chicken out and head downstairs.

In seconds, we were connected.

"Chey!"

At least, she looked happy to see me. Her dark blonde hair looked freshly highlighted and was pulled back with one of those large plastic clips we shared.

"Hi, Mom. How's things?" I figured start small and work my way up to 'hey, guess who got their own billboard this week?'

"Good. Quiet around here without you."

I smiled. Probably a good quiet.

We did the standard small talk—work, weather—and glossed completely over the topic of Dad before finally, I figured it was better to just spit it out and tell her. It would save my already fragile nerves.

"What's wrong?" she asked after one too many lengthy silences on my part.

"Now why would you think something's wrong?" I took a break by gulping down some of my strawberry smoothie.

"Because you look worried."

More anxious, actually. And nauseous.

"And your hair's changed."

I smiled, glad she could tell even though it was just an inch here and there and the streaks were meant to be more subtle rather than wham-bam in your face. "There's something I have to tell you."

"Oh, great. What's your father done now?"

"Daddy hasn't done anything." I played with my silver ring Mom had given me for my last birthday. "I uh..."

I cleared my throat and watched the cursor blink as it hovered over the *share file* button.

"I kinda got a job," I said as I clicked on it before I could back out and change my mind.

Mom was silent for a moment. "Doing what?"

"Modeling." Okay, so it wasn't the whole story, but I was working up to my new 'it girl' status. Really, I was.

She didn't move. And the only way I could tell she'd heard me was that little vein on the side of her neck began to twitch like it did when she was trying—unsuccessfully—to control her emotions.

"Chey..." There was a distinct audible sigh from her end. "How long's this been going on?"

I took another sip of my smoothie. "Not long. I did a charity fashion thing with Sorche a little while after I got here. Rico liked my look, and things sort of went from there, but really Mom, not long. Things sorta sped up the last little bit. It was like a blur between my shoot and my billboard went up this week and..."

So that last little bit ran together, and if she understood a word of it, I'd be stunned.

"Billboard?"

Good thing Mom understood Chey speak, I guess.

"Yeah. Rico was thrilled with how the photo shoot went, and—" I noticed she'd okayed the file transfer. "Sorche took the video. We went to watch it go up."

I let the *we* stay ambiguous. She didn't need to know Dad had missed my big moment. And she didn't need to know exactly when the billboard had gone up, either. I held my breath as she stayed silent for a few moments, then I heard the clip start to play.

Two minutes and forty-four seconds later, I caught the small smile on her face.

"Well?" I fought the urge to run from the room, not knowing what her reaction was going to be.

"You look beautiful, Chey. I only have one question. Make that two."

I braced myself. "Ask anything."

"Did your father have anything to do with you getting this?"

"None. All me. Rico saw me out with Sorche at that charity fashion show and thought I'd be perfect for his new line. The only thing Dad did was look over the contract for me and have his lawyer do the same."

"Then why didn't you tell me?"

I met her gaze straight on through the webcam. "Honestly? I was afraid you'd say no."

And pull the plug on my summer. Which could still happen, I realized as I bit the inside of my lip, waiting for her reaction.

There was another loud, audible sigh that seemed to echo in my room. "Chey, you're old enough to start making choices on your own."

Really? Since when? But I knew way better than to ask that. "So it's okay?"

She gave a slow nod.

"Send me some of the pictures if you have access to them, I'd love to see them." She looked like she was studying me intently. "I want you to have fun."

"I am." Most of the time. "Dad and I took some photos together at his party last night, so..."

"I'll probably see them somewhere." She smiled and gave a little head shake. "You're growing up, Chey. We've all got to get used to that."

I laughed a little. "So really, you're cool with everything?"

"As long as it's what you want and you're still hanging out with your dad, I'm fine."

I nodded quickly. "Definitely what I want."

And fingers crossed on the last one.

26

"Brought you something," Sor announced as I opened the front door to find her standing there, a large white cardboard box in her arms.

"What?"

"Let me in, and you'll find out."

I stepped back and waved her inside.

"Aren't you at least going to give me a hint?" I asked as I followed her back towards the kitchen.

She laughed and looked at me over her shoulder. "You're worse than a three-year-old."

Was not.

I was overtired. Exhausted. I'd been hanging out with JT pretty much every day this week since the party. We'd hit Malibu, hung out at his beach house, and played in the surf most of the week. I had a heck of a real California tan going for my efforts.

She set the box on the kitchen table and stepped back.

"Voila," she said with an exaggerated flourish.

I raised a questioning eyebrow and lifted the lid back to find the cover of a tabloid printed on the icing covering the large sheet cake. I leaned closer, not quite believing my eyes. Front and centre on the tabloid were none other than me and JT. Oh, this was a joke, right? It *had* to be a joke. Sor had found a pic somewhere and done a little work with Photoshop.

Because there was just no way...

Sorche laughed at the look of awe on my face. "I figured we had to celebrate such a historic event, no?"

"This is real?" My voice came out a rasp, and I stole a glance at her before looking back down at the cake.

"Oh, yeah. It'll be on every newsstand."

"Great." I was *so* not amused.

Who could blame me? This was just going to prove to Mom that I wasn't handling this summer out here like I'd promised her I would. She may have okayed me modeling. She'd probably thought the headline of 'Chey all grown up' on the ET website with the inset of me as a three-year-old perched on my father's shoulders at the beach was cute. But this? No way. I could almost picture her making her plane reservations as I stood here staring at the cover of a tabloid. *My* cover, to be exact. JT and I in full running mode, with a smaller inset picture of Dad and I arriving at the birthday party earlier.

"Relax, it's an advanced copy."

Like that helped any. I let out a dejected sigh and felt myself deflate a little.

"Autograph my copy, will you? I think I'll have it framed." She pulled an actual edition of the tabloid out of her tote bag, along with a silver marker. "I was thinking personalizing it would be best. After all, a simple *Chey* doesn't convey the deep meaning of our friendship."

I rolled my eyes. "You're a bitch."

"Yeah, yeah." She stuck her tongue out at me. "Small slice please. I'm modeling tomorrow."

I grabbed the knife from one of the drawers and cut a couple slivers of cake for us and set them on the plates Sorche had grabbed from the plate stand. Dad and Milo could obliterate the rest of the cake whenever they got back later.

"Here, let me read this to you."

"Oh, no. You mean there's more?"

Sor just smiled as she took the magazine and flipped it open to a page, probably already having the page number memorized.

"'All grown up. Where has Chey been hiding? Last we saw Sean's little girl, she was still in the single digits and taking in Disney movie premieres in full princess regalia'."

"Tell me there isn't a picture," I pleaded, leaning over to see that there wasn't one of me dressed up like Cinderella or Snow White gracing the glossy pages.

"Shush, I'm reading," she admonished, pulling the magazine further away from my view. "Where was I? Oh, yeah... 'but now she's back with a vengeance'."

I bit my lip to keep from interrupting her again. A vengeance?

Sor continued on, pausing for only a small nibble of cake. "Between the *House of Vanetti* billboards and a potential romance with reforming bad boy JT...she's also been spotted shopping at The Grove with fellow Hollywood daughter, Sorche..." She lowered the magazine. "That's about it."

I grabbed the tabloid away from her and flipped through it. Saw a nice photo of JT driving away, the top of my head visible next to the blurb she'd just read.

She pulled it back from me without a word.

"And here I thought he was a half-decent driver." I took a stab at the icing.

"Amazing what they can catch with the right lens. You know I need details."

"There are *no* details. It passed in a flash. Frankly, I was too concerned with my life to remember much of it. We left the club, guys chased us, we circled a block or two, finally got in the car, and sped off. Just like any other high-speed L.A. car chase."

Yeah, okay, so that was a bit of a fib. See, not a lie. A lie was purposefully misleading someone. A fib, on the other hand... Well, it was less than that. And more about keeping some info to yourself. And that's what I wanted. Sor didn't need to know about Malibu or our four a.m. breakfast. I needed to figure out this weird relationship...yikes, did I really just use the R word? Weird. Anyway, whatever JT and I had going—because honestly, I was a bit confused, and having a tabloid call us the latest summer fling on the index page...a hot summer fling...

I was going to take my confusion out on my slice of white chocolate coconut cake.

"You know, maybe I'm just not cut out for all of this," I mused.

She swiveled back to face me. "If you're talking about Rico putting you on a billboard, deal with it."

"I can't." Look at the fallout it was causing. A nice, neat domino effect. "This was supposed to be a summer-only thing."

And I knew from Trish that Rico was already talking about extensions, and what would happen if he took the *House of Vanetti* store to NYC? I'd been sitting there for some of that conversation that night at the restaurant, never figuring it would mean anything to me.

But now...

My life might never be the same again.

"So?"

"You don't get it. You're from a Hollywood family. They'd expect this from you."

"Your dad's—"

I knew she was going to say Hollywood. Yes, he was. *I wasn't.* I was still wearing my 'hello, my name is' nametag. Or at least, it sure as heck felt like it. What did it say when Milo fit better into this world than I did? I still didn't totally feel I belonged, and I was supposed to be the next 'it girl.'

"If I didn't know that one of these days it's all going to come crashing down around me."

"Now you're being paranoid."

"I'm not. If—*when*—my mom finds out about *all* of this..." I tapped the tabloid. "She'll go off the deep end."

"Well, then I don't know what to say, except for enjoy it while it lasts?"

If only I knew how long that would be. I closed my eyes and wished I could figure things out. I thought things were supposed to get easier as I got older, not even more pathetically complicated.

Sor left a couple hours later, leaving me the remains of the cake and the tabloid cover. Two, actually. The one she'd used for the cake and the second one, which proved almost as worrying since I knew it was one magazine Mom picked up regularly.

This wasn't good.

Any way you looked at it, the fact our—or more important, *my*—photo was splashed across the cover of a tabloid did not in any way, shape, or form, to quote Martha, constitute "a good thing." Not like this was a photo of Dad and me somewhere lunching with celebs, hinting I was about to meet the newest version of mommy dearest.

I wasn't even sure that would have been as bad. I mean, I could have easily gone into the 'evil stepdaughter-to-be' mode and banished her to a kingdom far, far away. (Okay, so I'd spent last night re-watching Dad's Disney collection that he'd amassed over the years for me). But the headline of *JT finds* love *with the 'Face of House of Vanetti'* just spelled disaster. With a capital D.

Just wait 'til Mom caught wind of this.

And she would.

This wasn't a little local paper anymore, or the local news reporting on the latest gossip that she could pick up on the satellite by accident.

Nope.

This was one even my grandmother would find in the 7-11 when she stopped to buy gas.

This so didn't bode well. My life as I knew it was over.

But I had a couple reason to think—hope—this wouldn't be as bad as it seemed. Mom was on the other side of the country. However, planes existed, and she could be here in under twelve hours from the moment she found out about this.

Let's not think that way, Chey, I told myself as I got tired of pacing my bedroom and moved onto my Romeo balcony, as Sor liked to call it.

It's just one *measly photograph.*

Not like we were getting engaged, or had eloped in some drive-thru Vegas chapel. Or that some random celeb-stalker-paparazzi had caught us hooking up in the back of some other celeb's car.

There was time for damage control.

Dad could help.

Trish.

They'd know what to do. Or what to say to Mom.

I hoped.

"Glad someone finds this amusing."

Dad looked at the extra copies of the tabloid in his hand.

And when I say extra, I don't mean one or two. It looked like a good dozen or more. He must have cleaned out the entire stock wherever he'd picked them up. He wanted me to sign them, for goodness sake. What was wrong with these people? Was there something in the water in California?

"You've got to look at the bright side in all this."

"Yes, every cloud has a sterling silver, or is it platinum, lining here in Los Angeles?"

I think I earned the right to impersonate Oscar the Grouch. I mean, hello—I didn't ask for this. I didn't want half this attention in the first place. This was supposed to be my low-key summer, just hanging out with Dad. I was, however, starting to doubt low-key even existed in L.A.

He sighed, setting the issues down on one of the chairs, and I caught sight of one folded and tucked into the back pocket of his jeans.

"What's got you in such a bad mood?"

Wasn't it obvious?

He lifted the knife and cut himself a slab of cake, taking it to the table where I sat.

"Oh, I get it. He hasn't called, has he?"

Was I that transparent?

"No call. No text. Not even a damn e-mail."

I examined my metallic blue nails. Sorche had even decorated them with little happy face emojis in an effort to cheer me up. Didn't work then; wasn't working now. I mean, shouldn't he have called? Or done *something*? I knew this wasn't the 'send flowers-type' of event or anything like that, but my best friend had brought a cake.

I stole a forkful's worth of icing from Dad's plate. I just wish it'd held JT's head instead of more of the lettering. I would have gotten a bit of satisfaction of smashing his head in, even if it was just an icing version.

"You know, you could call him."

My head shot up. "Me? He's the reason why I'm on that tabloid in the first place."

"And if he didn't matter to you, you wouldn't be that upset over it."

Here we go. Dad was going to go all Dr. Phil on me and ask what my payoff was. Well, there was none. I wasn't wallowing in my self-pity just to feel good. Besides, *this* wasn't feeling good. This was misery, plain and simple.

"Why don't you go body-boarding with Milo?"

I raised an eyebrow. "Why should I?"

"Get out of the house for a while. I doubt the paparazzi would care much. It's just Milo." He smiled, obviously teasing me. "C'mon. Where's my girl who said life in L.A. wasn't going to change her one bit?"

That foolish-minded individual had gone by the wayside the minute a naked teenager had streaked by her at her first Hollywood party—the same naked teenager she was waiting to hear from. It's not like L.A. was in the midst of a blackout and he'd have to resort to smoke signals to get my attention.

What I needed was to forget all about him as fast as possible.

"Body boarding, huh?"

Dad smiled. "I'll go give him a call."

"You ever done this before?" Milo asked me.

I looked at the mini boards in the backseat. "Not a lot of chances to go boarding at home, unless it's snowboarding."

"Gotcha." He tapped his hands on the steering wheel as we sat in traffic.

So much for getting anywhere any time soon; seemed like everyone had decided today was the ideal day to hang out at the beach.

"You know, if you don't want to do this, you can drop me off somewhere. I can call Sorche. I know my dad sorta shoved me off on you," I said, feeling a little uneasy.

I'm sure Milo had better plans than chaperoning me, or babysitting, whichever way Dad had called it during their little 'men' talk while I'd loaded the cooler full of drinks and snacks into the back of Milo's car.

"It's cool, really."

"You're nearly nineteen. Why would you want to hang out with a seventeen-year-old?" Like me, I wanted to ask. I didn't exactly see him doing this out of the goodness of his heart. I'm sure Dad had had to convince him to take on a little overtime work.

"You don't act like a seventeen-year-old," he said.

I kinda took that as a compliment. "Then what do I act like?"

"Well, when you're *not* freaking out over JT or something else pretty stupid, you could pass for a semi-normal twenty-something."

"Thank you." My voice rang with sarcasm as I rolled my eyes, and I slouched down in my seat a little, glancing at the cars around us.

"You're more mature than half the girls around here, and that probably includes Sorche."

That ticked me off. I thought Sor was pretty damn mature. She just had a fun side she let loose a lot more than I did. Hers was all nice and sun-kissed, and mine leaned more towards the never quite seen daylight pale look.

"You're just jaded," I threw back.

LISA CARDWELL

"I'm jaded? You're the one who throws a tantrum anytime someone gets close to your father."

"You just called me mature five seconds ago."

"Semi-mature. And that's only in some areas." He shot me a smile. "I'm teasing. But I know what it's like. I'm the same way with my mom. It's been her and me for as long as I can remember. And honestly, 'til she finds the right guy, I'd rather it stay that way."

I smiled, happy he understood where I was coming from. "So who do you think would be the right guy?"

"I'm not getting mixed up in some crazy soap opera scheme that you've got going on in that little blonde head of yours."

"Hey, it's not a scheme. I was just seriously wondering what you thought. I think they'd make a pretty cool pair, you know."

He focused his attention straight ahead, at the puff of exhaust coming out of the Ford pick-up ahead of us. "Right."

"Okay, fine, then." I shrugged. "Keep our parents from being happy."

"Do you want a wetsuit?"

I looked behind me where Milo was stepping into a black wetsuit with a bright blue chest.

"Do I really need one?" I'd grabbed a pair of board shorts I'd worn to the beach and my tankini. I thought that would be good enough. I wasn't planning on spending that much time in the water—so I hoped. Plus I planned on staying on top of the board as much as possible.

He shrugged.

"Do you have one for me?" I headed to the back of his car.

"As a matter of fact, Mom grabbed you one when we went to the board store to get your board."

Yeah, I felt the love in that statement. People were running *my* errands; 'people' being him and Trish. Nothing more endearing to him, I was sure.

"I could have done that," I offered.

"It was one of your dad's surprises," he said, holding out a shopping bag to me.

I looked inside and found a matching suit to Milo's. "Great, thanks."

"Just slip it on over your swimsuit and grab your board. We can leave your shorts with the cooler on the beach."

Minutes later, I was all zipped in, my pretty blue and silver board under my arm as we headed down the path to the beach. This wasn't the same beach Sor and I had been hanging out at. We'd hit Huntington Beach a couple of times, and I still couldn't remember the name of the one where we'd gone for the bonfire, but it had been further south.

I was a little more relaxed as we moved out of the water a couple hours later, my hair dripping wet from the knot I'd piled it in on top of my head after the first time I'd flipped into the ocean. I wiped the water off my face, smiling to myself. So maybe Dad did have a good idea, for once. And Milo really wasn't the worst male I'd ever encountered. He almost made me forget JT for the moment.

I dropped my board on the sand as he pulled out a couple canned drinks, holding one out to me.

"You look a million times better."

"Feel it." I took the chilled can from him. "He who won't be named is the furthest thing from my mind right now."

Milo actually smiled. "Glad to hear it."

I knew I should thank Milo for the great escape, and as Mom always said, the way to any man's heart was through his stomach. As we loaded the dry gear into the back of his car, I checked to make sure I had some cash in my wallet.

"You hungry?" I asked as he slammed the trunk.

"Why?"

"Oh, gee, just thought that rumble I heard was your stomach and not the next great earthquake meant to wipe out California."

He chuckled, running his fingers through his still damp hair. He'd gone back into the water one more time than I had. "I could eat a little something."

"Good, then I'll buy—on one condition."

I swear he muttered something about women under his breath as he unlocked my door and held it open for me. "Fine. What is it?"

"We go to Pink's. I'm craving a good milkshake."

Milo gave me the biggest grin I think I'd ever seen from him. "You're on."

We sat at one of the plastic tables, framed photos covering the wall beside us. My chili fries in front of me, his hot dog and fries in front of him. It felt different being there with Milo. No one knew who we were. No one cared. Just two normal, everyday teenagers out for something to eat.

"Why film?" he asked.

We'd spent the drive back talking about ourselves more than we really ever had before, and I'd casually mentioned that I thought about maybe going into it in college.

I shrugged. "It interests me."

I dragged a fry through a river of chili before popping it in my mouth.

"Enough to make a career out of it?"

Wow, when did he turn all guidance counselor? "Why do you fill in for Trish with my dad?"

"For the money." He smiled easily. "Why?"

"I doubt it's your life's ambition."

"It's not. I haven't really decided on anything concrete yet, but this lets me make good contacts going places with your dad."

Now that surprised me. Milo didn't have his whole life planned out? I figured he was the sort of guy who had everything down to the minute.

"You didn't answer my question." He stole a chili-soaked fry and pointed it at me. "Other than film, what interests you?"

"I really don't know. I like film. Dad's in film. I could make some decent contacts that way."

"Ah, using your daddy's name." He smirked, as if he knew everything.

I straightened up in my chair, mentally picturing him covered in the chili cheese fries and milkshake. Waste of good food. "I don't use my dad's name, in case you haven't noticed."

"I forgot. Sorry." He ducked his head a little, concentrating on taking a mouthful of his soda. "Must have been a nasty divorce," he said finally.

"It was."

At least, I'm pretty sure it was. They'd had everything sealed. I don't remember much. I probably blocked it all out. I'm sure I'll have horrible nightmares about it when I'm thirty and be forced into lifelong therapy.

"How serious are you about UCLA?" he asked, and I wondered if he really didn't want to be an investigative reporter with the way he was questioning me.

I glanced at him as I added more ketchup to the side of my fries. "I guess it's in my top five. Why?"

Okay, honestly, top two. Mom had her own choices for me, all of which were nowhere near California.

He shrugged, checking his cell phone. "Curious, that's all."

"Why don't you like me?"

"What?" He dropped his cell phone on the table.

He looked surprised I'd said it, let alone thought it.

"There's a distinct coolness you have towards me. Why don't you like me?"

That had been bubbling inside me the last few weeks. So my Dad did ask him to check on me when he was away and take me out body-boarding on the beach, but it wasn't like I required a babysitter. The last time I'd had one, I'd been in the single digits, thank you very much.

So I couldn't figure this out.

Milo sighed, shook his head, checked to make sure his phone was okay, then turned back to me. "I don't dislike you, Chey."

"Oh, really."

"Yes, really. I was about to offer to take you on a tour of the campus, if you want. I took some classes there last semester."

"Oh," came my soft and deflated answer. I took a long, long sip of my milkshake. Yeah, Chey steps in it again. "I'm sorry."

"It's okay. I'm used to hormonal—"

"What?" I cut him off, not believing what I was hearing.

"I just figured you were hormonal."

Okay, first off, it *so* wasn't his business if I was hormonal or not—which I totally wasn't, by the way—but that was just plain rude. I don't care if he was going to write my application essay himself and deliver it straight to the Dean of Admissions. Milo was being a jerk.

"I think I'm done," I said, pushing the last few fries away.

"You sure?"

I nodded. "Positive."

He shrugged and grabbed my remaining fries and shoved them into his mouth before getting to his feet. "Let's go."

I didn't want to hesitate as I let myself into the house. Milo had given me a pep talk before he drove past the gates, about being the best I can be...no, wait, that's the army. I mean, he told me I didn't need JT to be with me. Which I know was true, because I'd done amazingly well in seventeen years without him. But still...I'd checked every phone line in the house, checking the missed call numbers and all the voicemails before running upstairs in case my cell phone was acting up and I'd missed a message somewhere.

I checked all my emails.

Nothing.

Not a word.

'Course, I needed to think more like a guy, if that was at all possible. To him, it would probably be no big deal. Guys didn't care about this stuff, especially the supposedly bad boys like JT. He was intensely proud of his past; where he'd gone and what he'd gone through to be where he was today. Like breathing.

The last thing I wanted to do was stick around home, feeling sorry for myself. So I grabbed my car keys, scribbled Dad a note that I'd gone out for a while, and headed for the garage.

I hadn't meant to show up at JT's.

I'd gone out for a drive, a little window shopping. Get myself a sundae from Ben and Jerry's and to pick up a couple of pieces from Rico's.

I hadn't meant to take the scenic way home.

Way scenic, actually.

I took a chance he'd still be in L.A. and not have made the trip out to Malibu for some reason.

I sat in his parents' driveway, leading up to the gates, thinking the smart thing, the wise thing, the what-I-really-needed-to-do thing, was turn my car straight back around and go home like a good little girl.

Keyword being *good*.

Except right then, I wasn't really into good.

I looked at the address on the ripped piece of paper I'd found to write on in my wallet, then back at the gated house again. Rolling down my window, I leaned out to the intercom and pressed the button. "Hello."

Great, I sounded normal. I was afraid I'd either sound timid or like an animated cartoon character hopped up on helium. Who didn't want a girlfriend who sounded like that?

"Gate's open," JT's voice replied.

Right. I slid out of park and watched as he appeared at the front of the house. I really wasn't about to go charging through the gates (new car + paint damage = unhappy Daddy) and I didn't want to rush out of the car, either.

He must have figured that out as he came jogging towards the gates and hit a button on the other side. In one steady motion, the gates retracted enough for me to go through. I coasted inside and parked in the semi-shade of a palm tree and waited.

Before I could open the door and step out of the car, he was already heading my way.

Way too late to zoom out of the driveway like my sudden case of nerves were demanding.

I rolled my window down the rest of the way, taking a quick second to check I didn't have a hot fudge mustache or goatee going. How attractive would that have been?

"Hi."

Okay, so it just happened there was a copy of the tabloid lying oh so casually discarded on the passenger seat to my right, my purse next to it.

A girl had to get her message across somehow, right?

I didn't want to sound like the typical girl, all *why didn't you call*, but I figured this totally warranted some kind of a *why* moment. I was about ready to ask *did you see...?*

But he was already leaning in the open driver's window.

"So you saw, huh?" he asked as he swiped the magazine and began thumbing through it as he stood back up.

"Couldn't miss it."

You know, what between the cake, autographing the magazine for Sorche, and then Trish's copy and Milo taking a photo of the moment to capture it for eternity. I totally wanted to steal the camera and delete it, but I didn't want to hurt Trish's feelings.

He opened my door, and I stepped out, following him back around the side of the house.

"How about we play for something?" JT grabbed the basketball he'd no doubt abandoned when I pulled up.

"Like what?"

"You win, you're officially my girlfriend. I win..."

I sighed. "You make it sound like I need a title or something."

"You don't?" He arched an eyebrow. "First, you were obsessed over the official use of the term date—"

"Hey, you were the one practically stalking me like I was your next meal," I countered.

He laughed as he tossed the basketball in my direction. "What do you say? Unless you're afraid of a challenge?"

Ha! As if. Not likely. I was more likely a little more afraid of making a fool out of myself. Basketball was *not* where I excelled. And Google had told me JT was great at it, even playing in some Hollywood Celeb charity games.

"Chey?"

"Deal." I was glad I wore my sneakers and not a pair of my heeled sandals, like I usually wore.

I dribbled the ball like I knew what I was doing, and he looked half-impressed, so I knew I must have been doing something right. Nonchalantly, I brushed past him, did one of those moves I suddenly remembered from one too many gym classes, and watched the ball bounce off the backboard.

Just once, could I have done something cool and slightly impressive and have had it go in?

The karma gods were so against me.

JT grabbed the ball, a smile on his face. "Good try."

"Yeah, yeah..."

Might as well just brand a big *L* on my forehead right now, because there really was no way that ball was going through that hoop; well, thanks to me, anyway.

I tried my best to block him from going to the net, which honestly didn't do much but cause that amused smile of his to cross his face as he easily sidestepped me and sent the ball whooshing through the net.

"Nice one."

"Thanks." He caught the ball as it headed towards the ground. "Okay, how about a little amendment. You make this shot, you're my girlfriend?"

"How about this? I *miss* this shot, you go with me to some club opening next weekend?"

"Sounds like I win either way." He bounced the ball to me. "Go for it."

I moved a little closer, dribbled the ball once or twice before closing my eyes and shooting the ball in the air, hoping it went somewhere near the net.

"Well?" I asked as I heard the ball bounce back off the pavement.

JT laughed from nearby. "What time do you want me to pick you up?"

27

Things settled down to pretty quiet after the tabloid incident, which I was really grateful for. Rico kept sending over invitations, and Trish would leave me a stack every morning on the edge of my desk. Sor would look them over and pick a few, and we'd try to hit a place or two every night, even if it was just to pop in and look around. As she said, I had to earn my Vanetti pay check somehow.

It was usually Sor and I who went to the public places; I didn't want to go out with JT anywhere we'd end up being chased, so we tended to lay low and hang around the beach, or here in the theatre room watching old movies from Dad's collection or binging something on Netflix.

And even better, we all managed to avoid Adriana. Sor and I had spotted Fiona and some of the entourage the other night at one charity party, but the wicked witch of Hollywood hadn't seemed to be in attendance. After her comments at the birthday party, the last thing I wanted was to come face to face with her again. I didn't quite need any more time with her.

"Delivery!"

I looked up from my tablet as Trish walked into my bedroom, two dress bags in hand.

"What the..." I started, turning around in my desk chair to see better.

"From Rico, apparently." She handed me a small envelope and laid the black bags on my bed. "Just arrived. Didn't you hear the doorbell?"

"Thought it was Dad's trainer." I shrugged as I studied the heavy cream envelope, my name in copper gel pen. I figured the handwriting was Lorna's, since it had a definite feminine loop to it.

"So?" Trish took a seat on the edge of my bed.

"I wasn't expecting anything," I said with a shrug, using the corner of my nail to rip the envelope open. Looked like a note inside.

"Good news, I hope."

I nodded my agreement as I pulled the paper out and unfolded it to see Rico's note.

Chey,

Wanted to give you an update on the opening. Everything is moving well, and we're about to start putting the final touches on and bring in the clothing. Reminder to keep next Friday night open since the House of Vanetti launch party will be the place to be!

And it wouldn't be the same without our <u>face</u> there.

Expect a lot of fun and a few surprises!

Sent along a couple new pieces for you. One you should recognize immediately, and the second is one Lorna said was you the moment she saw it.

See you soon,

Rico

PS: Two more billboards went up this morning!

I'd been by the store once for a tour, wearing a hard hat while the crew worked to put the finishing touches on everything so Rico and everyone could start bringing over all the boxes and racks of clothes covering the offices. It was starting to feel exciting. I couldn't wait to see all the plans I'd heard about finally come to fruition. And it was something I'd get to be a part of.

I glanced towards the dress bags. I was definitely beginning to feel spoiled.

"What's he say?"

I tapped the envelope against my hand. "Not much. Reminded me the big opening's next week, and he sent along something for me to wear to the opening."

Trish smiled. "I thought he might."

"Did you talk to him lately?"

"No, just Lorna the other day. She wanted to check your schedule for the rest of your time in Los Angeles."

Time that I was suddenly reminded continue to slip away.

"For?"

"She didn't say. But she said she'd send a couple of invites my way to the party. For your dad, too."

I laughed. "I thought maybe I'd take him as my date."

"Ask him. I'm sure he'd love it."

"Yeah." I hoped so.

Just then, her cell phone went off. After taking a quick check, she sighed. "I gotta take this. See you downstairs?"

"Yeah, be down soon."

With a wave, she left, and I turned back to checking my silent phone. I had a movie premiere to get ready for in a few hours.

That same movie premiere Dad had invited JT to; he'd also invited Sorche and Milo and Trish. I tried not to take it personally it wasn't going to be just the two of us.

Sorche was already on her way over, and Dad's stylist was going to put in a repeat performance. My dress was already hanging on the back of the closet door. I just needed to kill time.

I had to admit, walking the red carpet was really exciting. Even when it had felt nauseating for a few horrible moments when I stepped out of the car and tried to ignore the sheer number of people there.

Dad kept waving at the crowd pressed up against the barricades, signing autographs and posing for photos, of which I took a couple of him with fans when they handed me their phone as I tried not to look around in too much awe. I mean, I thought I knew what Dad's life entailed, but this...well, this was like dropping me in the middle of it without a parachute.

The few places Sor and I had gone to, we'd been pretty well allowed to wander in freely, stopping for a couple photos, but that was about it.

Finally, he moved past the fans, and we headed farther down along the carpet, closer to the step and repeat as Sor had been trying to school me in the car. At first, I was sure she'd meant *take a step and repeat your pose*, which really seemed monotonous, but then, what did I know?

Anyway, we caught up to where some other people had stopped to talk to various members of the press. I took a deep breath and looked around, rubbing my bare arm anxiously. Dad got pulled away from us towards what looked like an *Access Hollywood* reporter, so I stood quietly a bit behind him when I heard someone shout my name.

"Chey!"

It happened again.

I glanced over at a perky blonde holding a microphone in the press line and who seemed to be waving me over. I looked to Sor for silent help, and she moved up to join me from where she'd been posing for pictures.

"Look, it's Chey *and* Sorche," she practically squealed. "How is your first Hollywood summer, Chey?"

"Hot!" Sor exclaimed with a laugh and a nudge to my ribs, which made me flash my well-practiced smile.

Blondie laughed a few seconds later, dipping the microphone closer to my face. "Chey, you're making a big name for yourself around here."

I blushed, and Sor squeezed in closer next to me as a couple people pushed by us to get to different reporters. I thought I saw a glimpse of JT further down the carpet, but I couldn't be sure.

"That, she is," Sor agreed, and I was thrilled she was taking over talking.

I wasn't sure I could make my voice work at will. It seemed I had a sudden impromptu case of stage fright.

I managed a small, more realistic smile at my friend and waited for the reporter to speak again.

"So, is that dress another product of the fabulous Rico Vanetti? I swear, every time I drive down the street, there is yet *another* billboard with your face on it."

"Yes, it is."

Wow, voice worked. Amazing. Sor elbowed me and raised an eyebrow, and I did a little twirl, showing it off.

"It looks amazing. Sorche, what about you?"

Sor rattled on about her dress for a few moments and did her own twirl while I caught sight of Dad moving to a few reporters ahead of us and waved as we made eye contact. I could see the corner of his mouth twitch up in a smile as he winked and started talking to another reporter.

Finally, Blondie was done with us, and we moved down the line. I joined Dad just as JT caught up to us.

"Cheyenne! JT!"

The reporter a few feet ahead waved Dad away, and the two of us got closer. I caught the quick flash of amazement on Dad's face before he disappeared into the thickening crowd, and I wanted to go after him, but JT caught my elbow and smiled reassuringly at me, leaning in close.

"He'll be fine," he whispered, pulling me towards the reporter. "Just let him go."

"If it isn't the hottest duo in young Hollywood right now. How did you two meet?"

My stomach tightened as I heard the question, and I let JT answer, his dimples appearing, and I managed a weak smile, trying not to strain my neck and go chase after my father. The one thing to be grateful for was JT kept the 'how we met' story very PG.

There was a party, we'd bumped into each other—literally—and been hanging out ever since.

We moved through the press row, continuing to be called over every few moments and posing for what seemed like a thousand pictures before we escaped and JT went in search of something to drink while Sor and I hung outside for a few minutes longer.

"You gotta go in sometime," Sor said softly as we watched Milo head inside.

"Do I have to?" I asked half-seriously.

Without a word, she grabbed my hand and pulled me towards the entrance.

The doors shut behind us and immediately, I started looking for two people. Dad and Trish. One to apologize to, and the other to ask for guidance, because I think I'd just committed the ultimate Hollywood Daughter faux pas—never, *ever* upstage your famous parent.

My mind kept flashing back to that look on Dad's face as the reporter dismissed him and wanted *me* and JT to come over.

Me.

Little old me, whose only claim to fame was being Dad's daughter and having my face on some highly popular billboards around the city.

Sor must have sensed my thoughts. "Come on. Let's go get some good seats before they're all taken."

Somehow, we made it past the crowd through to the theatre and found Milo already holding four seats halfway down near the aisle. I waved Sor ahead of me and slid into the aisle seat so I could keep an eye out for Dad and JT.

No luck on the first one, but my date for the night came strolling down a few minutes later, a smile on his face as he spotted us.

JT slid into the seat beside me. "Relax a little."

"Easy for you to say," I mumbled.

He handed me a chocolate bar from his jacket pocket. "What could you do? Ignore them? Rico's paying you to make nice. You gotta take the good with the bad, Chey."

"Right." I toyed with the wrapper. "I should just get over it?"

"Yes. You should." He grinned. "C'mon. Let's enjoy the movie."

I leaned on his shoulder as he wrapped his arm around me. The lights overhead began to dim, and within moments, the opening started.

Somehow, I managed to spend the next ninety-eight minutes staring blankly at the screen, barely concentrating on anything. Had anyone asked, I probably couldn't have even answered a single question about the movie, including who had been in it, even though two of the stars sat mere feet away in the aisle across from us.

28

The club was packed as I stuck as close to JT as possible, my hand securely in his as we weaved through the crowd and off the dance floor where we'd spent who knew how long dancing to what was supposed to be the hottest DJ in Los Angeles.

I had to agree—he was playing the best mix we'd heard yet, and I'd hit enough places lately. While JT had been out of town for a few days, Sorche and I had made a good dent in the invitations Rico had procured for me. I hadn't been home a single night this week, which was a blessing, since Dad was still a little off after that movie premiere.

"Drink?"

"You're a mind reader." I smiled, leaning in close so he could hear me over the music. "I'll meet you back here in a sec, okay? I'm just gonna cool down and touch up my make-up."

I was so warm, I was sure my make-up was slowly melting away no matter that I'd used that setting spray Sor had had me pick up the other day.

He nodded and headed to the left and the short few stairs up to the table area, and I pressed my way through the crowds towards the bathroom. I could definitely go for splashing some cold water on my face. With so many people on the dance floor, it had started to feel like a sauna.

Thankfully, there wasn't a line going into the ladies' room. I made my way to the half empty row of sinks. I grabbed a couple pieces of paper towel and ran them under the cool water before pressing them against the back of my neck.

I glanced in the mirror. The bathroom was done in black and silver, and it was actually pretty nice, with a couple of chairs to the far corner.

I opened my clutch, checked my cell phone to see a text from Sor that her auditions had run late but were over; she was going to try to stop by, but Milo had wanted to meet up. I had a feeling she'd be skipping me for Milo.

I texted a smiling emoji back and put the phone in my bag, taking out my lip gloss and reapplying to my dry lips. I'd be so happy to sit with JT for a while and have a drink. If Sor wasn't going to show up, maybe we'd bail early. We could all meet up for a pizza or something. I'd have to run that idea by him.

I turned to go and paused, seeing who was sitting with her back to me.

Fiona.

I'd recognize that hair anywhere. I faintly heard my name mentioned. What was it with them talking about me in bathrooms?

I almost stepped forward, but then shook my head. She hadn't seen me; I didn't want to ruin my night, and I had JT waiting for me.

I made my up the short few stairs up into the seating area. The big, muscular bouncer gave me a big smile as he stepped aside to let me through. I found JT easily, commandeering a small table and two tall silver chairs just by the railing and smiled, relieved he was alone with no Adriana brigade in sight.

With any luck, they'd be more in a dancing mood, and I wouldn't have to see my least favorite person at all.

"You found a table," I said over the music.

"I did. Managed to grab it before anyone else could." He waved for me to take a seat.

I sank into the chair and took a long sip of my drink. My favorite soda. I sank back against the chair, taking another long sip. It was so nice to cool down a little.

Maybe I could talk him into leaving soon. I didn't want to risk another run-in with Adriana like I'd had at Dad's birthday, not when there were so many people and press swarming the place outside. It just reminded me how big Rico was planning on making the store opening.

Why couldn't he have just done a couple small pop-ups somewhere?

Before I could bring it up, JT's cell went off.

"I gotta take this," he said, looking at the little screen. "I'll be a couple minutes, tops."

"Don't worry about me."

I watched him walk away and head down a small side hallway I knew led out to the parking lot.

I finished off my drink while I checked my text messages and waited for him to come back. Nothing back yet from Sorche. I was about to text her to ask about my pizza idea when I was interrupted by one of the waitresses.

"Can I get you anything?"

"Two refills would be great," I said, and the waitress grabbed both our empty glasses and walked off.

I picked my phone up again, deciding to text a quick message to Sor and check the time when JT's chair suddenly slid back.

"That didn't take..." I trailed off as I lifted my head from my phone to see who sat there.

"Well, well, well...an A-list club opening. How did you ever manage that?"

I sighed, drumming my copper nails on the table top as I put my phone down. "Same way you did, Adriana. I was invited."

"I know why *I* was invited. It's you I can't figure out."

"Having the hottest billboard in town gets me in a lot of places."

"Really? Hmm..." She took a long sip of her drink, stopping a moment to study me. "You still haven't figured it out, have you?"

"Figured out what?"

The waitress was a few tables over and caught my eye before nodding at me. Hopefully, this wouldn't take much longer. 'Course, I could just walk away now. There was always that option.

There was also the option of throwing *my* drink in her face.

That was one was awfully tempting.

Adriana smiled a pure sugary smile. I almost felt nauseated seeing it.

"You're really that clueless, aren't you? That Rico just saw you and suddenly everything came together? That billboards just happened to be available in the best spots in town? Didn't it all seem a little *rushed*? Like maybe, it had all been meant for someone else?" Her eyes sparkled darkly. "You weren't the first choice, Wyoming....so enjoy your little fifteen minutes, because when it's over, *so* are you. So is Rico. And I'll still be here. And so will JT."

She took a sip of her drink then, the corner of her mouth lifting up into a smirk as she set it back down on the glossy table. "Maybe when you're old enough, you can come back and try it again. Sorta like your dad."

I knew what response she wanted—my eyes to fill with tears, maybe a trembling lower lip, and me to go running out of the club. But I'd toughened up a little in the last while, and I wasn't about to give her what she wanted most. She'd have to do a hell of a lot more to intimidate me now.

I set my hand on the table and rose out of my chair just a little and leaned towards her.

"Funny you talk about my dad like that when I haven't even seen *your* parents' names in the trades at all." I tilted my head and looked at her. "And if you were Rico's first choice, evidently, you didn't measure up. But thanks for filling in 'til I got here, because it all just went so smoothly."

My smile was pure innocence as I stood up and headed towards where I last saw JT, my head held high as I knew Adriana would be watching me go. I needed something to keep me going; I honestly couldn't believe the performance I'd just put in. Adriana had wanted to hurt me, and maybe she had when she'd pointed out how naïve I'd been when I first signed on with Rico. But weeks had passed since then, and I'd been quickly schooled in things I never would have imagined.

I walked down the hallway but he wasn't there. There was a bouncer at the end of it, and I stopped outside the restroom doors.

Maybe he'd gone outside?

I pulled my phone out and checked. Nothing from him. I texted a quick 'where are you' and leaned against the wall, where I could see the hallway and most of the club. He'd have to pass by me either way.

For a moment, I found myself wondering if that oddly timed phone call had been from Adriana. I hadn't seen whose name had been on the screen, but it seemed like just the thing she'd do. Lure my boyfriend somewhere to talk trash about me. Or have her minions do it while she trash-talked me herself.

I clicked my phone on, but the reception was terrible. I took a few steps towards the bouncer.

"Can I just step outside for a moment?" I asked him. "My cell reception isn't working in here."

He looked at me. "Chey Morrow, right?"

I nodded. "Yeah."

"Sure, no problem. Just give me a double knock when you're ready to come in."

"Thanks," I said, though I wondered how he'd hear a knock over the loud music within. But whatever. I stepped out into the warm Los Angeles night and found a couple more people talking away on their phones. I scanned the area, but no sign of JT.

Where could he have gone?

Taking a few steps away, I hit JT's name in my contacts. It went straight to voicemail. Totally not a surprise if he was talking to someone. I kicked at a nearby pebble as I waited for his message to end. "Hey, it's me. I can't find you. I'm outside right now, Adriana's in the club, so if you find me, can we get out of here?"

I clicked the phone off and headed back to the door.

I tucked my phone in the back pocket of my jeans as I made my way back inside. The bouncer let me pass easily, and I walked back towards VIP. I could see the back of JT at our table, talking away with Adriana...

I squared my shoulders and headed over. "Hey..."

JT smiled as I approached. "There you are. Adriana said you took off..."

"Went looking for you."

"Must have just missed each other," she said sweetly, glaring at me. She had taken his seat, and JT was in mine, so I was left standing.

"Must have." I looked at the table top, two empty glasses, one of Adriana's and a Corona.

I glanced at JT. I was sure he wasn't drinking anymore.

But with Adriana lurking about, I wasn't about to say anything.

He slid off his seat. "Here, Chey. I'll grab another chair from a different table."

"Thanks."

I sat down, and she smiled sweetly, watching JT go to another table and steal a chair.

"Your luck isn't going to hold forever, Wyoming." She smirked into her drink. "There's a midnight for every Cinderella, you know."

JT pulled the chair up and sat beside me, both of us facing Adriana. She tried to be normal for about half a minute before it got too much for her, and she took off a few minutes later.

JT moved his chair to face me, and I leaned forward, looking at him. The more I looked, the more dishevelled I realized he looked. His hair was mussed, like he'd spent time running his fingers through it. At least, that what how I wanted to think it happened, not that Adriana had done it.

"Who ordered the beer?"

"Adriana...she said she thought I needed something a little...stronger."

"Yeah, I bet she did." I sulked back into my chair and eyed the bottle warily.

"I took one sip...to get her off my back, but I'm not drinking, Chey...I've got enough headaches tonight without that."

"Good." I pushed the bottle away. "What's up?"

"I didn't get the part, or any part I'd auditioned for this week. So my trip was a bust."

"I'm sorry."

"Yeah..." he trailed off, his gaze drifting to the beer bottle. He lifted his hand and waved over the waitress. "Can you take that away, and bring us a couple waters?"

"Do you want to stay?" I asked him, hoping he'd say no.

He glanced towards me, then back at his phone. "Actually...I need to stay for a bit. There's some people from the auditions coming in later around midnight..."

"You're going to have a meeting in a club?"

"Just hang out for a couple of hours. But they're probably not your type of people, Chey..."

Great. I had a feeling I knew what that meant. The type of guys JT *used* to be.

"Okay, then. I'll leave you here?"

"Probably a good idea. I'm sorry our night's messed up." He reached across the table and squeezed my hand. "I'll make it up to you this weekend, I promise. Maybe we'll go to Malibu?"

"Yeah, sure..."

I stood up and walked around the table. He gave me a big hug and kissed my cheek. "Besides, you don't want to stay here with Adriana around."

"That's true."

Decision made, I was definitely ready to leave. I checked the time on my cell phone, gave him one last kiss goodbye, and made my way back to the back entrance us *special people* were allowed to use.

The bouncer who guarded it smiled at me and murmured a "goodnight, Ms. Morrow". I gave him a soft smile and headed for the back door, my keys in hand. Didn't care who knew me anymore; I just wanted to get out of this place.

It seemed like everything in my life was going crazy at once. Dad and his career, not to mention his un-relationship with Trish;

Milo and Sorche's new little romance, and JT's sudden turn to-night...and I was still dealing with the oh-so-unstable Adriana.

As I walked towards my car, I realized it suddenly looked a little different, probably just because I was coming to it at an angle instead of straight on. Besides, when we'd parked, I'd been with JT and hadn't really been paying any attention to the car.

I stopped ten feet away, just past the last street light, and froze. Of course it looked different. My car was suddenly a low rider. As in, my tires were flat. And not because I'd driven over something, like say, broken glass. Nope, a good slash to my tires was to blame.

All four, I guess, since it wasn't lopsided in any way.

Dad wasn't an option, either. He and Trish were busy... That left me with Milo—if I could tear him away from Sorche.

I used my phone to take a few pictures of the car before dialing and heading back to the building. I mean, hey, whoever did this could still be lurking out there with a nice sharp blade. I'd snuck enough horror movies in my time to know that being alone in a parking lot with slashed tires and a crazed knife-wielder never boded well for the sassy blonde heroine, aka *moi*.

Two rings that seemed to take an eternity, and Milo picked up right as I reached the door and did my now familiar double knock-ing

"I've got trouble," I said in a hushed voice, not wanting anyone to overhear.

Milo made a sound that sounded like a muffled groan. "That should be your name, you know."

"Charming." I waved at the bouncer as he let me back in the tiny hallway that was suddenly even more crowded. "Look, I sent some pictures. Someone slashed my tires while JT and I were out."

"Where is he now?"

"The slasher? How should I know? I didn't see whoever did this."

"No, I meant the boyfriend."

My turn to get a little tee-d off as I sidestepped a couple of actresses I recognized from TV and tried to lean against the wall where I was still able to get a reception. "It's complicated."

"So you took off?"

"I'd rather not be a part of what sends him back to rehab. Look, can you just call someone or something? I don't know what to do." I wasn't about to start crying, even though the stinging of tears hurt like a blowtorch behind my eyes. I kept my head down and blinked them away.

"Hold on..."

I leaned on the neon flier-covered wall and wished for...well, what, I wasn't sure. A caring boyfriend who'd know what to do so I didn't have to call Milo all the time, like the pain-in-the-ass little sister he didn't want. If Trish and my dad ever got serious, I could be on my way to having a stepbrother. Milo as my stepbrother. There was a chilling thought.

"Wow, that's some slasher job."

"Thank you."

"Did you check the other side?"

"No, I didn't feel like it, in case, you know, the anonymous psycho was lying in wait." With the way my night was going, high chance that's exactly what would have happened.

"Good idea. Do you have a spare in the trunk?"

"Let me think...yeah, I think there is."

"I'll come get you and call a tow truck on the way. We can bring your car home. I'm sure Sean can get it all fixed up as good as new himself. *You* don't need the publicity, I'm sure."

"Me?"

"Uh huh."

I'd been thinking more of Dad's side of things. Like crazed teenage model stalks B-list actor's daughter. I'm sure I'd even make the top ten at ten o'clock on the news.

"Stay put. I'll see you soon."

And then, the phone went dead in my ear.

I walked back into the club itself, knowing it would take Milo almost an hour to get here in traffic. He'd text me the moment he reached the parking lot. The urge to have a drink hit me strongly, and I headed to the bar to order something nice, fizzy, and caffeinated.

I was on my third Diet Coke, thinking something stronger might just be in order while I watched the muscular bartender, Antonio—he'd introduced himself after my second drink—hand out drink after drink to the growing crowd of people crushing around the bar. No one seemed to care about the girl who kept jumping every time her cell phone seemed to vibrate on the shiny bar top, which happened more often than I'd ever imagined, thanks to the booming bass blaring over the speakers, combined with Antonio slamming down a drink nearby.

Finally, it buzzed for real, and I checked caller ID before clicking it on, amazed I actually had reception over here.

"Hello."

"It's me. I'm looking at the tires."

Milo let out a low whistle that had me pulling the phone away from my ear.

"Warn me the next time you wanna do that."

"Sorry. Look, I thought if maybe we combined both our spares and put them on, it would at least be drivable, but looking at the damage, I don't know, Chey. You feel comfortable enough leaving the club to come out here?"

"You alone?"

"I didn't bring a welcoming party."

"There's that sarcasm I know and love." I took a final parting sip of my drink and pushed back from the bar. I slid a small tip towards Antonio, thankful I'd had his muscles to distract me while I worried about the slasher waiting for me just outside the back doors.

"I'm on my way. Can you meet me at the back entrance?"

"I'll start heading that way, meet you there."

I pushed the door open and walked straight into Milo's waiting chest. At least, I was pretty sure it was Milo.

I looked way, way up.

Yup, definitely him.

"Thanks."

He shrugged. "Mom would kill me if I'd left you alone out here."

So nice to know he cared. Filled me with warm fuzzies just thinking about it. I walked beside him in silence. More people were streaming towards the back doors of the club, but no one seemed to notice the vandalized car.

"It doesn't look random," he commented.

"How can you tell?" I shivered in the warm night air. Fear must have gotten to me.

"No one else's car was touched. If it were someone out having fun, you'd think they'd hit a few more around here."

Right, I thought, looking around the packed lot. See, I figured. I was a walking target. Might as well get a bull's eye tattoo.

"From the look of things, you pissed someone off big time."

Great.

"Where was JT when this happened?"

"I told you, he was inside all night."

We reached my car, and I handed him my keys so he could check the trunk and do whatever it was guys did when people found their tires slashed.

"Did you talk to your mom?" I leaned against my car door, watching Milo crouch down to inspect the damage with a mini-flashlight. I looked away, not liking the sight of shredded rubber.

"Thought it would ruin the mood," he said, glancing up at me.

Trish and Dad had gone out somewhere together on what they termed a 'not-date,' but I knew better. And apparently, so did Milo.

"Good point."

We opted *not* to sit in my car and wait for the tow truck, thinking that would be just a little too weird. So we sat in Milo's instead and listened to the stereo. He tapped his fingers on the steering wheel to the beat.

"If it was just one, I'd change your tire, but with only two spares and all four out of commission..." he said, breaking the quiet between us.

I nodded. "I didn't take you away from Sorche, did I?"

"Nope," he said rather abruptly.

Wow, that was harsh. "You two fighting?"

"No, she just had other plans tonight."

I nodded, though I wondered how well I knew my new best friend. I mean, she wanted to be a model and here I was, a newbie, having Sor's dream handed to me on a silver platter. That'd be enough to make any girl snap. Look at what it had done to Adriana.

Speaking of Adriana...

I glanced back towards the club, where it might still house a lovely little group of suspects. I had spotted Fiona in the bathroom—she could have done it; she'd likely do anything Adriana asked of her.

Adriana. The one who, the more I thought about it, seemed awfully more likely to be slashing my tires.

Before I could reach for the door handle and go back inside to see if the wicked witch with the slasher side was still in there, Milo started the ignition.

"There's the tow truck. You stay here. I'll talk to him and give him the address. See if we can get out of here without too much attention."

Fingers crossed.

I sat there watching Milo talk to the guy, and then, the two of them headed off towards where my car was. Like that wouldn't cause too much attention when a tow truck with a blinking light started backing up towards my car.

Before I even knew what I was doing, I had slid out of Milo's truck.

29

I really had no idea what I was doing as I walked back towards the club, trying to stay close to the shadows instead of under one of the bright lights overhead that would no doubt shout 'hey, Milo! I'm over here!'

I was almost to the back door of the club when it opened and Adriana stepped out. I think we both froze for a second as we saw each other. She came to her senses—limited that they were—first.

"Isn't it past your bedtime, Wyoming?" she asked, her voice scathing.

I rolled my eyes, deciding to ignore her comment. Couldn't she come up with any new material?

"Just coming outside to check on your handiwork?" I asked as Fiona came outside to join her. I noticed Adriana glance towards the darkened parking lot several times. I doubted she was out there to use her cell; she didn't even have it in her hand.

"What nonsense are you talking about?" Fiona butted her way into the conversation.

"Don't tell me Adriana didn't tell you what she was up to tonight? Apparently, she thought I needed some new tires."

Adriana crossed her arms. "You're insane."

"No, pretty sure that's you, what with slashing my tires and all. But *don't* worry, I managed to snap some great pics and video on my phone. TMZ will be *so* thrilled to run with the story."

Okay, so that was a lie. I didn't want anyone to know about this little disaster, but the look of doom on Adriana's face right then was so worth a little lie.

"I'm sure it'll be everywhere by this time tomorrow."

"Huh?"

"What *are* you talking about?" More from Fiona, who looked a little uncomfortable about this whole face-to-face thing we had going.

"Oh, don't worry about it, you can find out all about it online shortly." I smiled sweetly and turned to go when Adriana grabbed a handful of my hair and gave it a great yank, pulling me back painfully. The sharp stinging on my scalp told me she'd managed to rip out some of my hair.

"You bitch!" she spat. "You aren't going to hurt me."

I caught myself from falling backwards and swung my hand out, connecting my palm with the side of her face. The first time I'd ever slapped someone, but damn, I had to admit this one felt good, even though my palm was stinging worse than anything I'd ever felt before. Hair rip included.

She released her grip on my hair as a pair of arms wrapped around my waist, pulling me back. Then, Milo's voice was in my ear.

"Come on, Chey. Don't cause a scene. That's the last thing *you* want. She's not worth any more attention tonight."

JT walked out of the back door then, phone in hand at the same time as mine buzzed.

Our eyes met, and he looked from me to Milo then the group in front of us.

"What's going on? Where have you been, Chey?" JT asked as he neared.

"Spent a fascinating hour out her in the parking lot, staring at my four slashed tires…" I motioned behind us with my free hand as much as I could. Milo's grip was unrelenting, like he figured I'd jump Adriana if given the chance.

Smart guy.

"What?" His eyes widened, and he turned to look back at Adriana.

"She's crazy."

"Again, I'm not the psycho who went at my tires with a knife."

She lunged towards me again, but Milo took a giant step back, taking us both out of reach. JT stepped in between us, a look passing between him and Milo as we moved backwards.

Adriana glared at me as Milo pulled me further out of her reach, my feet barely grazing the pavement.

"That's right. Run away, *Chey*," she mocked, but her voice wasn't as bitchy as normal. In fact, there was a definite wobble to it, like she was afraid of what tomorrow might bring.

I managed one last sneer and waved my cell phone tauntingly at her as Milo dragged me back to the safety of his truck.

"Milo," I called after him as he headed back towards the garage.

No one was home, and for once, I was grateful for that fact. I didn't want Dad to see the tow truck pull in with my awful-looking car behind it. It made a mind-numbing sight.

He turned back to me. "Yeah?"

I stuffed my hands inside my jean pockets, suddenly feeling a little overwhelmed. "Thanks."

"S'okay."

I looked at my car now nestled safely in the garage, not so sure I bought the *okay*. "Still..."

I chewed my bottom lip. I mean, if he hadn't come to my rescue, I don't know what I would have done. Calling Dad was *so* not an option, and I don't think I would have thought of calling a tow truck on my own. I'd probably have ended up at that club 'til closing, trying to figure out what to do and too unnerved to go back outside on my own.

Now look at me.

I'd gone back and told Adriana off once and for all.

My car was tucked safely in the garage, and I could only hope Dad wouldn't decide to take a good look around there 'til morning. Hopefully by then, I'd come up with a reasonable excuse as to why I needed four new tires, and why they looked like they did if he happened to see them.

Milo walked back towards me. "Look, it's cool. Don't worry about anything, okay? Now go on in, it's getting late."

I had the feeling he just didn't want to have Dad pull up and find the two of us standing there talking after two in the morning.

I stood there, biting my lip for a moment.

"Sorche will be here any minute," he reminded me.

Turned out he'd texted her when I'd gone back to confront Adriana, thinking I'd need someone to vent to.

"Thanks, Milo." I cracked a small smile, fighting back the tears that stemmed from being just too overwhelmed as I stood up on tiptoe and kissed his cheek. "I owe you one."

"Yeah, yeah. Just don't make it a habit."

30

We'd headed straight up to the rooftop patio the moment we got in the house. Even the height didn't bother me, for once. I just needed some space and privacy to let me get over my meltdown. My hands had still been shaking when we'd let ourselves inside. Thankfully, Milo had his own key and had let us in.

I'd grabbed one of the oversize loungers near the empty fire pit and closed my eyes, clearly drifting off to sleep at some point, because I woke up to the sound of Milo and Sorche's conversation from somewhere around me, but I kept my eyes closed.

"I've texted JT every five minutes since you told me what happened, and there's been no response."

Sor's voice wafted towards me. Milo made almost a growling sound in his throat. There were a few more murmured words I couldn't quite differentiate, and then, I smelled it...

Coffee.

I rolled over carefully, blinking my eyes open, and finding Milo's jacket wrapped around me. The first hints of dawn were lining up over the city. Sorche and Milo sat on one of the loungers across from me, sipping coffee and watching me anxiously.

"You awake?" Sor asked uneasily.

I yawned. "Yeah."

Milo got up and took a coffee from the nearby table and brought it over to me. "It's extra strong."

"Thanks." I grabbed it eagerly and took my first long sip. The warmth made its way through my body, the brain-sleep fog combo I had going on slowly melting away. I blinked a few more times and pushed myself to sit up, still wrapped in Milo's jacket. I leaned forward and set the coffee down by my feet.

Sheepishly, I set the jacket aside, but feeling the chilly air, I picked it back up and slid it on. "What's going on?"

"Oh..."

Milo nudged Sorche, and I could tell my best friend was a little uneasy. Well, that was likely the understatement of the year.

She got up and crossed the distance between us, sitting down beside me. "Milo's got someone coming by in a couple of hours to check out the damage."

I felt a numbness hit me. Of course. I couldn't hide the damage forever. Even I knew that deep down. Plus I needed to pay Milo back or the tow truck driver; I didn't even know who paid for getting the car back here in the first place.

"Thanks," I said, looking at Milo.

He nodded. "Yeah."

I guess that was as good as it was going to get. I saw a look pass between them that I couldn't identify.

Sorche cleared her throat, reaching behind us and picking up a soft fleece throw and wrapping it around our shoulders.

"I can't get a hold of JT. I don't know where he is or why he isn't answering. Did he see what happened? Maybe he went after Adriana?" she asked, and I could detect a tinge of hopefulness in her voice.

"I don't know. He could have," Milo offered.

I remembered meeting JT's gaze as Milo dragged me away and his words of *I got this.* So maybe he was trying to talk some sense into Adriana? I don't know. I did know he never kept his phone regularly charged.

"Second issue..."

"The bigger issue..." Milo corrected as he stood up. "I'm going to go pick us all up some breakfast. Chey, you need to eat. Sor..."

"I'll be here."

We watched him disappear down the steps, the door closing behind him. Sor sighed and retrieved her cell phone.

"Yours is still charging. I've got an extra power bank." She motioned to the table where my phone sat.

I took an extra long sip of my coffee, trying to somehow brace myself for whatever it was Sorche was going to try to tell me.

"That fight between you and Adriana..." She tapped a few things on her phone. I saw a bunch of notifications go flying by on her page, but my eyes were too tired to distinguish what they were saying.

"What about it?"

"It went viral."

I yanked the phone out of her hand. The screen blurred for a moment, and I blinked until it resembled something normal.

Oh.

My.

God.

I didn't really want to see the view counter, but I'd estimate it was already in the hundreds of thousands of views, and it had only been up a few hours.

Somehow, the video started playing, not sure how because I didn't touch the screen, but there it was. The fight. Everything in bright and vivid 4K. I handed her back the phone and tilted my head up to the sky. I was in a total brain fog, I was trying to think, but the words just weren't happening.

"Who..." I finally managed.

"I think one of her entourage...the angle looks right to be one of them. They're never far from her." She swiped her phone off, muting the notifications I noticed.

I raised an eyebrow.

"I've already had messages from half a dozen sites asking for comments."

"Fantastic." I fell backwards on the lounger. If I didn't drink before, I'd seriously think about having one right now. Something strong enough to numb myself through this mess. I could just imagine the nightmare this was going to cause.

If Trish knew...did Dad?

Worse, did Mom?

But she wasn't that social media savvy. Maybe, just maybe, this would blow over.

Milo came back with enough breakfast to feed a dozen people. We sat in silence on the rooftop. I barely picked at my hash browns as I watched the sunrise over the skyline. My stomach was hollow. I could hear Milo's phone vibrate every so often, but he didn't check it. Sor had turned hers off when Milo arrived, so who knew what was going on in the world. I wasn't about to turn mine on; I was too scared for what would be waiting for me.

Sor finally talked me into going to my room to lay down for a while, and she tucked me into bed like a little kid. She lingered in the doorway for a couple minutes, a worried expression on her face. "I'm gonna hang out with Milo for a while. You need anything, just call us, okay?"

"All I want right now is to sleep."

I'd never felt this exhausted in my life.

By the time I woke up hours later and snuck into the garage to check on the damage to my car, all had been miraculously taken care of. Four brand-new tires replaced the shredded rubber that had been there hours before. There wasn't a single sign of anything ever having been wrong in the first place.

"Told you I'd take care of it."

I jumped at Milo's voice.

"I just didn't expect it to be so soon," I said as I stood up from where I'd crouched down from beside the front right tire, examining it to make sure it wasn't a figment of my imagination.

It wasn't. They had that whole new-tire smell. And not a patch or a scar in sight.

I wondered how I was going to pay Milo back for all of this. My savings account was a measly one hundred and ninety-two dollars at the moment, and I doubted that would cover the tow, let alone the four new tires.

Dad had deposited my 'modeling fee' into some fancy new account out here that I barely knew how to get into, and asking now would just bring more questions that I didn't want.

"You need to be more careful, Chey."

"Thought I was." I followed him out of the garage. "Don't worry. I'm sure the tires will be the least of my worries from now on."

Milo cracked a smile. "Hope so."

"Where's Sor?"

"She went home to change. She said she'd pick up lunch and be back in an hour. You okay by yourself?"

"Why?"

"I got some stuff to do this afternoon now that all of this is taken care of. And your dad's out hiking all afternoon with his trainer. He messaged me while you were sleeping. I said your phone battery was probably dead."

"I'm fine. And thanks for covering for me."

I decided to spend the day hibernating at home, since Sor was going to pick up food that afternoon and bring it back. Milo was off running errands for Dad, and Trish was enjoying a day off, so with Dad out with his trainer for the rest of the day, doing some sort of hike or something, I had the place to myself for a while.

I stretched out in one of the patio chairs, propping my feet on the empty chair across from me, when I heard something from the patio doors.

I turned my head to see JT peeking through the open doorway. "Hi..."

I didn't know if I wanted to talk to him. "Hi."

He leaned against the doorway, tucking his hands in his jeans pockets and looking at me carefully. I watched him in silence. My phone...my silent phone...sat on the edge of the patio table.

He hadn't texted.

He hadn't called.

Not a word since last night.

He glanced around. "Milo let me in before he went out."

I nodded. Milo had left like fifteen minutes ago, so what had JT been doing? Lurking outside?

It seemed like he'd finally worked up the courage to walk over, and he joined me at the patio table. "So, about last night..."

"What about it?"

"After Milo took you out of there, I tried to talk some sense into Adriana and her little group."

I rubbed my forehead. "Did you do that before or after we went viral?"

"What?"

I slid my phone towards him. He swiped the screen to turn it on. My browser was set to the video. I saw him read the caption, then hit play.

Thank God I'd muted it about fifteen plays before.

A tick appeared in his jaw.

"I had no idea..." he said, lifting his gaze from the screen.

"Yeah, me, either, 'til I woke up to Sor and Milo mildly freaking out about it."

"Does your dad know?"

"Doesn't seem to. About the tires or that." I motioned to the screen. "I don't know..."

"About what?"

"Anything." I slid down in my chair a little, and JT put my phone down. He leaned forward.

"Look, I told Adriana she's lucky you didn't press charges."

"For?"

"Everything. The tires. The fight." He moved his chair closer to me. "She still says it wasn't her, but the way Fiona was looking at her, I think if she didn't do it herself, she definitely had one of her group do it for her."

"Great."

"I told her to lay off, or I'll make some trouble of my own for her."

I raised my eyes to his. "What?"

"Don't worry about it."

"She thinks everything of mine is hers."

"Well, it's not."

"Was she in the running for Face of Vanetti?"

"I think she was on a list of potentials, then she went to rehab, and Rico moved on..."

"And you?"

He laughed. "Not fond of females who play with knives."

"Sor's been trying to get a hold of you for hours."

He took his phone out of his pocket and handed it to me. Automatically, I swiped the screen.

Black.

Then, I noticed the cracked screen.

"What happened?"

"Adriana grabbed my phone during our little 'talk' and threw it down. I have a feeling it's a write off."

"Shit. I'm sorry."

"Not your fault." He took his phone back. "So that's why I didn't get any of Sor's texts or why I couldn't call you. I think Adri figured I was going to call the cops myself." He put the phone on the table. "Did you call?"

"No. But I think Milo was seriously thinking about it for a while. I heard him and Sor talking about security cam footage before I fell asleep."

"It would serve her right if you did."

"Right now, I just want to forget it ever happened. And have someone else in L.A. do something equally stupid so they take the limelight away."

"This is L.A., give it twelve hours."

I laughed.

"That's my girl."

I tilted my head to the side. "Your girl, huh?"

"Yeah." He leaned forward and brushed his lips against mine.

31

JT had been right. Things had seemed to die down within a few hours. Sor and I had decided to spend the weekend laying low at the house. We spent the day hanging out at the pool for a while. JT joined us for a late dinner on the rooftop with Milo. It was nice to relax again, and not a single one of us mentioned the wicked witch.

Sor left early Monday morning, having some auditions and meetings to go to. And I was finally feeling better, a little more like the old me.

I was in my room when I swore I heard the doorbell ring. We weren't expecting anyone. Trish and Dad were working from home. Milo was going to the beach later, and I thought I might tag along if he asked.

When the doorbell rang again, I set down my tablet and headed out of my room, down towards the main floor.

"Hello?" I called out, not sure if Trish was still here. Maybe she and Dad had taken off for a while without telling me. Last I'd seen her was when I grabbed my breakfast java and strawberry pop tart shortly after Sor left.

No response from anywhere in the house.

"I'll get it," I called as the doorbell rang a second time.

I hurried down the stairs, thinking maybe Sorche had gotten out of her appointment early with the new modeling agency she'd been so excited about.

I skipped the last step on the stairs and slid across the hardwood floor in my socks to the door. I threw one of the double panels open, the smile on my face freezing in place when I saw who stood on the step.

I blinked to make sure it wasn't a mirage or the sun playing tricks on me. "Mom?"

I totally didn't mean to make it into a question. But I was just so shocked to see her. I mean, I had time left in Los Angeles, and she wasn't even going to fly out to pick me up. I was going to be like a *real* grown up and fly back on my own.

She didn't smile when she saw me, and I didn't really get it. Why was she here? She hated California. Disneyland included. Which was why my summer vacations over the last many years had tended to happen somewhere suitably East Coast.

"Hi, Chey."

A small touch of panic rushed through me, knowing immediately something wasn't right for her to just show up out of the blue. No text, no phone call, nothing.

"What are you doing here?" And how did she get past the gate?

"I have the gate code in case of emergency. Can I come in?"

I nodded, moving back and waving her inside, embarrassed I'd said the gate comment out loud. She had on her favorite pair of jeans, I noticed, and a new tank top under her leather jacket.

"Dad, *Mom's* here," I hollered, hoping he'd hear and come out to join me from wherever he was.

She turned and gave me a thorough once over. "You look good."

"Thanks." I'd spent a lot of time out in the sun, and my at times Casper-like paleness was almost all but a distant memory thanks to Sor taking me for her weekly spray tan touch-ups.

"Do you want a drink?" I asked, not sure what to do but keep standing there. Nervously, I tucked my hands in my jeans pockets, my fingers in my left pocket finding that familiar piece of paper and toying with it anxiously.

It had been weeks since I'd looked at that first email Dad had sent about this summer.

I had no idea what to say. I mean, stunned to see her didn't even cover it. But deep down inside, I knew exactly why she was standing on our doorstep. Well, make that in our living room now as she surveyed the house. Maybe she expected some starlet to come giggling downstairs. Wait 'til she met Trish, who was as far from that as you could get.

I heard the back patio door open, and moments later, Dad's voice rang out.

"Who was it?"

He almost stumbled when he laid eyes on Mom as he came out of the kitchen.

"Guess I don't need to make introductions." I was totally uncomfortable. I would have been happy to even have Milo walk in. Someone save me from this Hell!

"Hi, Sean."

"What are you doing here? Chey's still got a few weeks left of vacation."

Nearly three and a half, but who was counting?

"Well, I was supposed to be Rico's big surprise for Chey for the opening this weekend."

I smiled. "Seriously?"

She gave me a half-smile. "Couldn't miss my girl's big night, could I?"

"What prompted you to ruin it?" Dad came a few steps closer.

I shot a glare his way at his choice of words. Mom didn't *ruin* it; she just sorta revealed it a little early.

I perched on the arm of the sofa. "Why are you here early?"

Her smile faded to a memory, and she started digging through her bag. "All was fine, until I saw this."

A folded tabloid came out of her purse. I wanted to cover my hands with my face. Somehow, I had an inkling. While I'd been concerned about that viral video finding its way to her, I should have realized that wasn't all I'd have to worry about.

"What, now?" Dad's tone was still a touch huffy. I guess that's what came from a couple decades with your face on magazine covers.

"This."

She tapped her finger on the glossy cover, and I could only stare blankly in shock. Adriana and I fighting behind the club. I had my head down like I was about to tackle her, and she had a handful of my hair. Just when I'd been threatening Adriana about the pictures on my phone, someone had evidently been busy snapping away on theirs.

Dad pulled the magazine out of her hands. He studied the image for a few moments then looked at me, obviously wanting an explanation. "When was this?"

I cleared my throat, glancing down at my chipped nail polish, trying to come up with an answer and an explanation of why I didn't tell him about it.

Thankfully, I was saved by Mom.

"That's just what I always wanted to see, Cheyenne, you and some Hollywood wannabe splashed all over the tabloids," she cut in.

Well, that aptly described Adriana.

Dad's hand went to my shoulder, giving me a squeeze of reassurance. "Let her talk."

"I knew, *knew*, something like this would happen when she came out here with you." She shook her head as I glanced up at her.

"'Chey gone wild!'" she read the headline. "Three months ago, that would have meant she'd done something stupid like forget her homework. Stayed out a little late. But not end up in a fight in the back alley of some stupid club."

I winced at the words, hating how true they were. Well, sorta—it was the back parking lot, not the back alley, but I doubted that would make it any better in her mind.

"Mom..." I started, hoping to talk some sense into her, if it was possible. I'd have to be truthful and tell her all about Adriana's attempts at ruining my summer and chasing me away.

"No, Chey. We had a deal. No L.A. if you couldn't handle it. And this proves you can't handle it."

"I *can* handle it. Adriana's been after me since I got the job as the 'Face of Vanetti'," I tried to explain. "And that night, she had my tires slashed. *All four tires.*" I turned to Dad as I continued. "I had to call Milo to help me out, and I was supposed to go sit in his truck like a good little girl. But instead, I went back to tell her off, to tell her enough was enough, but she walked out the door before I could go back in to find her. I turned to go after telling her off, and she grabbed my hair. *That's* the photo." I sighed as I looked at myself in mid-slap, my hair obscuring half my face in a second picture inset in the corner. "I thought..."

"I don't care about her right now, Chey. I care about you and the fact you're—"

"She's what?" Dad interrupted.

"Throwing her life away—or starting to. Nothing like this ever happened to her at home."

"That's because she never had the chance for anything like this to happen."

"Exactly!"

I slid off the arm chair and backed up a few steps, suddenly fading into the background, like it always seemed I did when these two got together. Without knowing how and without them noticing, I slipped up the stairs and around the corner, completely out of view.

I still hated hearing them argue—especially about me. It was like a time machine transporting me back to being nine years old again, crouched behind my bedroom door, listening to them fight.

I leaned my head against the wall, fighting back the hurtful heat of my unshed tears as their voices got louder. I'd gone through this once before, right before Mom decided she was filing for divorce. It had been the same decibel level.

"You're letting her run free!"

I cringed, waiting for my dad's reaction. "She's gotta grow up sometime."

"She was growing up fine *without* your influence."

I slid lower, not daring to peek around the corner, lest one of them spot me. I couldn't tell for sure if they were in the hallway or had moved the argument back to the living room. It had sounded closer for one brief moment. Either way, if they saw me, it would no doubt spell disaster with the mood Mom was in.

"I was right all along saying *this* was the complete wrong thing to do."

"Why? Because she's out here with me?"

That was enough for me. I crept up to my bedroom as silently as I could and grabbed my car keys and cell before heading down the back stairs and out of the house through the patio door in Dad's office. I doubted they'd even hear my car driving past while they kept arguing.

I needed air. I needed someone to tell me this was all going to be over soon. That I hadn't just messed my life up beyond repair.

The cell phone on the seat beside me began to ring, and I gripped the steering wheel tighter, doing everything I could to ignore it. The phone stopped for a minute, then the ring tone changed, and I knew it was Sorche. They must have gotten to her. I didn't care. Didn't want to talk to anyone at that very moment. I just wanted to be alone.

I didn't want to be someplace someone would recognize me or come over and want to talk. I didn't want to go somewhere Dad would think of finding me. Which meant my beloved Pink's was off the list.

I found my way out onto the PCH and just drove, letting the stereo blare, trying to drown out the echoes of my parents' argument in my mind.

I pulled off when I found a half-decent drive-thru and bought something to eat. I didn't feel hungry, but my stomach was growling. Who knew an emotional breakdown could be so draining?

I put my food on the passenger seat and headed back on the PCH, driving 'til I hit a deserted parking lot and stretch of beach.

Sitting there, staring at the waves crashing the shore and watching the darkening clouds coming in off the ocean, I picked at my French fries which held no taste whatsoever and grabbed my cell phone, scrolling through the missed calls. I didn't want to call Sorche, for fear Mom could talk her into anything. Milo would no doubt be super-cooperative—to Dad. And Trish was totally out of the question. Which left me with one person.

I hiccupped pitifully a couple times and took a long gulp of root beer, hoping to chase them away before I hit dial.

Moments later, Rico was on the phone. "Chey! You sound upset. What's wrong?"

I cleared my throat. "I'm sorry, Rico. I wasn't sure who else to call. Uhm, I need to get a hold of JT but I don't know where he is, and I don't want to call his cell or text him in case he's at my house."

"Where are you?"

"On a stretch of PCH."

"What happened?"

I heard Lorna ask who it was in the background.

"I shouldn't have called," I murmured, ready to hit 'end.' I mean, the last thing I wanted to do was worry anyone else.

"Wait!" Lorna came on the phone. "Chey? Rico looks very worried. What is it?"

I blurted out the truth before I could stop myself.

"I just don't want Mom or Dad coming out here right now. I need some space," I finished by saying.

"I understand, but why don't you call and just say you're okay?"

"I doubt they've noticed I'm gone yet." Okay, lie. Because that first ring tone had been Dad's, and it had been alternating between five people ever since. Dad, Mom, Sorche, Milo, and Trish. "Can you call JT for me?"

"Rico's dialing already. Do you know where you are?"

I looked back at the abandoned parking lot; I remembered seeing a sign as I turned off. "I think so."

I could use my GPS for the exact location if I had to. I just needed my eyes to stop blurring with those damn tears that kept coming every once in a while.

There was a muffled conversation on the other end for a moment. "He's at his place, heading for his car. I'll hang up, and he can call you."

"Thanks."

No sooner did I end the call than it rang again. Seeing JT's number, I clicked it on. "Hey."

"Where are you?"

I rattled off my estimated location.

"Stay put. Eat. I'll be there in a few," he ordered, and then the line went silent.

I clicked the phone off the second he said he was on his way. I reclined my seat back a little and leaned into it, reaching for my food. I was barely through picking at my chicken sandwich when I noticed his car pulling in the lot behind me.

"Did you break every traffic law in California?" I asked when he appeared next to my door.

JT laughed as he opened my driver's door and crouched down to my level. I must have looked worse than I thought, I realized when I heard his sharp intake of breath.

I pushed aside my urge to pull the sun flap down and look in the mirror. I didn't want to make myself feel any worse than I already did. And his reaction to however I looked right now was more than enough.

"Scoot over."

"It's my car."

He laughed again, softer this time.

"Yeah, it is." He leaned in and unlocked the passenger side before slamming my driver's door.

Before I knew it, he was in the other seat, taking a sip of my soda, my bag of food now on his lap.

"You look like crap," he complimented, as if I hadn't already gotten the message.

"That's what happens when my mother turns into the wicked witch of Los Angeles."

Who knew someone could eclipse Adriana?

He froze, his eyes searching my face. "Adri gave up her title?"

I fought my smile unsuccessfully.

"Apparently." I stole my soda back and took a long sip, my mouth suddenly desert-dry again. "According to Mommy dearest, I've made more mistakes since I've been out here than I have in my entire life, and now, the press is documenting it all so we can have a scrapbook of all these *beautiful* memories to look back on."

JT shook his head. "What did she say about me?"

I didn't think he'd want to know. "We hadn't gotten to you yet," I lied.

"Come on, let's go for a walk. You need some air."

I needed a lot of things at that moment, not quite sure air was one of them. For all I knew, my things were being packed up at Dad's and being sent back to Buffalo. I could have a brand new plane ticket awaiting my arrival.

Halfway down the beach, I pulled my sneakers off and dropped down in the sand. The wind was picking up, and there were dark, foreboding clouds overhead. I must have missed the whole creepy-dark-clouds-coming-in thing, being lost in my own personal dark cloud of doom. The ones I'd seen had been a pale, dusty grey. These were near black and downright scary.

JT sat beside me, completely blowing any thoughts of personal space away. I leaned my head against his shoulder as we looked out at the darkening sky and the dark water ahead of us.

"You know, eventually, you'll have to go home," he said softly.

Suddenly, he'd become the voice of reason? Never would have imagined that.

I nodded weakly. "Eventually."

Which, to me, meant a long time from now. And home no longer meant what it used to.

There was now Mom's and Dad's. And I just sorta existed between the two.

He turned his head, and his blue eyes met mine.

"You're going to ruin my bad boy rep, you know that, don't you?"

"Had an inkling," I said with the smallest trace of a smile.

He laughed, a low rumble I could feel reverberate through him. "This is..."

I waited.

"Nice."

"Wow, you really want to lose that bad boy label, don't you?"

He wrapped his arms around me, pulling me even closer to him. I wasn't even cold. And at least, I'd finally stopped crying.

"Storm's coming," he said, glancing up at the sky. The wind had picked up a little, but even that didn't bother me.

"Great. Matches my life. Not to mention my mood."

He grinned. "It'll pass, don't worry. Rico will talk to her. Your dad will talk to her. Heck, I'll even talk to her, if you want. All about how Adriana's a manipulative and jealous witch who wanted to drive you out of *her* town and used everything at her disposal to do it."

"Doubt she'd listen," I said sullenly. I'd tried and couldn't get through to her. I doubted JT's baby blue eyes would get to her. "Besides, you didn't help matters any. *You're* the reason I was in my first paparazzi chase."

The first drop of rain hit me square in the face. Followed by another. And then another. Each one stronger than the last.

"We gotta get out of here..." He hauled me to my feet, and we jogged barefoot back towards the cars, the strong scent of fresh rain hitting the air.

"You cool to drive?"

I shrugged, digging in my pocket for my keys. "Yeah, guess so."

"I'll lead. We should get to Malibu just before the storm hits big."

"Good. I'll call home from your place."

JT gave me a quick kiss on the forehead and opened his car door just as the first drops of rain began to fall, hitting me smack in the head.

I tilted my head back and took a deep breath full of the ocean air before I got into my car.

32

I told JT I'd be fine to drive, that I could handle it. I was a lot more cool-headed than earlier—not to mention, finally cried out—and besides, I still could use a little time to myself. We'd head up to Malibu. I'd call my parents. We'd wait for the storm to pass and then head back to the city where I'd no doubt be grounded for all eternity for taking off like I did. And that wasn't even worst-case-scenario—in which I'd be headed home on the next flight.

I flicked my headlights to signal I was ready to go. I was glad he was going to lead since I couldn't remember the way to his place. His lights flickered back at me, and then, he was pulling out of the parking lot. I started the engine and headed after him. The rain began to fall heavier the further we drove, and I gripped my steering wheel tightly as the pavement turned shiny and slick with the rain.

I turned the radio down just as my cell phone began going off again. I doubted I'd have any room left on voicemail before the night was through.

JT's tail lights disappeared around the curve, and I stepped on the gas to keep up, not wanting to lose him. I took the turn, and the car started to lose control, the tires not getting any traction as the rain pelted down. The wipers were working overtime, and I still couldn't see more than the blurred headlights up ahead of me, way up the curve.

My foot slammed down on the brake pedal to slow down as I tried to keep my eyes on the road and not squeeze them shut like I desperately wanted to do. My heart felt like it was in my throat, and the urge to throw up was getting harder and harder to ignore. Why hadn't I asked JT to show me some of that damn stunt driving? At least, learn how to handle things like this as I pressed harder on the brake, hearing the screech of tires as suddenly, I lost complete control of the car.

33

"We're live from outside the hospital where the latest Holly-wood 'it girl,' Chey Morrow, has been brought in. According to an unnamed source, she lost control of her BMW earlier tonight on a slippery stretch of PCH and spun out into oncoming traffic. No re-ports yet on whether or not alcohol was a contributing factor..."

The same perky blonde reporter from the premiere flashed a bright smile at the camera like my sudden downward spiral was the highlight of her day.

The screen split in two, and before the serious-looking anchor-woman could ask a single nauseating question, I clicked the televi-sion off, glaring at the darkened screen. Alcohol a contributing factor, my rear. I hadn't been near any all night. I'd been stone-cold-sober throughout the entire painful ordeal.

I'd been wide awake for the last hour, plucking a bald spot in the fur of the teddy bear JT had bought me from the hospital gift shop. I had a nice row of butterfly bandages near my temple from the impact of hitting my airbag, plain white ones which, according to JT, didn't scream 'it girl' to him. That's why there was a box of Disney Princess Band-Aids on the bedside table, a gesture that had actually made me laugh in spite of everything.

My door opened, and Mom walked in, dark rings under her eyes that I wasn't sure had been there the last time I saw her.

"Hi," I said meekly.

She pulled me into a careful hug. "Chey! You scared us to death taking off like that and then to get a phone call from the hospital saying you'd been brought in—"

"Took years off your life?"

"Most definitely." She sat on the edge of the bed, her fingers brushing my hair back, giving the slightest, almost imperceptible, shake of her head as she stared at the bandages by my right temple. What can I say, I must have hit the air bag hard. I was already thinking I was going to have a black eye or close to it the way the nurses were talking. "I talked to the doctor. They just want to keep you under observation for the rest of the night, make sure you really are okay."

"I'm fine." At least, for the moment. I pulled my gaze away from hers. "How's my car?"

"That's the least of your worries"

I slid deeper under the cold hospital blanket. "I know."

She sighed just as the door opened and Dad stepped in, the worried expression on his face matching Mom's.

"So, this is where the next stunt driver's hanging out?" he asked with a teasing grin.

"Ha, ha."

"JT said he'd give me the card of his instructor."

He smiled, but I wasn't so sure he was really kidding.

I suddenly felt a little defensive. "The road was slick from the rain, and those tires couldn't get a good grip. Before I knew it, I was fishtailing."

He moved closer to the bed, and instead of joining Mom on the edge, he took a seat in the room's lone chair. "You scared us."

"I know."

Truth be told, I'd kinda scared myself with the accident.

"Just glad you're okay." He leaned forward and patted my leg through the thin blanket.

Me, too.

"You should get some rest," Mom said, at last. "I'm going to go get some coffee. It's been a long day."

"You're leaving?"

"Not going far, Chey. There's one of those coffee machines near the waiting area. Your dad and I already decided we're taking turns sitting with you tonight."

I dozed off for a couple hours, or as much as I could with the nurses coming in to check on me what seemed like every fifteen minutes, my new teddy bear beside me as Mom and Dad alternated watching over me 'til dawn. I heard whoever was in the chair get up and head to the door where some sort of mini-conference took place. I was still half-asleep, my eyelids too heavy to open as I listened to my father's voice.

"I never expected..."

Right, me to take off. Not the best day of my life, considering where I'd ended up. I snuggled closer to my teddy bear.

"To take me up on my offer."

My shock and surprise grew with those words. I listened a little closer, doing my best Oscar-winning performance to look like I was still sound asleep. I couldn't hear who he was talking to, and I didn't want to risk a peek, knowing the conversation would come to a halt the moment someone saw my eyes open.

"A whole summer together; we've never had that. I figured she'd come out for a few days, a week, tops. But then, there she was, planning out an entire summer in L.A."

I bit the inside of my lip, fighting back the tidal wave of emotion. So Dad had never really wanted me to stay here at all? Or, at least, not this long. Wow, did everything ever click right into place. The entire summer made sense.

Trish. Sorche. Even Milo.

And most importantly of all, Dad's behavior.

I heard him walk away then, and the door shut behind him. Well, then, if that's the way he wanted it—a summer to himself—I wasn't about to deny him his wishes.

I opened my eyes slowly, blinked the sudden rash of tears away, and began to get dressed. At some point in the night, Trish had brought over a fresh change of clothes along with a baseball cap, and I wasted no time slipping into my yoga pants and tank top, pushing myself through the twinges of pain movement beyond blinking caused. Using the mirror in the tiny bathroom to gauge my appearance, I quickly grabbed a couple of JT's Band-Aids and covered up the plain, beige hospital-issued ones.

I took my purse and cell phone from the corner cabinet and peeked out the door, finding the hall absent of relatives. I just needed to escape.

I slid the baseball cap on and checked the butterfly bandage I was sporting on the side of my cheek and realized it could have been a lot worse. The 'overnight for observation' had been enough of a hospital stay for me.

But that was the least of my worries at the moment. At least, the cap would help disguise me, and I'd tucked my hair up underneath.

Hopefully, I could get through the front doors of the hospital without attracting too much attention.

One last deep breath, and I stepped out into the hall and hurried to the elevators

Once I got in, I hit the button to go down to the lobby and opened up my cell phone, texting a 9-1-1 to the only person I figured could help.

I was surprised when Milo peeked around the corner a few minutes later. One look at my tear-stained face, and I heard him swear under his breath.

"What do you need?" he asked quietly.

"I need to go home, *but* you can't tell my parents where I'm going."

He rubbed his face tiredly as his gaze darted around. "Chey..."

I knew he was going to say this was how this little accident mess of mine started, but I spoke before he could voice that thought.

"Just *please*, do me this favor?"

"I thought you weren't going to ask me for anything else?"

"So I lied." I looked at him pleadingly. "Please? Before they realize I'm not where I should be."

"You're breaking out of the hospital?"

I nodded.

He sighed and rolled his eyes skyward. Somehow, I didn't think he was praying.

"Come on."

We slipped out a side door, and I kept my head down as he hurried me past a few people outside and towards the parking lot. It surprised me when I heard the familiar beep and the sound of doors unlocking. I looked up to see he was driving Dad's SUV.

He held the door open, and I slipped inside, quickly doing up my seat belt. I figured I had an hour before anyone noticed I wasn't where I was supposed to be and that maybe, I'd taken off.

Waiting for Milo to get in, I finally noticed the darkly tinted windows of the Escalade. Were those new? Or had I just been so excited to be here, I'd never really noticed what was going on around me?

Milo pulled out of the parking lot in silence and stayed that way 'til we were halfway to Dad's.

"Do I want to know where you're headed?"

"It's not JT's," I said briskly, wishing I'd thought to grab the teddy bear. I'd been so determined to get out of there, I'd thrown on my clothes and put the pink bandages over the hospital-issued ones, not thinking about anything else.

I caught a hint of a smile on his face.

"Okay, good."

He pulled up in the driveway about five minutes later and parked near the front door. "You're not doing something stupid, are you?"

"No." I could tell he didn't quite believe me. "I'm going home, Milo."

"You *are* home." He motioned to the door.

"I meant the permanent one, back in Buffalo. This whole summer has been a mistake of epic proportions.'

"Now you're exaggerating."

"Uh, my car?"

"Not quite totalled."

"My life?"

"The same."

Evidently, Milo didn't see things the way I did.

"Look, it's seriously complicated, but the best thing for me to do is to get on the next flight out of here."

"Without anyone knowing?"

"Exactly."

He gripped the steering wheel even though we were in park. I had a feeling he wanted to give me a 'big brother'-like pep talk, which was stupid, because he wasn't exactly big brother material.

"And I can't talk you out of it?"

After what I'd overheard that morning?

"No," I replied firmly, my hand on the door handle.

About to push the door open and run inside the house, I leaned back and, for the second time in my life, kissed Milo's cheek. "Thank you."

That said, I slipped out of the vehicle and let myself in, running straight upstairs to my bedroom. I tried not to look at anything that would make me overly emotional. But in spite of myself, I sank down on the bed and grabbed my pillow and hugged it tight to my chest. Okay, eavesdropping was so out of my life. I couldn't take hearing things like that again. He hadn't meant to invite me out for the summer. A few days, maybe? What would he have done in a few days? No wonder he had orchestrated that invite to the party—how else was he going to get me out of his hair?

He must have been ecstatic when I made friends with Sorche. Not to mention that convenient gig with Rico. That had taken up more of my time.

With a shaky hand, I wiped the tears from my eyes and headed to the closet, grabbing my suitcase and tossing it on top of my bed. I had a feeling I needed to work fast, before they realized, a) I was out of the hospital and, b) I was probably already at home. Or even worse, Milo sold me out.

I made two trips back to the closet, yanking out my clothes—the ones I'd brought with me—off the hangers and tossing them haphazardly into my suitcase. Everything *he'd* bought me was staying behind; I didn't care what he did with them. Hell, sell them on eBay or give them to charity, I really didn't give a damn. I was finished with everything to do with him.

I slammed the lid down and snapped the locks in place. I turned on my cell phone and called for a cab as soon as possible as I glanced out the bedroom window and thought I saw the gates starting to open. I slid my phone in the pocket of the jeans I'd changed into, and my fingers wrapped around the familiar, crinkled paper.

I yanked it out and laughed bitterly as I saw the scrap that had at one time meant so much to me. However, that naïve Chey was long gone, and the one that stood there now knew too much about her father to care about anything to do with him ever again.

I crumpled the paper in my hand until it was nothing more than a small, crinkly ball and tossed it on my bed just as I swore I heard a car door slam in the distance. I pulled my two bags off the bed, causing a sharp intake of breath as I was suddenly reminded by my body of that wonderful collision with the airbag. One more deep breath, and I hurried downstairs, hoping I could be up front and in the cab before anyone came in through the back patio doors.

If I didn't have bad luck, I'd have no luck at all.

Dad was coming down the hallway when I stepped off the last stair.

"Chey!" His voice was full of relief as he saw me.

"Don't!" I put my hand up to keep him from coming anywhere near me.

He hesitated, confusion clearly etched on his face.

"What…" He looked at my luggage behind me, the wheels of my suitcase bopping off the last stair and running into the back of my legs, but I didn't flinch at the sudden jolt of pain.

"I'm leaving." So I was stating the obvious, but what else was there to say?

I saw Trish walk up behind him and Mom behind her, both looking at me in a mix of awe and relief. Awe that I was ready to go, and relief for finding me safe and sound, I guess.

"Chey, what are you doing, honey?" Trish squeezed past Dad to look at me. I hoped Milo hadn't filled them in on my plan.

"Leaving," I said plainly.

"Why?"

I let out a pained laugh that I put a stop to before it could turn into uncontrolled sobbing. "Ask Dad."

They looked at him, and he shrugged cluelessly before they all stared at me again.

"I think the 'best by' date on my summer passed a long time ago," I said, shifting my carryon bag to my shoulder.

"Chey, where's all this coming from?" He took a cautious step towards me.

As I stood there staring at him, I suddenly realized my father wasn't the most important person in my world. He actually never had been. He was just the one whose attention I kept trying to attract. Maybe that was my sole reason for agreeing to the job with Rico.

"You don't get it, do you?"

I took a deep breath, but it wasn't helping. It was all about to come pouring out, whether I wanted it to or not. I didn't care Trish and Mom were there. I didn't care if Milo was within hearing range, either. This was between me and my father, and he was going to hear it for once in his damn life.

"This whole summer was supposed to be about spending time *with* you. I didn't give a damn about meeting anyone or making new friends or having my face splashed on billboards. I didn't need a so-called bad boy boyfriend. I didn't need some jealous eighteen-year-old out to make my life miserable. I didn't need a damn single one of those things. I *needed* my father. But he was too busy chasing some project, he didn't even get to see that."

I hoisted my bag higher on my shoulder, lifting my chin as I tried to control my emotion.

"So you know what?" I fished the keychain out my pocket and tossed it his way.

He caught it, keeping silent. The sound of the keys jingling echoed through the oddly silent house.

"I don't need you. I *never* have." I gave a pitiful little laugh that sounded awful sad. And warbled. Great. Now I'd have to fight back tears on top of it all. "And this summer just proves it all."

He stepped forward, but I put my hand up.

"Don't bother. I know you've got a meeting somewhere...about some part...some..." I shrugged. "Whatever. I don't even care anymore."

I took a bit of a shaky breath but pushed forward. The faster I was out of there, the faster the tears could fall and I could realize the only thing that this stupid trip had brought me was palm trees and broken dreams.

Lifting my chin, I headed for the front door and stepped out into the suddenly bright L.A. sunshine. I heard someone's footsteps, but I didn't dare to look behind me, afraid I might lose all control if it was Dad. Or Mom.

Trish appeared beside me and wrapped her arm around my shoulders. "I'm not letting you go to the airport in a cab."

Thanks, Milo.

"I already called." I hurried down the steps, not bothering to look back. I wanted to put as much distance between everything as possible.

"Milo can take care of it." She opened the passenger side of her SUV. "Get in."

What else was I supposed to do?

Funny enough, I didn't even feel like being alone right now. Even though if I had taken the cab, I would have been curled up in the backseat, my suitcase beside me on my way to freedom.

I opened the back door and pushed my luggage inside, before getting in beside Trish.

She blared the air conditioning as she headed past the gate, and I knew she kept watching me, but I refused to look over.

"I wish you hadn't heard that," I said, wiping my eyes with the piece of tissue I'd grabbed out of my purse. Out of everyone in L.A., Trish was the one who I thought was actually genuine.

"Took a lot of guts for you to get all that off your chest. You've been holding that inside for a lot of years."

Again with the weak laugh. "Only about eight."

I concentrated on shredding the damp tissue in my hand. I didn't want to look up or even outside the window; not that I wanted anyone to see me, anyways.

"Feel better?"

"Hardly." I leaned my head back against the head rest, wincing at a small jolt of pain. My head was starting to pound, and I was looking at a few hours of wait time at the airport.

All I wanted was to be alone with my misery.

Trish turned the radio down. "You know, I've never seen anyone stand up to your father like that before."

Great, leave it to me to break new ground. "Good."

"What prompted it?" she asked softly as we left the Hills.

I stopped my shredding and glanced at her, wondering if I should tell her the truth. Before I could stop myself, the words came tumbling out. Every word I'd heard him say, every word that felt like a knife in my heart.

"He didn't mean it the way you're taking it," Trish tried to soothe me as she turned off onto a road I hadn't seen before.

I blinked back the burning hot tears that stung behind my eyes like someone was trying to strike a match. Why wouldn't they stop? I was used to being the last thing on his mind. Why should it change now?

"I was an idiot to come out here," I hiccupped pitifully.

"You weren't. Look at everything that's happened this summer."

"Yeah, just *look* at the train wreck my life's become."

My mother was upset. My parents were fighting like they hadn't done in years. And I'd made an enemy out of *Little Miss Hollywood*. No doubt she'd love to know I was hours away from being packed up and shuttled home on a plane. She'd be the first one to break the news to JT that his little girlfriend was *bye, bye, bye*.

"It's had its bumps in the road. And at times, your father's been an absolute idiot."

The corners of my mouth twitched up into a temporary smile. "I'll agree with that."

"But you should go back. At least so you don't go on a plane as upset as you are. Did you book a ticket?"

I shook my head, wiping my nose with the remains of a shredded piece of tissue. "No, I was hoping I could get on standby."

"At least go back to Sean's for a bit, and if you're really sure you want to go, let me book a ticket back. I don't want you alone at the airport in the mood you're in. I doubt your parents would, either."

I bowed my head. "I don't want to see him."

She took a turn. "You could stay in the car, but I think it'd get awfully warm awful quick."

I sighed, leaning my head against the cool glass of the passenger window and noticed we were headed back towards the Hills and Dad's.

"That's sneaky of you, Trish," I said, tapping the window as we passed a familiar street sign.

"Just give him an hour, okay?" she asked, glancing at me, her eyes filled with a sadness I didn't quite understand. "That's all I ask."

I sighed, not sure I could cry one more tear.

"One hour," I relented.

34

Dad was standing on the front steps when Trish pulled back up, and I slid lower in my seat, suddenly wishing I hadn't agreed to her request. I should have waited for my cab down by the gates and gone to the airport like I'd originally planned. I'd probably be half-way to LAX by now.

I watched Trish go in, but I wasn't ready to go back inside. In fact, I really wasn't sure I was ready to be *there*, period. I leaned back in my seat and closed my eyes, trying to will myself to get enough nerve to go in. For some odd reason, I was a little embarrassed by what I'd done earlier. Not for getting it out—because I'd had to do that; Dad so deserved it—but doing it like I had...maybe not the wisest decision.

But what was done was done, right?

I opted to stay put a few minutes longer, maybe hoping somehow, I'd disappear.

No such luck.

There was a rap on the window, and I looked up to see Milo standing there. *Sorry*, he mouthed. I shrugged, and he opened my unlocked door.

"I didn't say a word," he whispered as I stepped out, and I actually believed him.

"S'okay."

He put an awkward arm around my shoulders as Dad headed back inside the moment we neared the steps. Apparently, he didn't want another confrontation any more than I did.

Mom was nowhere in sight as we walked back in, and I was a little relieved. Facing Dad was going to be weird enough, but Mom, too? That would be enough to send me back into a major meltdown. Not only had I learned the truth about my little summer, but I'd also screwed up majorly in my mom's eyes. More than enough to give me a complex right there.

Milo left me in the living room with my suitcases. He left them by the couch and headed off to Dad's office where Trish had no doubt disappeared to. I had a feeling he'd probably be playing the role of my chauffer to the airport if Trish succeeded in getting me a flight out.

I spun around and kicked my luggage absently as I pulled my cell out of my purse and scanned it for messages. Looked like there was one from Dad, but I scrolled past it—it was probably from when I'd taken off from the hospital. I'd turned my phone off as soon as Milo had appeared that morning. Stuffing the device into my pocket, I reached for one of the magazines on the coffee table, waiting for Trish to appear and tell me she had me on a flight out.

"Rumors are true then, huh?" Dad asked.

I was surprised to see him standing in the doorway.

"More rumors?"

What was it this time? Couldn't I even leave town without someone talking about me?

"This one looks like it's based in truth, though. You're actually leaving?" He cast a glance at my stack of luggage.

"Adriana throwing a party yet? Or are the invites still being engraved?"

Dad crossed his arms over his chest, which was when I noticed the crumpled piece of paper in his hand. A very familiar piece of paper.

"Where did you get that?" I asked in a small voice. The last time I'd seen that, I'd been throwing it away.

"Your mom found it upstairs on your bed after you left with Trish."

"Oh."

"Chey..."

"Hmm?" I felt so incredibly awkward. Embarrassing for me to have him see that horribly crumpled piece of paper.

"Trish told me all about the e-mail before we got home, why you carried it with you. Apparently, I've been the biggest ass of a father there can be." He ran a hand through his hair, causing it to stand up in spikes, and I suddenly noticed he looked more tired and older than I'd ever seen him. "I didn't know how much this meant to you, Chey. I should have seen it, but I didn't. I thought what you wanted was the L.A. lifestyle. I didn't get you wanted less of that and more of me."

I sniffled. Damn teenage hormones. I turned my gaze away from his, not wanting to see the shine there that implied unshed tears and that he meant what he was saying.

"Yeah, well..." I kicked the edge of my carryon. "That was then; this is now."

"And you want to go home."

Wouldn't you, I was tempted to ask.

He walked a few steps farther into the room. "I wish you'd opened your eyes at the hospital when I was talking, to see who I was talking to."

"Does it matter?"

He nodded. "It does. I was talking to your mom. About how having you out here has made me realize how much I've missed."

"So?" I purposely put a defiant edge in my voice, trying to keep the emotion back.

"I wish you'd heard the rest of the conversation we had. Chey, I know I missed a lot of time with you. And this summer, I wanted to give you back all the things I never got to give you. The friends. The lifestyle. The car. Everything that I could. And I know I might have been a little well, shocked, when you said you wanted to spend the summer together. But I didn't mean that I didn't want you here, because I did. *I do*," he said emphatically. "I just never expected the most important part of your summer was me. I guess I should have, when the most important part of *my* summer was you."

"Me?" I couldn't quite keep the disbelief out of my voice as I took a seat on the couch, suddenly feeling a little overwhelmed.

"It might not have looked like it, but you were. I wanted to give you what I thought your mom didn't. Freedom. You could do what you want. Fit me in whenever you wanted. I guess I should have tried more." He gave me a weak smile. "I just hate the thought of your summer ending like this."

"Me, too," Mom said.

We both looked up to see her standing in the doorway to the kitchen, a can of soda in her hand. "Sorry, I didn't mean to interrupt, but I heard the last couple minutes between you guys."

"That's okay," Dad said as he waved her in, and I saw a look pass between them I don't think I'd ever seen before. Something like acceptance.

Mom came over and took a seat beside me. "I know I was a bit of a catalyst here. If I'd gone with Rico's original plan to be the surprise this weekend, things would still be good between you two."

I shrugged slightly. Okay, so it was a little true. My outburst never would have happened. I wouldn't have taken off—twice. I'd be busy prepping for Rico's opening and bugging Sorche over how nervous I was getting.

Instead, here I was, waiting for Trish to book me a flight home so I could wallow in my room for the next month before trying to figure out the rest of my life..

"For my part in this, I'm sorry. I need to deal with the fact you're growing up, and out here, it's more accelerated. I know from talking to Trish and Milo, and even JT, that this whole Adriana situation was going to blow up at some point. It's not your fault someone captured it with their phone and some so-called magazine decided to run with it."

"So what now?" I asked softly.

"That's up to you."

I looked up at the two of them.

"Me?"

"You're almost eighteen, Cheyenne. It's time for you to make some decisions on your own."

"Do you want to go home?" Dad asked, looking at me carefully.

The funny thing was *this* still felt like home. Sometime over the last few weeks, this had become my home.

I leaned my head against my hands, trying to think.

I felt my mom's hand on my back, rubbing gently.

"What do you want?" I asked, looking up at him.

He looked down at his hands. "I'd like you to stay, for the summer. Longer if you want. Rico's opening is coming up. He's got plans, he'd probably love to see you stay around here. Your mom and I talked...whatever you think is best for you, we're a hundred percent behind."

I glanced between them again, catching Mom's nod.

"So if I wanted to stay..."

"Then you stay. And I'll stay..." Mom said. "For the opening, at least, and maybe a couple days after. See those billboards of yours and maybe go out to dinner a few times. See a show. Trish said she could get us some concert tickets."

I bit my bottom lip, catching Trish and Milo in the kitchen doorway, Sorche and JT standing behind them, JT holding my teddy bear in his arms.

I locked eyes with him for a moment, and the corner of his mouth lifted up into that smile that sent my heart skipping a beat.

That's when I realized...

This was my home.

This was my *family*.

Sorche, Trish. Even Milo.

And JT...

How could I leave? And how could I let Adriana chase me away from a place and people that made me happy? No way was I going to just hand her everything on a silver platter.

I turned back to Dad. "Then it's a done deal. Dad, you've got yourself a roommate. I'm staying."

The End

ABOUT THE AUTHOR

Lisa Cardwell loves the sun, sand and a good read.

A good day involves at least one.

A perfect day involves all three.

Most days you can find her behind her tablet writing—and dreaming of warmer weather.

Find Lisa online at
www.lisa-cardwell.com

CPSIA information can be obtained
at www.ICGtesting.com
Printed in the USA
BVHW031704230119
538501BV00001B/1/P